Ralph Nicholson Wornum

Some Account of the Life and Works of Hans Holbein, Painter, of Augsburg

Ralph Nicholson Wornum

Some Account of the Life and Works of Hans Holbein, Painter, of Augsburg

ISBN/EAN: 9783337394110

Printed in Europe, USA, Canada, Australia, Japan

Cover: Foto ©Andreas Hilbeck / pixelio.de

More available books at **www.hansebooks.com**

SOME ACCOUNT

OF THE

LIFE AND WORKS

OF

HANS HOLBEIN.

Painter, of Augsburg.

WITH NUMEROUS ILLUSTRATIONS.

BY

RALPH NICHOLSON WORNUM,

KEEPER AND SECRETARY NATIONAL GALLERY.

LONDON:

CHAPMAN AND HALL, 193, PICCADILLY.

1867.

To my Friend

JOHN RUSKIN.

PREFACE.

THE accompanying volume, as I have perhaps fully explained in the text, is not called a "*Life of Holbein*" because I feel that we have not as yet materials sufficient to justify such a title. Neither does it constitute a "*Catalogue Raisonné*" of the painter's works, real or reputed: such an undertaking presents two difficulties of some magnitude; it would involve an amount of physical work that is not only beyond my means and opportunities, but is in itself a compilation requiring too much of the mechanical system and patience of an appraiser not to be repulsive to a literary or historical taste: as all the pretended works, as well as the real, demand an examination, if not a notice, if one is to speak with any authority or absolute decision as to quantity as well as quality.

I have endeavoured only to give an adequate conception of Holbein's career and qualities as an artist, by a succinct relation of all the known biographical events of his life, and by a detailed and chronological review, as far as possible, of all his characteristic or capital works.

I have attempted to present to the mind of the reader, a definite and true image of my hero, both as an artist and as a man; and to do this as compactly, and in a form as agreeable and as little fatiguing to the reader, as lay within my powers to compass. That I have omitted to notice some good genuine works is not only possible, but very probable; and I shall feel grateful for any corrections, and for any new information concerning any undoubted works by the painter, that have escaped my knowledge.

In the illustrations of this volume I have, with one exception, adopted nothing but what is by common consent or tradition, ascribed to the painter's own hand: the reader may therefore consider this Essay as an Account of the Life and Works of Holbein, illustrated by himself. The exception is the shield on the title-page, which is a free copy of that published by Chr. von Mechel in his "*Oeuvre de Jean Holbein,*" from the Painters' Guild-book at Basel. I have selected the illustrations with a view to showing the vast range of Holbein's art, and the comprehensive character of his capacity or genius, as an historical painter and designer. He was very far from being a mere portrait painter; he had, evidently, dramatic powers of composition of the highest class. He is unsurpassed in his best efforts at ornamental design; and is, I think, quite unequalled in his faculty of drawing the human face, in lines or in light and shade with the mere point, whether soft or hard. His own hand is shown in the two photographs in this volume; one, the portrait of a young man, the other that of an old man.

The woodcuts executed by Messrs Dalziel have been carefully drawn, under my direction, by Mr. Andrew Reid: they are from pictures, drawings, designs for silver work, jewellery, typographical embellishments, and other ornamental manufactures.

For the readiest mode of attaining to an adequate idea of Holbein's taste, style of composition, and powers in drawing the human figure, I strongly recommend the reader to consult the fine series of photographs, from his designs in the Basel Museum now in course of execution in Germany by Adolph Braun of Dornach; they are printed the size of the originals, by Swan's carbon process, and are supposed to be permanent: they are very forcible, and constitute a magnificent series of designs.*

October, 1866.

* They are, or shortly will be, published in this country by Messrs. Charles Hauff and Co., No. 4, St. Benet's Place, Gracechurch Street, London.

CONTENTS.

THE FIRST BOOK.

INTRODUCTORY—OLD BIOGRAPHIES AND NEW DISCOVERIES—A FAMILY OF PAINTERS AT AUGSBURG.

CHAPTER I.

CHAPTER II.

CHAPTER III.

THE SECOND BOOK.

HANS HOLBEIN THE YOUNGER. IN AUGSBURG, AND IN BASEL.

CHAPTER IV.

CHAPTER V.

CHAPTER VI.

CHAPTER VII.

CHAPTER VIII.

CHAPTER IX.

CHAPTER X.

THE THIRD BOOK.

HOLBEIN IN ENGLAND.

CHAPTER XI.

CHAPTER XII.

CHAPTER XIII.

CHAPTER XIV.

* See also note, Appendix, p. 392.

CHAPTER XV.

CHAPTER XVI.

LIST OF ILLUSTRATIONS.

THE FIRST BOOK.

INTRODUCTORY—OLD BIOGRAPHIES AND NEW DISCOVERIES—A FAMILY OF PAINTERS AT AUGSBURG.

CHAPTER I.

OLD BIOGRAPHIES.

Chap. I.

Introductory.

N commencing at this late day an account of the Life and Works of Hans Holbein, it will not be uninteresting to the reader, to peruse as a prologue a brief analysis of the substance of the accounts given us by early writers; from which indeed nearly all that till quite recently was known of his life has been mainly derived. Three accounts are more especially prominent, but even the oldest of them was not compiled till about a couple of generations after Holbein's death, and has accordingly no great historical weight. Documents unfortunately have not entered into the balance before the present century; and what we have in that way even now, is remarkably little compared with what we might wish; however, I can safely promise the reader some

CHAP. I. *Introductory.*

genuine matter of considerable value or I should not have ventured on the present attempt. I flatter myself that even the general lover of art-history will follow me with patience; to the lover of Holbein's art in particular, I need make no apology, for he must follow me with interest, even though he should not be altogether satisfied with the results. This first book was originally in the form of an introduction to my volume, but it has run to such a length, and contains incidentally such a mass of information that is essential to the subject, that it has developed itself into an integral part of the biography. It constitutes an essay on Holbein's life, in itself complete; some may consider it as in a measure forestalling my work, but I give it as a necessary thesis, laying before the reader the subject he has to study, and as an inducement for him to enter upon the task with curiosity as well as interest. I do not offer this volume to the public as a "Catalogue Raisonné" of Holbein's works; I have not the slightest inclination to undertake so laborious a task, which at most could only be used as a book of reference. I have done only what it has given me pleasure to do, and have attempted to produce a readable volume on the remarkable career of a remarkable man. I have placed before the reader all I have been able to learn concerning Holbein's Life, and have given some account, with more or less detail as circumstances have dictated, of all his principal works, more especially however as a painter and draftsman; and I have endeavoured in the investigation, to separate the true from the false. The subject is not without obscurity even now (1865). There is no plot to spoil, and the knowledge picked up in this preliminary review, will enable the reader to follow the various discussions in detail, as they arise, with some feeling of previous acquaintanceship.

Carel van Mander. 1604.

The three writers above referred to are CAREL VAN MANDER* a painter of Meulenbeeke in Flanders; JOACHIM VON

* *Het Schilder-boek*, or *Het Leven der doorluchtige Nederlandsche en Hoogduitsche Schilders.* Amsterdam, first published in 1604, small 4to; then in 1618; and again in 1764, in two vols. 8vo. Van Mander was born in 1548, only five years after Holbein's death.

SANDRART* another painter, of Frankfort on the Main; and CHARLES PATIN† a French physician settled in Basel.

Carel van Mander. 1604.

The earliest of these, and of any notice of Holbein, is that of Van Mander, published at Amsterdam in 1604, sixty years after Holbein's death, and it was compiled probably not much before that date. He says Holbein was born at Basel, or at Augsburg, in 1498, but he leaves both year and place in uncertainty. The rivalry therefore as to our painter's parentage, whether Swiss or German, is an old one; it is however at length firmly established that Augsburg, in Bavaria, was not only the abiding place of his family for a generation or two, but was also his own birth place: the date of his birth was not later than 1495, as will be presently shown.

To continue Van Mander's account, we are informed that the young painter was at least established very early in life at Basel, and there made the acquaintance of Bonifacius Amerbach the son of a well-known printer of that name, and acquired also the friendship of the celebrated Erasmus of Rotterdam, who had finally settled down at Basel in 1521. Both these acquaintances were very serviceable to him: Amerbach was a connoisseur and collector.

Holbein never visited Italy, says our biographer, and I have found nothing to contradict this statement; but to escape from the pesterings of an ill-tempered wife, he was very glad to venture his fortunes in England: the greater field open to him in England was of course part of the inducement to leave Basel. He brought with him a letter of introduction to Sir Thomas More, from his old friend Erasmus, together with a painted portrait of the great scholar, which he was by Erasmus himself justified in saying was much more like him than the portrait taken by Albert Dürer.

Through Sir Thomas More, with whom he remained nearly

* *Accademia Todesca*, or *Teutsche Academie der Edlen Bau—Bild—und Mahlerei-Künste.* 4 vols. folio. Nürnberg, 1675.

† Μωριας Εγκωμιον. *Stultitiæ laus. Des. Erasmi Rot: Declamatio. Figuris Holbenianis Adornata.* Basiliæ, 8vo. 1676.

CHAP. I.

Carel van Mander. 1604.

three years, continues Van Mander, and this tradition seems now to be corroborated by facts, Holbein was introduced to the king, Henry VIII., and was afterwards taken into that monarch's service. This brings us to the anecdote of the painter's throwing an obtrusive nobleman down stairs who persisted in forcing himself into his study after being warned that he could not be admitted, and we have a record of the compliment afterwards incidentally paid to Holbein by the king, at the nobleman's expense.

Van Mander notices portraits of the king, and of his children —Edward, Mary and Elizabeth; besides other works; and he singles out the admirable full-length figure of Henry VIII., which was still to be seen at Whitehall in his time. It is not easy to thoroughly follow him and identify all the works enumerated, but this portrait of the king is apparently the celebrated picture which was painted on the wall of the Privy Chamber at Whitehall, and of which there is a small copy at Hampton Court by Remigius van Leemput, one of the scholars of Vandyck. A portion of the original cartoon for this picture is still preserved, and is now in the possession of the Duke of Devonshire.

He notices also the large portrait piece of Henry VIII., and some members of the guild, belonging to the Barber-Surgeons; and he refers to, but doubts, the report that this picture was left unfinished by Holbein, and completed by another hand. At the same time, he remarks that it is wonderful how many pictures Holbein did paint, considering the immense number of his designs for goldsmiths, silversmiths, engravers in wood, and sculptors. He notices further, the two cartoons or *tempera* pictures, on canvas, the well-known compositions of "Riches" and "Poverty," which Holbein executed for the Hanse merchants, in the *Stahl-hoff* or *Osterhuis*—the Steelyard of the Easterlings, in Thames Street—from which, he says, Federigo Zucchero made two drawings, about the year 1574, pronouncing them, as reported by Goltzius the painter, quite worthy of, if not superior to, Raphael. He mentions likewise the full-length portrait of a Countess, dressed in black satin, which was then

Carel van Mander. 1604.

in the house of the Earl of Pembroke, and of which this same Zucchero declared that he had seen nothing so good in Rome. As an Earl of Pembroke presented or bequeathed some pictures to the Arundel family, we may safely infer that the admired picture in question is the excellent full-length of the Duchess of Milan, now at Arundel Castle.

Further we have an account of one Andrew or Andries van Loo, an enthusiastic admirer and buyer of Holbein's works, living in London: he possessed portraits of Master Nicolas (Kratzer) the king's astronomer—now in the Louvre; of the old Lord Crauwl (Cromwell); of Erasmus of Rotterdam; of the Archbishop of Canterbury (Warham); and of Sir Thomas More and his family, a large painting in water-colours (*tempera*) on canvas, which was after Van Loo's death bought by one of Sir Thomas More's grandsons—the example now at Nostell-Priory in Yorkshire, seems to answer to this description, though repeated repairing and varnishing may have rendered its method a question. The portrait of the archbishop, says our author, passed afterwards into the hands of Master Coop, in London*—query, now in the Louvre, or at Lambeth?

In Amsterdam was a Queen of England in cloth of silver, of wonderful workmanship; and a small round miniature of Holbein himself, in water-colours, then in the possession of one Jaques Razet.

Holbein worked equally well, says Van Mander, in oil and in water-colours; and he executed many drawings; he painted also miniatures of especial excellence; which last art he learnt from one Master Lukas, then in London, whom however he very soon far surpassed; in fact as the sun exceeds the moon in brilliancy, says our biographer, an assertion we must accept *cum grano salis;* and it is a pity that on so interesting a point, he was not more explicit as to what Luke he referred to. I assume Luke Hornebolt to be the man; he,

* "Sir Walter Cope, who lived without Temple Bar, over against the Lord Treasurer Salisbury, and had several of Holbein, which passed by marriage to the Earl of Holland, and were for some time at Holland house." *Oxford MSS. Vetert.*—Walpole.

CHAP. I.

Carel van Mander. 1604.

his father Gerard, and his sister Susannah, were all distinguished miniature painters: Luke Hornebolt was in England in Holbein's time, and was not only domiciled here, but was also "a servant of the king's majesty."*

Van Mander tells us that he tried to get some authentic information concerning Holbein, from a Dr. Iselin at Basel; but the Doctor answered his Dutch correspondent that it would be somewhat laborious to find out all he required, and that he could not undertake it, unless he were to be well paid for his trouble: at which Van Mander was very much disgusted.

He closes his account with the statement, only in part correct, that Holbein died poor in London, of the plague, in 1554, aged fifty-six; thus placing the painter's death eleven

* There were three painters of the name of Luke living at this time—Lucas Van Leyden and Lucas Cornelisz, called the Cook-De Kok, completing the trio. The first may be dismissed at once, he was never in this country; the second, assumed by Vertue and Walpole to be alluded to, was here, but he in all probability came at a later time. He was the son of Cornelis Engelbertsz and was born in the same year as Holbein, 1495; but as he came to this country through the pressure of the wants of a family of seven children, he can scarcely have come as a young man, and accordingly he too may be dismissed: we know nothing of any miniatures by him. We have no alternative therefore, but to adopt Lucas Horenbout or more correctly Hornebolt, as the master who taught Holbein miniature painting. He was settled here in 1529 and perhaps earlier; his skill in this department of art may have incited Holbein's emulation. Holbein possibly came here before Hornebolt, but Holbein may have first adopted miniature painting during his second visit to this country, after 1532, when in the king's service, as Sandrart distinctly states.

Luke Hornebolt of Ghent, was some years in Henry's service, and was in receipt of a higher salary than Holbein ever had—namely 55*s.* 6*d.* per month. He died in the spring of 1544, surviving Holbein about six months only. His Will was proved in the Consistory Court of Westminster, May the 27th, 1544, with administration to Margaret Hornebolt his relict. See the paper on the "*Contemporaries and Successors of Holbein*" by Mr. J. G. Nichols, in the 39th volume of the ARCHÆOLOGIA.

In this paper is also the following, from the *Roll of New Year's Gifts* 30th Henry VIII., "By Lewcas paynter a skrene to set afore the fyre, standing uppon a fote of woode, and the skrene blewe worsted." This was in 1539, and this Luke received in return for his present, a gilt cruse weighing 10½ ounces. Holbein and Anthony Toto, an Italian, received similar presents for their gifts; but there is no mention of Hornebolt—he was clearly this "Lewcas paynter," there was no other Luke of any distinction. See further about this painter in the XIth chapter of this volume, where the Will is given in full.

Carel van Mander. 1604.

years too late, and making him eight years older than he really was. This erroneous record, in the course of more than two centuries, many times repeated, has been the source of a multiplicity of misconceptions, involving the history of Holbein and his works in a very deplorable confusion. There is a document among the archives of Basel, only recently discovered by Herr His-Heusler of that city, dated the 19th November 1545, which speaks of our Holbein as already deceased.* This date may have been communicated to Van Mander, and by a common but unlucky fatality the 4 and 5 have changed places in printing or in transcribing, and thus led to the long confusion. The document I refer to, is a letter from the Burgomaster Adelberg Meyer, to Jacob David, goldsmith in Paris. The restoration of this letter to light, gives us one more authentic record, proving the earlier death of Holbein than the popular error gave him.

The next account we have is that of Sandrart, in his *Teutsche Academie*, 1675. He substantially copies Van Mander, but also adds some original and interesting matter.

Joachim von Sandrart. 1675.

The family, he says, was of Augsburg, but as the father had settled in Basel, Holbein was there born. After praising his style and some of his genuine and reputed works at Basel, including the "Dead Christ," the painter's "Wife and Children," and also Christ's Passion in eight compositions, an oil painting on wood, and the "Dance of Death," a fresco series in a churchyard there; he observes that as far as he knows, Holbein never visited Italy. He relates Holbein's friendship with Erasmus; the vexation he suffered from his wife's bad temper; the sending of the portrait of Erasmus, by the painter to Sir Thomas More, whom and his family he most successfully painted; and he notices the ultimate presentation to the King some three years after his arrival in England, at a banquet where Henry was shown, and had

---

* Speaking of Philip Holbein, it says—"*von wylandt Hansen Holbein seligen, sinem Vater,*" &c.

CHAP. I.

Joachim von Sandrart. 1675.

expressed his admiration of, the painter's excellent portraits. We then have a repetition at length of Van Mander's anecdote about the assault on the unlucky nobleman who wilfully interrupted the sturdy painter at his work.

Among the most prominent of the few works enumerated by Sandrart, are two which were at Whitehall; one was a wonderful portrait of the King, full length as large as life; and the other picture he merely speaks of as showing the painter to be a real Apelles. The portrait of Henry was that already mentioned of which we have the small copy by Remigius van Leemput, and of which a portion of the original cartoon is now in the possession of the Duke of Devonshire. The second picture I cannot guess at.

Sandrart also says that Holbein commenced miniature painting in the King's service, having been incited to adopt this branch of the art by the excellence of the works of Master Lucas, repeating the account of Van Mander. He enumerates the portraits in possession of Van Loo, and adds that the Earl of Arundel had a large collection of Holbein's pictures and drawings, some with the pen and washed, others in chalk; both from profane and sacred history; as well as portraits; all executed with an ease and precision almost supernatural. He further mentions that "Sir" Inigo Jones had shown him a book of pen and ink drawings of designs for silver-work, dagger-sheaths, vases, and other ornaments of figures, and scroll work, for almost every purpose, for furniture and the person, from a cap ornament to a shoe-buckle: this was apparently the Sloane volume.

Michael Le Blon or Blond, agent of the King of Sweden in Amsterdam, where Sandrart had settled after his return from Italy, was a celebrated collector of works of art and an engraver himself, unless there were two of the name. He possessed several pictures and drawings by Holbein—among them "a learned Doctor, behind whom was Death with an hour-glass" (this is perhaps the picture now at Munich, called *Sir Brian Tuke Miles*, in the catalogue); some other portraits; and a Venus and Cupid. Sandrart added another to his

Joachim von Sandrart. 1675.

collection, a present for services rendered, a "beautiful" round portrait of Holbein himself. Le Blond had possessed the picture of the "Meyer Family," but when Sandrart was in Amsterdam, about 1640, he had already sold it many years before, to the Banker John Loessert of that city for 3,000 florins.* Sandrart possessed what he calls an original drawing of this picture; and also a "Passion in folio," but from which two compositions of the series were missing; and he offered any one 200 florins who should procure them for him, in order that he might show the work complete—this in honour of Holbein.

Sandrart tells us an anecdote in illustration of the high admiration in which Holbein's designs were held generally by distinguished artists, many of whom he says appropriated them. When Sandrart was studying with Honthorst at Utrecht, in 1627, Rubens paid his master a visit, and they went all three in company together to Amsterdam. While in the canal-boat they entertained themselves with the book of wood-cuts of Holbein's "Triumph of Death," (first published at Lyons in 1538,) and Rubens took the opportunity of impressing on Sandrart's young mind the great merit of the designs as works of art, adding that he himself had diligently copied them in his young days. This is an anecdote which though now more than two hundred years old will, I think, bear repetition, and should prove highly interesting to most of my readers. Rubens probably made large studies in his own way from these lively and dramatic compositions. The great Fleming was then a veteran hero in art, fifty years of age, Honthorst was a man of thirty-five years and now reaping the fruits of his labours, Sandrart was a youth of twenty and only just starting into life and activity, but such is the abounding spirit of the little book that old and young alike may equally derive a store from it. Honthorst and Sandrart were possibly then on their road to this country, where they were employed this year painting the large picture

* Le Blond was born in Frankfort in 1590, and died in Amsterdam in 1656.

CHAP. I.

Joachim von Sandrart. 1675.

of Charles I., his Queen, and the Duke of Buckingham, which is still to be seen at Hampton Court.

Sandrart gives the same account of Holbein's death as Van Mander gave, that he died of the plague; and he adds that the Earl of Arundel, Thomas Howard, was very desirous to erect a monument to the painter's memory, but could not ascertain where he was buried: this difficulty Sandrart supposed to have arisen from the circumstance of his having fallen a victim to the pestilence and having been accordingly buried together with others. Holbein lived in the parish of St. Andrew Undershaft and was no doubt buried in that parish; the parish church is that in Leadenhall Street, and it still bears its old name. St. Catherine Cree (Christ) Church in which some accounts say he was buried, is close to that of St. Andrew Undershaft.

Charles Patin. 1676.

To the above accounts there is little to add from the "Life of Holbein"—*Vita Joannis Holbenii Pictoris Basiliensis,* prefixed to Erasmus's *Praise of Folly,* already mentioned, published at Basel in 1676, the authorship of which is ascribed to one Charles Patin a French physician and accoucheur settled in that city. This account is commonly quoted as an early picture of our painter, but we must not overlook the fact that it appeared one hundred and fifty years after Holbein left Basel, that is no nearer to his time than we are now to that of Queen Anne and the succession of the House of Hanover; further, I think I shall be able to lay before the reader a circumstantial account which will clearly show it to be improbable if not palpably false and scandalous.

The author speaks of the painter as a native of Basel, but adds that some have assumed Grünstadt in the Palatinate, to have been Holbein's birthplace, and that others have supposed Augsburg. He describes him as living in great poverty, owing to his disorderly life and too great a fondness for wine; and states that Erasmus, and his patron Bonifacius Amerbach frequently relieved the painter's necessities. This is a picture

Charles Patin. 1676.

not quite consistent with the letters of introduction with which Holbein was furnished to Peter Ægidius and to Sir Thomas More when he set out on his English journey in 1526. It is very improbable that a cautious man like Erasmus would introduce a dissipated scamp to his renowned and distinguished friends. Patin also would lead us to believe that Holbein did not leave Basel so much on account of a very natural desire to find a larger field for his labours in England, but to escape from the constant curtain lectures of his imperious wife. He arrived in this country almost destitute, as it were begging his way, but was kindly taken into his house by Sir Thomas More, and remained with him about two years. He was then introduced to the king and entered his majesty's employment. After a visit of about three years' duration altogether in this country, Holbein returned in 1529 to Basel and renewed his old habits with his former boon companions, still apparently finding his wife's society anything but agreeable to him: he had recourse to his old toping friends and again wasted his time and his money in disgraceful dissipation. Yet if such were his life, where did he get his money from?

In 1538 says Patin, the Council of Basel settled a pension of fifty florins a year on Holbein on conditions that within two years he would return to his wife and family: he never returned. The account of the painter's death is a repetition of that of Van Mander.

Such is the dismal swamp this worthy doctor has led us into, and he seems to have had no compunction in the matter. It is certainly not an agreeable history of a great painter's life, but it is fortunately untrue: we have no evidence that this is even an approximately true picture of Holbein's character; his early marriage, on the other hand, and his accomplished art both bear witness against its general truth; it seems to have been founded mainly on the fact that Erasmus, in a spirit of retaliation, jokingly wrote the name "Holbein" under the well-known sketch of a coarse boor drinking and caressing

CHAP. I.

Charles Patin. 1676.

a girl, which the painter has drawn on the margin of one of the pages of a copy of the "Praise of Folly."*

Patin follows up the memoir with a catalogue of the painter's works, which is the basis of Vertue's and Walpole's; he enumerates eighteen pictures at Basel, comprising the two skulls now assigned to the brother Ambrose, and some forty others in various places, including several religious pieces for the Augustines at Lucerne. We shall be able to trace some of them in the following pages, but not all. Patin speaks also of his numerous wood engravings, taking it for granted apparently that Holbein was the actual engraver of all such designs as are known by his name.

Van Mander, and Sandrart, and Patin after him, all remark that Holbein painted with his left hand; which I imagine to be a fable that may have arisen from a circular print engraved by Lucas Vorsterman, which being reversed, as is common in old engravings, necessarily puts his brush in his left hand:—*Joannes Holbenius Pictor Regis Magnæ Britanniæ, sui cæculi celeberrimus. Anno* 1543, *ætat.* 45—is the legend. This may possibly have been engraved from some lost portrait or miniature of the Arundel collection; it has been repeatedly copied since, by Hollar and others with various alterations, but we have no evidence either that it represents Holbein, or that should such be the case, the back-ground inscription is an autograph. It represents an oval-faced man with a short beard, and a black skull-cap on; of this more hereafter.

* There is really something shocking in the manner in which both this gossiping French accoucheur and his daughter Caroline speak of Holbein, and all without any given justification. Some of the father's charitable observations are recorded above; the daughter was quite as bad. In her "Tabellæ Selectæ," Paris, 1691, where in page 192, she speaks of the family picture of Sir Thomas More, by way of contrast between the painter and the great statesman whom he painted, she terms the former, "this rude man, a pauper and a drunkard," &c. Dr. Patin was forced to leave Paris from some misconduct, and could not return; he seems to have spent his exile at Basel and at Pavia: he died in 1684.

CHAPTER II.

New Discoveries.

ITH Patin ends our list of original biographers of Holbein. Such is the complete substance of all that was commonly known about him, before Horace Walpole digested George Vertue's "Notes" for his so-called "*Anecdotes of Painting in England*," the first edition of which was published in 1762, and the last, my own, in 1849. In this later account of course the substance of the other three appears in full, but expanded into a much more interesting body of matter, though still vague enough throughout, and quite erroneous in many essential points. This work accordingly only confirmed the embroilment of Holbein's biography, notwithstanding the efforts of Dallaway to rectify and complete it. The whole matter has lately, and especially in a critical sense, been thrown still deeper into the abyss of confusion by Dr. Waagen, not only in his popular "Art Treasures," but also in his later "Handbook of Painting."* Both through his unfortunate attribution of impossible works to Holbein, and by the arbitrary fixing of certain years for the production of pictures

Chap. II.

Recent confusion.

1861.

* "*Treasures of Art in Great Britain*," with Supplement, 4 vols. 8vo. London, John Murray, 1851-57; and "*Handbook of Painting. The German, Flemish, and Dutch Schools*," &c. 8vo. London, John Murray, 1860.

CHAP. II.

Recent confusion. 1861.

which the painter himself had already differently dated for us. "About the year 1546," says Dr. Waagen, "another and final change in the master's colouring took place, consisting of a light yellowish local tone in the flesh, though retaining still the grey shadows. Portraits of this character are those of Henry VIII., at Windsor Castle, and of his son Edward VI., in the same place. This period also includes the large picture of Edward VI., as king, in Bridewell Hospital. The bad state and high position of this, *the most important work of Holbein's latest time*, permit no opinion, properly speaking, upon it."*

If Dr. Waagen has really looked at the last picture, he should have seen that it has not a trace of the hand or style of Holbein in it, apart from the fact that it was painted some years after Holbein's death. The Henry VIII. mentioned in the above quotation, he has in his "Treasures" suggested to be a copy of the Warwick portrait, which he assumed to have been painted in the year 1530; the two pictures have really no resemblance to each other, the costumes are quite distinct; and the king is quite fifteen years older in the Warwick picture than he was in 1530.

In another place ("Treasures," &c. vol. i., p. 245), though we are told of the "yellow tone" adopted in 1546, the Doctor notices a portrait in Mr. Neeld's collection, inscribed—"Æt. suæ 48, Anno Domini 1547," as executed in a "powerful brown red tone," with the animated air of Holbein, and the admirable drawing of the hands which distinguishes the painter's later works.

There is a half-length of a man in armour at Longford Castle, which used to be ascribed to Lucas de Heere, from the monogram it bears—HE; it is further inscribed ÆTATIS XLII. MDL., with the initials T. W. below. This picture was of course not painted by Lucas de Heere, who was in 1550 only sixteen years old; but it was certainly not painted by Holbein either, to whom Dr. Waagen has awarded it, for that

* Handbook, p. 201.

Recent confusion. 1861.

painter had been dead already seven years in 1550. It is needless to add further justification of my remarks on this matter of impossible pictures.

With reference to the subject of arbitrarily, though no doubt unconsciously, altering the years of dated pictures, the examples are somewhat remarkable. The Doctor assumes the portrait of Sir Henry Guildford, at Windsor, to have been painted in 1533; Holbein has inscribed it "*Anno D:* MCCCCCXXVIJ., *ætatis suæ;* XLIX."

Archbishop Warham, he has assumed to have been painted "next in order," after that of Sir Richard Southwell, at Florence, dated he says on the 10th July, 1528. The painter has not left us in doubt about these pictures; he has inscribed the archbishop "*Anno Dm̄.* MDXXVIJ. *ætatis sue* LXX.;" and the Southwell portrait has in the middle of the back-ground the following exact date and the age:—X°. JULII. ANNO. H. VIII. XXVIII°. ÆTATIS SUÆ ANNO XXXIII., that is, on the 10th of July, in the 28th year of Henry VIII., which was 1536. The portrait of Nicholas Kratser, astronomer to Henry VIII., in the Louvre, is not dated 1527, but 1528.

In the next example, that of the so-called "Ambassadors," at Longford Castle, I am not surprised that the real date escaped Dr. Waagen, for it was not known to Lord Folkestone himself, and it cost me half an hour's search to discover it.* The Doctor however, notices this fine picture as the portrait of Sir Thomas Wyatt and another, and he assigns it the year 1529;† yet he has mentioned the legend on Sir Thomas's dagger—ÆT. SUÆ 29,‡ which should have warned him to inquire into the year of Sir Thomas Wyatt's birth, before he brought age and date together: if the picture represents Sir Thomas Wyatt, who was born in 1503, it cannot have been painted in 1529, but some time in 1532 or 1533. Holbein has come again to our rescue in this case; the picture has in its lower right-hand

* I was enabled, through the kindness of Lord Folkestone, to thoroughly examine the various pictures ascribed to Holbein at Longford Castle; having had several of them down from the walls. October 13th, 1865.

† *Handbook*, p. 196.

‡ *Treasures*, vol. iv., p. 359.

CHAP. II.

Recent confusion.

1861.

corner, just under the ermine edging of Sir Thomas's overcoat, the following most interesting inscription:—

JOANNES HOLBEIN, PINGEBAT, 1533.

The words slope from the right to the left, following the perspective lines of one of the divisions of the parquetted or marble floor, and vary little in colour from that portion of the floor itself; still the words are distinctly visible to the naked eye, when it knows where to look for them—Dr. Waagen describes this picture, on panel, as 8 ft. high by 9 ft. wide; it is just 6 ft. 9 in. high by 6 ft. 10 in. wide.

As a last illustration I may mention the portrait of the Duchess of Milan, at Arundel Castle, which the Doctor says was certainly painted in 1539. The picture, or drawing, taken from the Duchess herself at Brussels, "very perffight" says John Hutton, was executed by Holbein in the short space of three hours, between 1 and 4 o'clock, on the 12th of March in the xxx[th] of Henry VIII., which is 1538. The full-length portrait therefore, doubtless painted from this life-study, was, as there was so much hurry for it, painted most probably in 1538, not in 1539.*

There is another category of pictures, and a very interesting one, only too few in examples already, which Dr. Waagen has run his pen through, to bring in additional numbers to the already encumbered Holbein catalogue; namely, the list of pictures preserved by tradition under the names of distinguished foreign artists rarely met with, yet who are known to have been employed in this country. One of the great misfortunes in art-criticism is that the reputations of secondary painters are so often absorbed by first-class names, to the certain injury of both. Luca Penni and his brother Bartolomeo, both worked in this country, and Lucas Hornebolt was domiciled here, yet how rarely are their pictures met with. When tradition, notwithstanding the mischievous activity of presumptuous ignorance, has still handed down works with comparatively obscure names attached to them, the fact alone should go a great way

* See the extract from Hutton's letter in the XVth chapter of this volume.

towards its confirmation as truth. In Lord Normanton's collection is a good female portrait called Lady Jane Grey, and ascribed to Luca Penni; this picture Dr. Waagen has unhesitatingly pronounced one of Holbein's finest works; now if it is Lady Jane Grey it cannot possibly be Holbein's, as when he died she was but a child six years old. Again, the Marquis of Bute has a portrait of Henry VIII., now at Cardiff Castle, ascribed to Hornebolt; this also Dr. Waagen has taken from that master and given to Holbein. Hornebolt most probably did paint the king, and the fact of his name being connected with such a portrait is most interesting, and should be cherished, not ignored. Holbein has already more than enough of Henry-the-Eighths ascribed to him, which he certainly did not paint.

CHAP. II.

Recent confusion.

1861.

As it is a long lane that has no turning, so at last light has been let in on to the biography of Hans Holbein. His age and his birthplace have been hitherto unknown, both his topographical and his chronological position have been false, and it has been impossible to know him correctly. German writers, apparently under the impression that he was a Swiss, have until lately done nothing or little for him; since he has been acknowledged as a German they show much more interest in his career. It will, however, long remain difficult to know Holbein well; no man perhaps, with the exception of Philip Wouverman, has had proportionably so many works of other men ascribed to him, as Hans Holbein. I should calculate about three out of every four, if not four out of five, of the pictures ascribed to him to be misnamed; and it is not likely that the tares will now ever be wholly separated from the wheat. If we may judge from the National Portrait Exhibition at South Kensington (1866), it would be no exaggeration to say that not more than one portrait in ten, on an average, of those ascribed to Holbein, are the veritable work of his own hands. Hampton Court Gallery may serve also as an illustration of this abuse of his name; of some thirty works attributed to Holbein in this royal collection, very few can be absolutely depended on. His father and mother, on the same panel;

New light.

CHAP. II.

False attributions.

1861.

Frobenius and Erasmus, as a pair, and the latter writing, are perhaps, unquestionable; the Reskimer, and the Henry VIII. with the scroll, may be questioned, the latter particularly: of the whole mass we cannot accept more than one-fifth as genuine; a second fifth may be considered doubtful, and the other three-fifths not doubtful at all, but very certainly not Holbein's. A portrait called Holbein himself, has the monogram, somewhat rubbed, certainly, of Hans Baldung, commonly called Grien, and is dated 1539. In the wardrobe accounts of the effects of Henry VIII., preserved in the Manuscript Department of the British Museum, is a catalogue of pictures, &c., drawn up in 1547. The names of the painters are not mentioned; but among the hundred and thirty-one pictures here enumerated that belonged to Henry, are certainly a few that can be traced to Holbein, as for example two portraits of the Duchess of Milan, and perhaps some one or more of the four portraits of the king himself.*

In Vander Doort's catalogue of the pictures of Charles I., eleven works only are ascribed to Holbein, and in these are comprised four miniatures. The large picture of Henry VIII. and his family, now at Hampton Court, though noticed in the catalogue, is not given to Holbein; it remains nameless. The half-length of Queen Elizabeth, as a girl, holding a book in her hands, now in St. James's Palace, and ascribed to Holbein by Vander Doort, but certainly not by him, appears to be the only picture of the eleven which occurs also in the inventory of Henry VIII.

All the pictures, however, falsely ascribed to Holbein are not unworthy of him: there are several excellent portraits dated but not signed, both in this country and elsewhere, which were painted about and before the year 1550, which

* MSS. *Harl.* 1419. Inventory of Hen. VIII. Guard-robes, &c., Plut. xlii. 1. See the Catalogue in this volume. This Inventory, I believe, has never yet been published, and the account of it given by Dallaway in his "Walpole," is not accurate: it seems to comprise 131 paintings, on wood and canvas; 21 specimens of fine embroidery (not hangings); 14 painted terra-cottas; 11 carvings and other works; and 2 framed slates to write upon: total 179 articles, in the charge of Sir Anthony Denny.

False attributions. 1861.

would do no discredit to Holbein's best time; and some of these pictures I imagine must have been painted by Justus Van Cleef, an Antwerp painter, and according to Van Mander the best colourist of his time. He visited this country, and certainly survived Holbein several years. I may instance as an example, the fine portrait engraved by Dibdin in his "Antiquarian Tour,"* which he saw in the possession of Herr Dom. Artaria, in Manheim; a half-length of a man with a beard, in cap and furred cloak, holding out before him his right hand, and resting his left, in which he holds his glove, on a table, and on which is lying the other glove. This portrait has the following inscription, in a cartellino:—AETATIS SUAE. ANNO xlviii. *Anno dm̄. vero* 1547. Very similar in style and attitude is the portrait No. 97 in the Munich Gallery, *once called Luther and now called Calvin*, and ascribed to Holbein in the catalogues. This subject I have treated on more fully in later chapters. The injustice of a false attribution of course remains the same whether the picture be worthy or unworthy, the real painter is in the former case defrauded, though it be done in ignorance, not wilfully.

In this country the various portraits of Henry VIII. afford the most obvious illustration of the injustice that has been done to Holbein, in making him answerable for the shortcomings of others. I may be mistaken, but I imagine that there is scarcely a portrait of this king in England which is not ascribed to Holbein; yet the great majority, or nearly all of them, were painted after his death, and are certainly mere *roba di bottega*, contract work supplied from the shops of the sergeant-painters or others; this has been a practice of all countries, of all times. Portraits of reigning monarchs abound everywhere, yet perhaps not five per cent. are painted from the august personage himself; most are mere copies of copies. Philip Reinagle, the Academician, was the pupil and assistant of Allan Ramsay, sergeant-painter to George III., and he used to relate how for two years of his time, he did nothing what-

* Vol. III. Sup. p. liv. 1821.

CHAP. II.

False attributions.

1861.

ever but manufacture portraits of George III. and his Queen for presents or for the dealers, to supply the country market; all of which were launched into the world as genuine portraits of their Majesties by the sergeant-painter: their source was probably some original sketch or portrait by Ramsay, but that was the extent of their authenticity; and so much authenticity we may safely allow to some of the portraits of Henry ascribed to Holbein, though they may be mere copies of copies. I have only to deal with the genuine works of Holbein, as far as they can be ascertained; the proof of authenticity of reputed works rests with those who claim it.* In those days of splendid costume of course much labour was bestowed over the royal dress, this is, however, mere mechanical work; the dresses are varied, but the face is commonly the same, with more or less of ill drawing and bad painting. The very identity of the view of the face, a full front in these portraits, is alone enough to stamp them as spurious copies, independent of their general worthlessness as paintings. The majority of these portraits represent him in the last period of his life.

However, I make no pretension whatever of having accomplished the task of altogether separating the genuine from the spurious works of Holbein, in the following pages; I know that I have not done so. I have seen many of Holbein's works, but certainly not all, and I find him exceedingly difficult to pronounce upon. This difficulty arises probably from the vast comprehensiveness of his powers of observation; he had nothing of what the Germans have styled the subjective operation in his practice; he at once comprehended the indi-

* Among the mass of portraits of Henry VIII., now on exhibition at South Kensington (April 1866), one only certainly by Holbein—the large drawing contributed by the Duke of Devonshire—the Kimbolton example is perhaps the best of the half-lengths; Lord Yarborough's is not there. Lord Galway's is dated 1547, not 1543, as stated by Dr. Waagen, and it is not a whole-length, but a half-length—2 ft. 11 in. *h.* by 2 ft. 3 in. *w.* It bears the following inscription—HENRICUS. VIII. DEI. GRACIA. ANGLIAE. FRANCIAE. ET. HYBERNIAE. REX. FIDEI. DEFENSOR. ET. IN. TERRA. SUB. CHRISTO. SUPREMŪ. ECCLESIE. ANGLICANAE. ET. HYBERNICAE. CAPUT. 1547.

Criticism not dogmatism. 1861.

viduality of his subject, and added nothing of himself to the representation of the object to be reproduced, displaying an extraordinary contrast to the ordinary proceeding of Rembrandt, and a still greater to that of Rubens.

Hence this essay is called "Some Account of Holbein and his Works." There are not yet the materials of what may justly be called a "Life of Holbein," though I have found subject matter enough for a somewhat bulky volume. I have been unavoidably compelled to place my own views before the reader with a degree of prominence which I should have preferred to avoid; not that I do not feel justified in giving an opinion; on the contrary, a man who devotes his life to a special department of study is commonly supposed to have acquired some experience which may be made useful to his fellow-students and workers. It is now two and thirty years since I commenced my first extensive tour on the continent (April 1834) with a view to acquiring, from experience, some definite ideas about foreign art and artists, and right or wrong, I have gathered a few. Such views may be communicated without dogmatism; the assertion of a fact is one thing, the assertion of an opinion is another. The critical opinions in this volume are to be accepted as opinions, and nothing more. A critic has every right to say that he doubts the ascription of a certain work to a certain master, without being pronounced dogmatical. As the impressions and convictions produced by works of art on the minds of people vary infinitely, in accordance with the nature and experience of the individual, so must the judgments vary where the mind exerts itself so far as to shape its impressions into a judgment; but the value and influence of that judgment depend upon the experience of the judge. The opinions of inexperienced people may sometimes be sound, but they are commonly without influence and remain harmless if incorrect. Still there is no doubt that there are what in the common sense of the word may be called experienced people, whose opinions if not harmless are certainly worthless; and that is because they have sufficient vanity to wish to be considered judges, yet are

CHAP. II.

Criticism not dogmatism.
1861.

almost wholly deficient in the faculty of seeing, and in the power of comparing impressions on the mind. The chief essential to a good critic is perhaps honesty; if a connoisseur will endeavour not to deceive himself, or imagine he knows what he really has but the vaguest ideas about, he is not very likely to deceive others. If he be honest and laborious at the same time, that is supposing he start with fair average abilities, he will not be long before he has stored up a few impressions which will assume gradually a very definite shape, and become useful capital in the acquisition of other impressions like them. These impressions in time become convictions, and as such are facts in the critic's mind, and they constitute his real stock-in-trade. It is no dogmatism to give expression to these convictions, he does not assert a fact about a picture, but a fact about his own mind, an impression. At all events I desire the reader in this light to accept any opinions or *dicta* that he may dissent from, which he may meet with in this volume, with reference to the works of Holbein. I do not intend to assert that Holbein never painted such and such a work, but simply that I do not perceive his hand in it.

Having derived certain convictions from the careful and repeated observation of works which have a history as well authenticated as such matters commonly can be authenticated, and in applying these convictions as tests to certain reputed Holbeins, the critic will find his mind more or less vigorously repelled or attracted, and naturally draws his conclusions accordingly; how far others are to allow themselves to be influenced by such conclusions depends upon their own estimate of the quality of the experience out of which they arise. Each must decide for himself, according to his own lights. The judgment may be rejected without there being any necessity for condemning the judge. In a professed research such as this, into the history of a painter's works, it is not the business of a critic to suppress his convictions out of respect to prejudices; on the contrary, *coute qu'il coute*, it is his proper business to put such convictions on record. All judgments find their level in the end, and such as arise from imperfect

Criticism not dogmatism. 1861.

knowledge, hasty conclusions, or inadequate comparisons affect only the critics themselves; the true work is sure to maintain its position. I do not pretend to be altogether guiltless of either hasty conclusions or inadequate comparisons, but I trust notwithstanding, that I shall be treated with more charity of opinion by my critics, than one of my heroes in this book, the Chancellor Thomas More, indulged the Protestants with, whom he has written of as "abominable heretics, and against God and his sacraments and saints, very blasphemous fools."*

Documentary evidence is generally the only evidence that sound criticism can spring from; works with their documents are the fundamental data to raise a superstructure on; but documents are only positive, not negative evidence; they show certain works to be by a certain master, but nothing more; they do not prove that others are not by the same master, though they may by inference lead sometimes to that conclusion.

The characteristics of a master's style are founded on analysis and synthesis, applied to his works, not on documents; and it is this analysis and synthesis which constitute the special province of the critic; the proper weighing of the documents belonging to the historian's province. But documents themselves require as careful a testing as opinions. Many erroneous attributions have gained credit and notoriety, from the mere echo of a positive affirmation about some spurious or imaginary document, each repeating in placid confidence the same refrain, till some sounder or more curious inquirer discovers that the whole web is made out of a mere rope of sand. We are apt to believe almost any silly tale that flatters our vanity or self-love, and consider those who unde-

* Roper's "Life of More," Ed. Revd. J Lewis, 1731, Preface. This was apparently the general orthodox opinion in those days; in the Bishops' Reply to the Petition of the Commons containing accusations against the disorderly conduct of the clergy, in November 1529, the Heretics or Protestants are thus spoken of—"Truth it is that certain apostates, friars, monks, lewd priests, bankrupt merchants, vagabonds, and lewd idle fellows of corrupt intent, have embraced the abominable and erroneous opinions lately sprung in Germany." Froude, *History of England*, &c. Vol. I.

CHAP. II. 1861.

ceive us exceedingly rude. But justice surely does not require us to leave people in the peaceful solace of their delusions, should even charity be supposed to do so. I certainly, in the following inquiry cannot claim to have much respected either tradition, or prejudices, and I have accordingly found the whole popular fabric of Holbein's biography and artistic career to have been the veriest house of cards imaginable.

Holbein's Will.

The first very important discovery with reference to Holbein's life, is that of the period of its termination, through the most welcome finding of his Will in St. Paul's Cathedral by Mr. W. H. Black, which was communicated by him to the Society of Antiquaries, on the 14th of February, 1861; the absolute truth of this discovery has been clearly demonstrated by Mr. A. W. Franks in his remarks upon it, communicated to the same society, in a letter to Earl Stanhope, in 1863. This last was supplemented by another valuable contribution to the "Archæologia," in the same year, by Mr. J. G. Nichols, in his "*Notices of the Contemporaries and Successors of Holbein*," to which Mr. George Scharf added some "*Additional Observations on some of the Painters contemporary with Holbein*," containing further matter of interest.

His birth.

Another very important recent discovery is that of the true time and place of Holbein's birth, made public by Dr. Alfred Woltmann, in a Latin Dissertation on the "*Origin, Youth, and Earliest Works of Holbein*," held in the University of Breslau, on the 26th of November, 1863, and since published—"*De Johannis Holbenii celeberrimi Pictoris, origine, adolescentia, Primis operibus, &c.*"* Another valuable paper upon Holbein has appeared in the *Beiträge zur vaterländischen Geschichte herausgegeben von der historischen gesellschaft in Basel*, vol. viii., 1866, entitled—"*Die neuesten Forschungen über Hans Holbein des Jüngern Geburt, Leben und Tod.*" Mitgetheilt von ED. HIS-HEUSLER. Some of this gentleman's discoveries are of the highest interest and importance.

* See also the *Fine Arts Quarterly Review*, No. V.

These new data, perfectly reliable, and fixing incontrovertibly the beginning and the end of Holbein's life, have mainly given me courage to attempt the present undertaking, having previously made two extensive tours on the continent, and having had the advantage of a personal inspection of the many important works ascribed to Holbein, authentic or reputed, scattered in various localities over Germany, Switzerland, France and the Netherlands; more especially in Augsburg, Basel, Munich, Vienna, Dresden, Berlin, Darmstadt and Paris. Though in the first tour, comprehending Berlin and Vienna, I had not decided on attempting such a work, and accordingly did not make such precise observations of the various reputed Holbeins I saw on that occasion, as I should have done had my work been already resolved upon. The proper way for the curious amateur to study Holbein, and follow his development is—first to visit Augsburg, then Munich; in these two cities are his earliest works, and also many of his father's: whether the Munich Gallery has any other picture by the son, besides the triptych of the "Martyrdom of St. Sebastian," is questionable. From Munich he should proceed to Basel, where a rich feast is provided; then let him go by way of Darmstadt to Dresden. At Darmstadt, in the palace of Prince Charles, is the admirable picture of the "Burgomaster Meier and his family:" at Dresden are a repetition or rather copy of this picture, and the wonderful portrait of "Mr. Morett," jeweller to King Henry VIII. of England, besides some other good pictures. From Dresden he may proceed to Berlin to see the superb picture of "George Gyzen," commonly ascribed to Holbein. I do not believe that there is any other picture by Holbein in the fine collection of the Berlin Museum, though Dr. Waagen's catalogue describes eight works ascribed to him. This museum however contains some interesting early drawings by him. In the Belvedere Gallery at Vienna, are several good examples, and conspicuous among them are—"John Chambers," physician to Henry VIII., and the portrait called "Queen Jane Seymour."

CHAP. II.

Holbein topography. 1861-6.

It is a curious fact that among all the pictures possessed by

CHAP. II.

Holbein topography. 1861-6.

Henry VIII., at his death, there was no other portrait of any one of his six wives, than that of Queen Jane joined with himself in a diptych.*

The Louvre, in Paris, is rich in fine portraits by Holbein, all of which were probably at one time in this country; here are capital pictures of—Erasmus, Anne of Cleves, Archbishop Warham—1527, Sir Richard Southwell—1536 (apparently a copy of that in the Uffizj, at Florence), Sir Thomas More, and a few others of inferior quality. In England perhaps the greatest treasure we have, as an illustration of Holbein's powers, is the portfolio of drawings in the Royal Library at Windsor, where also are a few miniatures. In the Queen's Closet, likewise, are some fine portraits by him, of Sir Henry Guildford and others. There are also the half-dozen or so of genuine works at Hampton Court. At Hardwick Hall, Derbyshire, is the Duke of Devonshire's fine cartoon of Henry and his father; and at Longford Castle in Wiltshire is one of the most important of all his pictures, the so-called "Ambassadors," two large full-length portraits, in the same piece, of Sir Thomas Wyatt and another, painted in 1533. At Arundel Castle, Sussex, is that of the Duchess of Milan, taken in 1538, and also a fine portrait of the third Duke of Norfolk, painted in 1540. In the British Museum is an excellent and varied collection of his drawings, in different departments of art, showing the versatility of his powers as well as the unusual thoroughness of his execution as an artist. Indeed, with the Windsor drawings and the Museum drawings together, Holbein is on the whole better represented here than in the Museum at Basel, at least in this province of his art, not only in powers of execution, but also in invention and in

* "Item, a table like a booke, with the pictures of Kynge Henry the eight and Quene Jane." Of their son Edward he had three portraits, two of which were whole-lengths; he had one of the Princess Elizabeth, but not one of the Princess Mary, though the fine portrait of this princess belonging to the Society of Antiquaries, was probably painted during Henry's life-time, and when she was about 30 years of age. This picture and that of the Princess Elizabeth as a girl, at St. James's Palace, were I imagine painted at nearly the same time and by the same hand, but that hand was not Holbein's.

composition; as well in historical subjects, as in portraiture and in ornamental design. CHAP. II.

Holbein's drawings. 1861-6.

The various drawings ascribed to Holbein, in this country and elsewhere, and the numerous prints and woodcuts after his reputed works, I have not made a special study of; these are noticed only incidentally; but I have neglected no works of these classes which are in any way materially concerned in demonstrating the character and progress of Holbein's career. Even in the matter of pictures my labours have been circumscribed by short means, and by a restricted liberty of locomotion, to say nothing about time, the most precious element of all.

Documentary authorities.

In the matter of documents, or biography itself, in which however the supply of materials is still deplorably defective, without reference to art or æsthetics, I am, besides the works mentioned beholden also much to Ulrich Hegner's "*Hans Holbein der Jüngere.*" 8vo. Berlin, 1827; this is, or perhaps rather was, now, the chief source of our information respecting Holbein's life in Switzerland; and the book is well done, though the author had no critical knowledge of art. The references in Dr. Waagen's "*Art Treasures*" have been useful; and I have derived some slight help too from the Doctor's "*Kunstwerke und Künstler in Deutschland.*" 12mo. Leipzig, 1843–45, where many Augsburg pictures are described: and I am indebted in some degree also to J. D. Passavant's "*Beiträge zur Kentniss der Alten Malerschulen Deutschlands, bis in das sechzehnte Jahrhundert,*" published in the *Kunstblatt*, Nos. 45 and 46. 1846: these last papers, notice besides the Holbeins, many of their principal contemporaries. But unfortunately some of the documents relating to the Holbeins published both by Waagen and Passavant have turned out to be spurious; the details are given in their proper places. I am indebted likewise to the catalogues of the various picture galleries containing Holbein's real or reputed works; but unfortunately the two most interesting collections, namely those of Augsburg and Basel are not yet catalogued (1865); for the mere numerical list of drawings and pictures, sold at Basel, is of but

CHAP. II.

Documentary authorities. 1861-6.

very little service: it does not even give the dimensions or materials of the pictures.

The chief authority for the history of the Holbein woodcuts is C. F. von Rumohr's *Hans Holbein der Jüngere in seinem Verhältniss zum Deutschen Formschnittwesen.* 8vo. Leipzig, 1836; with which may be consulted Passavant's *Peintre Graveur. Contenant L'Histoire de La Gravure sur Bois, &c.* Vol. III. Leipzic, 1862.

Just before going to press I have received the first part of Dr. Woltmann's promised "*Holbein und seine zeit;*" this gives the painter's career from his birth to his departure from Basel for England. The volume contains much interesting matter relative to Holbein's works in Augsburg, and I received it just in time to be spared falling into the same errors respecting these Augsburg pictures, which the false documents referred to led the two German writers into. In the *Beilagen* constituting an Appendix to this first part of the work, is a series of interesting documents, relating to Basel as well as Augsburg, those discovered by Herr His-Heusler, and others. As regards pictures, the author has left undisturbed several attributions, which I have ventured to reject altogether. And though we do not vary in facts, the inferences drawn from these facts vary materially in several instances, as for example as regards the time of, and the individuals represented in, the picture of "Holbein's wife and children," and in the details of the pedigrees of the two pictures of the so-called "Meyer Madonna."

On the other hand the Doctor not only questions the fact of there having been any grandfather Hans Holbein, but also denies the journey of the father to Basel. Though there is no document to prove the removal or journey of the father, it is still a possible and even probable incident; and the absence of any positive proof is not a proof of the contrary conclusion. I am content, therefore, to let the matter rest as a tradition, leaving it to time to clear up all obscurities. As regards "old Holbein," his existence appears sufficiently established, unless we are to imply another gross case of forgery; that he

Documentary authorities. 1861-6.

was the grandfather of our great painter, is certainly not established. It is in fact immaterial whether he were his grandfather or great-uncle. The two volumes are certainly very different in their character, but I must say that I consider Dr. Woltmann's an admirable work, though it is quite German in its view and treatment. My main objects have been to arrange my facts in an orderly succession; to give a critical review of the painter's works; and to interest the reader personally in his career, without reference to his nationality or the school that produced him. Holbein belongs to Europe, not to Germany.

Were I restricted in this account of Holbein to saying only what would admit of positive documentary demonstration, I should certainly not have had much to say, and I should probably have adopted the safer alternative of saying nothing. As it is, if the reader derives only one tenth of the pleasure in reading this essay, that I have had in writing it, I shall be content. I flatter myself that he will derive both pleasure and instruction from it.

Kindred painters.

To give some notion of the confusion into which modern want of criticism has thrown us with regard to Holbein, it is certain that works of all the following painters besides some others have been and are ascribed to him:—QUINTIN MATSYS (1466—1530), and JAN VAN HEMESSEN (*painting* 1530); BARTHOLOMAEUS BRUYN (*painting* 1533), and HANS VON MELEM (*painting* 1530); also HANS MIELICH (1515–72), HANS BALDUNG commonly called GRIEN (*died* 1552), GEORG PENCZ (1500–50), CHRISTOPHER AMBERGER (1498—1568), and HANS ASPER (1499—1571); besides the following, most of whom visited this country:—JAN DE MABUSE (1470—1532), JOOST VAN CLEEF (*painting* 1554), LUCAS HORNEBOLT (*died* 1544), ANTHONY MORE (1525–81), LUCAS DE HEERE (1534–84), PETER POURBUS (*died* 1584), NICHOLAS LUCIDEL or NEUCHATEL (*painted* 1561), and our own NICHOLAS HILLIARD (1547—1619). All these men except the last, were Holbein's contemporaries, though some few were his juniors by a generation. The majority were his proper contemporaries, and there is nothing

CHAP. II.

Kindred painters. 1861-6.

in the costume of their portraits that should necessarily detach them from Holbein's period and thus spare us the confusion of masters. Quintin Matsys, De Bruyn, Von Melem, Mielich, Amberger, Asper, and Pourbus, painted in a taste very similar to Holbein's, though there is an evident distinction in the handlings when their genuine works are brought into close comparison. Several of the above men, of whom I shall have occasion to speak again as we advance, are admirable sometimes; and Amberger, if the painter of some works ascribed to him, is occasionally very free; he is considered a follower and imitator of Holbein, though I do not feel quite satisfied about this. Holbein left but little for him to imitate at Augsburg, and Amberger was only 18 years of age when Holbein left that city; his opportunities of studying anything else than what Holbein left at Augsburg must have been few indeed. The portrait of Sebastian Münster, in the Berlin Gallery, ascribed to Amberger, is a superb picture, and the painter of this work I imagine to be also the painter of the small picture of an old man at Dulwich, which is ascribed to Holbein. No. 353, a small half-length of an old man, in black and sable, with a small ruff or plaited white collar round his neck, somewhat of an Elizabethan pattern; he has a short grey beard nearly white, a black hat brimmed, and holds a book in his hands. On oak 1 ft. 9 in. *h.* by 1 ft. 3½ in *w.* There seem to be two other portraits, now on exhibition at South Kensington, by the same German painter; viz., the reputed Sir Thomas Boleyn, Queen Elizabeth's grandfather, contributed by Mr. W. B. Stopford, a bust portrait, in black dress and furred overcoat with close ruff, and two shields of arms; inscribed *Aetatis suae* 60. This is a very clever picture but is much later than Holbein, and can have nothing whatever to do with Sir Thomas Boleyn: the coats of arms should be able to settle the question. On oak, 1 ft. 8 in. *h.* by 1 ft. 5 in. *w.** The second

* I was pleased to read in the 'Builder' of May the 18th, the following remarks by Mr. Planché on this picture, fully, from an independent source, corroborating my view:—"It must be obvious from the armorial ensigns painted on this picture, that the portrait is that of some Master or member of the Company of

Kindred painters. 1861-6.

picture is that called "Ambrose Dudley Earl of Warwick," exhibited by the Marquis of Salisbury, on oak, 3 ft. 1 in. *h.* by 2 ft. 4 in. *w.* A half-length, in dark cap and jewelled dress, with small white ruff round the neck and ruffles at the wrists; holding a book in his hand. I am not aware whether Amberger was ever in this country, but the Augsburg Gallery possesses a portrait of Henry VIII. ascribed to him; if his it may be a copy after some other master. Of course both this reputed Sir Thomas Boleyn, and the Earl of Warwick, are ascribed to Holbein; but he cannot possibly have painted the latter.

Merchant Adventurers, and has no claim whatever to be considered a likeness of Sir Thomas Boleyn, K.G. I hope to be able to show whose arms are those on the left of the picture: but they are not to be found in the three principal ordinaries of arms at the Herald's College, and may be foreign coats." "Besides the fact that no insignia of the order of the Garter are visible in this picture, the costume indicates a period posterior to that of the death of Sir Thomas Boleyn (1538) by nearly twenty years." "On the right are the arms of the Old Company of Merchant Adventurers, and on the left, the arms of the person represented impaling those of his wife."

CHAPTER III.

A Family of Painters at Augsburg.

Chap. III.

Old Holbein.
1459–1499.

N a wall, in the new "Maximilian's Museum," of the ancient city of Augustus, or Augsburg, an interesting old imperial Suabian town, now Bavarian, once as famed for its Commerce as for its Protestantism, is hanging a large picture of the "Virgin Mary seated on a bank, and holding in her arms the Infant Christ;" signed—

HANS HOLBEN
C. A.
1.4.5.9.

It was, according to report, originally painted for the world-famous Fugger* family in Augsburg, and placed in their chapel in the St. Annenkirche; it passed into the Augsburg Museum from a Herr Samm, of Mergenthau. The authenticity of the signature is now questioned.

This picture, uninteresting as a work of art, in itself, and quite inconsiderable as a painting, though apparently carefully

* The Fuggers rose and throve on the manufacture of linen, during the fifteenth century. Anthony Fugger who entertained the Emperor Charles V., was supposed to be the richest man in Europe: he died worth 6,000,000 golden crowns in ready money besides estates and other property. They are still one of the richest families in Europe.

studied from nature, when compared with contemporary works which were starting rapidly into existence, in Holland, Flanders, and in Italy, has if the signature be genuine a great historical value in our present investigation. Hans Holbein the painter, and citizen of Augsburg (C. A. *Civis Augustanus?*) who painted this Madonna in 1459 is commonly supposed to have been the grandfather of Hans Holbein the painter of Henry VIII., who was domiciled in London, in the parish of St. Andrew Undershaft, and was carried off by the plague here, in 1543. But from what I have just stated in the last chapter, we must assume some other relationship than father, to the second Holbein; that of uncle for instance.

Notwithstanding the C. A. interpreted as citizen of Augsburg, this old Hans Holbein is not mentioned in the Register of the painters of Augsburg. If not a myth, he belonged probably to some other town, in which case the letters C. A. are misinterpreted.

The painter was not yet master of his art, the work is hard, but careful and not without intelligence; in its character it displays something of the taste of Martin Schoen's pictures at Colmar, whence he may have migrated to Augsburg. In a second work, in the Picture Gallery at Augsburg, executed forty years later, in 1499, a long interval, he displays a somewhat more finished mastery over his materials; but in this picture the figures are small, while the Madonna of the Museum is large life-size. It is one of a series of six remarkable works, ordered by the nuns of St. Catherine in 1496, on the occasion of the reconstruction of their convent. In 1484 his Holiness Innocent VIII., had, through the intercession of their confessor Dr. Ridler, granted these nuns certain indulgences, acquired by those who paid their devotions at the altars of the seven principal ancient Basilicas or churches, of Rome. It was however, on condition that certain prayers were repeated, rationally allowed that pictures of the churches, &c., would answer the same purpose as the Roman altars themselves, which was certainly very convenient for the

CHAP. III. *Old Holbein.* 1459-99.

Augsburg nuns. They accordingly decorated their chapter-house with six votive pieces, from the hands of the best masters of the city. Apparently, from the evidence of the works as follows:—Old Hans Holbein; Hans Holbein the father; Thomas Burgkmaier, and his son Hans Burgkmaier.

Old Holbein undertook the Basilica Liberiana, or the church Santa Maria Maggiore; Hans the father undertook the Basilica Ostiense of St. Paul—San Paolo fuori le Mura; to Thomas Burgkmaier, according to Passavant, though there is neither document nor signature to show this, fell the Basilicas San Lorenzo and San Sebastiano, both in one picture; Hans Burgkmaier painted the other three — St. Peter's, or the Basilica Vaticana, San Giovanni in Laterano, or the Basilica Lateranense, and the Basilica Sessoriana, of the Holy Cross, or Santa Croce in Jerusalemme. The foremost figures in all these pictures are about one third the scale of life, or about the ordinary size of a student's academy figure.*

The donors, and prices of these several pictures are recorded in some Annals of the Convent, preserved in the Episcopal Library at Augsburg. They were: — Barbara Riedler, the donatrix of the St. John picture, which cost 64, or 54 florins: Helena Rephon, of the St. Lawrence and St. Sebastian piece, at the price of 60 florins: by Veronica Welser, two pieces were contributed, those of the

* I received many details respecting these and other pictures at Augsburg from Herr Eigner the Conservator or Keeper of the Picture Gallery there. They are reputed to be originally derived from a Dr. Von Ahorner, physician to the convent, and taken from two volumes of archives or extracts from the archives of the convent, which were reported as lost, but supposed to be still in the Royal Library at Munich. Dr. Woltmann after patient investigation has been fortunate in finding them in the Episcopal Library of Augsburg, and they consist of an abstract of the archives of the Convent of St. Catherine made by Dominica Erhardt, a nun who died in 1756. The extracts communicated to Passavant were materially altered by the interpolation of names of the artists of the pictures described, as part and parcel of the original records, whereas only here and there a name has been written by a modern hand on the margin, suggesting the painters or supplying their names from another source; but even this does not account for the principal changes. Passavant and Dr. Waagen have evidently been victims of a deliberate hoax or something worse. The extracts referred to are in Waagen's *Künstler und Kunstwerke in Deutschland*, 1845; and in his Handbooks of 1860 and 1862; and in Passavant's articles in the *Kunstblatt* for 1846.

Holy Cross, and St. Paul, for 187 florins: Dorothy Roelinger gave the Virgin Mary picture, at a charge of 60 florins: and lastly Anna Riedler gave that of St. Peter, at an expense of 45 florins.

Here we have to do more particularly with the works of the two Holbeins. Old or "Alte Holbein's" Santa Maria Maggiore, is signed and dated on two bells; on one are the letters HANS HOLBA, and there being no room for the rest of the name, the two remaining letters are placed on the second bell, with the date,—IN 1499. This picture has also on a tombstone an H. It was the commission of Dorothy Roelinger for the considerable remuneration of sixty florins. "*Item Dorothea Rölingerin, hat lassen mahen unser liebn Frauw taffel, die gestatt oder stett* 60 *gulden.*"*

Sixty Bavarian florins at the present day are equivalent to about five pounds of our money, which in those days represented twelve or twenty times the amount of commodities such a sum would now procure: in many cases the old florin was certainly much more than the equivalent of our pound.

In the upper part of the picture, which is in oil and on wood, and in parts gilt, is an abundance of Gothic tracery, it being divided into compartments by Gothic pillars, and the church itself is represented in the same style. Above is the Coronation of the Virgin, with a representation of the Trinity in three similar persons; below, on the spectator's right is the "Nativity of our Lord," on the left the "Martyrdom of St. Dorothy," the nun's patron saint. There is a dryness and meagreness about the forms, also a flatness of effect through want of relief of light and shade, and an affectation in the postures of the figures, but the colours are well manipulated, and altogether the picture quite reaches the average excellence attained by German artists in the fifteenth century, though not approaching the delicacy of execution and richness of colour, not at all uncommon in the pictures of the Westphalian school of this time. Were it not for a very marked difference in the

* *Verzaichnus wer die Taflen in den Capitl oder die siben haubt Krichn hat machen lassen.* Woltmann, *Beilagen* III., p. 360.

CHAP. III. *Old Holbein.* 1459-99.

style, one would naturally conclude that this picture were the work of the younger or second Hans Holbein, as the date accords perfectly with his time; but the styles are distinct. Sandrart naturally speaks of this altar-piece as the work of Holbein's father, as there was in his time no question about a third or older Hans Holbein. Passavant has written very decidedly of this "Alte Holbein," but he seems to have been altogether misled by words purporting to be in the old records, which are *not to be found there.* If the father Holbein signed and dated this picture, he must have employed some other master to paint it for him; and this is not impossible or improbable, as he was, as we shall see, very much occupied; and there are some known cases of the kind on record, where painters have undertaken commissions, and entrusted their execution to their assistants. Further the Basel Museum possesses two pen drawings of portions of this composition, the "Coronation of the Virgin," and the "Martyrdom of St. Dorothy," dated *Anno d.* 1499. These drawings are similar in style to other sketches ascribed to Hans Holbein the father.

I have given above the authentic entry respecting this "Santa Maria Maggiore" votive piece; in Passavant's notice it is materially altered into the following:—"*Item, Dorothea Rölingerin, hat lassen machen unser lieben Frauen Taffel, die gestatt* 45 *gulden,* VON ALTEN HANS HOLBEIN HIE." This was thought by Passavant to establish the existence of Hans Holbein the grandfather, more especially when this statement was apparently corroborated by other records which the writer quotes in the same article. He refers to two passages, one from the convent annals, where the father is, on one occasion, referred to as "Maler Holbein;" and in another record of the time with reference to the presentation of an apprentice from Passau, are the words "1497 hat Hans Holbein, Jun.," &c., where a child two years old could certainly not be referred to, and this was our hero's age at that time. Dr. Woltmann has been unable to find any such record: the reference is certainly sufficiently vague, and Passavant's entire case for the existence of the grandfather Holbein must be considered as fallen to

Old Holbein. 1459-99.

pieces. The mere signatures on the two pictures, and the variety of handling in that dated 1499 from the known works of the father are hardly sufficient data to come to any satisfactory conclusion on. That there was such a painter as this oldest of three Holbeins called Hans, though not an established fact, is just possible, and he may have been the uncle of the second of the name, if not his father. There is the alternative that there was no such person and that the signature on the Maximilians-Museum picture is a forgery. What Dr. Woltmann considers especially suspicious is the spelling of the name Holbein instead of Holbain, as it occurs in the register and in nearly all other cases at this time. The spelling however of surnames is no criterion, as we find in the case of this very name: the spelling on the picture is not HOLBEIN but HOLBEN with a dot over the first stroke of the N, which may be either design or accident, or the work of the restorer.

Michel Holbein. 1454-86.

As regards the Holbein family in Augsburg, a MICHEL HOLBAIN is found in the Register of Taxes as early as 1454, and in 1469 he appears to have been a householder; he is on one occasion entered as a *Lederer* or currier, in 1468. His name occurs on the register for the last time in 1486. The name of Hanns Holbain occurs first in 1494. We have further Michel Holbainin, Anna Holbainin, which signify apparently the daughter and the widow of Michel, the mother of Hans, our Holbein's father. Anna is noticed as late as 1522, and this must be Holbein's aunt noticed in Sigmund's will, also the Margreth noticed in these records must be another of the aunts. Sigmund's name occurs; and possibly also our hero is referred to or included in the entry of 1499 which speaks of *Holbain's Kind.* The names Endlin for Anna, and Otilia Holbainin likewise occur. Whether the same name always refers to the same person is doubtful, but it is not a matter of much importance in this history. There is but one Hans Holbain mentioned and he was the son of Michel.*

* Woltmann, *Holbein, &c. Beilagen* IV., p. 361.

CHAP. III.

Holbein the father.
1492-1508.

HANS HOLBEIN the second of the name born at Augsburg, probably, in 1459 or 1460, was one of a family of five, two sons and three daughters—Johannes (Hans), Sigmund or Sigismond, Ursula, Anna, and Margaretha; the respective order of these sons and daughters is not known.*

Portraits of both Hans and Sigmund are engraved in Sandrart's "Academie," from supposed original drawings by Holbein himself, dated 1512; apparently on one piece of paper. They are both good-looking men, Sigmund appearing of prime middle-age; Hans has a long beard and may pass for a man between fifty and sixty years of age, but neither head is conspicuous for individuality; this however may be the fault of the engravings, made after copies by Sandrart.

Under these heads was written—*Contrafät von Hans Holbein dem alten, Mahler;* and *Sigmund Holbein, Mahler und Bruder des ältern*—Portrait of Hans Holbein the old, Painter—Sigmund Holbein, Painter, and brother of the elder. I imagine that Sandrart a known collector of such things, and a man of property, was liable to be imposed upon, by the shrewd dealers of his time; the demand created the supply, and the portraits may have been fictitious.† We have the father's and mother's reputed portraits, in a very remarkable picture, supposed to be genuine, of this very year, 1512, on the small panel at Hampton Court, long since ascribed to our painter.‡ The father has in this picture no beard whatever; his age is marked as fifty-two, he was

* According to Dr. Woltmann, the father of this family was MICHAEL HOLBEIN, a currier or leather dresser in Augsburg. Schauer's *Holbein Album* 1865, for which Dr. Woltmann has supplied the text.

† These Sandrart drawings may or may not have been genuine; the father may have been copied from a figure in the "Martyrdom of St. Sebastian," now at Munich; that of Sigmund has certainly some resemblance to the Imhof drawing still preserved in the Museum of Berlin, a profile, photographed in Schauer's *Holbein Album*, and which may be the source of Sandrart's drawing. It is not presumed that the descriptions are by Holbein himself, even if of his time, which may also be questioned. The inscription on the Imhof drawing is simply *Sigmünd Holbain maler.* The Duke D'Aumale has a drawing of the father corresponding with this of Sigmund, also the reverse of the print, but it does not quite correspond with Sandrart's, the upper lip is shaven, and the inscription likewise—*Hans Holbain maler, der alt*—is not in agreement with Sandrart's.

‡ Hampton Court Gallery, No. 336, "Holbein's Father and Mother. 1512."

Holbein the father. 1492-1508.

therefore born in 1459–60: the mother's age in the same picture is marked as thirty-five.

There is another drawing by Holbein, still preserved in the Print Room of the Museum at Berlin, long supposed to represent Holbein and his father. It is one of the "Imhof" collection or book of Holbein sketches, is signed and dated, and the date has been commonly read as 1511, a reading which has been assumed to finally fix the year 1498 as that of Holbein's birth. The fact however operates quite against the common assumption.

This drawing is very interesting; it contains two heads, over the younger head is written "Hanns 14," between the heads is the name "Holbain," over the other head, on the right of the first, is a writing now all but illegible; the name has been hastily interpreted as *pr ejus*, that is *his father*, and against the name are two figures indicating the age, of which the second figure only is now ascertainable—a 5. Above the two names is the date which has been read as 1511, but which Passavant already, twenty years ago, admitted to be illegible. The second head is that of a man much too young to have been the father of the first, and Dr. Woltmann's investigations of the drawing have resulted in the discovery that this second portrait is that of Holbain's brother Ambrose, the letters interpreted as *pr ejus* being the remains of the name Amprosy, the supposed *j* being a long *s*: the age he has supplied as 25. The date of the year he reads 1509, the two figures interpreted as 11 being both curved, and portions only of the figures 0 and 9.*

With the exception of the age assigned to Ambrose, probabilities are all in favour of Dr. Woltmann's reading, and his conclusion as to the age may also be quite correct, but it will involve the necessity of assuming the two brothers to be sons of different mothers, if we accept the Hampton Court picture,

* A photolithograph of this drawing is given in Dr. Woltmann's first volume, and the disputed figures are there obscure enough: the date appears to be near enough to 1511 to be read as such, and the age of Ambrose is quite invisible.

CHAP. III.

Holbein the father. 1492-1508.

just referred to as genuine: the details of this question however belong to another place. What is important here is the date of the drawing 1509, and the fact that it does not represent Holbein the father.

Thus apparently has a little patient investigation, exposed a long-established theoretical reading, founded on foregone conclusions. The injuries to the date may certainly have been accidental, but they may also have been wilfully made, in order to harmonize the testimony of this interesting drawing with the popular assumption that Holbein was born in 1498, and thus obviate any question as to the authenticity of the drawing itself.

Rejecting the idealized head published by Sandrart as an authority, owing to the difficulty of the long grey beard, there is no authentic portrait to interfere with the genuineness of the Hampton Court picture, and I assume therefore that Hans Holbein the father, for so he is commonly called from the far greater reputation attained by his son, was born, at Augsburg, in the years 1459-60, as he was fifty-two years old in 1512, according to the inscription in this picture, in which I am inclined for various reasons to have faith; the date, the style, and the tradition are all in its favour.*

The name of Hans Holbein Maler occurs in the Register of Taxes, for Augsburg, eleven times—1494 Hanns Holbain, *Vom Diebollt;* in 1505, he is entered as Hans Holbein Maler, with Sigmund sein Bruder: and the name occurs for the last time in this register, in 1516.

The earliest known work we possess by the hand of this painter, is the small "Madonna and Child with angels," in the "Moritz Kapelle" at Nürnberg, which is signed HANS HOLBON and dated apparently 1492: The picture is said to be finished with great care, but I have not seen it. This was

* For a description of this piece see the 5th chapter—*Early Works at Augsburg.* There is a bearded head, that of one of the spectators in the back-ground in the picture of the "Martyrdom of St. Sebastian," which is a good deal like Sandrart's portrait: it is the first head on the spectator's left; I have already suggested that this head may be the source of Sandrart's.

CHAP. III.

Holbein the father. 1492-1508.

done in the artist's careful time in the elaborate style of the good Westphalian painters, when he was seeking a reputation. Later he either painted simply for money; or, indifferent, sent forth his pupils' work as his own. His name occurs in the Augsburg Register of Taxes for the years 1494–95, under the heading von Diebolt or Diepold, the name of the street, when he was living apparently in the house of Thomas Burgkmaier, near the Zucht-haus. He was according to Von Stetten,* but this is not otherwise established, married to old Burgkmaier's daughter, and was accordingly the brother-in-law of his pupil Hans Burgkmaier. As he was living at this time with his father-in-law, he had probably not very long been married, two or three years at most, for we learn from the Hampton Court picture referred to, that his wife was seventeen years younger than himself; she was born in 1476–7, and can hardly have been married before 1492 or 1493. She was four years younger than her brother Hans.

There are three pictures by Holbein the father, in the Augsburg Gallery, and though not his first in the order of time, they are those by which he has recovered in modern times his former reputation in Germany.

The picture of the Basilica of St. Paul, BASILICA SANCTI PAULI, already mentioned, and representing that church and the life and death of the saint, was painted in or before 1504, perhaps 1503, and was the donation to the convent of the Sister Veronica Welser, a lady of a distinguished Augsburg family; and the painter it is said has introduced her, seated, as the most prominent figure of the chief fore-ground group. He has however not painted her portrait, for from modesty, or perhaps from a principle of consistency, her back is turned to the spectator, and she shows only her head and a pretty neck, she herself being only a spectator of what is going on in the picture—the saint's preaching. The identity of this lady however is indicated by the name *Thecla* which the painter has

* Paul von Stetten, *Kunst-gewerbs-und Handwerks-geschichte der Reichsstadt Augsburg.* 8vo. Augs. 1779-88. I., p. 269, &c., quoted by Hegner.

CHAP. III.

Holbein the father.
1492-1508.

conspicuously written on the back of her chair, and this name has probably nothing whatever to do with Veronica Welser, for it is an historical name connected with the story of St. Paul himself. In the next division, on the left hand of this lady, who is in ordinary, not in conventual costume, are a middle-aged man with beard under the chin only, and two boys; and near them, is a female figure of somewhat sharp features. These four are now said to represent the painter, his wife, and two sons—Ambrose, and Hans our hero. This is however impossible if we allow Ambrose to have been born in 1484, for the elder of the two is but a boy of ten years old or so. This older-looking boy is somewhat more slightly built, and in features resembling a little the presumed wife, old Burgkmaier's daughter: the other boy on whom the father has laid his hand, is a large-headed round-faced boy, and may be eight or nine years old. The explanation of this supposed grouping of the painter and his family with the donatrix of the picture is a little romance; he is said to have been an admirer of hers before she entered the convent: this is the tradition I received from Herr Eigner, there is however not one particle of authority either for the story or for calling these four figures the painter and his family. Even if young Hans himself be there, and there is an amount of likeness between this head and that of the Berlin drawing dated 1509, it is not imperative to assume the older-looking boy to be a brother; Holbein had however a second brother, Bruno.

This work, an ordinary conventional altar-piece of the time, is like that of "Old Holbein," divided by the painter into compartments, and abounds in Gothic tracery and the usual gold enrichments. In the upper portion is "Christ crowned with thorns, scourged, and mocked by the people:" one of the most brutal of the actors is clothed with pantaloons, or hose rather, of blue and white stripes, with the veritable Bavarian cheques on the seat, showing the contempt of the imperial city of Augsburg for the Bavarians, with whom the Augsburgers were in constant hostility. In the lower compartments are—the Conversion, Baptism, and Martyrdom of St. Paul.

Separated from its historical interest this is a picture that would scarcely arrest a spectator many moments, in a picture gallery, but its associations indue it with great attractions. Though abounding in merit for its time, and well coloured yet not transparent, it is hard and eminently Gothic or rather German in its style, as we are familiar with that school in our own Gallery. It is superior to the reputed grandfather's work, in the Santa Maria Maggiore picture, in all respects, more especially in the relief of the figures, through a more vigorous contrast of light and shade, giving a sharper modelling, and by a variation in the male and female carnations. The tints are very clean and the impasto is solid, and is manipulated without difficulty. The weakest parts are of course the extremities, and it is disfigured by that resource of incompetent masters, histrionic exaggeration, in the place of true dramatic action—the protruding chin to which here is added a peculiarly projecting bristling beard; we have also the straightened leg, and pointed thrust-out toes, &c. The draperies are however simple without any offensive angularity or multiplicity of folds. The figures are somewhat more than one third the scale of life.

Besides this St. Paul picture the Sister Veronica presented also Hans Burgkmaier's work illustrating the Basilica of Santa Croce, with various pilgrims and the legend of St. Ursula and her eleven Martyr Virgins (XI. M. V.), which is signed—*Hans Burgkmair M. von Augspurg Anno* 1504. M. signifies Mahler-painter. This inscription gives us also the approximate date of Holbein's picture, for the two works were apparently ordered together, master and pupil receiving simultaneous commissions, as recorded in the annals; and the payment for the two was 187 florins,* a sum however which may be now as I have said, under-estimated in value, considering it even as 187 pounds sterling.

Burgkmaier had already produced a better picture in the

* Item, Veronica Welserin hat lassen zwu taffeln machn, die ainen von Heillig Creiz, die andre von Sanct Pauls—haben gestandn mit allem Dingen 187 gulden.

CHAP. III. — *Holbein the father.* 1492-1508.

Virgin in glory with the Patriarchs and Apostles, &c., and the fathers of the church below, signed—

J. BURGKMAIR
PINGEBAT
1501.

It is very brown and coarse in its manipulation but there is a good deal of manly vigour about it, and some firm modelling and decided expression; the preliminary drawing showing itself in many places through the thinly driven colour: it was no doubt expeditiously executed. The painter was then twenty-nine years old, according to the portrait of himself and wife in the Belvedere Gallery in Vienna, which is inscribed—

JOANN BURGKMAIER MALER LVI JAR ALT.

ANNA ALLERLAHN GEMAHEL LII JAR ALT. MDXXVIII.

Burgkmaier died three years afterwards, in 1531.

As a painter, on the whole, Holbein shows to greater advantage than Burgkmaier in the Augsburg Gallery and churches, though the latter was a more modern and vigorous artist; he had been in Italy, and had acquired some taste for the revived art of antiquity. His Basilica Vaticana, one of his best here, represents the façade of the old church of St. Peter, with the Transfiguration above, and the Apostles below; St. Peter holds in his left hand the keys of Heaven and Hell, and in his right a cartel inscribed "*Auctoritate Apostolica dimitto vobis omnia peccata.* 1501."

The other two works by Holbein the father in this gallery are:—

1. The Trinity, with six scenes in two rows from the Passion of Christ, below; which was ordered and perhaps painted in the year 1499, for the small sum of 26 florins; by Veronica, Walburg, and Christina Voetter, three sisters, sixty years inmates of the convent, whose portraits, according to the general custom, are introduced; though the only one living when the picture was finished, was Walburg, and she died in 1500.

2. The large picture in three divisions, painted in 1502, for

Holbein the father. 1492-1508.

the donor Ulrich Walther, whose daughter Anna was then prioress of the convent. His family and kindred are introduced in the fore-ground of the centre picture, a representation of the "Transfiguration:" on one side of this is the "Feeding of the four thousand;" on the other, "The casting out a Devil." This picture is remarkable for its rich and still well preserved colouring.

This Ulrich Walther died in 1505 aged eighty-six, and left behind him his widow and the vast family of one hundred and thirty-three children, grandchildren, and great-grandchildren; and the many figures in the three pictures are supposed to be all from his own family. The "Feeding of the four thousand" is one of the few subjects suitable for such a family. All this painting was done for 54½ florins, about four guineas of our money! and it is not among the painter's more careless works. When we think of the prices he received it is wonderful what this old painter accomplished.

It is however in the Cathedral of Augsburg that the really respectable ability of the elder Holbein is fully displayed, in the four works formerly in the convent or old abbey of Weingarten in Württemberg, recently restored by Herr Eigner of Augsburg, and now fitted up with handsome gilt Gothic carvings, richly pinnacled, over four altars in the body of the church. They were painted as early as 1493, and their superiority over his later works, especially those in the Munich Gallery, shows that the painter was tempted by success to neglect quality for quantity.

His pictures are numerous, in other cities besides Munich and Augsburg; the churches or galleries of Frankfurt, Nürnberg, Basel, and Schleissheim, all having several examples; but in Munich their abundance is oppressive, because with very few exceptions, they belong eminently to that class of work, which the Italians have stigmatized with the designation of *Roba di Bottega*, shop-rubbish, the greater part of their execution having been left to prentice-hands.

It is however not very easy to judge of pictures at Munich, that is, those hung in the large rooms, or so-called Säle, of the

Pinakothek; the windows of which are few, small, and very high. The glass has turned purple and the light is further excluded by the aid of dirty blinds, seldom drawn aside, and the rooms have the effect of gloomy caverns. As if these were not difficulties sufficient, the pictures are hung all above the eye, the bottom of the lowest frames being full five feet from the floor, so that even the smallest-sized portraits are so much above the eye as to be out of the reach of a proper investigation. This difficulty of seeing pictures is perhaps the main cause of the provoking practice of taking down and removing out of the gallery all pictures permitted to be copied. This leads to endless disappointments. Some of the best works of the collection are repeatedly absent for weeks and hundreds must go away without seeing them. On the two last occasions that I visited Munich, in 1863 and 1865, the fine early Canigiani Raphael, the so-called Pyramid, was away in the copying-room; in 1865 the two pictures I was most anxious to see were also away in the copying-room, the "Adoration of the Kings," by Memling, and Holbein's "St. Sebastian." As the attendants cannot pass visitors into this room it is necessary to procure the personal introduction of the keeper of the gallery, who is not always on the premises. Even the Louvre obstruction, of easels and scaffoldings, though they stand before the pictures the whole of the five days of the week that the gallery is open, is far preferable to this Munich practice. The Munich rooms have no rails certainly, so that you are not kept away from the walls as you are in Paris, or at Hampton Court, where the rail in some parts is at the impracticable distance of four feet from the wall, and all close examination is made impossible: but when the pictures are all hung over your head there is no advantage in being near the wall, nor is there any need of a rail: the Munich pictures were much better seen thirty years ago in the unpretending old rooms on the north side of the Hofgarten.

The pictures are now spread over the walls at arbitrary architectural intervals, reaching to the top; anywhere but opposite to the eye, as if they were mere pieces of ornamental furniture to display the damask, and set off the rooms. There is not even the help of the masters' names on the frames, the very numbers are or were so small, that many of them are invisible from below, though this defect has been in some cases remedied. As there is no explanation offered anywhere the visitor naturally had recourse to a catalogue, and there he met with the most vexatious disappointment of all, he found that he had paid two shillings for a book that gave him the barest modicum of information, that abounded in false attributions, and was not furnished with so simple an aid as an alphabetical index, and this has been allowed to go on for years.*

Holbein the father. 1492-1508.

In the first Saal, that devoted to the old German school, and containing seventy-six rather large pictures, are sixteen works on panel by the elder Holbein, part of a numerous series which he painted, by the assistance of pupils, in 1502, for the convent of Kaisersheim near Donauwörth; others of the series are in the Moritzkapelle at Nürnberg and at Schleissheim; the subjects are from the life and passion of Christ, and the history of the Virgin, with some passages also from the lives of the

---

* I refer to the well-abused *Verzeichniss der Gemaelde in der Königlichen Pinakothek zu München.* Preis 1 fl. 12 kr, of 1860 and other years: this anonymous book is something less than a reprint of the Catalogue of 1838 of the former Director G. von Dillis, with the most useful parts of it, the Introduction, and the Index at the end, omitted. This year happily (1865) the want of a guide in the gallery has been at last supplied, though the first copy I procured of the new work *had no Index.* However on my farewell visit to the pictures, the day before I left Munich, the 24th of July, I procured a copy with an Index, the first copy sold — *Verzeichniss der Gemalde in der älteren Königlichen Pinakothek zu München. Neue vollständig umgearbeitete und mit einem Register versehene ausgabe, von Prof. Dr. R. Marggraff.* 12mo. Munchen 1865. Pp. 265. The arrangement is numerical, and it is sold in the gallery stitched, for about half-a-crown, 1 fl. 24 kr. This gallery should not be visited without an opera-glass, and that a good one. The pictures in the Säle at Munich have the distinction of being probably the worst hung in Europe; the Salon Carré at Paris is hung on much the same architectural principles, but it at least is well lighted. Except on a cloudy day the temporary rooms of the National Gallery, at South Kensington, with their outside fixed blinds, I know no rooms so badly lighted as those of Munich. For *showing pictures* the much-abused rooms in Trafalgar Square are by far the best I have ever seen; they have crowded into them two or three times the number of pictures they were built for but that is no fault in the construction of the rooms, we simply require many more of them.

CHAP. III.

Holbein the father.
1492-1508.

Apostles: they are most of them about 6 feet high by nearly 3 feet wide. They have all the bad characteristic conventionalities of the ordinary German art of their time, and are what I consider come under the category of mere *roba di bottega*. One of this series, the "Annunciation," he has signed HANNS HOLBON.

There are works ascribed to him also at Frankfurt and at Basel, but were it not for the better examples at Augsburg his reputation would have to rest almost wholly upon the glory of having been the father of so able a son; happily these works give him a claim to our respect as a painter also, he was certainly the best of his time of the school of Augsburg, if not of all Germany.

The four pictures formerly, till 1715, in the abbey of Weingarten, now in the cathedral at Augsburg, were originally two wings of a shrine, the panels having been painted on both sides, a very common practice in the fifteenth century; when the shrine was shut you saw one side, and when open the other; they have now been sawn asunder the backs from the fronts and constitute four altar-pieces, of a very agreeable effect for German quattro-cento work; the panels are about 7 ft. 6 in. high, and 4 ft. wide; the subjects are—1. Joachim's offering in the Temple rejected; with the vision of the angel in the distance. 2. The Birth of the Virgin Mary; in this the nurse is testing the water with her naked foot, before washing the infant. 3. ThePresentation of the Virgin in the Temple: and 4. The Presentation and Circumcision of Christ. The figures are rather more than half the scale of life, and the influence of the Van Eyck school is decided; there is perhaps less effort at individuality in detail, than in the St. Paul picture of the gallery, but there is more dignity; they are more monumental works; the draperies are carefully hung and modelled, and undamaged by an over-abundance of lines and angles, as is too often the case in German draperies. The colours are well driven and blended and solid, there is no mere scumbling showing a brown under-painting below, as is seen in Burgkmair's work, and the effect is brilliant, though the colours

Holbein the father. 1492-1508.

are without transparency. Some very similar designs, indeed almost identical, have been engraved by Israel Van Meckenem, as part of a series of twelve scenes from the life of the Virgin, of which it is possible that the original designs were by this older Holbein; they may be seen in the Museum Print Room.* These interesting pictures are fortunately signed and dated, and we have the name of the old carver of the shrine or altar decoration as well as that of the painter; namely, Michael Erhart, sculptor. The girdle of one of the female figures in the composition, is inscribed—Michel. Erhart. Pildhauer. 1.4.93 Hanns. Holbain. Maler. O Mater Miserere Nobis.

These pictures were purchased by the present Bishop of Augsburg, Pankratius von Dinkel, for the comparatively large sum of 6,000 florins, 500*l.* sterling, and by him fixed in their present prominent places in the centre of the old cathedral.†

In 1499 Holbein left Augsburg, and we read of him in the same year as at Ulm, where he also had the rights of citizenship: he is noticed in an Augsburg document, dated the 6th November of this year, respecting the sale of a house, in which he is mentioned as—Hans Holbain the painter, now burgher of Ulm.‡

In 1500 and 1501 our painter was engaged in Frankfurt, working for the church and convent of the Dominicans, and living with those monks there. He has signed four of those pictures formerly in the refectory, representing the patriarchs from Abraham Isaac and Jacob, to Joseph; and the various generals of the Dominicans—Hans Hoilbayn de Augusta me pinxit, and has indicated the date 1501, in the following

* These prints are $10\frac{1}{8}$ in. *h.* by $7\frac{1}{4}$ in. *w.*; they are signed Israhel V. M. The following are the titles given by Bartsch, *Peintre Graveur*, VI., p. 215. *La Vie de la Vierge*—1. Le Grand-pretre refusant l'Offrande de Joachim. 2. La Naissance de la Vierge. 3. La Presentation au Temple. 4. La Circoncision.

† Dr. Woltmann who saw these pictures in their primitive damaged state, bears testimony to the skilfulness and faithfulness of Herr Eigner's restorations. I saw them after they were restored, in July 1865, and was certainly astonished at their good general effect and excellent details. They came lately from Bregenz, and had previously belonged to an Austrian General, von Wocher.

‡ Woltmann, Vol. I., p. 81.

CHAP. III.

Holbein the father. 1492-1508.

words—Ano a partu Virginis salutifero M° V^c Primo. It is remarkable that in the few instances in which he has written his name in full, we have four different spellings—Hollbain, Holbein, Holbon, and Hoilbayn (printed Hollbayn in some accounts).

At the suppression of the religious houses in 1803 the ancient repose of this convent was disturbed, and in 1809, about twenty of these Holbein pictures, together with many others, were dispersed, but some few were saved, and placed in the town museum, and they are still in the Frankfurt Library: two others, very ordinary, are in the Städel Museum; "Christ's entry into Jerusalem;" and the "Driving the money-changers from the Temple." They formed parts of an altar-piece, the centre of which, the "Last Supper," is now in the St. Leonhard's church. Others which were in the possession of Dr. Schäfer in Darmstadt, are now also in the Städel Museum.*

In 1506, 1507 and 1508 Holbein was still engaged in Augsburg, executing some works for the St. Moritz Kirche and Convent, as is shown by some still existing documents in the city archives, in which the name is written Holpain, containing some interesting though not very clear money accounts, but no accurate description of the works: the chief however consist of side pictures or wings for two shrines or altar-pieces.

On the 25th January 1506 he received 32 florins;

On the 28th October, 10 florins, on account of the 100 florins that he was to have for the four wings of one altar-piece;

On the 14th January 1507, 10 fl.;

On the 29th March, he borrowed 3 fl. of the wife of the steward;

On the 10th of June he received 10 fl.; on the 15th,

---

* See the account of these works and the history of their dishonest dispersal in Dr. P. F. Gwinner's, "*Kunst und Künstler in Frankfurt am Main,*" &c. 1862. In Hüsgen's time, 1780 (*Artistisches Magazin*), they were all still reposing under venerable dust in their original places. It seems that C. G. Schütz a landscape-painter and picture-cleaner to whom they were entrusted in 1809 for the purpose of being cleaned and restored, repaired a few only, and sold the rest for his own benefit.

20, and on the 27th of the same month 27 fl., through persistently urging his great need.

On the 2nd October, 40 fl.

By an entry of the 16th of March 1508, it appears that he had undertaken a contract to paint some altar-wings, the centre probably being a carved shrine, for the large sum of 325 florins; of this amount he had then received 240 fl., leaving a residue of 85 fl.; he then received 11 fl. besides a present (drink-money) of 5 fl. to his wife, and 1 fl. to his son.* The remaining 74 fl. were paid on the 31st March 1509, to Thomas Freihamer, to whom Holbein was to that amount indebted.†

It is about this time that he is reported to have been invited to Basel, to be consulted concerning the decorations of the new town-hall, then about to be undertaken,‡ and which was carried out between the years 1508, when the old house was pulled down, and 1521 and following years, when the paintings of the new house were finished: those of the council-room however being carried out by the son Hans, not the father.

He is commonly reported in 1516 to have settled in, or at least visited, Basel with all his family, consisting of three sons: this seems however to have been inferred chiefly from the circumstance of his having left Augsburg in that year. His two elder sons Ambrose and Hans both acquired the rights of master-painters in Basel; the former in 1517 and Hans two or three years later. Hans appears to have been the only one who took up the rights of citizenship, but of this more hereafter.

The third son Bruno was also a painter according to Dr. Patin, but he is scarcely known, he is supposed to have died young. The father was living in 1521, but both time and place of his death are as yet uncertain, though it is recorded

* Perhaps Ambrose.

† *Auszug aus den Zechpflege-Rechnungen von St. Moritz.* Woltmann, *Holbein, &c., Beilagen* V., vol. I., p. 364.

‡ Ochs, *geschichte der stadt Basel, &c.* V., 396-7; Hegner, *Hans Holbein, &c.,* p. 70. These statements are not authenticated by any documents, and I give them as I find them as mere reports. That Sigmund Holbein however migrated to Switzerland is certain; but he settled in Bern not in Basel.

CHAP. III.

Holbein the father. 1492-1508.

that he died, or was dead in 1524. He never became a citizen of Basel, and therefore never settled there. I have given evidence of his having been still in Augsburg in 1516, but there is no further notice of him till 1524, when his name occurs among the deceased artists, in a register of painters in the Maximilian's Museum at Augsburg—*Handwerks buch der Maler*,—"1524 Hannss Holbain Maler."*

In the museum of Basel are exhibited nine drawings and three coarse indifferent Passion-pictures assigned to him: whether they are by him or by Hans Scheuffelin, or by anybody else, is not worth the labour of the inquiry.

The only work in the museum at all resembling him in his best style, or approaching in merit his good works at Augsburg, is No. 25 in the catalogue (1863)—"The History of Christ's Passion," in eight small compositions, some of them showing great spirit and energy, forming an altar-piece; each picture is somewhat more than 2 ft. 2 in. high, and about 13 inches wide. The subjects are—

1. The prayer of Christ in Gethsemane.
2. The kiss of Judas.
3. Christ before the High Priest.
4. The flagellation.
5. Christ mocked.
6. The procession to Mount Calvary.
7. Christ on the Cross.
8. The deposition in the Tomb.†

* Woltmann, *Holbein &c., Beilagen*, p. 357. Dr. Woltmann notices two portraits of an Augsburg merchant, Anton Rehm, of the year 1522, with green backgrounds, similar to the works of the son, as the productions of the father; one is in the Library of St. Gallen, the other in the possession of Herr Herberger in Augsburg. The first mentioned is inscribed ANTON: RHEM EQUES S. SEPULCHRI: ET S. CATHARINAE. ANNO 1522.

† Lithographs of these compositions by various artists, but much modernized, may be seen in the Print Room of the British Museum; they were published by Merian in Basel in 1829. These prints, apparently the same size as the pictures, average about 27 inches high by 13 inches wide. If compared with the fine drawings of the "Passion" by Holbein, in the same collection, or in the British Museum, of which one is engraved in this volume, their great inferiority will be evident to any one, and they are still more inferior, considered as paintings.

Holbein the father. 1492-1503.

In the last we have something of the scheme of the "Entombment" of Raphael, in the Borghese.

These pictures are accredited to Hans Holbein the son, but they have nothing of his brownness, of his transparency of colouring or of his freedom of execution, or of his power in any way. On the contrary they have quite the impasto of the St. Paul picture of the convent of St. Catherine, though they are more finished and delicate, but hard and without elasticity in their modelling, and more uniform in execution; but they have the same histrionic attitudes, hooked noses, and even the same peculiarity of beard noticed; they are hard and wooden and altogether without transparency. The compositions have some of them sufficient energy and occasionally a Holbein character, but the *painting* is certainly not the work of a great master. There is no such mastery in this "Passion" as to preclude its being a careful early work of the father, and its ascription to his more celebrated son may have arisen simply out of a confusion of the two painters through identity of name: it may even possibly be a work of the successful Sigmund Holbein of whom examples are so singularly rare that he must be said to be an unknown master. Men are prone to reproduce themselves in their pictures, and the prevailing nose of these compositions is certainly the nose of Sigmund.

Granting it to be by a Holbein, and supposing it to be by the younger Hans, it is almost impossible to assign it a time; for it is not like anything else by him either at Augsburg or in Basel. In attempting to classify the works of the Holbeins, it should surely not be overlooked that there were certainly two other painters of this family, besides the father, who lived and produced pictures, and yet of whom we have now but one single authentic example—Sigmund the uncle and Ambrose the brother or half-brother; what has become of their works?

This "Passion" is not one of the Amerbach pictures; its history is unknown, and there is no authority for giving it to Holbein beyond popular rumour, and the incidental gossip always found attending such rumours in books; we first meet with it in the town-hall about a hundred years after Holbein's

CHAP. III.

Holbein the father.
1492-1508.

death, and it has been assumed that it was one of the few relics of the cathedral rescued from the Iconoclasts of 1529, of whose doings Erasmus has given us a melancholy picture. It remained in the town-hall until 1769 when it was thoroughly *restored* by a painter of Stuttgart of the name of Grooth, and in the following year, 1770, it was removed to the public library, in the museum of which it is now preserved. How far its present uniform *wooden* aspect may be owing to Herr Grooth's restorations I cannot say, but I am quite satisfied that such a wooden uniformity of texture as some of these figures show cannot have proceeded from the pencil of Holbein, whatever may have been the source of the compositions. A solution of the difficulty, and not a bad one, is that the picture was entirely repainted by Grooth in 1769: finding it perhaps difficult to match the new with the old, he made it all new.

Sandrart, not seldom wrong in matters of criticism, going along with the rest of the world, took it for granted that the celebrated Hans was the Holbein who was the reputed painter of the series, and he relates that in 1644 while painting the portrait of the Elector Maximilian of Bavaria, he spoke so highly of it, that the Elector sent a commissioner to Basel to buy it; the sum of money however, or amount of salt, offered for it, was no temptation to the civic authorities of Basel, and the picture remained in Switzerland. The real sum is not known, modern exaggeration has raised it to an extravagant amount. There is a record noticing the refusal to sell, but Sandrart has somehow confused the story, it happened in 1641 according to the documents, not in 1644.* However I speak of the work as we now see it. My impressions were ingrained while standing before the picture itself, in spite of Herr His-Heusler's endeavours to efface them. When we are once familiar with example upon example, both in drawing and in painting, such as we have in England, of the stupendous power of Holbein in seeing and representing individual character, in its most superficial and in its profoundest elements, it is

* Hegner, *Hans Holbein*, &c., p. 81.

Holbein the father. 1492-1508.

impossible to believe that he could at intervals have let those powers slumber and have debased his art to the level of the handicraft of a mere image or puppet-painter.

As Mr. Ruskin has well said, Holbein was complete in intellect, what he saw he saw with his whole soul, and what he painted, he painted with his whole might. "His work is true and thorough; accomplished in the highest as in the most literal sense, with a calm entireness of unaffected resolution, which sacrifices nothing, forgets nothing, and fears nothing!"

The figures of this Passion do not belong to such a master. We are all supposed to seek the truth, and criticism should it only lead to the sounder investigation of a subject, does good service. The works of the successful Sigmund Holbein have yet to be hunted out, and it will require researches among the archives of Bern. This Passion has however all the appearance of being a careful work of the father's, though it is certainly better than anything we know to be his, more especially in its grouping and character.

Sigmund Holbein, living 1540.

SIGMUND HOLBEIN, the brother of Hans the father and Holbein's only uncle, was some few years younger than his brother, but his order in the family of five is not known; about 1465–70 is perhaps not too late a date to assign him: he was probably never married, or if married he had no family as all his property was left to his nephew in London and his three sisters in Augsburg. When Hans Holbein and the other male branches of the family left Augsburg on their presumed journey for Switzerland, the females remained behind, at least the three sisters, who were probably then married and settled in their own country. Of Burgkmair's daughter the elder Holbein's wife we have no record beyond what has just been stated.

Sigmund is noticed in the Register of Taxes for the years 1505 and 1509, not afterwards, his final wandering from his home supposing Augsburg his home, may have accordingly taken place in 1509. He did not settle in Basel; if he visited it, he removed to Bern and obtained the citizenship of that place, where he acquired a house and other property. It is

CHAP. III.

Sigmund Holbein, living 1540.

even possible that Sigmund's settling in Switzerland was the cause of his nephew's visiting that country.

There is only one signed painting of Sigmund Holbein's yet known and that is an early work on a gold ground, now in the Burgh, formerly in the collection of the Landauer-Brüderhaus, at Nürnberg, at present a School of Design and Manufactures: it represents the "Virgin and Child enthroned," with a choir of angels above, two hovering angels crowning the Virgin, and a third holding a green drapery behind her: it is signed S. HOLLBAIN F., but the signature is written from left to right. I do not recollect having seen this picture.

Two other works of a much more modern character, which have been ascribed to Sigmund, but are not signed, are two very good small portraits on wood, companion pieces, in the Belvedere Gallery at Vienna; one representing an old man, the other a young man, both in black, and both without beards, the two heads covered, rather less than life size, and of what may be termed perhaps the Holbein school, though the style belongs generally to most of the good painters of the north in the earlier part of the sixteenth century. Many portraits ascribed to Holbein are inferior to these two heads.

In our own Gallery is a good portrait, ascribed hypothetically to this painter; it was presented by the Queen in 1863, and represents a Swiss lady in a large white cap on which a fly has settled; her maiden name was Hoferin or Hofer, GEBORNE HOFERIN is inscribed on the picture, the foregoing words have been cut away. She shows both hands, in one of which she holds a piece of forget-me-not. Bust, life-size, on deal, 1 ft. 9 in. high by 1 ft. 3½ in. wide.

Both this picture and that of the Landauer-haus at Nürnberg were formerly in the collection of Prince Ludwig von Oettingen-Wallerstein. The Landauer collection was lately dispersed, and this picture has been placed in the Burgh or Castle of Nürnberg.

Passavant* compares Sigmund Holbein with Martin Schoen,

* *Kunstblatt, l. c.*

CHAP. III.

Sigmund Holbein, living 1540.

by whom there are several works at Colmar, of a hard dry character.

Among the drawings at Berlin, is a capital head, a profile, of Sigmund Holbein, by his nephew: he has long hair, an aquiline nose, and a short bushy beard. The forehead is full and high, and the whole countenance intelligent and handsome. The head of Sigmund engraved by Sandrart, is similar to this drawing, and perhaps derived from it, but it is idealized and not in the least improved; it is on the contrary very inferior.*

There must be authentic works by Sigmund still in Bern, and no doubt at Basel also: he was a prosperous painter, as he possessed property in Bern and at Augsburg. His Will made September the 6th 1540, is preserved among the chancery records at Bern. He bequeaths all his property in Bern—house and grounds, in the Brunngasse, furniture, plate, and all *painting materials*, comprising colours, painter's gold and silver (malergold und silber) to his "beloved brother's son Hans Holbeyn the painter, citizen of Basel, as his born blood relation, of his own direct line, and name; and from the great love and friendship he bore him." Whatever he possessed in Augsburg was to be divided equally among his three sisters—Ursell Messerschmid in Augsburg, Anna Elchinger by St. Ursell-am-Schwall also in Augsburg, and Margreth Herwart at Esslingen. He gives as the reason for making his Will that he was about to set out on a visit to his own people in Augsburg, and might die before his return.†

There is no positive record of his death, and whether his nephew in London ever inherited personally or derived any direct benefit from it is not known.

As neither Ambrose nor Bruno Holbein are mentioned in the Will, they were probably both already deceased, in 1540, and they had apparently died without leaving any family

* See the photograph in Schauer's *Holbein Album—Hans Holbein der Jüngere.* Text von Dr. Alfred Woltmann. 4to. Berlin, 1865.

† Hegner, *Hans Holbein der Jüngere.* This contemplated journey was apparently never made; it seems to have been interrupted by his death very soon after the making of this will, namely, before the 18th of November 1540. The will is given in the original in full by Dr. Woltmann.

CHAP. III.

Sigmund Holbein, living 1540.

behind them. Sigmund himself was already dead on the 18th of November of that year. The property left to his nephew Hans in London, who had visited him perhaps in 1538, was enjoyed by the wife, who was thenceforth possibly independent of her husband.

There can be little doubt about the distribution of the property, for among the archives of Bern, there is a document bearing date January 10th 1541, which shows that Holbein's step-son Franz Schmid was sent to Bern with letters of administration, by his mother Holbein's wife—*Elssbeth, meyster Hansen Holbein's des maler's, Burger's zu Basell, Eeliche Hussfrouw*—to take up the inheritance of her husband.

This discovery that Holbein's wife ELIZABETH SCHMID was a widow and a mother when he married her is very important; it is most probable that she was several years older than our painter, and it is also possible that she had some means or occupation of her own, independent of such assistance as her young German husband could give her. These circumstances should materially modify the judgment that has been formed prejudicial to Holbein as regards his leaving this woman and ceasing to cohabit with her, from the time of his first journey to England. He had but one child by her that we know of, and a future chapter will show that the education of this child was not neglected.

That Franz Schmid and Philip Holbein were only half-brothers is shown by a letter from the Burgomaster of Basel dated 19th November 1545, to a Swiss goldsmith in Paris, where he is mentioned not only as his brother but as his guardian also, showing that mother and father were both dead at that date: Philip as he had a guardian was of course under age; but at that time and even now, in Basel, civil majority is not attained until the completion of the 25th year.*

* His-Heusler, *Beiträge, &c., l. l.* "Dem Erbarn, unserm lieben Burger, Jacoben David, dem goldschmid zu Paryss."— * * * * "*Philipp Holbein, noch under sinen jarenn, durch Frantzen Schmid, sinen bruder, unsern Burger vervögtigett, &c.* * * * * Datum Donstag denn XIX. tag Novembris A° XLV." This Franz Schmid was then quite thirty years of age, at the least.

Ambrose Holbein. 1517

Ambrose or Ambrosius Holbein, is commonly reported as much the elder brother of Hans, but as I have come upon no grounds beyond a vague assertion, for the assumption, I must either disregard it or adopt the suggestion already made, that Ambrose and Hans were only half-brothers, and this is the conclusion my inclination tends to: he was no result of the marriage of Hans Holbein the elder with old Burgkmaier's daughter. If we might depend upon ordinary custom, and were compelled to judge exclusively on conjecture, we should be justified in assuming Hans to be the elder son of the marriage referred to, as he bore his father's baptismal name. The thinner built boy in the St. Paul altar-piece described, seems much about the same age as the other, but if there is any difference he looks a little older; it is impossible to judge within a year or two from mere appearances of this kind: he is probably Bruno, but as I have already remarked there is no necessity for his being a brother at all.

It is remarkable that German writers have so long followed vague speculations as to the ages of several of the painters of this family, when such very good data exist to set aside such speculations. Von Mechel, who arranged, and compiled a catalogue of the Belvedere Gallery in Vienna in 1781, has suggested 1450 and 1456, as the birth dates of the elder Hans and Sigmund, and 1484 as that of Ambrose; and the German writers to the present day retain some of these old speculative dates, not excepting even Dr. Waagen, and Passavant.*

Dr. Waagen, thirty years ago, in 1835, published in his *Kunstwerke und Künstler in England*, the ages and date on the Holbein family picture at Hampton Court, without a question as to its authenticity, and yet has made no use of the information such dates confer: the style of the picture, independent of its dates and tradition, sufficiently proclaims it, I think, a genuine work to any who have carefully studied Holbein's pictures at

* It is just possible that this birth year 1484, may have been derived from the Berlin drawing mentioned, before it became so much obscured as it is at present.

CHAP. III.

Ambrose Holbein. 1517.

Augsburg and at Basel. Passavant however, though in his *Kunstreise durch England und Belgien*, published in 1833, he has noticed some pictures hanging near this piece at Hampton Court, has omitted to mention this very interesting pair of portraits.

To complete the account of Ambrose here I must repeat what I have already given in substance. Accepting the evidence of the figures in this picture of the father and mother, the latter was not born before 1476, and can only have been married at the earliest about 1493; Ambrose therefore cannot have been born much earlier than 1494, or have been more than a year older than Hans, if the son of Burgkmaier's daughter. If the figures already spoken of which Dr. Woltmann found over the head of "Amprosy" in the Berlin drawing, do not lead us to this conclusion, I have no hesitation in adopting a compromise, and if we must not infer that the lost unit before the 5 is 1 and that Ambrose was 15 years old when his brother Hans drew him, in 1509, we have the only alternative left, that the missing figure is a 2, that Ambrose was 25 years old in 1509, and accordingly that he was only the half-brother of Hans; either by a former marriage, or illegitimate.

Ambrose went apparently in 1516, if not earlier, to Basel, and was admitted a member of the Guild of Painters there, on St. Matthew's Day, February 24th, in the year 1517; but he did not according to custom take up the rights of citizenship.* He may have moved elsewhere, or more probably he died shortly afterwards; in 1518 or 1519?

There are four pictures attributed to Ambrose, in the Gallery of the Museum of Basel, which formed part of the Amerbach

* "Ambross Holbein Mahler von Augsburg." Ochs, *geschichte der stadt Basel.* Vol. V., p. 394, quoted by Hegner; and more fully by M. His-Heusler:—"Item es hatt entpfangen die Zunfft uff Sant Mattistag Ambross Holbein maler von Augspurg in dem xvij jor."

It is a rule enforced in many German cities that a trade cannot be practised except by a member of the guild, or under the employment of some member, and therefore as a journeyman only; and this explains the necessity of this constant taking up of the freedom of guilds by artists and others, making even short stays only in the cities they visited. In Basel they were obliged to take up also the rights of citizenship within a certain limited period.

Collection, purchased by the city council in 1661, for 9,000 thalers, about 1,350 pounds sterling.* CHAP. III.

Ambrose Holbein. 1517.

These pictures are No. 36, a "Salvator Mundi," after Albert Dürer; Nos. 37 and 38, two delicately painted heads of two boys; and No. 39, two human skulls. The two last are very carefully painted, in a smooth elaborate style, much in the taste of the works of Hans Holbein, but without any special excellence or vigour: Dr. Patin enumerates them among the works of Hans. Worse work, however, still passes under the name of his brother, in many galleries.

Three drawings also are exhibited under the same name, and from the same collection:—a man's portrait dated 1517; a woman's portrait, of the following year; and another female portrait without date.

A small "Portrait of a man in black," a very well executed head, in the Belvedere Gallery at Vienna, is likewise ascribed to this painter, by Von Mechel: now No. 17 among the old German pictures; it is on wood, about 17 in. high by 12 in. wide.

The monogram ÆH found on some drawings and woodcuts of this time is supposed in some cases to indicate Ambrose Holbein. The same mark was used by Augustin Hirschvogel. This monogram occurs with the date 1517, in a large book-title border, 10 by 6¾ inches, of the *Des. Erasmi Roterodami in Novum Testamentum, &c., Annotationes*, published by Frobenius in Basel in 1519. The design contains above, the Battle of Arminius; and below, the "Calumny of Apelles," inscribed *Apelles hujusmodi pictura Calumniam ultus est*; it is treated much as the subject, which was popular in the sixteenth century, is commonly treated. No doubt many other such decorations, comprising some attributed to his brother Hans, were executed by Ambrose. Rumohr † notices two others similar in style, and of nearly the same size: one the "Hercules Gallicus;" the other the "Imago Vitae aulicae," about 9½ in.

* That is computing the thaler at three shillings; if the crown dollar is signified, the sum will be raised to 1,875*l*.

† Von Rumohr, *Hans Holbein, &c.*; Passavant, *Pientre Graveur.* Vol. III., p. 421.

CHAP. III.

Ambrose Holbein. 1517.

high by 6¾ in. wide. The first is signed HF and dated 1519; the second, of which there is a copy in the Museum Print Room is in the *Max. Tyrii Sermones*, and also in some later works published by Froben. The same monogram ÆH occurs in Froben's *Velleius Paterculus*, 1520; in the *Opera Divi Caecilii Cypriani Episcopi*, &c., fol. 1521; and in the title decoration of the *Adagia* of Erasmus, published at Basel in 1523.

Bruno Holbein.

Of BRUNO HOLBEIN I have met with no account, except the incidental mention of him as a painter at Basel by Patin in his memoir of Holbein prefixed to the *Moriae Encomium* of Erasmus, published in 1676, showing that it was a Basel tradition. Patin's authority was probably Herr Fesch.*

* Dr. Woltmann quotes the following from a MS. by the collector Remigius Fesch—"A. 1651 mense Aug. cum admissus essem ad inspectionem Musaei Amerbachiani, ab heredibus, vidua Basilii Iselii Amerbachiade p. m. (per Matrem) audivi in schedis Amerbachianis reperiri tres fuisse fratres Holbeinos pictores omnes, hunc Johannem, Ambrosium, Brunonem." Vol. I., p. 187.

THE SECOND BOOK.

HANS HOLBEIN THE YOUNGER. IN AUGSBURG, AND IN BASEL.

CHAPTER IV.

BORN IN AUGSBURG IN 1494–5.

OHANNES or as the Germans in olden times invariably contracted the name, HANS, was, according to tradition, his father's second son, but, failing any document to the contrary we might assume him to have been the eldest son; both from his name, being that of his father, and from the almost extreme youth of his mother, as such, when he was born. However, from the circumstances detailed in the notice of Ambrose, we may as well leave this matter as we have found it. In order to make my account of each member of this family as complete as possible I must reiterate a few facts in this place that have been already substantially given before, in the notices of the father, and of Ambrose Holbein.

The "Strasse zum Diebold." 1494-5.

CHAP. IV.

The "Strasse zum Diebold." 1494-5.

The question as to the locality where Holbein was born may be considered settled; it was in or near Augsburg, and if we place it in the house of his reputed maternal grandfather Thomas Burgkmair, in the "Strasse zum Diebold," near where the Zuchthaus now is, we shall probably be not far wrong: this is where his father and mother were living in 1494 and 1495.

The date of his birth is not so easily fixed, as from the commonly vague fashion of recording dates in inscriptions, we may be as much as a whole year from the exact day. For instance in the case of Holbein we have two inscriptions purposing to fix the date, namely that of the Imhof Sketch-book in the Berlin Museum—"1509, Hanns Holbein 14," and that on a picture in the Augsburg Gallery, to be described presently—"1512, Aet Suæ 17." In subtracting the age from the date we have in each case 1495; but do the inscriptions signify in his fourteenth and seventeenth years respectively, or when fourteen and seventeen years of age: that is, in his fifteenth and eighteenth years?

Here at once is the difference of a whole year. Again a man will be in his seventeenth year the day after he has completed his sixteenth, or the day before he enters upon his eighteenth, also giving nearly a year's latitude. Accordingly we cannot fix the date of Holbein's birth within a year, but we know that he was born either in 1494 or 1495. If it could be shown that Holbein was the second son, then we might safely infer that he was born late in 1495; but in any case, from the extreme youth of his mother at the time, who we learn from the Hampton Court portraits, was born in 1476–7, probabilities are in favour of the later date.

This drawing of the year 1509 is interesting as the earliest known work of the painter, it marks also the coincidence of his career as an artist commencing with the reign of Henry VIII. of England; and in that regnal system not uncommon in earlier times and officially in use now, of reckoning events by the year of the ruling monarch's reign, we have in the case of Holbein and Henry identical numbers,

CHAP. IV.

The "Strasse zum Diebold." 1494-95.

though while the painter's dynasty reached only the 35th year, the king's extended to the 38th.

There is still a third inscription known in engravings, which implies 1498 as the year of Holbein's birth; but the authority for this statement is not to be found. There is a circular print by Luke Vorsterman, 4¾ inches in diameter, without date; a head and shoulders, but both hands are seen, he has on a skull-cap, and has a beard, and he is *painting with his left hand*, the print, as was common in those days, being reversed. The ground of this portrait has no inscription of any kind, but around the outside is engraved the following legend:—*Joannes Holbenius Pictor Regis Magnae Britanniae sui caeculi celeberrimus anno* 1543 *aetat.* 45. This print has been copied the same size by Hollar, but the painting left hand is omitted, and we have for the information of the legend—a monogram, the age of painter and the date, on the *ground* of the picture, as if it were all autograph, thus—HH Æ 45—AN° 1543. Below is the legend—*Vera Effigies Johannis Holbeinij Basiliensis Pictoris et Deliniatoris rarissimi. Ipse Holbeinius pinxit, Wenceslaus Hollar aqua forti aeri insculpsit. Ex Collec: Arundel:* 1647. It is a round, 4 in. in diameter.

Here much more is said than in the simple legend of Vorsterman; it would indeed be difficult to be more positive or circumstantial, yet as the Arundel picture, or drawing, in question is apparently lost, it is quite worthless as evidence, though some such picture may have existed, as the following note quoted by Walpole, testifies—"In the Arundelian Collection, says Richard Symonds, was a head of Holbein in oil by himself, most sweet, dated 1543," but observe, nothing about the painter's age.

This portrait can, possibly, be the round miniature mentioned by Van Mander, as at Amsterdam in his time, and it may also be the very portrait given by Sandrart to Le Blond, from whom it could have passed to the Earl of Arundel, before 1647.

A round oil miniature on oak, 4⅞ inches in diameter, or 4½ inches sight measure, is in the possession of Mr. R. Verity, of

CHAP. IV. *The "Strasse zum Diebold."* 1494-5.

South Woods, Thirsk; it was formerly at Rutland House, Knightsbridge, the town residence of the Dukes of Rutland, the collections in which were dispersed in about 1835. This clearly represents the head seen in prints, a middle-aged man, with short brown beard, and brown eyes, in a black skull-cap and jacket, with a white shirt, edged with a small frill. Parts of both hands are seen, and he is in the position of a man sitting at an easel painting his own portrait, with his right hand, and possibly holding with his left some small palette or utensil for painting, which is nearly covered by the hand. The back-ground is of a raw umber colour, and is inscribed, not with gold, but with dirty yellow:—H. H. above, one on each side of the head, with AN°. 154×. and ÆTA. 45. beneath the two letters. The fourth figure of the date may have been a 3, but it is not legible now. The face is expressive, but imperfectly drawn, the right eye being incorrectly placed and insufficiently foreshortened; the painting is rubbed, is softer than Holbein in manner, and is probably a century or more later. It has some resemblance to the reputed head of the painter, at Florence; but in that there are no hands. The head itself though not identical with, corresponds mainly also with Hollar's print, but the writing which does not look old, is very different in its form, as the comparison of the two inscriptions here given will show. Hollar's head is seen a little more in profile, otherwise as this miniature belonged to the Rutland family, it may have previously formed part of the Arundel Collection, as the Arundel and Rutland families were connected by marriage; but it is most certainly not identical with Hollar's print either in its form or in its inscription.

A small round finely executed miniature, of the painter himself, a man with a short beard, likewise supposed to represent Holbein, and not unlike Vorsterman's print of him, was sold at Strawberry Hill in 1842, for 13 guineas.* It is 1½ inches in diameter, and has a deep blue back-ground; the

---

* See Cat., p. 116, No. 40.

painter has on a black coat and skull-cap, and is working with his right hand; it in fact corresponds very well in *reverse* with Vorsterman's print, except that it has the following legend in gold, on the ground:—on one side of the head is AN°. 1543—on the other ÆTATIS SVÆ 4×; the last figure of the age having perished; and over each inscription is an H, certainly retouched: the eyes of the picture are grey, also possibly retouched. In comparing the above inscription with that of Hollar's portrait, the difference is obvious; and we are certain that this miniature is not the original of Hollar's engraving, unless we infer that the inscription was the arbitrary addition of the engraver. I am not only of opinion that Hollar is the sole author of his back-ground legend, but that he copied Vorsterman's print, not any picture; or otherwise he would not have omitted the painting right hand. Of course my opinion amounts to the belief that Hollar's print is an imposture, yet so far an innocent one that he was not aware that the legend he transformed into a presumptive autograph, was erroneous: but any invention of a signature is sufficiently mischievous, and is essentially a forgery.

CHAP. IV.

The "Strasse zum Diebold." 1494-5.

The miniature in question passed from Strawberry Hill into the possession of the eccentric Mr. Blamire, of the Adelphi, and is now in the collection of the Duke of Buccleuch; there is however nothing really to identify it with Holbein, though it may possibly be of his period, nor is the inscription necessarily an autograph. I have examined it very carefully; though the age may once have been 45, it is positively irrecoverable now: Holbein's true age requires a 7 or an 8 to supply the place of the missing figure. An old copy apparently of this same miniature, in oil, or simply varnished, is in the possession of Mr. Mackay of the firm of Colnaghi and Co., the eyes are decidedly grey: the inscription is quite rubbed out.

Many other prints have been issued since Vorsterman's, with some of the details of the two above described, but with slight variations, and evidently not a single one from any authentic

CHAP. IV.

The "Strasse zum Diebold." 1494-5.

picture.* Should the original Arundel picture ever be found, for if Hollar's print be genuine, it cannot be the above described miniature, and the whole inscription be considered autograph, 45 may still prove a misreading for 48, for I can scarcely imagine that Holbein can have been so forgetful as not to know his own age, or so weak or vain as to wilfully misrepresent it. However the fact may be, until the original be forthcoming there is nothing to shake the sure testimony above recorded, in favour of the earlier date. A bird in the hand is said to be worth two in the bush, here we have two in hand against only one in the bush.

Fictitious signatures.

As one illustration of the pernicious character of fictitious signatures under false impressions, where mere hearsay has been gratuitously embodied into an ostensible autograph I may instance the portrait of Edward VI., at Wilton, which is signed E. VI. R. HANS. HOLBEEN. P. This we now know to be false, though the writer may have been unconscious of its falsehood. Another striking instance is that of another picture at Wilton which is a copy of the small panel with portraits of three children, by Mabuse, now at Hampton Court. This picture is inscribed—K: HENRY VII.

THREE OF HIS CHILDREN. HÄNS HOLBEEN P: 1495
ye Father

and over the three heads respectively, are the names HENRY, ARTHUR, MARGARET.

The information thus boldly placed on the *face* of the picture at Wilton is copied from the *back* of the picture at Hampton

* All are made up from previous prints; as for example, one by R. Gaywood from Hollar; another by And. Stockius; that engraved for Patin's *Moriae Encomium*, 1676, said to be from a drawing in the Fesch collection at Basel; and that in the edition of Van Mander's *Lives, &c.*, 1764. Vorsterman's seems to have been copied, in another shape, for Bullart's *Académie des Sciences et des Arts*, Brussels, 1695; but it has the simple legend beneath, no monogram or other writing on the ground; the painter is however at work with his left hand. The small portrait on paper, about 15 in. *h.* by 11½ *w.*, said to be that of Holbein, in the Uffizj, at Florence, has the legend "JOANNES HOLPENIUS BASILEENSIS SUI IPSIUS EFFIGIATOR. Æ 45," but no year, this however has no pretension to being autographic, it is evidently spurious.

CHAP. IV.

Fictitious signatures. 1494-5.

Court, on which is written:—*Henry huit^{me} Roy d la Grande Bretagne, avec ses deux seùres. Marie espousa Louis XII. Roy de France, en suitte Brandon. Margarite espouse Jaques IIII. Roy d'Escosse.* This inscription is clearly not pretended to be an autograph, but its information is turned into a spurious autograph in the Wilton example.

The portraits are really those of the three children of Christian II. King of Denmark; the original belonged to Henry VIII., and is thus described in his catalogue:—"*Item, a table with the pictures of the thre children of the Kynge of Denmarke, with a curteyne of white and yellowe sarcenette paned together.*"*

* This error of substituting the children of Henry VII. for those of the King of Denmark, seems to have arisen from a note in Vertue's transcript of the Bodleian MS. of Charles the First's Catalogue, which was published by Bathoe in 1758. The mistake has been pointed out by Mr. George Scharf, in a paper read at the Society of Antiquaries, in 1862, ARCHÆOLOGIA, Vol. XXXIX. Mr. Scharf who has collated the book with the Bodleian MS. finds even the description incorrect; where Vertue writes oranges the MS. has, correctly, apples. The little girl called Margaret, is really Christina afterwards Duchess of Milan, whose name will appear again in these pages, in connection with important events, and one of Holbein's most celebrated portraits. Mr. Scharf has obliged me with the following copy of the entry in the MS.:—

No. 60. A Whitehall piece *thought to be of Jennet.* Item, under the said picture another picture, wherein two men children and one woman child playing with some *apples* in their hands, by a green table. Little half-figures, upon a board, in a wooden frame.

In Bathoe's printed Catalogue, p. 110, we have:—

No. 60. A Whitehall piece *curiously painted by Mabusius.* Item, under the said picture another picture, wherein two *men children and one woman child, playing with some *oranges* in their hands, by a green table; little half-figures upon a board, in a wooden frame. *Less than the life, now engraved by G. V.*

* *Prince Arthur, Prince Henry, Princess Margaret.*

CHAPTER V.

Early Works at Augsburg.

Chap. V.

In the convent of St. Catherine. 1510-16.

F the pupilage of Holbein there is little to be said, he was brought up in his father's workshop or studio, and seems at first to have derived considerable benefit from the companionship and example of his reputed uncle Hans Burgkmair, who had visited Italy, and who though he has not shown much taste in his works was a man of great energy; and young Holbein was I imagine more influenced by him than by his father; but no doubt he was employed to do much of the heavy work of his father's pictures, when he had attained to years of strength and activity, and by the time he was fifteen he was either receiving independent commissions, or was allowed by the father to execute some of his commissions.

The Augsburg gallery possesses four compositions on two panels one above the other, which are said to be his earliest known works; they were commissioned for the convent of Niederschönefeld near Augsburg, by the prioress Lucia Zenner about 1510. The subjects are the "Annunciation," and the "Nativity," the "Coronation of the Virgin," and the "Death of the Virgin." They are coarse brown energetic works, similar to the coarse productions of the father, with something of the grotesque in them, showing already considerable skill but no promise whatever of what was to come, and there is nothing to be said about them as paintings; their interest is purely historical. They are probably works of the father in which he was assisted by his son.

CHAP. V.

In the convent of St. Catherine. 1510-16.

There is another series of religious pictures in this gallery, of a date two years later, and here the progress shown is prodigious; indeed I know nothing so agreeable in the field of German art of this period, as the great advance from a dry conventional medievalism to delightful nature, which is exemplified in the picture of the Education of Christ or "St. Anne and the Virgin teaching the Infant Christ to walk," when compared with his own father's work or with that even of the sturdy Burgkmair. These pictures were long exhibited as the works of the father, owing to the date 1512 which is inscribed on one of them, but Dr. Waagen agreed with Herr Eigner, twenty years ago, in ascribing them to the son, owing both to the variety of style and the total change of spirit indicated in them; notwithstanding it seemed unaccountable that such works should be produced by a boy of fourteen. This last difficulty however is I trust now surmounted; he was a boy of seventeen instead of fourteen.

These four pictures originally on two panels, but now sawn asunder, the backs from the fronts, were the insides and outsides of the wings of an altar-piece or shrine, which were painted for Veronica Welser, then prioress of the convent of St. Catherine; the centre picture or shrine has disappeared. The subjects are as follows: on the outsides of the doors—the "Martyrdom of St. Peter," and the "Education of the Infant Christ;" on their respective insides—a "Legend of St. Ulrich" the patron and bishop of Augsburg,* and the fourth, the "Martyrdom of St. Catherine." On the last picture is an inscription with the

* This saint at a supper after midnight on a Thursday, that is on a Friday morning miraculously converted the leg of a goose that he had supped from into a fish, in order to avoid the accusation of breaking the fast. A messenger from King Otho to the bishop, had received a leg of the bird for his reward, but instead of eating it, he carried it to the king to expose the profanity of his bishop, but to his astonishment when he took it from his pocket he found a fish in his hand. This incident is represented in the back-ground.

CHAP. V.

In the convent of St. Catherine. 1510-16.

date MDXII.,* and on the old frame was written in gold letters HANS HOLBA . . Its reverse was the picture on which a very valuable inscription has been discovered in an open book in it. The long concealment of this inscription is owing partly to the dirty state of the picture, which has been only recently cleaned, partly to its being upside down or nearly so, and written in abbreviated Latin with words arbitrarily divided; and partly also to the fact probably that no learned German, familiar with all kinds of Latin, had before thought of giving it a minute attention. It is plain enough when known, and runs over the two pages of the inverted book thus:

IVSSV. VENER.	H. HOLBA
PIENTQVE MA	IN AVG.
TRIS VER	ÆT SVÆ
ONI . .	XVII.
W . . . E.	

That is "By the command of the venerable and most pious mother Veronica Welser. Hans Holbain of Augsburg in the seventeenth year of his age." The few missing letters of the name Welser are covered by the fingers of the left hand of St. Anne as she holds the book on her lap.†

The other three pictures are of less importance, but this with the inscription has much more than an historical interest, it has a charming grace and sentiment, and is drawn in a large manner leaving all Gothic angulosity and affectation behind it. It is indeed wholly free from convention and superstition, and the genuine religious sentiment of the picture has rather gained than lost by what blind superstition may condemn as profane innovation. The Virgin and St. Anne are seated on a bench with the Infant standing up on the seat between them, holding a hand of each, perhaps learning to step out, and on the lap of his grandmother seated on the child's

* It is a prayer to St. Catherine the patroness of the convent: — Quid. devotis. laudibus. tui. memoriam. virgo. recolimus. ora. pro. nbis. virgo. beata. M.D.XII.

† Jussu venerabilis pientissimaeque matris Veronicae Welser. Hans Holbain Augustanus aetatis suae XVII. Alf. Woltmann, *De Joannis Holbenii, &c., Dissertatio.* And in *Holbein und seine zeit.*

left is lying the open book on which is the inscription quoted: angels are seen above supporting a green drapery.* The upper part of the panel which is not much more than three feet square altogether is enriched with some very bold cinque-cento arabesques in gold, mingled with amorini; executed evidently *con amore,* his natural love of art for its own sake, even now rebelling against the trammels of tradition. And this practically sudden rejection of the geometrical vagaries of the ecclesiastical stonemason, which overwhelm the works of his immediate elders, for the rich play of floriated curves intertwined with living nature is not one of the least indications of Holbein's ability and originality. He never lost his love for cinque-cento ornament, no man has applied it in a more masterly manner for the decoration of silver work.

In the convent of St. Catherine. 1510-16.

The figures appear to have been first drawn carefully with a strong outline, in brown, showing hatched or lined shadows; they have then been thinly scumbled over and modelled in detail with a brownish flesh tint, and whiter lights. The drawing and modelling are in parts masterly, and everywhere simple: the whole picture is admirable, though there is no real transparency of colouring in it, such as is found in several of the Basel examples of Holbein's early work. Much of the prominence of the preliminary drawing may be owing to a darkening of the colour through time. There is certainly a good deal of the taste of his uncle Hans Burgkmair in this series, as is evident from a comparison of the works of the two painters hanging almost in juxtaposition here, but the influence was transitory; the nephew's works at Basel leave the uncle's far behind.

His father and mother. 1510-16.

Another important work of this early time is the small panel at Hampton Court No. 336, dated 1512, containing two bust portraits of a man and his wife, known by tradition as the painter's father and mother. They show nearly full faces, turned towards each other, the woman being on the man's left:

* Engraved in slight outline in Förster's *Geschichte der Deutschen Kunst.*

CHAP. V.

His father and mother. 1510-16.

against the man are the figures 52; he has a cap on, is close shaven, and is rather muffled in a large coat, seems old for fifty-two though not grey, his face gives no indication of strong character or of unusual intelligence; he was, as his last works show, content to do pretty much as his fathers had done before him. The woman is very different, she has a large round white cap on her head, has rich brown piercing eyes, a finely formed nose, like her son's, and must have been very handsome when young; she still exhibits in her countenance strong indications of great energy and intelligence; she is as yet only thirty-five as indicated by the figures written against her, and was accordingly seventeen years younger than her husband. The back-ground is very hard: it represents a landscape, in the neighbourhood of some mountainous country, as seen through an open window, or something to the same effect. On the right side of the picture behind the father, is seen the entrance to a château, with moat and bridge; further in is the gable of a small house, and beyond this is a church, near which is a road with a bridge over a small river. The painting appears to be executed on paper attached to oak, the panel being 13¼ in. high, by 24¾ in. wide; sight measure. Even in this work, notwithstanding the evident ability it displays, there is no striking promise of the power that was developed even only three or four years later. The style of the heads is not so large in manner as that of the "Education of the Infant Christ," he had here no place for generalizing, his business was to represent given individualities, and one may be satisfied that he has succeeded: in transparency of colour this picture is superior to that at Augsburg, especially in the carnations, and in the eyes of the mother. It has been somewhat rubbed, the hands have especially suffered, but only one of either figure is seen.

This very precious little picture belonged to King Charles I., and is noticed in his "Catalogue," as having been "brought out of Germany by Sir Henry Vane, Treasurer of the Household, and given to the King."

To his Augsburg period belongs also an interesting little

picture of the "Madonna and Child" belonging to a Catholic priest in Ragatz in Switzerland.

Madonna and Child. 1510-16.

It is a small panel of Holbein's ordinary size, measuring about 17 inches by 13 inches, and may belong perhaps to the year 1513 or 1514. The Virgin, a half-length figure of the same type as the Augsburg Madonna, dressed in blue with a jewel on her bosom is supporting the Child on a brocaded cushion which rests on a stone coping before her; he holds a hanging rosary in his right hand, and with his left is taking a peach from the hand of his mother; and on this side is a vase containing lilies of the valley. The back-ground is enriched with Renaissance architecture and ornament, with a pilaster on each side, as in the small portrait in Mr. Thomas Baring's collection, constituting a setting for the figures: in two medallions are the initials—I. D.—I. H. This picture independent of its own charm and merits, which are represented as considerable (I have not seen it) is particularly interesting for the inscriptions it bears:—on one pilaster is written — CARPET. ALIQUIS. CICIUS. QUAM. IMITABIUR.; on the other is—JOHANES HOLBAIN. IN. AUGUSTA. BINGEWAT.*

The word *bingewat* for *pingebat* is curious. The young painter has evidently got his Latin from some one of his learned friends among the monks of the neighbouring convent of St. Ulrich, and has either misread them or put them down at hazard from the sound only. The first is more remarkable than the second; this line he has decidedly got from some one acquainted with an anecdote told by Pliny, and by Plutarch, who says that Apollodorus was in the habit of writing upon his works—"it is easier for one to find fault than to do the like"—*μωμήσεταί τις μᾶλλον ἢ μιμήσεται.* Pliny gives the saying to Zeuxis—*invisurum aliquem facilius, quam imitaturum.* The slight variation of sound in the two Greek words in antithesis gives the saying infinitely more point in that language. I

* Described by Dr. Woltmann, in the Vienna *Recensionen und Mittheilungen über bildende Kunst.* March 1865.—Engraved on wood in his *Holbein und seine zeit.*

CHAP. V.

Early portraits. 1510-16.

prefer to Pliny's even Holbein's sentence—*Carpet aliquis citius quam imitabitur.**

The Count Lanskronski in Vienna possesses according to Dr. Woltmann a portrait of this period, in a similar taste and size with this "Madonna mit den Maiglöchchen" as the Germans call it, "the Madonna of the May-lily." It represents the bust portrait of a man with light brown hair, in fur cap and furred gown, seen nearly in full face, and holding a roll of paper in his right hand; with a red carpet hanging in front; the back-ground shows a portion of blue sky. It is dated 1513, and inscribed on the two pilasters—ALS. ICH. WAS. 52 JAR. ALT. DA. HET. ICH. DIE. GESTALT. Such was I when I was 52 years old: the person is unknown.

Dr. Waagen describes also as an early Holbein a small half-length portrait which was at Corsham Court in 1835, inscribed —"1514. *Franciscus de Taxis annorum* 55." This Franz von Taxis was a man of distinction; he first established the Post Office in Germany: he is seated at a table, holding a sealed letter in his right hand, and a roll or staff in his left; before him on the table are gold money, and writing materials.

The Darmstadt Gallery possesses a small panel with the head of a young blond-haired man dressed in red, full face, of a very fair florid or ruddy colour, and with bright blue back-ground. It is inscribed—H. 1515. H., and has much of the force and accuracy, but not the freedom, of some of the early portraits of Holbein, even of a later date than this; and the characteristic brown carnations of these earlier pictures is wanting; this however may have been owing to the peculiarly fair and florid complexion of the individual represented: it is possibly by Holbein, but conveys the impression of being somewhat too delicately executed for him for so early a date as 1515.

A very interesting historical picture commonly attributed to the father but now by Dr. Woltmann ascribed to our painter, as belonging also to this early period, is in the possession of the Augsburg banker Paul von Stetten. Unfor-

* Plutarch, *De glor. Athen.* 2; Pliny, *Hist. Nat.* xxxv. 36. See my *Epochs of Painting*, p. 35. 1864.

Ulrich Schwartz. 1510-16.

tunately when I visited Augsburg in July 1865, this gentleman had left town for a short time, and as the picture was locked up it could not be shown, and I have no opinion to give upon it. This is a votive picture to the memory of Ulrich Schwartz, painted years after his death, for one of his sons. Schwartz was a member of the Carpenters' and Joiners' Guild, and was seven times Mayor of Augsburg, but by his overbearing manners and tyrannical acts he made himself many uncompromising enemies among the patrician families, and he was at last seized and thrown into prison by the authority of the emperor; and on the 18th of April 1478, was publicly hanged, in the rich costume he had been in the habit of wearing. The lower part of the composition represents Schwartz and his family—his three wives and many sons and daughters, the males on one side the females on the other, all in prayer; and above appears the Almighty as judge, surrounded by cherubim, and sheathing his sword of justice; Christ showing his wounds and the Virgin Mary baring her bosom, are interceding in behalf of the sinners represented below.* The various members of the family have their names attached. The prayers of the Saviour and of the Virgin, and the answer of the Father are given, in the following words:—

Christ.—Vatter sich an mein wünden rot,
Hilf den menschen aus aller not,
Durch meinen bittern tod.
The Virgin.—Her thun ein dein schwert das du hast erzogen,
Und sich an die brist die dein sun hat gesogen.
The Father.—Barmhertzigkait will ich allen den erzaigen,
Die da mit warer rew von hinnen schaiden.†

Another interesting early production, in parts excellent, and about which I have no doubts whatever, is the altar-piece

* On the knob of the hilt of the sword is a monogram, an H within an H. There is a woodcut by Urs Graf of a very similar composition. See Paul von Stetten, *Kunst und Handwerks-geschichte*, &c., I., p. 272.

† *Christ.*—Father look upon my red wounds, save these people from all their suffering for my bitter death's sake.

The Virgin.—Lord put up thy sword that Thou hast drawn, and look upon the breasts that Thy Son has sucked.

The Father.—Mercy will I to all those extend, who die in true repentance.

CHAP. V.

Martyrdom of St. Sebastian. 1510-16.

of the "Martyrdom of St. Sebastian," now placed in the Pinacothek at Munich. This picture was also long attributed to Holbein the father, until a forged document circulated by Dr. Waagen and Passavant, caused the general public to look upon it as unquestionably the work of the son. The quotation referred to and by which these two writers were imposed upon, is a singular instance of effrontery: it is complete in assertions for which the genuine passage on which it is founded does not give the slightest justification. The record itself is contained in the abstract of Dominica Erhart already referred to and is as follows—"*Item, Sw. Magdalena Imhoff hat hergeben an S. Sebastian den Neyen zu dem heil. Kreiz auf dem altar,* 3 *gulden. Und de lay Schwestern* 2 *f. Sovill is dasselb bildt gestandten, od. zu teutsch dass es kost hat.*" Which seems to signify that the sister Magdalen Imhoff contributed 3 fl. and the lay sisters 2 fl. for a figure of St. Sebastian to be added to the Holy Cross, (or group of the Crucifixion), on the altar of the church. Now in the place of this simple statement we have the following elaborate history about a picture by Holbein:—

"*Item, Magdalena Imhofin hat den Sebastian den Neyen von dem kunstreich mahler Holbein* 1515 *mahlen lassen, und dafür* 10 *gulden geben, weiters noch jede Lay Schwester* 2 *gulden dazu; so vill ist dasselb Bildt gestandten, wurde am Kreuz altar aufgestellt im Jahr* 1517, *nachdem die Kirch neugebaut war.*" Which is—Magdalen Imhof had the "Sebastian den Neyen" *painted, by the skilful painter Holbein, and gave* 10 *florins for it,* besides 2 florins contributed by each lay sister; so much did the picture cost; *it was placed on the altar of the Holy Cross, in the year* 1517, *after the rebuilding of the church.*"

This is certainly a most satisfactory record, and had greatly delighted me, until I learnt its one great fault from Dr. Woltmann, namely that it is a fabrication pure and simple: and for more than twenty years the art world has been misled by this forgery. The picture however remains untouched by it; though we cannot fix its time and price by documents, Holbein's authorship of it is proclaimed by its intrinsic merit and handling, and circumstances establish its period sufficiently

ST. ELIZABETH OF HUNGARY.

P. 95.

close. Until of late years it has always remained in the convent, and was possibly fixed in its place in 1517 after the reconstruction of the church: it may have been painted in 1515–16, not later, because the latter is the year in which Holbein removed to Basel; but we can no longer feel sure that it was painted for the convent of St. Catherine.

CHAP. V.

Martyrdom of St. Sebastian. 1510-16.

The picture is a triptych, measuring altogether about 5 ft. in height and 7 ft. in width; in the centre is the saint bound to a fig-tree, surrounded by his executioners, and spectators, in all nine figures: the executioners are four in number, and three of them have cross-bows, three are shooting their bolts, the fourth is kneeling in the fore-ground, bending his bow; this one is clothed in stripes of blue and white, the colours of Bavaria, another illustration of the dislike borne by the patriotic burghers of the imperial city for their Bavarian neighbours. On the right wing is St. Barbara (SANCTA BARBARA) with the cup and wafer; on the left, is St. Elizabeth (SANCTA ELIZABET) of Thüringen, giving food and drink to the poor and sick, represented by three unfortunate wretches, covered with blotches, crouching at her feet. On the back or outside of the St. Barbara picture is the angel Gabriel; on the back of the other, the Virgin Mary receiving the good tidings of the coming of our Lord, a dove in glory hovering over her head. The figures are about half the scale of life.

As I observed, this altar-piece was, until of late years, ascribed to the elder Holbein, and the centre composition of the martyrdom has certainly too many of the traces of the father's *Bottega*, but the wing of St. Elizabeth helping those sick of the leprosy* is a fine picture, abounding in natural truth, and very evidently by the same hand as the "St. Anna selb dritt" or "St. Anne and the Virgin with

* Dr. Virchow, *Archiv für pathologische Anatomie*, &c., vols. xxii.-iii. Berlin, 1861, has remarked on these figures of the sick in this picture as having been certainly painted from leprosy patients; there were in Augsburg in Holbein's time hospitals for this plague; and these figures are the only middle-age illustrations of the disease. See Woltmann, p. 170. This circumstance would lead one to imagine that the picture was painted rather for a hospital than a convent.

CHAP. V.

Martyrdom of St. Sebastian. 1510-16.

the Infant Christ," in the Augsburg Gallery, and much superior in style, for broad naturalistic effect to anything by tne father.

The centre picture, the actual martyrdom, is said by Passavant to be inscribed 1516, I certainly did not see the date, though I searched for it, nor do I find it in any print or photograph, but such things are easily overlooked. No such fact however, is noticed in the new catalogue of the Munich Gallery by Dr. Marggraff, and one of the special advantages of this book over the old catalogue, is, that as a rule it notices signatures and inscriptions.*

* It not only notices inscriptions, but goes to the extent of criticising their authenticity. So in the case of No. 105, Cabinet VI., the author, following Dr. Waagen, deliberately attributes to Memling a small solidly painted dryly executed picture of "St. John the Baptist in the Wilderness," which is inscribed in gold letters H. V. D. GOES 1472, setting aside this interesting inscription as spurious. Hugo Vander Goes appears to be a painter whose reputation has been absorbed by the greater name of Memling, and I believe that the singular rarity of this painter's name in collections arises from the fact that his pictures are commonly ascribed to his greater contemporary. Munich is the last gallery in which such a mistake should occur, with the extraordinary work of the celebrated "Seven Joys of the Virgin" to serve as a key to determine the hand of this famous master. If this Vander Goes signature be not genuine, we have the remarkable instance of the possessor of a work by a painter of great reputation, forging upon it the name of an obscure master of the same school, unknown in auction rooms and one whose name very rarely occurs in old records! This was an inexpert possessor indeed; and I find it less difficult to believe in the signature, than in the forgery; and more natural to infer a false designation of other similar figures, as for instance, of the two Louvre figures called Memling—Nos. 288 and 289, than to assume this name of Vander Goes to be an imbecile counterfeit. The picture has not a trace of the hand of Memling in it, to judge from the Châsse of St. Ursula at Bruges, or the famous Munich example of the master just referred to. There is of course a certain school affinity. The same St. John certainly occurs in other pictures besides that ascribed to Memling in the Louvre, as for example—in the Duke of Devonshire's so-called Van Eyck, a triptych exhibited this year at South Kensington, containing the portraits of Sir John and Lady Donne (said to have been painted in 1470!); also in the picture No. 66 in the Frankfort Gallery, ascribed to Roger Vander Weyden—the Virgin and Child enthroned, with John the Baptist and St. Peter on one side, and Saints Cosmas and Damianus on the other; in the centre of the foreground a lily in a vase, and the arms of the city of Florence (where the picture was no doubt painted)—and likewise in the pair of saints No. 747, ascribed to Memling and lately purchased for the National Gallery. All these works I imagine to belong to this now neglected painter, though in his own time he was held in high consideration: he is supposed to have died in 1479.

CHAP. V.

Martyrdom of St. Sebastian. 1510-16.

This altar-piece is now commonly cited as the best of all Holbein's Augsburg pictures; perhaps as regards the wing of St. Elizabeth of Thüringen, it is so. The saint herself is what may be termed an Iconic portrait, she is standing between two pilasters, and the back-ground is an architectural landscape; the relief of the sick is necessarily rather indicated than represented, by the three figures kneeling, in the lower part of the picture, one indeed is but a head, looking up to the saint with a supplicatory expression; she is pouring something from a jug into a bowl held in the hand of the foremost figure. The heads are all very fine in character; the boy with the eruption on several parts of his face, is remarkable.

The composition of the centre piece, the death of St. Sebastian, is dramatic and impressive as a whole, but the execution in detail is coarse and careless; the naked figure of the saint though in a fine attitude is ill-drawn, especially about the neck, and the raised right shoulder; the hands are throughout coarse and badly modelled, the fingers and nails particularly so; and these are parts which Holbein afterwards greatly excelled in painting.* The outside pictures of the wings (which however few have ever seen, as they are not shown) representing the "Annunciation," though in chiaroscuro are in drawing and composition, among the superior parts of the altar-piece: the Virgin kneeling and slightly turning her head to receive the announcement from the descending angel, is really beautiful; the attitude is particularly graceful: she has a white cloth on her head, but her long hair falls in thick clusters over her right shoulder. The scene is placed in a temple of Renaissance architecture.†

Merz and wife.

I may here notice also two other pictures called Holbein's, of uncertain time, preserved at Augsburg: two life-sized portraits comprising the bust and hands, of one Merz a dis-

* Dr. Waagen says that an excellent original drawing with the pen and washed, of this composition is in the collection of drawings at Florence. *Kunstwerke und Künstler in Deutschland*, II., 26.

† There are photographs of the five compositions of this interesting altar-piece in Schauer's *Holbein Album*. 4to. Berlin, 1865, and a woodcut in Woltmann's *Holbein*, &c.

CHAP. V.

Merz and wife. 1510-16.

tinguished citizen of Lindau, and his wife, a lady of Augsburg, hanging opposite the already described Madonna by the painter's so called grandfather, in the Maximilian's Museum. They are good genuine pictures, and appear to be by the hand of Holbein, but not of the highest class of his portraits; they have the Holbein brown carnations, thinly driven colour and careful modelling, but the handling is not perfectly precise and masterly. They have evidently been much repaired. However at a little distance the effect is natural almost to illusion, more especially of the wife's portrait, Afra Rehm.* They belong possibly to the painter's Basel period, but they have the general character of his works of some few years later, though wanting in the force and in the delicacy of his best Basel works. Holbein may have visited Augsburg during his sojourn in Switzerland. If these two portraits are not the work of Holbein, they are close imitations of his style, and may be the productions of Amberger. They are inscribed on the back, but these back inscriptions are not to be relied on, as they are seldom by the painter himself. The wife's portrait is a better picture than the husband's.†

The Museum at Berlin possesses the Imhof collection, of three volumes of early drawings, seventy in all, executed by Holbein from 1509 to 1516 inclusive; portraits, some washed, but most in pencil, of people of all ranks, of the city and of the neighbourhood of Augsburg:—Emperor, abbot, fool and prostitute; and especially the monks of the monastery of

* Afra Rehm was Merz's second wife, and the date of the marriage seems to have been certainly 1534. In the Diary or *Tagebuch* of Lucas Rehm published by Greiff in Augsburg in 1861, is a notice of a present to his relative jungfrau Afra Rehm on the occasion of her marriage to Merz in 1534. In the Museum of Würtemberg Antiquities at Stuttgardt is a similar portrait of this lady dated 1524, that is ten years before her marriage, and this is the time that both portraits may have been painted, and their being brought together may have been a mere consequence of the marriage.

† On the back of Merz's portrait, as I am informed by Dr. Woltmann, are painted his arms and those of both his wives, with the dates of his two marriages, the first wife's name was Kraft, from Ulm; 1534 is given as the date of the second marriage, on the picture, and thus agreeing with the date in the diary quoted.

The Imhof drawings. 1510-16.

St. Ulrich, Augsburg's patron saint; and many of these drawings show the ready hand of the master.

This collection is just such an illustration of Holbein's early career, as the drawings of the Windsor portfolios are of his mature years. Among them is the drawing described of himself and brother 1509, and one of his uncle—"*Sigmund Holbain Maler;*" also the sculptor and carver Hans Schwartz; a tailor named Grün, of great force. Further, Abbot Merlin—"*Conrat Merlin abt zu Sannt Ulrich*" from 1496 to 1510, and a great patron of the arts: likewise his successor Abbot Schrott, who notwithstanding his scandalous life, enjoyed the favour of Lang, Cardinal Archbishop of Salzburg; and through him of Pope Leo X.: the learned Leonhard Wagner: the convent fool—"*Hans nar zu S. Ulrich:*" and the notorious impostor "*Lomenitly,*" who first shocked the good people of Augsburg by her profligacy, and afterwards by the gross imposture of her pretended reformation and sanctity; she professed to live without food.

The collection contains also drawings of the celebrated merchant Jacob Fugger the *Rich*, who shows a shrewd intelligent face but by no means a handsome one; and of other members of that distinguished family, still the most prominent in Augsburg—there are Anton Fugger; and Ulrich the younger, with his bride, drawn in 1516. It was Anton Fugger who enjoyed such high favour with the Emperor Charles V., whose portrait also, as a youth of fifteen, is among the series.* There is a sketch of the Emperor Maximilian, inscribed "*Der Gross Kaiser Maximilian.*" This must have been done from memory as the young painter, one of a crowd of excited spectators, had seen him passing by while on a visit to the imperial city; the drawing of the grandson, afterwards Charles V., shows a falcon on the prince's wrist, and by the bird is written "Kaiser's falck;" the young prince himself is described as "*Herzog Karl võ Burgundy.*" Charles became

* This must have been a copy from some other drawing or picture, as it seems that Charles never visited Augsburg at this period.

CHAP. V.

The Imhof drawings. 1510-16.

Duke of Burgundy in 1515, and this fixes the date of the drawing. This was the year of the accession of Francis I. of France. In 1516 Charles became King of Castile.

This is a motley gallery worthy of the versatile pencil of Holbein, many of the drawings are described* as well exhibiting the painter's general accuracy of observation, and his singular power of drawing the eye. Holbein seems to have been quite at home in the cloisters of St. Ulrich, and his familiar intercourse with the many varieties of men, learned and otherwise, brought together in an old religious house, such as this famous Augsburg monastery, cannot but have been of great use to him as a fruitful source of education and a safe and enlarged knowledge of the world : and it is not impossible that he here also acquired some of that taste for good living which the world has attached to his memory.

We must now follow his fortunes to Switzerland, where, in Basel, we shall find him almost at once developed into the great portrait painter. What particularly took our successful young painter to Basel, we cannot say, if we adopt the popular tradition, which however has indeed not much in its favour, one must conclude that he simply followed his father to that city; if we reject this we may assume that he took Basel incidentally in his wanderings in search of experience and employment. What detained him in Basel may have been its unusual amount of religious and political liberty, or the attraction which resulted in his afterwards unhappy marriage.

* Woltmann, *De Joannis Holbenii, &c., Dissertatio:* see also Schauer's *Holbein Album*, which contains photographs of four of the drawings—the fine head of SIGMUND HOLBEIN; JACOB FUGGER; the monk LIENHARD WAGNER, a good-natured but exceedingly gross physiognomy; and KUNZ VON DER ROSEN, one of the Emperor Maximilian's councillors. All these drawings show great mastery, and prove the young painter's remarkable precocity, for he was but twenty years old at most when they were made: he had however perhaps been drawing from his childhood. It has been already noticed that the earliest date, and perhaps the earliest drawing, is of the year 1509. A similar but smaller collection is preserved at Copenhagen, and of these there is a set of photographs:—*Quarante feuilles d'un Livre d'Esquisses de Jean Holbein le Jeune, tirées du cabinet Royal d'Estampes à Copenhague.* 1861.

CHAPTER VI.

Removes to Switzerland, and Settles in Basel: Works at Basel and Lucerne.

VER since his name was established tradition and popular belief have at Basel persistently assigned nearly all works of painting in that city to Holbein; comprising not only those executed in his own time, but before and after him, as:—The Dance of Death in the churchyard of the Predicants, a work of the fifteenth century, which was painted by Hans Kluber, in commemoration of the plague which in the spring of 1439 carried off 5,000 people: it was during the sitting of the council of Basel, and many dignitaries perished: Kluber's son Hans Hugo repaired the paintings in 1520, or 1568. He has also the credit of painting what was saved from the Iconoclasts of 1529, in the cathedral; all the paintings of the town-hall; the painted glass of the old house with the arms and shields of the twelve cantons, refitted in the new; and Hans Bockh's picture of the "Last Judgment," of the new house, painted in the staircase, and which was so conspicuous for its Lutheranism even before Luther,* as it was fondly

Chap. VI.

Works at Basel.

1516-26.

* In this composition is the figure of a crowned pope burning in hell; the town council after the toleration of this rude moralizing for about a couple of centuries, at last early in this present century, shocked at the indecency of the thing, ordered the crown to be painted out, but left his holiness to burn, when degraded of his insignia. Hegner, p. 76.

CHAP. VI.

Works at Basel. 1516-26.

imagined. So also nearly every picture and drawing good bad and indifferent, of the Amerbach collection, formed during the sixteenth century, was taken for granted to be the work of our painter, Boniface Amerbach having been the personal friend of Holbein, who yet did not reside altogether perhaps ten full years in Basel.

A blind hero-worship, for Holbein has been commonly supposed to have been a native of Basel, has precluded all discrimination, and what popular belief sanctioned in olden times, must not be called into question by the sceptical criticism of the moderns. Even Hegner, the painter's intelligent biographer, willingly throwing over those attributions which documents prove to be impossible, adheres to others almost as palpably proclaimed impossible by the nature of the works themselves. And he very simply remarks, that it is only of late times that people have thought of questioning the genuineness of the assumed authorship, of some of the most admired of the Amerbach works and others in the Basel Museum. Yet no one knew better than Hegner that these assumptions had not a rag or a thread of a document to support them. Such matters were in former times not only indifferent to the masses, but few people indeed were capable of judging, or even ventured to think for themselves at all. Thousands passed their whole lives in a single town or village; the very element of criticism, the power of comparison had no standing-place. Railways have changed all this, any man with a will can now extend his wanderings over his own frontiers and learn a little from his neighbours as well as his forefathers, and contribute to them his mite in return.

We in England have acted much as the people of Basel; for generations nearly every historic portrait, of the time of Henry VIII., and of times before and after him too, have been indiscriminately given to Holbein; as if he were the only portrait painter of that age, and as if, setting aside natives, such men as Mabuse, Anthony Toto, Van Cleef, Luke Hornebolt, Gerome of Treviso, Anthony More, Lucas de Heere, and William Stretes had never lived and painted in England:

Early Works in the Museum. 1516-17.

there we have at once a list of at least eight able masters who we know were busily employed in this country in the time of the Tudors; yet all the portraits assigned to these painters combined do not approximate the number ascribed to Holbein alone.

The time of Holbein's arrival at Basel can be pretty nearly established. Among the drawings at Berlin has been already mentioned a portrait of the wife of Ulrich Fugger the younger; records show that this lady was married on the 10th of June 1516; in the summer therefore of that year Holbein was still in Augsburg, but before the end of the year we find that he had already painted some portraits at Basel; as those of Jacob Meier (zum Hasen), the burgomaster of the city, and of his wife Anna Tschekapürlin; two busts life size, almost in profile, both on the same panel, and signed H H. 1516. He has a red cap on and shows both his hands, holding in his left a piece of gold money; this has reference to a new privilege just granted by the Emperor Maximilian, in January of this year, to the city of Basel, empowering it to issue a gold coinage.* Her hands are concealed in a cuff; she has a large cap on, and is richly dressed in a low body.†

These heads are brown and transparent, freely yet carefully executed, and marked by individuality; but they have nothing approaching an enamelled appearance. They have much the character of his best Augsburg pieces, of a somewhat richer brown and more transparent: this brownness so common in Holbein's early works is I imagine partly owing to darkening through time. There is another picture of this year in the Basel Museum, but without the monogram, which is ascribed to Holbein; as a work of art it has no value, nor has it any resemblance with the picture of the burgomaster and his wife; it is a small schoolmaster's sign, was originally painted on both sides, and has been sawn into two panels. If the work of

* Ochs, V., p. 319.

† This picture was engraved by B. Hübner in 1790, for C. von Mechel's "*Œuvre de Jean Holbein.*" Folio, Basle, 1780-92. And again, in wood, in Woltmann's *Holbein*, &c.

CHAP. VI.

Early works in the Museum.

1516-17.

Holbein, it is either some careless hasty sketch made for an acquaintance, or done in the way of business for a few pence only. Of much the same class and not much better are two Last Suppers, ascribed to him; one on canvas, the other on panel; one measuring about 4½ ft. by 5 ft., evidently a very early work if by him; and that on wood about 3½ ft. by nearly 4 ft. These things are contemptible as paintings when associated with such a name as Holbein's at the time we have now reached, though they show vigour enough, and may belong to earlier years, when he was still in Augsburg; that on canvas is certainly quite an early work. It is true, no absolute judgment should be formed of the second picture, because it was destroyed by the religious Iconoclasts in February 1529;* some only of the pieces were saved by Boniface Amerbach and were so unskilfully put together again, that in 1750 it was decided to have them reset by one Nicholas Grooth, and the picture was then restored to the state we now find it in.† Passing by a few other indifferent pieces we come to one of the following year, of great interest; this is a small picture on paper, fixed to panel with the busts and hands of Adam and Eve, the latter with the apple, nearly life size. It is similar to the picture of Meier and his wife, but is still bolder in the execution, and is very brown. In this the future great master is conspicuous, it is decidedly able; the lines of the drawing are seen distinctly through the thin paint; the finger-ends are well modelled, with large lights upon the nails; and these are the earliest examples of a good quality, I have noticed in Holbein's work; good extremities however often occur in later pictures. It is signed 1517 H H., and is described in the Amerbach Inventory as—*Ein Adam und Eva mit dem üpfel H. Holb. uf holz mit ölfarb.*

We have a good example of this period also in this country,

---

* Both are catalogued in the Amerbach Inventory,—that on canvas as—*Ein gross nachtmall H. Holbeins erste arbeiten eine uf tuch mit ölfarb*; that on wood—*Ein nachtmall uf holz mit ölfarb, H. Holbein, ist zerhouwen und wider zusammen geleimbt aber unfletig.*

† It was engraved by Hübner for Von Mechel, *l. l.*

Early works in the Museum. 1516-17.

in Mr. Thomas Baring's small portrait of John Herbster, a painter of Basel. He was the father of Oporinus the printer, and was, says Füssli, in the battle at Pavia in 1512: his name occurs in the book of the Basel Guild of Painters, the "heavenly guild"—*zunft zum Himmel.* We should bear in mind that this gives us another H. H. among the painters of Basel; Herbster's works are quite unknown.

The portrait, a bust, represents a middle-aged man, with a large brown beard and long hair, and showing a three-quarter view of the face; he has on a red cap set on one side, and a black or grey coat. The back-ground is an open archway, of Renaissance architecture, showing the blue sky immediately around the head and shoulders of the man. From the centre of the arch hang two festoons of fruit and leaves, the opposite ends being held by amorini, seated on capitals, before the spandrils of the arch; and above the heads of these two boys also in the spandrils, are two tablets supported by festoons, containing date, and signature of the painter. The date, on the right tablet, is ·1·5·16·, the signature on the other was apparently H. H., but it is injured and is now illegible. On a sort of cornice or plinth below is written in capitals JOANNES HERBSTER. PICTOR. OPORINI PATER. On paper attached to deal, 16¼ in. high by 11 in. wide. In 1529 during the reform troubles in Basel, this Hans Herbster, falling like Fra Bartolomeo and Lorenzo di Credi before him, under the influence of the fanatic zeal of the reformers against works of art, forswore his profession, under the impression that all *imitative works* were a desecration, as contrary to the spirit of the Second Commandment.*

With respect to the dates on Holbein's pictures we must not forget that the year in his day commenced from the 25th of March, the Annunciation day, at least for the ecclesiastical and legal year, and it was accordingly used in common for dates. This custom prevailed very generally, but not univer-

---

* See Hegner, *Hans Holbein*, &c., p. 240, who quotes Theod. Zwinger in *Theatr. vitae hum.* Bas. 1586.

CHAP. VI.

Early works in the Museum. 1516-17.

sally, not excepting England, and it continued until the year 1752.* Upon this principle, the picture of Meier and his wife, may have been painted in the spring of 1517 though it bears the date of 1516, this would give us a little more latitude for the transition period between Holbein's last known works in Augsburg, and his first in Basel.

In the Pinakothek at Munich are two companion full-length portraits on panel, about 6 ft. high by 3 ft. wide, on each of which is written Anno MDXVII.; one is conjectured, from a book of arms, to represent Conrad Rehling, of Hainhofen near Augsburg; he is standing, dressed in a black robe edged with fur, and above is an angel in the clouds, with a legend: the other is supposed to represent Conrad Rehling's children; in the upper part of this picture the Madonna and Child are seen in the clouds. It is somewhat strange to see these two pictures hanging in the same room as the St. Sebastian altar-piece, and painted within a few months of each other, ascribed to the same painter. The two portraits are only a weak approximation to Holbein's style of about twelve years later; the children are flat and appear to be unfinished: these portraits certainly bear no resemblance to Holbein's authentic works of this very period just described, as Meier and his wife, for instance, or the Adam and Eve. Setting aside the divergence of style, in itself an obstacle sufficient, the assumed fact that the family is of Augsburg creates its own difficulty; Holbein was not at Augsburg in 1517. He was then at Lucerne.

The Church Reformers.

This year 1517 is memorable as that in which John Tetzel commenced the public sale of the gross and infamous indulgences of his Holiness Leo X.; granting for a few pence wholesale remission of sins, past, present, and future, however heinous their nature. The commotion created by such eccle-

* Much confusion was occasioned in consequence, and Granger notices the remarkable fact, that the year 1667 had two Easters, one on the 27th of April, and the other on the 22nd of March following: and state documents are not free from this confusion. See Granger, *Biographical History of England*. Preface; and *L'Art de Vérifier les Dates*.

The Church Reformers.

siastical scandals did not reach Basel, until some years later, and Holbein though he has the credit of having been a Protestant, and this fact is pretty certain, from the part acted by the clergy in his "Dance of Death," was never mixed up with religious disturbances in any way. There is not however a single authentic portrait of any of the more conspicuous reformers by Holbein, nor does he appear ever to have met Luther, Calvin, or Melanchthon; Luther was not thoroughly famous until he was honoured by Leo's happy excommunication January the 6th, 1521. This was the year of his triumph at Worms.

This year also, one Wilhelm Röblin an enthusiastic priest and reformer preached against the abuses of the church to the people of Basel, and him Holbein may have known, though scarcely painted: he was soon expelled the city by the municipal authorities. Holbein may possibly have painted Zwingle, when he was in Basel in 1529–31. Oecolampadius preached and resided in Basel in our painter's time, and may easily have been painted by him, but I am not acquainted with any authentic portrait of this reformer by Holbein. It was during the preachings of Oecolampadius, in 1524, that the authorities of Basel had the good sense to break up the nunneries, and give the nuns permission to marry, and thus perform the natural duties imposed on them by their Creator, instead of entombing themselves alive in furtherance of the wicked devices of priestcraft.*

Wanderjahre. Lucerne. 1517-19.

The time that Hans Holbein the father went to Basel is not known, nor indeed is there any evidence that he ever went there, but he seems to have left Augsburg in 1516. If however it should be a fact, notwithstanding want of evidence, that he was invited to Basel in order to be consulted about the

* In Longford Castle is a portrait called Oecolampadius, but it is not by Holbein. In the Welfen Museum at Hanover is also a small round portrait of Melanchthon, given to Holbein, but there is no evidence that Holbein was ever in the same place with Melanchthon. The portrait is described as a good one. The small round portrait of Melanchthon which Walpole had, and which was sold at the Strawberry Hill sale, in 1842, for fifteen guineas, was probably a copy of this Hanoverian picture.

CHAP. VI. — *Wanderjahre. Lucerne.* 1517-19.

decorations of the new Rath-haus as recorded, his visit there may have been the principal cause of the visit to, and the establishment of his sons in this city. However this may be, the decorations of the council-chamber appear to have eventually fallen altogether to the lot of his son Hans. As already observed, his brother Sigmund did not settle in Basel, but in Bern; whether he spent any time, or worked in Basel, we have no accounts. Ambrose, as already shown, joined the Basel guild of painters in 1517, while Hans did not join until two or three years later. The latter seems to have been absent from Basel for about two years, from this very time; and we will now follow some traces of his journeyings in neighbouring towns. He was called away in 1517 by the bailiff of Lucerne, Jacob von Hertenstein, to decorate his new house for him, which Holbein painted both inside and out; and he entered the guild of painters there. This house with its decorations was still in existence as late as 1824; when it was wilfully destroyed by a banker of the name of Knörr, to make place for a structure more in accordance with modern comfort and requirements. One would have thought that room for a new house might have been found without destroying this interesting old monument; however such sentimentalism may be unsound; this old house met only with the natural fate of decaying tenements which have done their work, or are meet only for the simpler wants of a bygone age.

Some imperfect drawings from Holbein's paintings were made for a Colonel May von Büren, and are now preserved in the Library of Lucerne. The house was decorated after the fashion of the old houses of Augsburg, Nürnberg, and other cities: some of the old painted façades of Nürnberg still exist; and the present residence of the Fugger family in Augsburg, has been recently painted from top to bottom, with cheerful frescoes by Herr Wagner a native painter of that city. A good architectural effect produced by strong contrasts of light and shade may be æsthetically preferable, but I suppose the painting is much cheaper, and a flat façade is immensely enlivened by successful colouring.

The decorations of this Hertenstein house consisted of subjects from the ancient stories of Greece and Rome; as Leæna the mistress of Aristogiton before her judges, after the murder of Hipparchus; the stories of Tarquin and Lucretia, of Mucius Scævola, and of Marcus Curtius and others; also a Triumph of Julius Cæsar, which was freely copied from the famous series by Mantegna, taken from old prints probably. Besides the sports of children, armorial bearings, &c. This Hertenstein had had four wives, and the arms of all were emblazoned by Holbein on the façade, and the dates of the several marriages added to each. One remarkable composition, forming the principal outside group, was a story from the *Gesta Romanorum* representing the settlement of a disputed succession, in the form of a shooting contest between three royal brothers, as to who was best entitled to succeed to the father's government; the target being their own father's body, the heart the point to be reached. The first and the second sons had shot their arrows, and the turn of the third came, but he rather than shoot at such a target, broke his bow in two, and gave up the contest; he was however at once declared the victor, and the succession was awarded to him by acclamation.*

In one of the rooms of the house, was the date 1517, the year probably of the completion of the building, and fixing also approximately the date of Holbein's paintings. The Museum of Basel contains among its drawings (No. 82) the original sketch of the composition of Leæna before her judges, when, rather than betray her lover, she bit off her tongue. The Library of Lucerne contains sketches of all the compositions. One of the descendants of this bailiff Hertenstein, says Hegner, had still, in 1826, a portrait of him by Holbein, of the year 1517.

Holbein was likewise employed at Altorf in the canton Uri, from which district some have supposed the painter's family to have originally come, as the Holbein arms are nearly identical

* See Woltmann, *Holbein*, &c., I., p. 217.

CHAP. VI.

Wanderjahre.
Lucerne.
1517-19.

with those of Uri; they are found in the book of the painters guild at Basel.

The works he executed at Altorf were destroyed by fire in 1799; they comprised an altar-piece of the "Crucifixion," in the parish church; it was painted on canvas, a material rarely used by Holbein. A large "Ecce Homo" also in the possession of M. Tillier at Bern, in 1821, was assumed to be a work of Holbein; Hegner mentions other supposed works of the period of our painter's wanderings, but of which we have now no positive data, and no conclusions are to be drawn from notices so vague.

Patin mentions five pictures which Holbein painted for the Augustines of Lucerne:—a "Nativity;" the "Adoration of the Kings;" "Christ disputing with the Doctors;" a "Sancta Veronica;" and a "Taking down from the Cross," the thieves still hanging. There was no trace of any of these works at Lucerne in Hegner's time.

Of many of the portraits ascribed to Holbein in Switzerland, no doubt Hans Asper of Zürich, his reputed pupil and imitator, is the author. The Swiss in their enthusiasm for their imagined art-hero, were not aware that they were robbing a countryman of their own to add to the glories of a stranger. It seems to have been a common practice at one time in the country about the Swiss borders to give pictures which could not be reasonably assigned to Albert Dürer, to Holbein. The monogram of Hans Asper HH, is one that a very little wear would reduce to a form often given to Holbein himself HH. Asper was born in 1499, so that the signature IH AN° 1543 AETATIS 45, would accord well with the circumstances of Hans Asper, though not with Hans Holbein. H. H. will answer also for Hans Herbster, another Swiss painter: and it was the mark also of Hans Holzmüller, and of a few other somewhat later masters, but of no special repute.

CHAPTER VII.

SETTLES IN AND BECOMES A CITIZEN OF BASEL. THE HISTORICAL PAINTINGS IN THE TOWN-HALL OF BASEL.

CHAP. VII.

Painter and citizen of Basel. 1519-20.

UR painter had returned in the course of the year 1519 to Basel, and we have some important works of this date, when he seems to have reached the vigour of his powers, though as he grew older, contrary to the ordinary proceeding of artists, he appears to have become more careful and minute in his execution. He now entered the zunft or guild of painters at Basel, and did more, he took up the rights of citizenship, which his father and brother never did. He entered the guild on Sunday before Michaelmas, that is towards the end (the 23rd) of September, either in 1519 or 1520, for both years are given, in different extracts from the record in question, though I suppose we must assume the second or later reading to be the right one. The following is the entry in the guild-book according to Hegner:*—" *Item, es hat die zunfft enpfangen Hans Holbein der Moller uff Suntag vor Sant Michelstag im XVXIX.* (1519) *Jor, und hat geschworen der zunfft ordnung zu halten wie ein ander zunfft bruder der Moller.*" This passage had been previously quoted by Peter Ochs† as

* *Hans Holbein der Jungere*, p. 49, who remarks, "Auch bei Ochs, er hat, 1520."

† *Geschichte der Stadt und Landschaft Basel.* 8 vols., 8vo., 1786-1822. Vol. V., p. 394.

CHAP. VII. *Painter and citizen of Basel.* 1519-20.

XVXX., and which Hegner altered into 1519. Recently however Herr His-Heusler has again examined the document, and reports the date to be $XV^{C}XX.$, thus restoring the 1520 of the earlier historian.*

Before this, on the 25th of July of this year he had been named *Stubenmeister*, that is something similar to Housekeeper, but there was another officer who kept the accounts, namely the *Seckelmeister*.

Further, in the Rathsbuch of Basel, which is preserved complete from the year 1490 to 1525 inclusive, is the following entry, with reference to Holbein's citizenship, which he took up, swearing the usual oath, on the 3rd of July—on Tuesday before St. Ulrich's day, 1520:—"*Item, Zinstag vor Ulrici anno XX. ist Hans Holbeinen von Augspurg dem Maler das Burgrecht glichenn, et juravit prout moris est.*" From which it appears that the father Holbein was certainly not a citizen, or the son would have been the same by right. Holbein must have paid the usual fees, on his registration.

In the cathedral of Freiburg in Breisgan, in the chapel of the university, are still two altar-wings which are by Dr. Waagen and others assumed to have been painted in the year 1519. They are in very bad condition, and have indeed had many wanderings to make, both in Germany and in France. They were lastly carried off by the French in 1796, but were again restored to Freiburg in 1808.† It has been doubted whether they were painted in Basel or in Freiburg, during the painter's *wanderjahre*, but they appear to be well authenticated works of Holbein, and to have been painted at Basel for the Oberriedt family, one of which was a member of the Basel council in 1513.

One of these pictures represents the "Nativity of our Lord," in which the painter, as Correggio and Hans Baldung Grien have also done, has made the light proceed from the

* *Beiträge zur Vaterländische geschichte*, &c., vol. VIII., 1866. *Die Neuesten Forschungen*, &c., p. 353, note. Hegner must have mistaken the C for I: but he has put it in the wrong place.

† Schreiber's *Geschichte des Münsters zu Freiburg*, &c., quoted by Hegner.

Painter and citizen of Basel. 1519-20.

Divine Infant; the second is the "Three wise men of the East bringing presents." In both of these compositions, in the lower part, the painter has introduced portraits of the family of the donor, with the two shields of arms of the Oberriedts, and the Tscheckapürlins, the female branch. The Oberriedts were settled in Freiburg long before 1529, yet it is supposed that in this instance Hans Oberriedt the assumed donor, and councillor, was driven from Basel during the religious riots of that year, and that he contrived at the time to save these pictures from the fury of the Iconoclasts. They are supposed to have been originally in the convent church of the Carthusians, of which Hieronymus Tschekapürlin was prior.*

Boniface Amerbach.

In 1519 Charles V. succeeded his grandfather as emperor of Germany; and this year was also an important one in the career of our painter: one of his most brilliant portraits and one of his most remarkable compositions, both bear this date; and it is perhaps the year of his developing an acquaintance with his valuable friend Boniface Amerbach, whose name is henceforth inseparably connected with that of Holbein. BONIFACIUS AMERBACH at once the friend and patron of Holbein was the son of the eminent printer, Johann Amerbach of Reutlingen, who settled in Basel, and died there in 1515. Amerbach was a distinguished lawyer and eminent citizen, and was an antiquary and lover of art; he was a tall thin blue-eyed man, and was of the same age as Holbein, having been born in 1495. The qualities of the antiquary and those of the connoisseur or genuine art amateur, are not often combined; one passion generally overrides the other, and the love of the old too frequently supplants the perception of the beautiful. Of course the race is in the main to the long purse, but the hot competition for works of art is caused not by the intrinsic merit of the pieces, but by their antiquity or rarity. Amerbach had sufficient independence and judgment to bestow his money and labour on the collection and preservation of the

* Woltmann, *Holbein*, &c., p. 241.

CHAP. VII.

Boniface Amerbach. 1519-20.

works of a contemporary, even before he had emerged from the ranks of the, in a worldly sense, obscure. Boniface Amerbach may perhaps justly be considered the founder of the Basel Art-Museum, through his timely acquisition and preservation of so many of Holbein's drawings and pictures; and these still constitute the chief, if not the only attractions of the collection. The most beautiful work in it, though not the most important, but certainly one of the most admirable of all Holbein's paintings is Amerbach's own portrait, a bust somewhat under the natural size, on a blue ground, the face seen little more than in profile, turned to his right, the right eye being just visible. He has a slouching cap on, with a small cross on it, a furred cloak and embroidered vest, and is looking intently before him; he has a ruddy short full beard, and the blue eyes are brilliant and piercing. The complexion is of a rich transparent brown tint, and the whole is modelled with the minute accuracy of a photograph. In the back-ground on the right side is the stem of a tree, with a tablet hanging to a branch, containing some complimentary verses spoken by the picture itself; and the painter's signature. Holbein must have been content with his work, as he has signed it in an unusually complete manner, having added even the day of the month as well as the year—October the 14th, 1519—

BON. AMORBACCHIVM
JO. HOLBEIN. DEPINGEBAT
A. M.D.XIX. *Prid. Eid. Octobr.*

This head I believe the painter has never surpassed, his art as a portrait painter, perhaps here culminates in technical execution, especially as regards transparency: it was painted in his twenty-fifth year, Amerbach being of nearly the same age as the painter; just completing his twenty-fourth, according to the third line of the inscription—while on the point of completing the eighth term of three years—*τριετής*.*

* Picta licet facies, vivae non cedo, sed instar
Sum domini, justis nobile lineolis.
Octo is dum peragit ΤΡΙΕΤΗ, sic gnaviter in me
Id quod naturæ est exprimit artis opus.

Boniface Amerbach. 1519-20.

Erasmus speaks of Amerbach as a man of but one fault; he was excessively modest. Of his collection of forty-nine pictures, and he collected many other things besides, his son Basilius, in an inventory made in or before 1586, but many years after the father's death, ascribes no less than seventeen to Holbein: some of these ascriptions however are assuredly wrong: and it is certain that many of the drawings also enumerated are by another hand than Holbein's. It is singular how rapidly misunderstandings and misconceptions crop up in such matters. We do not know how many of these seventeen pictures Amerbach got from Holbein himself, some passed to him from Erasmus, others would be bought after Holbein left Basel, and no doubt several, perhaps the majority, were procured after Holbein's death. Between the departure of Holbein from Basel, and the drawing up of the inventory, about sixty years elapsed, time enough for considerable confusion and error to have been developed in the various ascriptions, and a very long time to preserve a scrupulously true classification of a mixed collection of works of art. Besides these seventeen pictures the Amerbach collection is supposed to contain one hundred and four original drawings, large and small, by Holbein; besides the book of eighty-five sketches, and the copy of the *Moriae Encomium* or Erasmus's "Praise of Folly," with Holbein's marginal pen and ink sketches.

Amerbach was Erasmus's principal heir: his letters and correspondence are preserved in the public library of Basel, and Hegner has suggested that if these letters were carefully examined, something trustworthy might be found in them concerning our painter, especially respecting his life in Basel. Amerbach died in 1562.

His portrait is thus entered in his son's inventory—"Meins vatters conterfehtung in der jugend, H. Holbein's uf holz mit ölfarb."

The original drawings by, and prints after, Holbein were preserved in two distinct drawers in a cabinet containing many other drawers, in which were arranged the works of various schools and masters, and this distribution turns out to be

CHAP. VII.

The Amerbach Collection. 1519-20.

important, in helping our classification of the drawings and woodcuts ascribed to Holbein.* These drawers were numbered V. and VI.:—

V. *H. Holbeini imitatio aliena non propria ejus*, 64 (*i. e.*, sixty-four pieces, all copies after Holbein). Getruckt 111 (*i. e.*, one hundred and eleven prints after Holbein's designs, there being no doubt several impressions of some). Biblica historia, &c., 2 (*i. e.*, two printed copies of Holbein's Bible illustrations). Totentantz 2 expl. (*i. e.*, two copies of the "Dance of Death").

VI. *H. Holbeini genuina*, gros, klein, von seiner hand, 104 (*i. e.*, one hundred and four original drawings and sketches by Holbein's own hand, and from this distinction we may assume that he was certainly not the engraver of the cuts in the two series of illustrations mentioned above). "Moria Erasmi," hin und wider mit figurlin (*i. e.*, the copy of Erasmus's "Praise of Folly," in which Holbein had made some marginal illustrations in pen and ink; which were published by Patin in 1676). Ein buchlin darin by 85 stucklin gerissen (*i. e.*, a little book containing eighty-five sketches). Ein anders permentin mit eim stuck (*i. e.*, a drawing on parchment; this is Holbein's portrait noticed in the inventory among the pictures, where it mentions the frame belonging to it, but explains that the portrait itself was lying in the cabinet among the Holbein drawings). Erasmi effigies in eim rundelin mit ölfarben (*i. e.*, the round so called oil miniature of Erasmus, in the museum).†

* This arrangement of Holbein's works, was first published in the Kunstblatt for 1843, by Herr Peter Fischer, see p. 63. Dr. Woltmann has since published much more complete extracts. *Holbein*, &c., Beilagen, VI., p. 365.—*Inventarium der stucken oder sachen so in der nüeren cammer gegen miner studierstuben über, begriffen dessen in min Testament meldung beschicht.* Indorsed—Autographum Basilii Amarbachii vor A. 1586 ververtigt; und nach diesem jar supplirt, &c.

† The Basel Museum Catalogue ascribes no less than thirty-two pictures, or fragments of pictures, besides drawings, to Holbein. Sixteen of these, counting the schoolmaster's sign as two, were in the Amerbach Collection. Of these sixteen the only pictures in my opinion of

CHAP. VII.

The "Fountain of Life" at Lisbon.

1519-20.

I have already spoken of Holbein's power as culminating as a portrait painter in this year 1519, by which I mean simply that his practical skill in mere painting reached its highest at this time, and in the portrait of his friend Amerbach: no other work of his shows better execution, indeed in richness of colouring and in transparency of effect it remained perhaps unrivalled; in the portraits painted afterwards in this country he was incontestably dryer. Considering Holbein's general precocity there is nothing remarkable in his having attained his full manhood in his twenty-fifth year; Masaccio had nearly run his course at this age, he was only twenty-six when he died, at Rome in 1428-9; and yet he had contrived to live long enough to influence generations of painters that came after him. Raphael was but twenty-five when he was invited to Rome by Julius II. to decorate the Stanze of the Vatican, and when the works of living men old enough to be his father were sweptaway to give place to his works. 1519 is the date of our "Raising of Lazarus" by Sebastian del Piombo; and it is the date also of Raphael's last picture, the "Transfiguration," now in the Vatican: Raphael died on the 6th of April, 1520.

And it is to this year 1519 that belongs a very remarkable picture now at Lisbon in the palace of the king of Portugal: I have not seen this picture but I have a photograph of it,* and it is a sufficient reproduction of the original to enable one to perceive some passages of a very strong similarity to known works by the painter, though it is more complicated and more varied in its composition than any of Holbein's previous

characteristic power or merit are Nos. 4, 10, 12, 13, 15, 16, 17, 18, 19, 30, and 33; that is not including the very coarse early, and as art comparatively worthless, productions. These to avoid numerical confusion, I will also name:—"The Last Supper," on wood; "Adam and Eve," 1517; "Boniface Amerbach," 1519; "The Burgomaster Meier and Wife," 1516; "Erasmus writing;" "Miniature of Erasmus;" the same in a round; "Dead Christ," 1521; "Holbein's Wife and Children;" Head of a King, a fresco; and the "Portrait of Froben." Lastly the admirable portrait of Holbein himself, in body colour, noticed in the inventory, as placed with the drawings:—"*Item, ein tafelen gehort darin ein conterfehung Holbeins mit trocken farben, so im grossen Kasten under Holbeins Kunst ligt.*" It hangs now in the "Salle des Dessins," and is numbered 15.

* Schauer's *Holbein Album.*

CHAP. VII.

The "Fountain of Life" at Lisbon. 1519-20.

works. The picture, known as the "Fountain of Life"—*Der Brunnen des Lebens*, it is inscribed PUTEUS AQUARUM VIVENCIUM, represents an eastern landscape, nearly the whole of the upper half of it being covered by a rich temple or triumphal arch of Renaissance taste in variegated marbles; the lower half is occupied by an almost semi-circular group of small figures, about one third the scale of life, symmetrically arranged. The centre of this company is the Madonna seated, on a throne, in front of the temple which constitutes a kind of canopy to it, holding the naked Infant in her arms, and in the fore-ground in front of her is the fountain of life coming from a cherub's mouth at the base of her seat, and springing into a well in which are swimming fish: by the side of this well is a vase, in which a tall lily is growing, bearing three buds, and three flowers in full bloom. Behind the Madonna are standing Joseph and St. Anne, and on each side of her, ranging to the lower corners are three female saints—behind each of these principal groups are other female saints, and in the extreme back-ground beyond the temple are three groups of winged angels, singing and playing musical instruments, one in the centre seen through an archway of the temple, and the other two, one on either side of the temple.

Of the figures in this composition, the Virgin bears a strong resemblance to the Virgin on the exterior of the St. Sebastian altar-piece; the St. Anne calls to mind strongly the portrait of the painter's mother at Hampton Court; and the foremost saint on the left of the Virgin with roses, apparently St. Dorothy, has a striking likeness to the St. Elizabeth of the St. Sebastian altar-piece, engraved in this volume. The foremost saint on the other side opposite to St. Dorothy, with a dragon at her feet is St. Margaret; on her left is St. Barbara; on the right of St. Dorothy is St. Catherine who holds the left hand of the infant Christ. These four saints are the principal accessory figures.

The architecture is extremely rich, and more careful and elaborate than anything else we have by Holbein; the draperies are large and elegant, and quite free from that charac-

CHAP. VII.

The "Fountain of Life" at Lisbon. 1519-20.

teristic littleness of arrangement of fold, which too commonly disfigures German art. The picture is said to be signed with the painter's name and to bear the date 1519. The whole composition is easy and beautiful; the lower half contains eighteen figures, and the three small groups of angels beyond the temple in the back-ground add about eighteen more. It will be observed that in this composition we have nothing ecclesiastical; we have the Lord as the "Fountain of Life," and the more popular female martyrs as representing the virtues and affections—no priests, no church dignitaries, no dogmatizers, no monks with their bald crowns, shaven in the pride of ostentatious humility.

This picture was formerly in England, and is possibly one of those collected by the Earl of Arundel, though I find no mention of it in any of the early accounts; it seems however to have been in the possession of Charles II., and it was through this circumstance that it found its way into Portugal, whither it was carried by his widow Queen Catherine; Pietro Guarienti saw it early in the last century in a royal chapel in Lisbon. There is an interesting note upon it, published twenty years ago, in Count A. Raczynski's "Arts en Portugal,"* "BEMPOSTA (*près de Santa Anna*, 26 Mars 1844). —Dans la sacristie de la chapelle du château, au-dessus d'une armoire, est placé un tableau signé, de Jean Holbein. Il porte la date de 1519. Il a à peu près 2 mètres de hauteur sur 1,30 m, de largeur [6 ft. 6 in. high by 4 ft. 3 in. wide]. Les figures du premier plan ont un tiers de grandeur naturelle. C'est un admirable ouvrage, et il est d'une conservation parfaite. Les bourreaux, appelés restaurateurs, n'y ont pas touché.† Le sujet est *La Sainte Vierge assise sur un trône* tenant l'enfant Jésus dans ses bras et entourée de beaucoup de saintes. Derrière le trône se voit une riche et belle architecture dans le style de François Ier. Ce fut la fille de Jean IV., la reine

* *Les Arts en Portugal, Lettres adressées a la société Artistique et Scientifique de Berlin et accompagnées de Documens.* 8vo. Paris, 1846, p. 295.

† Il serait superflu de dire que je n'appelle *bourreaux* que les mauvais restaurateurs de tableaux.

CHAP. VII.

The "Fountain of Life" at Lisbon. 1519-20.

Catherine de Portugal, sœur de Pierre II., et femme de Charles II. d'Angleterre qui, étant devenue veuve, rapporta ce tableau d'Angleterre et en fit présent a cette chapelle. Je tiens ces renseignemens des ecclésiastiques qui la desservent."*

The Town-hall, Basel.

We may now return to the paintings of the Town-hall or Rath-haus, the *Richt-huss* or Judgment-hall as it was then called. The old house was according to Ochs, pulled down in 1508, and the new was completed by March 1521. In June of this year Hans Holbein the painter (not the father but the son) was commissioned by the council, his friend Jacob Meier being still burgomaster, to paint the council-room. One of the four walls of this room was completely pierced by windows, and was unfit for paintings: the entrance was at the end of this wall and as you entered the hall, on your left hand were the windows, and on your right hand was, at a right angle with these windows the only sound wall in the room;

* The picture is signed JOANNES HOLBEIN FECIT 1519, on the rim of the well in the fore-ground, in small dark letters; but according to the convictions of M. Fournier, *Secretaire interprète* of the Prussian embassy in Lisbon, this inscription has been repaired or renewed: such is his opinion communicated to Dr. Woltmann. The inscription cannot have been very perfect in about 1735, for Guarienti, with a strange want of sagacity not only read the name as HOLTEIN without any misgiving, but conjectured from the style and time that the painter must have been a scholar of the celebrated HOLBENS, and stranger still, Guarienti published this conjecture after he had been appointed superintendent of the Dresden Gallery, and which then already contained its "Meyer Madonna." He enters Holbein's name in his continuation of Orlandi's *Abecedario Pittorico* (Venice, 1753) as OLBEIN. The passage is interesting as recording a high opinion of the drawing, colouring, and execution of the picture.—"GIO: HOLTEIN, nome da me veduto in un quadro, ch' è in una Regia Capella di Lisbona, in cui si rappresentano gli attributi di Maria Vergine, il qual quadro è *perfettamente bello*, ben disegnato e colorito, con quantità di figure. Dalla maniera, diligenza, e composizione di detto quadro, e del anno 1519, posto sotto al nome di lui, pare che possa dirsi, esser esso stato scolaro dell' Holbens, che circa a quel tempo fioriva, e che morì nel 1554. Non ho potuto raccovre di lui altra notizia." This passage coming from a *Keeper of the Dresden Gallery* shows how singularly little was known or thought of Holbein in the middle of the last century. His name on one of his finest works is misread, and one of the principal connoisseurs of his age speculates as to who the painter can have been. Our great painters had need have biographers, if notwithstanding their fine works such is the obscurity into which they can fall a century or two after their decease.

The Town-hall, Basel. 1519-20.

both the others being pierced with doorways or windows, but leaving several spaces where decorations might be introduced: the room was about 60 feet long by 35 feet wide, but only 12½ feet high; and in the middle of it were three pillars supporting the ceiling.* It was therefore little calculated to display paintings, yet it was here that Holbein made his highest historical efforts, and produced his largest compositions, on three of the four walls.

The Frescoes of the Council-room.

In the course of the years 1521 and 1522 the painter received in seven separate payments, the sum of 120 florins, though he had painted two of the walls only; and the original contract for the whole three seems to have been but 120 florins (*hundert und XX gulden*). Holbein maintained that he had earned the money, notwithstanding the bare third side; and this the council seems to have acceded to, and as no immediate arrangement was made for prosecuting the work, it was suspended, and it remained suspended for some years, partly through a want of decision of the council, and partly through Holbein's departure for England. The third wall, the unbroken one on the right hand on entering, and for which Holbein received an additional sum of 72 florins, was not painted until 1530, after the painter's return to Basel from his visit to Sir Thomas More in England.†

The insignificant fragments of fresco from this chamber, which are preserved in the Museum of Basel, are, with the exception of a single head, that of a king (No. 30, a head in profile with a spiked crown), quite unimportant, and display nothing worthy of Holbein's reputation; but the head in question is really a fine work of art. The Museum however pos-

* A plan is given in Woltmann's *Holbein*, &c., p. 303.

† These are the discoveries of Herr His-Heusler. The payments are given in the volume referred to, p. 353. The account is somewhat obscure as it is given in two currencies, in florins and in pounds and shillings, that is Basel pounds—of copper. The florin was one pound five shillings, the pound being divided into twenty shillings: the florin was accordingly $\frac{25}{16}$ of a pound of copper, equal to twenty of our old pennies, supposing the weights to be equivalent. This is about the value of the florin in the south of Germany and Holland at the present day. Our own shilling was in the Norman time the twentieth part of a troy pound weight of silver. See Jacob's *Precious Metals*, 1831.

CHAP. VII.

The Frescoes of the Council-room. 1521-2.

sesses among its drawings five washed sketches which were presumed to be original when in the Amerbach cabinet, but there is nothing to proclaim the originality in the drawings themselves. They are certainly interesting as giving the subjects and compositions,* namely—Samuel reproving Saul; King Rehoboam; the legislator Charondas; King Sapor and the Emperor Valerian; and the legislator Zaleucus. There are also some indifferent sketches of the state of the paintings in 1817 by one Jerome Hess.

Portions of the frescoes were in an ordinary state of preservation in 1577, as they are mentioned in a local history of that date, quoted by Hegner,† and some were still to be seen in Patin's time, a century later: he notices the three walls of this hall as painted by Holbein. The subjects were comprised in several compartments or divisions, an arrangement of course necessitated by the nature of the spaces as described above. The painter adapted his designs to the spaces, introducing large compositions, smaller groups, and single iconic representative impersonations. The frescoes appear to have been altogether eleven in number, five figures, and six compositions. The five single figures were :—Our Lord, with the legend—*quod tibi non vis fieri, alteri non facias;* David with the harp; Justice; Wisdom; and Temperance, a young woman pouring wine into a small flask. All with appropriate Latin inscriptions.

Three of the stories, painted in illustration of justice, are

---

* They are thus noticed in the unsatisfactory catalogue of Basel :—

35. Le Prophète Samuel reprend le Roi Saul.

36. Le Roi Roboam.

37. Le Legislateur Charondas, et les Rois Sapor et Valérien.

38. Le Legislateur Zaleukus et la Justice.

In the "Inventory" they are described as follows :—

Item, Der Prophet Samuell und Achab, getouscht, auf einen langen bogen.

Item, Der König Rehabeam mit vielen bildern, tuscht, auf einem kleinen bogen.

Item, Zaleucus } getuscht, auf
Item, Charonda Tirius } quart bögen.

Item, Valerianus et Sapor rex Persiarum, getuscht, auf einem quart bogen.

The old catalogue is a little more explicit than the modern compilation made nearly three centuries later.

† *Epitome Historiae Basiliensis. aut. Chr. Urstisio.* 8vo. Basil, 1577.

Chap. VII.

The Frescoes of the Council-room. 1521-2.

those of three celebrated ancient legislators—The Roman consul Manius Curius Dentatus; the Locrian Zaleucus; and Charondas Thurius; painted in 1521. When some Samnite ambassadors visited Curius Dentatus, bringing presents of gold, in order to bias him in their favour, they found him in his cottage cooking his own dinner; and he asked them if they thought a man who lived as simply as he did, could have any use for gold.

The laws of Zaleucus were noted for their severity, and the punishment for adultery was deprivation of sight by putting out the eyes; when his own son was convicted of this crime, Zaleucus in compassion and through love of his son, put out only one of the young man's eyes, but in justification of the law put out also one of his own.

Charondas Thurius of Catana in his laws had decreed punishment of death for whoever should enter the assembly of the people armed; and on an occasion when he had returned from the pursuit of some robbers, he inadvertently entered the assembly without having laid aside his sword. It was pointed out to him that he had himself broken his own law. "On the contrary," he replied, "I enforce it," and he immediately pierced himself through the body with the offending weapon.

Whether true or not the above are well chosen examples for the pictorial illustration of the majesty or the inviolability of justice, however barbarous: a semi-civilized people require strong illustrations. The terrible punishment for adultery imposed by Zaleucus contrasts singularly with the slight penances and small fines exacted by the Roman priests for the same crime, in Holbein's time in this country.

The fourth subject was Sapor the Persian king, using the captive Emperor Valerian as a step to mount his horse from.

The two principal compositions however, were apparently on the end wall, which afforded an unbroken field; these were two scenes from Jewish history:—Rehoboam; and Samuel reproving Saul, after his victory over the Amalekites. These are assumed to be the pictures which Holbein painted after his

CHAP. VII.

The Frescoes of the Council-room. 1521-2.

return from England in 1530, and for which he was paid, in four instalments, 72 florins.* This was after all not very great encouragement for him to remain at Basel, considering that painters in England at this very time, were receiving about as much for a single portrait as Holbein was paid for two historical pictures, one about 15 feet wide, the other about 19 feet; the smallness of the sum does appear somewhat astounding, twenty pence for a large figure in fresco. Holbein must have found an agreeable difference in the pounds and shillings he received in England as compared with those he received in Basel. The English pound was then just sixteen Basel pounds.

The subject of Rehoboam is a fine composition, but in the sketch the proportions of the figures are somewhat unrefined, like too many of the painter's earlier figure pieces; though there is great dignity in the arrangement and in the figures in the back-ground. The moment represented is when Rehoboam seated on his throne, following the advice of the young men, utters the terrible words to Jeroboam and the Israelites, when they went to him on the third day as he had appointed:—"My father made your yoke heavy, and I will add to your yoke." "My little finger shall be thicker than my father's loins." "My father hath chastised you with whips, but I will chastise you with scorpions." (1 Kings, ch. xii.) Rehoboam, in a spacious hall of Italian architecture, is raising himself on his throne, and leaning forward, his body is just seen above the Israelites in the fore-ground, some still looking at the king and others turning away from him and thus showing their faces to the spectator. The king with a ferocious countenance is threatening them with the little finger of his left hand, while with the index of his right, he points to a scourge in the

* His-Heusler, *Beiträge*, &c., p. 358. Woltmann, *Beilagen*, p. 373. These several payments to Meister Hans Holbein dem Moller, were made as follows:—

Uff mitwuchs noch Ulryci (6th July) im 1530 jor . . . fll. 12.
Uff donstig noch sant laurenzen dag (11th August) im 1530 jor fll. 20.
Noch frene (Verenatag, Thursday 1st September) im 1530 jor . fll. 24.
Uff fritag noch sant Martis dag (18th November), im 1530 jor . . . . fll. 16.

CHAP. VII.

The Frescoes of the Council-room. 1521-2.

hands of a slave standing by the throne. In the back-ground on each side of the throne, but behind it, are the councillors of the king—on his right "the old men that stood before Solomon, his father," who gave the good counsel—on his left "the young men that were grown up with him," who gave the bad counsel. In the back-ground on one side is seen a piece of hilly country where Jeroboam is being crowned king of Israel.

In the meeting of Samuel and Saul, we have a crowd of foot- and horse-men met by the prophet, who addressing Saul, says, "What meaneth then this bleating of the sheep in mine ears, and the lowing of the oxen which I hear?" And Saul said, "They have brought them from the Amalekites," "to sacrifice unto the Lord thy God;" and Samuel said, "Hath the Lord as great delight in burnt offerings and sacrifices, as in obeying the voice of the Lord? Behold, to obey is better than sacrifice, and to hearken than the fat of rams." "Because thou hast rejected the word of the Lord, he hath also rejected thee from being king." (1 Samuel, ch. xv.) Samuel is pointing with his left hand to the sheep and oxen which are seen in the middle distance.*

There is something striking in the change of subject from the stern virtues of the heathens to a sentiment of religion derived from Scripture, during the interval of eight years which passed between the suspension and completion of these decorations of the Council-hall—and a great change had come over the religion of the people, the ordeal of 1529 had been passed; the church was no longer to be a school of ceremonies and burning of incense; the exhibition of relics, or the counting of beads; the denunciation of the prophet had reached the ear of Basel—*Behold, to obey is better than sacrifice, and to hearken than the fat of rams!* This is an indication of the presence of what after events more clearly showed, that the spirit of our own Puritanism had found its biding places among the sunny vales of Switzerland.

* Woodcuts of these two compositions are given in Woltmann's *Holbein und seine zeit.*

CHAP. VII.

The Frescoes of the Council-room. 1521-2.

As the works themselves have perished it is impossible to give any opinion on their merits; the sketches show dramatic vigour, and no doubt the works had many excellences. Whether Holbein was a good practical fresco painter, means of judging are wanting; the fragments in the Museum of Basel are quite insufficient to give any adequate idea; one of the heads is certainly fine, but the others are indifferent.

The great efforts however, and perhaps they were more successful in their execution than most such efforts are, and almost unique in Germany in their time, were destined to but a short duration.

This council-hall seems to have been ill secured against damp; this was the destroyer of the frescoes, not the Iconoclasts—the mischief was caused by imperfect construction and deficiency of proper precautions. Already in 1576 the paintings of one wall were so seriously decayed that a painter of the name of Hans Bockh, was employed by the town council to make an oil copy of them on canvas, and the copy occupied him the long days of no less than six and twenty weeks. His application for payment for his half-year's labour, is still among the archives of Basel, and bears the date 23rd November 1579: considering that the work copied contained about one hundred figures as he estimated it, he demanded 100 florins—a moderate remuneration certainly, about eight guineas, making a little more than a shilling a day, yet by no means contemptible pay for those times. There was however no picture which contained one hundred figures, even the Rehoboam and the Samuel and Saul together, do not contain so many.

This canvas copy was placed on the wall over the original, yet such was the fatality of the place, that it too perished in the course of not many years, and the walls were finally furnished with hangings of cloth and old tapestry. It was so lately as 1817, when some changes had to be made in the hall, that in removing the tapestries, some traces of these old frescoes were discovered on the walls, very nearly quite oblite-

The Frescoes of the Council-room. 1521-2.

rated. There were remains of the stories of Curius Dentatus, and Zaleucus, dated 1521; and it is from these ruins that the seven fragments of the museum were saved, among them some heads of the Samnite deputies, which are now treasured as valuable relics of Holbein's frescoes. The crowned head specified is masterly and interesting.

To Holbein also has been commonly ascribed the painting of the "Last Judgment," in the staircase, the work that was so long vaunted for its Lutheranism before Luther. It is now shown from documents that this work was not executed till nearly a century after Holbein left Basel, and as many after Luther's famous revolution in ecclesiastical polity. Several accounts and records of payments are preserved in the town archives which show that this work was executed in the years 1609-10 by the above-mentioned Hans Bockh, and his sons; who was accordingly a young man when he copied the frescoes of Holbein for some thirteen pence the day.

The twelve painted windows or panes of glass which were transferred from the old council-room to the new, were all painted before Holbein's time; they represent the arms of the twelve cantons, and Appenzell which was only added in 1513 is not included; while the shield of Solothurn bears the date of 1501.*

Rarity of his easel-pictures at Basel.

No doubt Holbein in so circumscribed a field as Basel, more especially in the unsettled times of the Reformation, was compelled to turn his hand to many kinds of work which on the present system of the division of labour, the cultivators of high art would consider derogatory. But great artists commonly led simple lives at this period, even in Rome the very centre of corruption. If Holbein's so called easel-pictures are few for the considerable number of years that he was residing in Basel, it is not so much that his pictures are lost as that he must have been busily occupied in every branch of his profession, as a mere house decorator, as a fresco painter, as a designer for stained glass, and for the silversmiths. Several

* Ochs, III., 218; Hegner, p. 77.

CHAP. VII.

Rarity of his easel-pictures at Basel. 1521-5.

sketches of these various classes are preserved in the Museum of Basel, and his designs for silver work, for arms, for heraldic devices for glass, and mere ornament, perhaps even for embroidered muslin, show a perfect Italian taste, and in fact that he was a consummate master of the ornamental design of the cinque-cento period; some of his foliated and floriated scroll drawings are not only perfect in their forms but are executed with all the ready ease of a consummate master.

Among his decorations recorded is one of the façade of a house in the Eisengasse, painted from top to bottom, in the fashion of the rich architectural back-grounds which at a later time distinguished the pictures of Paul Veronese, and of which a sketch is preserved at Basel, on which he had painted the story of Marcus Curtius leaping into the gulf; and also a very popular peasant dance, which as the most sympathetic and intelligible incident of the whole composition gave its name to the house itself, the house of the *Bauerntanz* or "*Haus zum Tanz:*" for this work says Theodor Zwinger, an old writer quoted by Hegner,* Holbein was paid 40 florins: it is very rarely that we are able to report the prices Holbein received for his work. Even Albert Dürer was content at this time to draw a portrait for a florin, and the 40 florins mentioned were probably a satisfactory remuneration to the younger painter, for a work that might have occupied him even for forty days.

There is somewhere a large water-colour copy of the *Bauerntanz* referred to, made by one Wilhelm Stettler, which passes for the original drawing by Holbein himself. The museum possesses drawings or sketches of the whole façade, and of some of the parts; but all, if any one is, are not original.

Considering that Holbein was painting in Basel at least eight years, and the museum there contains the works belonging to his intimate friend and patron Boniface Amerbach, the

* *Methodus apodemica.* Basil, 1577. Domus Privata in platea ferri (Eisengasse) choream rusticam exhibet, a J. Holbenio XL. florenorum stipendio depicta. Hegner, *Hans Holbein*, &c., p. 143.

rarity of his easel-pictures at Basel is remarkable. Some belong to the purchased Amerbach Collection, some to that of Remigius Fesch, likewise a lawyer, made in the following century, and acquired through bequest; and some few isolated examples have been purchased by the town-council.

CHAP. VII.

Rarity of his easel-pictures at Basel.
1521-5.

All these works combined must constitute but a small portion of Holbein's labours while in Basel, even if we deduct another two years or so for the time he was occupied in preparing designs for and in painting the council-hall itself—1521-2. Some few however of the pictures of this museum are invaluable, as showing the painter's early style and progress; and we have certainly authentic examples extending over the whole period of ten years that Holbein was more or less domiciliated at Basel; from 1516 to his departure in 1526: viz.—Jacob Meier and his wife, 1516; Adam and Eve, 1517; the portrait of Dr. Amerbach, 1519; all already described. Further, the exquisite small portrait of himself, engraved in this volume, a drawing in body-colour, when about one or two and twenty years of age; a small portrait of John Froben the printer; a similar portrait of the celebrated Erasmus, writing, on parchment; a large life-sized picture of the "Dead Body of Christ lying in the Tomb," signed and dated H. H. 1521; and the very remarkable portraits, on paper attached to wood, of his wife and his two children, which were probably painted in 1525 or 1526, certainly not long before he started for England.

Here are several years unrepresented; of 1523 and 1524 we seem to have nothing whatever; but a few links may certainly be supplied from foreign collections; as for example Hampton Court Gallery, which contains several examples of this time. Elsewhere it is not so easy to lay one's hand on examples; the two portraits in the Maximilian's Museum at Augsburg, appear to be Basel works, as I have already surmised. The magnificent "Meier Madonna" to be described presently, and the remarkable picture of 1519, the "Brunnen des Lebens" at Lisbon, described already, are also Basel works. The altar-wings at Freiburg may possibly belong to these later

CHAP. VII.

Rarity of his easel-pictures at Basel. 1521-5.

years, that is after the painting of the council-room rather than before.

Still all these works do not account for very much of the time of so able a master as Holbein. He must have been greatly occupied with mere decorative work for old walls, and for stained glass, which has mostly perished. He appears to

Glass-painting.

have been frequently employed in preparing drawings for stained glass; the Basel Museum possesses several examples:* a great deal of his time also must have been given to the preparation of drawings for woodcuts; such as his "Dance of Death," and the Bible series. He appears to have made more than one important series of drawings for the Passion of our Lord; there are ten in the "Salle des Dessins" at Basel, which according to the catalogue were made for glass paintings; they have some bold back-grounds of coarse Renaissance architecture, which has much of the ordinary character of such work designed for glass.

The Drawings of the Passion.

The "History of the Passion" constitutes a very important series of designs, showing great power both in drawing and composition, yet in some few instances they exhibit a coarseness of treatment almost amounting to caricature, though he has not approximated the hideous deformities of many of his celebrated countrymen, not excepting even Albert Dürer, occasionally. Seven of these scenes, apparently without variation but reversed, outlined with the pen and washed with Indian ink, are among the drawings of the British Museum, and have been for some time exhibited in the King's Library; they were purchased at the sale of Sir Thomas Lawrence's collection.† The execution is masterly and beautiful, but they appear to have been made from some other drawings, they

* Dr. Woltmann has given a woodcut of one of these studies, from a coloured drawing in Berlin, in his first volume, a couple of Landsknechts, reposing, and holding a shield, left blank for some inscription or coat of arms; a landscape in the distance, and some rich Renaissance architecture serving as a framework to the two soldiers, p. 253.

† See the catalogue compiled by Mr. Carpenter, *A Guide to the Drawings and Prints exhibited to the Public in the King's Library*, 1862. The subjects, about 15 in. by 12 in., are:—

1. Christ brought before the High Priest.
2. The Mocking of Christ.
3. Christ brought forward and shown

"ECCE HOMO."

P. 130.

CHAP. VII. The Drawings of the Passion. 1521-5.

want the carelessness and imperfections of original sketches; they have been possibly traced in some way from those at Basel; their effect is if anything superior to that of the Basel drawings.

Among the best drawings also of the museum at Basel may be particularized the fine sepia sketch for the wings of the organ of the cathedral there. The wings themselves are preserved in the museum, painted in chiaro-scuro, in brown, but they are injured, and their effect is gone. The drawing is a genuine Holbein work, with dignified figures and bold effective draperies: on one wing is the Emperor St. Henry, and behind him the Empress Cunigund holding the cross, with a model of the Cathedral of Basel on the ground between them: on the other wing, symmetrically arranged, is the Madonna crowned, holding the Infant Christ in her arms, and behind her is St. Pantalus, bishop; between them is a choir of winged cherub angels with musical instruments. The whole is further enriched with elaborate and highly foliated cinque-cento scroll-work.†

Dead Christ. 1521.

The "Dead Christ in the Tomb," mentioned above, a life-sized figure, is in a very different taste from all Holbein's after pictures, of this or any other period: some have professed to have been greatly shocked by the *naturalism* of this picture. It is in a very different taste from his life-like portraits, and necessarily so. The painter has turned from life and intelligence to death and decay, and he has further adopted a

to the people by Pilate (engraved for this volume).

4. Pilate washing his hands.
5. Christ led to Execution.
6. Christ divested of His garments.
7. The Crucifixion.

The following is the Basel series, as given in the catalogue of 1863; they were formerly in the Amerbach Collection; those marked with the asterisk are the three missing designs of the Lawrence series. The Inventory notices them thus—Item, *Zehen stuckh vom passion getuscht, Jedes auff einem Bogen Papyr.*

39. Le Christ devant Caïphe.
40. La flagellation du Christ.*
41. Jesus insulté par les soldats.
42. Le Christ couronné d'épines.*
43. Pilate se lavant les mains (engraved for Dr. Woltmann's first volume).
44. Ecce Homo (No. 3).
45. Le Christ conduit au Calvaire.
46. Le Christ dépouillé de ses vêtements.
47. Le Christ cloué à la croix.*
48. Le Christ en croix entre les deux larrons (engraved for Dr. Woltmann's first volume).

† A photograph is given in Schauer's *Holbein Album.*

CHAP. VII. Dead Christ. 1521.

peculiar lighting of the body, to produce as ghastly an impression as possible, and thus enhance our abomination of the act of the Jews.* The corpse is lying flat on its back on a cloth, the chin and small beard pointing upwards; it is emaciated and of a cold greenish grey colour, and thrown mostly into shadow by the artifice of lighting it by a horizontal ray of light supposed to be coming through some small aperture low down; it therefore strikes the soles of the feet, putting the upper sides in shadow, and so on along the body to the chin, illuminating the lower or under side of every prominent part, and darkening the upper; producing altogether a most revolting effect: and all is done with a horrible realistic power. He has inscribed it JESUS NAZARENUS REX JUD. H. H. 1521. It is one of the Amerbach pictures, and is noticed in the Inventory thus:—"*Ein todten Bild H. Holbeins uf holz mit ölfarben* cum titulo Jesus Nazarenus Rex, &c."

The drawing of himself on vellum, in crayon or body-colour, already noticed in pages 116 and 129, which Mr. C. W. Sharpe has engraved as a vignette for this volume, will not require much description. In the original both the sleeves and a part of the right hand are shown; the loose over-coat is of a pale drab, the facings appear to be of dark brown velvet; the cap is red; the eyes are a rich brown. The effect of the whole is magnificent.

* Engraved in von Mechel's *Œuvre de Holbein*, &c.

CHAPTER VIII.

Friends and Patrons at Basel.

Frobenius and Erasmus. 1521-5.

HEN Holbein arrived in Basel, the printer Froben or Frobenius as he is commonly called, had already a European reputation; he seems as well as Amerbach to have been an early and good friend of the painter. It was probably through the first that Holbein became acquainted with Erasmus, who was settled in Basel in 1521, and lived in the house of Frobenius; these two were in the double relationship of publisher and editor, and landlord and tenant. Frobenius had printed works of Erasmus before this time, and Holbein had already illustrated several volumes for him. The "Colloquies" of Erasmus were first published in Basel in 1522. It was, it is said, the great reputation of Frobenius as a conscientious man, and able printer, that induced Erasmus to settle in that city: he had previously dwelt chiefly in Antwerp; but Basel held out the additional inducement of liberty of conscience and a freedom from priestly domination. And here in the house of the famous printer and publisher, the young German painter in his ordinary visits respecting possibly some woodcut design, some ornamental initial or title-margin, though his general art reputation would be a better introduction, became acquainted with, and gradually acquired

CHAP. VIII.

Frobenius and Erasmus. 1521-5.

the friendship of, the great commentator: Erasmus had some appreciation for art; he himself tried painting in his youth.

Rumohr assumes* that Holbein was employed as a wood-engraver by Froben; this is possible, but from the general inferiority in the execution of the woodcuts referred to, I find it very difficult to adopt this opinion. Holbein may have tried to cut, and having failed once or twice, or found the process too slow or mechanical for him, have given it up. But it is quite certain that so good an artist in every way as Holbein was, could not possibly have gone on producing bad woodcuts; this would have been an æsthetic violation of his taste and judgment: even as regards the designs, I do not believe Holbein is the author of one quarter of those ascribed to him. But to be even tolerably perfect in wood-engraving a man must make it his business, and we know that Holbein did nothing of the kind. He was certainly much too fine an artist to have produced or at least tolerated when produced by himself such essays as the very bad early cuts that are ascribed to him; and he was certainly too unpractised an engraver to have produced the excellent cuts of later years, which have been given to him; such for instance as those of the original "Dance of Death," which some writers insist on being his own handiwork.

The conclusion my impressions impel me to, is, that he engraved neither the good nor the bad: and the prints seem to show that even as a designer on wood, he was really not much employed by Froben, who had other artists who worked for him besides Holbein, whose time could not be turned to so good an account as our consummate painter's, and who were in no proportion in such request for other work: Holbein seems to have worked for Froben in the first years only of his sojourn in Basel. Among other artists living at Basel at this time we

* *Hans Holbein der Jüngere in seinem Verhältniss zum Deutschen Formschnittwesen.* 8vo. Leipzig, 1836. This volume contains an elaborate investigation of woodcuts ascribed to Holbein. See also *Zur geschichte und Theorie der Formschneidekunst*, 1837, by the same writer.

Frobenius and Erasmus. 1521-5.

know that Urs Graf and Ambrose Holbein were both employed on woodblocks by Froben.

Erasmus was probably too much absorbed in his own pursuits, to have noticed the humble efforts of an obscure designer, though embellishing or at least attempting to embellish his own works. Froben however must have known the man he employed, and by some means or other, either through the father or the uncle engaged in Basel before the son's arrival, or otherwise, Holbein's talent for designing in the Renaissance taste, was soon made known to the great printer and publisher, who seems to have employed him immediately after he settled in Basel.

The marginal decoration of the dedicatory page of this volume was first used by Froben according to Hegner in 1516.* The cut is used in various publications from 1516 to 1520 inclusive; and first in *Erasmus de Octo orationis partium constructione,* 1516, and again in 1517. It is used also in Sir Thomas More's "Utopia," November 1518.—*De optimo Reip. statu, deque nova Insula Utopia,* &c., for title and at p. 17. This cut is more particularly interesting as being one of the earliest of its class designed by Holbein; he was only twenty in 1516; and as bearing his signature, virtually in full, in the two tablets at the top—HANS. HOLB. A few others have the initials H. H., as in the title to the *Epigrammata clarissimi Disertissimique Viri Thomæ Mori,* &c., 1520: in this design is the composition of Mucius Scævola and Porsenna. The engraver of the majority of these book cuts is supposed to be an artist of Basel who signed J. F.†

Froben seems to have afterwards, for a few years employed both Ambrose and Hans, as ordinary designers for the ornamental blocks for his publications, but he required no great

* *Hans Holbein,* p. 344. Passavant says 1515, but this must be an error; Holbein was not then in Basel, and as the cut contains Froben's trade-mark of the Caduceus, it would appear to have been expressly designed for him; therefore after Holbein's arrival in Basel.

† See Passavant, *Peintre Graveur,* Vol. III., p. 355; and Peter Vischer, *Kunstblatt,* 1838, No. 53, where there is a list of the superior cuts ascribed to Holbein, as the designer, not as the engraver.

CHAP. VIII.

Frobenius and Erasmus. 1521-5.

number, as he commonly used the same cuts in several volumes—Initials, borders, vignettes, &c., of which I have given examples in this volume. They are unhappily coarsely and even badly engraved, as a rule, but some of the more ornamental scrolls do not suffer by this, their sentiment remains in full force; the more ambitious efforts however in cinque-cento design require careful engraving to preserve the spirit of the drawing. I have already noticed Holbein's preference for the Renaissance style of ornament and architecture over the Gothic, in noticing the early picture of the Infant Christ, at Augsburg; and he shows the same preference in all the woodcuts attributed to him in the publications of Frobenius; the designs themselves are free enough, it is the engraving that is at fault. Still, all the defects of these early works must not be laid at the engraver's door, Holbein's ornamental sketches generally of this period are not to be compared with some of his later designs, especially some of those for silver work which were executed in England; these are unsurpassed. He adhered to his first love, the cinque-cento, or rather the Renaissance, throughout. But if we compare, for instance, the *amorini* in Mr. Baring's portrait of Hans Herbster, with those of the design for Sir John Denny's clock, now in the British Museum, the distance between the skill of the 'prentice-work and the master's is enormous.

One of the best and most interesting of these old blocks, a piece of pear-tree, is still preserved in the museum at Basel; it represents the portrait of Erasmus, full-length, resting his right hand on the head of a truncated Terminus, which is placed immediately in front of him and hides his feet. He is surrounded by an ornamental border, in the form of a triumphal arch, of rich Renaissance architecture and ornament of elegant design. Above, in a tablet, are the letters ER. ROT., Erasmus Roterodamus, and below, in another ornamental space, in the earliest impressions from the block, are the two following lines:—

Corporis effigiem si quis non vidit Erasmi
Hanc scite ad vivum picta tabella dabit.

Frobenius and Erasmus. 1521-5.

This cut, altogether 11¼ in. high by 6 in. wide—the triumphal arch itself is only 9 in. high—is commonly ascribed to Hans Lützelburger, the drawing being assumed to be by Holbein, and it is said to have been first used in 1519: it is quite worthy of Holbein. Lützelburger is the assumed engraver of the "Dance of Death" series of cuts, published at Lyon in 1538. There are several impressions from the Erasmus block in the Print-Room of the British Museum, in the original and in a later state : the later print has four lines instead of two, in the lower space referred to, viz. :

> Pallas Apellaeam nuper mirata tabellam
> Hanc ait, aeternum Bibliotheca colat.
> Dedaleam monstrat Musis HOLBEINNIUS artem
> Et summi ingenii magnus Erasmus opes.

John Froben or Frobenius according to the then habit of Latinizing surnames as well as the baptismal, was invited to Basel by Amerbach the father, to assist him in his arduous printing operations. He became the most distinguished printer of his time; his publications are numerous, but his *opus magnum* is perhaps, the complete edition of the writings of St. Jerome, in several volumes folio, first published in Basel in 1516, and reprinted in 1520 and 1524, under the superintendence of Erasmus: the period when Holbein gradually developed his great powers in Basel, then a renowned centre of liberty, learning and the arts; and no doubt the patronage and friendship of John Froben and his learned editor contributed, as did the intercourse with the monks of St. Ulrich, at Augsburg, not a little to completing the education of Holbein as a man of the world, and grinding out the littlenesses almost inseparable from a restricted provincial bringing up; though Augsburg was a city of great importance in those days.

In October 1527, to the despair of Erasmus, his friend Froben died suddenly, aged sixty-seven. This famous printer and publisher fell down on the pavement struck by apoplexy, and so seriously injured his head by the fall, that he never recovered his senses, but died six hours afterwards. Erasmus

CHAP. VIII.

Frobenius and Erasmus. 1521-5.

in a letter to his friend John Emsted, wrote a feeling lamentation on Froben's death, and a sincere eulogy on his life and character.*

Erasmus and Froben seem to have been repeatedly subjects for Holbein's pencil, though from the uniformity of character in the various portraits of them, it would appear that they did not often sit to him. Holbein seems to have had the wisdom to spare his sitters the ceremony of sitting, as much as possible. Many of his portraits are evidently painted from chalk sketches, indeed some of them are simply these sketches varnished over and heightened with a little colour. A man who possessed the power of seeing as Holbein possessed it could afford to do this, there was no fear of either hand or eye failing him.

I assume that all the genuine portraits of Erasmus by Holbein, were drawn or painted in Basel, between the years 1521 and 1526, that is when he was still in the prime of his maturity, when about fifty-five years of age; he is grey, not white, and the eye is still brilliant. It would be difficult to determine any number for the genuine portraits; they may be several, but not many. These genuine pictures have been again multiplied by copies: most of the so-called miniatures I imagine to be careful copies or studies, made by various painters, for some of the more enthusiastic of the many admirers of Erasmus's extraordinary learning; not only in Germany but also in England, where he held the Greek professorship at Oxford, for many years. Erasmus died at Basel, July the 12th, 1536, in his seventieth year.

There is a pair of portraits of Froben and Erasmus at Hampton Court, which are evidently companions, and which have hitherto been preserved as inseparable; and I take them to be the two which were presented to Froben by Erasmus. They were given to Charles I. by the Duke of Buckingham; they are Nos. 323 and 324: on the back of 323

* See *Epistolarum D. Erasmi Roterodami.* Libri XXXI., &c. Folio. London, 1642. Lib. XXIII. Ep. 9. 1527.

was pasted a record of the gift, but the following words are all that now remain legible—

CHAP. VIII.

Frobenius and Erasmus. 1521-5.

"*This picture of Frobonus was delivered to his M^y by * * * Buckingham before * * *.*"*

The original size of these pictures was 18½ in. high by 12½ in. wide; but for some reason not very evident, unless it were to make them fit two old carved frames, two inches and a half have been added to the top of each, injuring, not improving, the effect of the portraits, and involving the necessity of repainting the back-grounds, which instead of some simple foil to the heads, as Holbein commonly supplies us with, now consist of cold minutely elaborated Gothic pillars and arches, as if the two friends were in some gloomy church or other dismal Gothic apartment: Steenwyck the architectural painter has the credit of having furnished these back-grounds in 1629, possibly when the pictures were in Le Blond's possession. The king's brand is on the back of the added pieces.

Froben's is the freer and more careless portrait of the two, and was probably first executed, but both of them appear to have been original drawings perhaps on parchment. It was Holbein's custom occasionally to attach his crayon or body-colour drawings, whether on paper, parchment, or vellum, to panels and finish them in a rough way as pictures; the heads, and hands perhaps, being the only parts thoroughly elaborated: the parchment covering acting as the priming of the panel. Mr. Baring's Hans Herbster is an example of this practice; a paper drawing has I imagine been attached to wood, and is finished as an oil picture. Of course such drawings however masterly they may originally have been, would lose immensely by accumulations of dirt and varnish; a varnished crayon drawing might easily be scumbled and glazed into an effective picture.

Erasmus seems to have had these two pictures hinged

---

* The words to be supplied are "he went to the Isle of Rhee." See Walpole, *Anecdotes*, &c., Vol. I., p. 76, note.

CHAP. VIII. *Frobenius and Erasmus.* 1521-5.

together, as he had done in the year 1518 with two other portraits of himself and Peter Aegidius which he sent in that year from Antwerp to Sir Thomas More. They were joined as a diptych, and as a type of the friendship by which the originals were bound; he gave the right-hand place to Froben, who is accordingly made to be looking at Erasmus. Patin saw them in London in 1672, hinged together as described, they were then in the royal possession. He says that Le Blond, the collector already noticed, bought them in Basel for 100 gold ducats, that is he bought the Erasmus, the Froben going with it. They passed probably from Le Blond to the Duke of Buckingham.

Froben is uncovered and in full profile, the portion of the ground immediately behind the head being a marine green; on one side are a box for printers' types, and a small ink dab. Below is inscribed, though scarcely by Holbein, IOANNES FROBENIVS TYP. HHOLBEIN P.

Erasmus is painted nearly in full face and looking down, being turned a little to the right, that is towards Froben; he is dressed in a black furred coat, and has on a black cap; his hands, admirably drawn, are resting on a red book; his mouth also is exquisitely modelled; the eyes are small. Both pictures are very brown, and neither can be looked upon as a first-class example of the painter's works even at this time, though sufficiently characteristic in style; the Erasmus is the better picture: under all circumstances however they are very precious both on account of their subjects, and of their painter. And they might be to some advantage relieved of their additions, encased together in one frame, and for old association's sake, be for evermore inseparable.

At King Charles's sale these pictures were valued at 100*l.* each.*

* Ulrich Hegner, writing in 1827, says that he possessed copies of them painted in oil by Sixt Ringlin in 1648, for the Fesch Museum: it would be interesting to compare the back-grounds of these two sets of portraits, they should be identical if copied in 1648, when the originals were in the king's possession. King Charles's pictures were sold and dispersed in 1649—1651.

Frobenius and Erasmus. 1521-5.

There are other portraits of Froben; the Basel Museum possesses one similar in character to that at Hampton Court, but not exhibiting so decidedly the distinctive features of Holbein's style at this time: it is a comparatively recent purchase.* Another small portrait in oil of Frobenius, ascribed to Holbein, was sold in 1842 at the Strawberry Hill sale for nineteen guineas.

Among the prints of Erasmus, by far the finest head is that engraved by Vorsterman from a portrait formerly in the Arundel Collection, and now said to be in the possession of Mr. oward of Greystoke Castle, Cumberland; the first is dedicated to the then Earl of Arundel. The picture was bequeathed by Alathea, Countess of Arundel, to her grandson, Charles Howard, an ancestor of the present Duke of Norfolk. It is a three-quarter face looking down, the hands only partly seen are clasped in front.

This Greystoke picture, a small portrait, which I have not seen, has been assumed to be that which Erasmus sent to England in 1525 as a present from him to Sir Thomas More, and of which Erasmus wrote that it was more like him than the portrait of him painted by the famous Albert Dürer. It is a pity he has told us nothing about the portrait painted of him by Quintin Matsys. All the heads of Erasmus by Holbein are very similar, as they could not avoid being, coming from the hand of a man who saw as Holbein saw. That of Dürer is not at all like them.

There is a fine etching by Dürer himself, of his portrait of Erasmus, in the British Museum, 10 in. high by 7½ in. wide. The philosopher is standing, writing, with a reed in one hand and an ink-bottle in the other; a vase with a few flowers and some leaves in it is standing on the table, and some books

* The Basel Catalogue, 1863, is one of the worst of a very worthless lot yet sold in the German galleries; it is not only not descriptive but does not even mention the materials or dimensions of the works enumerated; there is literally no help in it. There is yet no catalogue whatever of the Augsburg Gallery. The men of the last century made much better books than are now sold in some galleries.

CHAP. VIII.

Frobenius and Erasmus. 1521-5.

are lying on a bench in front. The etching has the following legend, in a tablet:—

IMAGO ERASMI ROTERODAMI AB ALBERTO
DURERO AD VIVAM EFFIGIEM DELINIATA
THN KPEÍTTΩ TA ΣΥΓΓΡΑΜΜΑΤΑ
ΔΕΙΖΕΙ*
MDXXVI
AD

1526 is of course the date of the etching, not of the picture, or rather drawing, as that was executed before 1525.

The mechanical work is admirably done, but the drawing is mannered, especially in the crimped draperies, and the effect is metallic; but for the inscription one would not know that it represented Erasmus at all; compared with such work as this the head engraved by Vorsterman, is life itself. Such a portrait, however great the manipulative skill it may display, should strongly induce us to doubt Albert Dürer's power of seeing thoroughly what was before him. We have not only Holbein's portraits to judge from, and they are quite enough, but Erasmus himself in another place tells us that Dürer's was not a bit like him.†

The "Erasmus writing," at Hampton Court (No. 331), may also be looked upon as a fine genuine portrait, though so dark and dirty, that much of the expression of the eyes is obscured. The philosopher is seated, or standing, in his ordinary cap and coat, writing in a book, he has a ring on his fore-finger, and

* ΔΕΙΞΕΙ? "What is written will show the better," that is reading δείξει for δειζει; the reader perhaps will find out the meaning for himself.

† In writing to H. Botteus after Albert's death, in 1528, Erasmus says—"Pinxit me, abhinc aliquot annis, Durerus, *sed nihil simile*," quoted by Hegner, p. 142. It is notable here that Erasmus speaks of this portrait as a *picture*, "pinxit" he says, while Albert himself describes it as a drawing; at least so I understand the words "imago deliniata." This portrait if in existence as a picture is surely discoverable somewhere; but I imagine it was simply one of the many pencil drawings he made during his tour in the Netherlands in 1520-21. Pingere seems to have been used indifferently in medieval Latin, either for to paint or to draw.

Frobenius and Erasmus. 1521-5.

this, the right hand, is in a good state, and is a fair example of Holbein's manner of painting a hand at this time. The background represents a shelved recess or cupboard, with six books in it: on the topmost book on the edges of the leaves, are the letters HOR—for Horace; on one beneath is NOVVM TESTAMENT.; on another is the name of Lucian—ΛΟΥΚΙΑΝΌΣ; and on a fourth is written the name of Jerome—HIERONVMVS. By the side of the books is hanging a pair of pointed scissors, of very modern fashion: all reminding very much of Quintin Matsys.

Everything in this picture is well defined, and the lines and touches of the original drawing are still visible beneath the brown film which covers all; there seem to be even distinct pen hatchings among the shadows, and the whole gives the impression of a varnished drawing on paper or rather parchment, being merely strengthened by an oak backing. The sight measure is 19¼ in. high by 17¼ in. wide; and on the back is the brand of Charles I.—C. R. surmounted by a crown.

Turned the opposite way, that is showing his left side, is another smaller "Erasmus writing with a reed," which belonged to Charles I., but is now in the gallery of the Louvre. It is less brown and apparently more minute in its details than those above described, approximating to the character of Holbein's so-called miniature work, of which the examples are so rare, that it is difficult to acquire a satisfactory notion of it.

This is a small panel of deal 16½ in. high by 12½ in. wide; it has on the back the brand of Charles I., twice, and a memorandum on paper partly destroyed, similar to that at the back of Frobenius, given above, and about as incomplete: it says—*Of Holbein, this * * * of Erasmus Rotterdamus was given to * * * Prince by * * * Adam Newton.* There is besides a red seal on the back, with the arms of the Newton family, and the device *Vivit post funera virtus.*

This is the portrait which Charles I., through the French ambassador the Duc de Liancourt, gave to Louis XIII., in addition to a "Holy Family" by Titian, in exchange for the fine picture of "St. John the Baptist" by Leonardo Da Vinci,

CHAP. VIII.

Frobenius and Erasmus. 1521-5.

which is also now in the Louvre. At the sale of King Charles's effects, a French banker of the name of Jabach purchased the St. John, for 140*l.* sterling, and he ceded it to Louis XIV.*

In the Basel Museum are three portraits of Erasmus; one is the often repeated composition, where he is seen in profile, writing; this is on parchment attached to wood, and is a dull, brown picture; it is one of the Amerbach purchases. The other two are what are improperly termed oil miniatures; one upright; the other, very good, a round about four inches in diameter, already noticed as being preserved with the Holbein drawings in the Amerbach cabinet. These are carefully and solidly painted heads, but have nothing in common with miniatures strictly so called, such as professed miniature painters execute on card, ivory, and vellum; they are simply small oil paintings, the heads occupying as much as three square inches, while the strict miniature head is often no more than half a square inch. About 17 in. by 12 in., sometimes a little more, sometimes a little less, was a favourite size with Holbein for his small portraits; about the ordinary size of a folio of parchment, or half a skin.

Patin notices that Erasmus was often painted by Holbein for England, France, and elsewhere, and he enumerates six examples: the three in the Basel Museum, and the companion to the Frobenius now at Hampton Court; one at Vienna, and that in the Louvre. The Greystoke picture and the portrait in which he is writing, at Hampton Court, making a seventh and eighth; there is a drawing ascribed to him, at Stafford House. This is a considerable number, but neither the Longford picture, nor that at Windsor, nor that at Turin are yet accounted for, to say nothing of numerous copies.

That at Vienna is a small picture of no remarkable character, the sage is seated, in his doctor's cap and furred coat, with an open book before him. On wood, about 15 in. high by 10½ in. wide.

---

* Villot, *Notice des Tableaux du Louvre.*

There are several other portraits of Erasmus, smaller and larger, some of which may be original; he was compelled to have some painted to please his friends, and it was apparently not quite so unpleasant to himself as he would lead us to believe, in a remark he has made on the subject. All these portraits have probably been copied, more than once; it is however not to be supposed that even all the originals are by Holbein, for we know that he was painted not only by Albert Dürer, but also by Quintin Matsys, and this last name introduces an interesting inquiry.

CHAP. VIII.

Frobenius and Erasmus. 1521-5.

The portrait of Erasmus, certainly enjoying the greatest reputation, is that at Longford Castle, Wiltshire, the seat of the Earl of Radnor. Dr. Waagen says that this picture alone is worth a pilgrimage to Longford Castle: Walpole on the other hand terms it stiff and flat: I had rather in this case second Dr. Waagen's opinion. This picture was formerly in Dr. Mead's collection, and at his sale more than a hundred years ago, in 1754, was sold as a work by Holbein for one hundred and five guineas, 110*l.* 5*s.*: it then passed into the possession of the Earl of Radnor, who also bought the Aegidius for ninety-one guineas, 95*l.* 11*s.* The composition is much the same as that at Hampton Court, No. 331. He is seated in his black cap and furred coats, the under-coat lined with sable, the upper with black fur, resting his hands on a very handsomely bound book before him, and on the gold edges of the leaves of this book, are the words, partly in Greek and partly in Roman letters—HPAKΛEIOI ΠONOI ERASMI ROTERO—the rest of the last word being cut off by the yellow sable cuff of his coat—the Herculean labours of Erasmus of Rotterdam. Behind is a green curtain on a rod, a rich Renaissance pilaster on one side, and on the other a cupboard or shelved recess, in which are a small bottle or carafe and three books; and here, on one of the books leaning against the bottle is the date, which is at present distinctly MDXXIII. On the edges of the leaves of this same book is a damaged Latin legend which comprises the names JOANNES HOLBEIN: it would be difficult to read all the other words.

CHAP. VIII.

Frobenius and Erasmus. 1521-5.

There is also at Longford Castle, a companion picture to this, one which has been its companion a long time, a portrait of Peter Giles or Aegidius, a celebrated traveller, of Antwerp, and a friend of Erasmus's. He is dressed in a furred coat, and holds in his left hand a letter addressed to himself, in Antwerp, his right touches a book on which is written ANTIBAPBAPOI in Greek capitals, his left elbow rests on this book: in the back-ground are some shelves with a gold cup and several books, ancient classical authors—Plutarch, Seneca, Suetonius, &c. On the table before him is his sand or pounce-box. The address on the letter, in which we have a facsimile, as will presently be seen, of the handwriting of Sir Thomas More, the English Chancellor, is considerably injured, but appears to be as follows:—*Viro Literatissimo Petro Egidio Amico Charissimo, Anversæ.* (?) When these pictures were in Dr. Mead's possession, he had the following inscriptions written on labels attached to their frames; and they remain there still:—

On that of Erasmus—"E tenebris clarum doctrinae attollere lumen
Qui felix potuit, primus Erasmus erat."
On that of Aegidius—"Aegidium musis clarum dilexit Erasmus;
Spirat ab Holbenio pictus uterque tuo;"

and these two pictures have passed as a matter of course as portraits by Holbein, and even as exceptionally excellent examples of that painter. What follows will show that they are most probably two capital works of the "Smith of Antwerp," Quintin Matsys. Their dimensions are precisely the same—2 ft. 5 in. high by 1 ft. 8½ in. wide. That of Aegidius is certainly by Quintin, about the Erasmus there may be a doubt, although the two panels are so precisely the same in character that it is difficult to believe that their similarity can have been the result of accident.

It appears from a letter of Erasmus, written some time in 1517,* when he was living in Antwerp, that he promised to send to Sir Thomas More two portraits, on the same piece (in eadem tabula), one of himself, and the other of his friend Aegidius.

---

* "*Epistolarum D. Erasmi Roterodami.*" Libri XXXI., &c. Folio. London, 1642. Lib. VII., Ep. 24.

Frobenius and Erasmus. 1521-5.

In October 1518, these two portraits, by Quintin Matsys, were already in the possession of Sir Thomas, and on the 6th of that month he writes news of them to Aegidius in Antwerp: they were however not on *one piece*, but on a *double piece*, a *tabula duplex;* these portraits were therefore not painted together on the same panel; they constituted in fact a diptych, such as that afterwards presented by Erasmus to Froben, and of which the two panels are now preserved at Hampton Court.

In this portrait Aegidius held in his hand a letter to himself, from Sir Thomas More, and the direction was so skilfully imitated by the painter, that the simple connoisseurship of the learned chancellor was quite fascinated; in the letter referred to* he goes into raptures at the wonderful imitation of his own handwriting, considering Quintin, the painter, to have outforged the most skilful of forgers, and he declares that he could not have so exactly reproduced the address himself. These pictures were evidently painted, or at least finished, in 1518, and this MDXVIII., may have been the true reading of the date MDXXIII. marked on the portrait of Erasmus; the error of substituting 1523 arising either from the imperfect preservation of the inscription, or from too great zeal to harmonize it with some year when Erasmus was known to have been living in Basel, and to make Holbein its possible painter: I throw this out as a mere conjecture, the date is now clearly MDXXIII. The false reading of X for V, and V for X is not unusual, especially in manuscript of this time. The date of the Papal indiction, in the inscription of the cartellino on Antonello Da Messina's picture in the National Gallery, of

* *Epistolarum D. Eras.*, &c. Lib. III., Ep. 7., where More says—"Mi Petre cum omina mirifice QUINTINUS noster expressit, tum mirificum in primis falsarium videtur praestare possenam ita inscriptionem literarum ad te mearum imitatus est, ut ne ipse quidem idem iterum possem itidem." This restitution of his work to Quintin Matsys, shows that Dr. Waagen's ground for supposing that Holbein had made a lengthened stay in Antwerp, painting this very Ægidius, is purely imaginary: there is no other foundation for his notion that the "Lais Corinthiaca," and the "Venus and Cupid" at Basel, were painted by Holbein at Antwerp.

Frobenius and Erasmus. 1521-5.

Christ as the "Salvator Mundi," has been read VIIIe instead of XIIIe, which it is, and should be to be correct, for the year 1465. So also a similar ambiguity occurs with reference to the date of a book of sketches ascribed to L'Ortolano, the years of the studies being read both MDVII. and VIII. and MDXII. and XIII.* We can by historical parallels decide upon the correct figure in these two cases, and so also the positive historical data in the case of the above described portraits determine MDXVIII. as most probably the proper reading of the date on the book in the portrait of Erasmus. A copy of this picture was in Archbishop Tenison's Library, and there is another at Oxford. The dimensions of the panels, 2 ft. 5 in. by 1 ft. 8½ in., are the same, and they are of the same thickness: that of the Aegidius is oak, the back of the Erasmus has been painted, but it has the same ring and appears to be also of oak. The coincidence of the preservation of these two panels together, and their agreement with the account in the correspondence of Sir Thomas More, of the two sent from Antwerp is sufficiently remarkable to justify the assumption that they are the same, yet there are points of disagreement that must not be altogether overlooked, and I notice them to enable the reader to form his own conclusions.

What has been stated above is strong evidence in favour of the conclusion that they are the same, and consequently that both pictures are by Quintin of Antwerp. A record so precise and remarkable as that of Sir Thomas More's letter cannot be set aside; as regards the Aegidius it is conclusive, but not so as regards the Erasmus; with reference to this picture it gives us only presumptive evidence. Two arguments against the inference in question are the date 1523, and the name of Holbein occurring in the legend on the edge of the book on which the date is written; but these are still far from being infallible evidence, both date and legend may have been

* See National Gallery Catalogue—under L'Ortolano—the title is "*Studio di me Zoane Bapta d. Benvegnù fatto in Bologna suxo le dipinture del Rapi ac° e del Sangio da Urbino, a li anni*, MDXII. and MDXIII.:" common sense demands the X.

Frobenius and Erasmus. 1521-5.

added by anybody; no date can easily carry its own proof of authenticity with it. Holbein has very seldom signed his pictures, and the great majority of those that he dated are marked with Arabic numbers: the ordinary signature used at Basel was H H with the year commonly in Arabic figures. In dating Augsburg and London pictures he has occasionally used Roman numerals. The name *Joannes Holbein* in full as autograph is also exceedingly rare, and here it is certainly no autograph. Further, the using of Greek letters in inscriptions has we see, been had recourse to by Matsys, but there is no instance of Holbein's having used them, except once in the name of a Greek author: Greek words and characters occurring in both these portraits is an additional argument in favour of identity of authorship. Somewhat more important evidence may be suggested by the difference of style in the two pictures, not that there is anything in the Erasmus which could not have been painted by Quintin, for he was at times a really admirable painter; his finish is often remarkable, being much more minute than Holbein's; but there is a difficulty in the difference in scale of two pictures supposed to have been painted at the same time, and as companions.

The colouring, and especially the carnations of the faces are much the same in both, but the portraits are not companions for a diptych: they both look the same way, to the right; and they are painted on a different scale, the Erasmus being much larger, and the superiority of this as a painting, over the Aegidius, is most striking. The hands of the Erasmus are vigorous masculine hands, such as we have found in other of his portraits, and in other pictures, by Holbein, while the hands of the Aegidius are meanly painted and not at all like Holbein's work. The accessaries are all better painted in the Erasmus, especially the book on which his hands rest, and his yellow fur cuffs which are exquisitely managed. The head itself is infinitely superior, though the drawing of the eyes does not show that precise mastery which we often find in the eyes of Holbein's pictures. It is not however that I believe

CHAP. VIII.

Frobenius and Erasmus. 1521-5.

Quintin incapable of having painted such a picture as this, for the picture of the man and his wife counting their money, at Windsor, known as "The Misers" bears a strong resemblance to it in its details; but that he should have been so unequal to himself in so brief an interval of time, a few weeks or months at most, is the point which tells chiefly in favour of Holbein's authorship of one of this pair of portraits. As it is, we can only safely pronounce this picture to be an admirable Erasmus, but were it not for the record in question, we might have as positively pronounced it an admirable Holbein also, though my own impression now is that it is the work of Quintin Matsys.

This, as well as the small Greystoke portrait, has been assumed to be the picture sent by Erasmus to Sir Thomas More in 1525, though we have no specification of any particular picture or painter either.

The chancellor acknowledges the receipt of some picture and praises the painter, in a letter from Greenwich dated the 18th of December of that year. Erasmus sent of course only one portrait of himself by Holbein to Sir Thomas, and this may have been in 1525; just seven years after the sending of the portraits from Antwerp. Sir Thomas More was not acquainted with Holbein's name before this time; he knew nothing whatever of him when he wrote, so highly praising the handiwork of Quintin. A portrait sent from Basel may safely be assumed to have been painted by Holbein.

The fine portrait of Erasmus at Windsor by Georg Pencz of Nürnberg, but for his monogram on it, composed of a P on and above a G, might pass for an original by Holbein; Pencz was the scholar of Albrecht Dürer and acquired the delicate execution of that master: this copy has clear grey eyes, but the nose is disagreeably pointed, it has however many admirable parts. Pencz is another of a dozen painters whose portraits pass for those of Holbein; he died at Breslau in 1550, about fifty years of age, and though an excellent portrait painter, is more celebrated as an engraver, especially for his imitations or copies of Marcantonio.

Frobenius and Erasmus. 1521-5.

The copy of Erasmus at Windsor was painted in 1537, the year after Erasmus's death, and is inscribed—

D. Erasmus Roterodamus,
Vixit An. LXX. Obiit
V. id. Jul. Anno
MDXXXVI.
15 PG 37.

On oak 23 in. by 18 in. It was formerly in Charles I.'s collection, to whom it was presented by the Duke of Hamilton, who bought it in Nürnberg.

It is a bust portrait, with a plain green back-ground, showing a part only of the hands, clasped, not well executed: the dress is the same as that of the Longford picture, an under-coat trimmed or lined with sable, and an over-coat edged with black fur. There is a cast shadow of the head on the back-ground. In composition it accords with the picture engraved by Vorsterman: the colouring agrees with that of Matsys, who may have been the painter of the original; Vorsterman's print is reversed.*

Already in 1525 Holbein seems to have required a larger field for the exercise of his ability, and what could be more natural? how could a man of his great powers be content with the scope or with the publicity of a small provincial town like Basel? He apparently even now contemplated a visit to England, whether spontaneously, or urged to the step by some passing Englishman who may have seen his works is immaterial. Erasmus appears this year to have sent Sir Thomas More another portrait of himself, that is, the picture I have

* This print is of great technical excellence, and has an admirable effect as a work of art: it is $7\frac{1}{16}$ in. high by $6\frac{3}{4}$ in. wide, and is dedicated to the then Earl of Arundel, in whose collection the original picture was. It would be interesting to discover where the picture was when Penez copied it; Holbein was then alive, but Sir Thomas More's property had been confiscated. It is just possible that William Fitzalan Earl of Arundel, who was probably the nobleman who advised Holbein to come to England, may have become possessed of some of Sir Thomas More's Holbeins, soon after More's death. There is a copy of the Vorsterman print by A. Stockius, engraved in 1623, and published at the Hague.

CHAP. VIII.

Frobenius and Erasmus. 1521-5.

already had occasion to refer to more than once, and with this picture was sent some intimation that the painter was about to follow it, though that this painter was Holbein is a mere conjecture. However on the 18th of December 1525, in the letter just mentioned,* More replies to his friend—"Your painter, dear Erasmus, is a wonderful artist, but I am afraid that he will not find England quite so prolific or fertile as he anticipates, although I will take care, as far as in me lies, that he does not find it altogether barren." That this visit was not a mere project the events will presently show. What the picture was that Sir Thomas refers to, must now unfortunately be a mere matter of guess-work.

This year 1525 is memorable as that in which Luther showed his opinion of the folly and the wickedness of monastic vows, by boldly marrying the nun—Catherine Bohra. And common repute gives Holbein the credit of having painted both these remarkable characters. It is pretty certain however that he painted neither.†

---

* *Opera*, 1703. III. App. Epist. 334.

† There is a portrait in Windsor Castle, which used to be called "Luther, by Holbein," but it is now registered as Dr. John Stokesly, Bishop of London. "A man," says Hall, in his Chronicles, "of greate witte and learning, but of lytle discretion and humanity." There is also at Longford Castle a portrait of a hook-nosed man in a black cap, called Luther. The accessaries in this picture are remarkable; he holds with his left hand on his knees a painted ball, to which he points with his right hand; the ball is divided horizontally into four equal parts, on each is a landscape representing one of the four seasons—at the top, ploughing and sowing; then a figure reclining among trees; thirdly, the vintage; and lastly, encamping by a fire. On the right corner above is the following legend, on the instability of all things in this life—"Lux tenebris rursus Luci tenebre fugienti succedunt. Stabilis Res tibi nulla manet." On wood 3 ft. 5 in. *h.* by 2 ft. 9 in. *w.* The Windsor picture, a small oak panel 20 in. by 15, is still ascribed to Holbein; it represents an ecclesiastic, also a hook-nosed man, in black cap and gown, with a pen in his right hand and a book in his left, with a green ground, and in the left upper corner is a curious armorial device: a man with a scarlet cape holds a green shield, a silver bar dividing it horizontally; above the bar are two gold rings, and below it is a third. The history of the picture is not traced, it is branded behind with W. R. 124. In 1833 it was engraved by C. E. Wagstaff as Luther for the *Gallery of Portraits.* I do not know why hook-nosed men are chosen to bear Luther's name, a medal of him in profile gives him a straight nose: see the Gallery of Portraits, l. c. In his portrait by Cranach the nose appears to be slightly aquiline.

CHAPTER IX.

THE PAINTER'S CHARACTER AND MARRIAGE. "PINGUIS ET NITIDUS EPICURI DE GREGE PORCUS." HIS WIFE AND CHILDREN—ELIZABETH SCHMID. LAIS CORINTHIACA. THE MEIER MADONNA.

CHAP. IX.

"Epicuri de Grege Porcus."

E have already seen that Patin has had no mercy on Holbein's character, and it is but just to the great painter's fame that some effort should be made if not altogether to explain away, at least to modify this evil reputation which has more or less tainted all subsequent sketches of his career. That his character was not immaculate is certain, several circumstances of his life are sufficiently well authenticated to show this; but the chief circumstances of this same life show even still more prominently that his career on the whole cannot have been disreputable; his great art, his great friends, of many degrees and kinds of greatness, and the remarkable impression he has made on his age, one conspicuous for vigour and intellect, all proclaim it. It is folly to suppose that Holbein can have been an ordinary or an inferior man in any sense. It is not a little to a man's credit to have been honoured and distinguished for any noble qualities in such a period of ecclesiastical abuse and social tyranny, as that of Charles V. of Germany: he was fortunate perhaps in his choice

CHAP. IX.

"Epicuri de Grege Porcus."

of a domicile, but in his case, as in many others, the good fortune was not nearly so much the upshot of good luck as the natural result of a sound judgment.

The most prominent charge against him, and it appears to be true, is, that he separated from his wife, but as incompatibility of temper has been allowed to be the justification of others, we cannot deny the same justification to Holbein. Another serious charge against him, but of which there is no evidence is, that he was fond of drinking to excess, indeed that he habitually squandered his time and means in taverns; I believe the long years of excellence in his art to be a sufficient denial to this slander: it is assuredly false; the two things are incompatible, physically antagonistic. I think it will not be difficult to track the source of this bad repute to its origin —namely, the painter's own illustration of a quotation from Horace, made by Erasmus in his "Moriae Encomium," where he speaks of a hog of the herd of Epicurus.

Hegner says that Holbein's friend Oswald Müller (Molitor) of Lucerne, who at one time kept a school at Basel, used to entertain the painter with readings from Erasmus's Μωριας Εγκωμιον, or Praise of Folly. The book belonged to this Molitor, but he lived at Zurich in Holbein's time, not at Basel. It is more probable that Erasmus himself read the work to Holbein; the book belonging to him before Molitor had it. Molitor has written on the second title *Hanc Moriam pictam decem diebus, ut oblectaretur in ea Erasmus habuit.* On the first page he has written *Est Osualdi Molitoris Lucerni.* The wit of this then popular volume, which perhaps belonged to Holbein even before it passed to Erasmus, so delighted the painter, that he gave vent to his satisfaction by sketching in pen and ink on the margin free illustrations of the various passages that most attracted him: on the whole he made eighty-three such sketches on the margins of the printed pages; all in ten days. Among these illustrations Erasmus found a page which appears to have not altogether pleased him—his own portrait labelled, complete, is with more than ordinary finish drawn as the illustration of a passage which

"*Epicuri de Grege Porcus.*"

reflects with some severity on the want of common sense and energy in the learned; in contradistinction to the general success and world popularity of fools. Dr. Woltmann considers Hegner's story about Molitor's reading the book to the painter, to be imaginary; how the sketches came there it is not easy to explain, but there they are, and certainly by the hand of Holbein. From the singular mistakes in the Latin of some of Holbein's pictures I cannot imagine that Holbein was himself capable of reading the book; granting this, somebody must have read it to him: all the sketches are certainly in their right places.*

The passage opposite Erasmus's portrait, is as follows, I use the words of Bishop Kennet's translation. Folly speaks:—

"But I forbear from any further proverbializing, lest I should be thought to have rifled my Erasmus's Adagies.† To return therefore, fortune we find still favouring the blunt, and flushing the forward; strokes and smooths up fools, crowning all their undertakings with success; but Wisdom makes her followers bashful, sneaking, and timorous. And therefore you commonly see that they are reduced to hard shifts, must grapple with poverty, cold, and hunger, must lye recluse, despised and unregarded." The philosopher is drawn in profile, as we see him in his pictures, seated at his desk writing, in an arched cell, with an open casement, over which

* Page 53 of the original volume, which is now preserved in the library of Basel. Patin reproduced these sketches, cut in wood, in a reprint of the original work, in 1676—see pp. 193 and 196. ΜΩΡΙΑΣ ΕΓΚΩΜΙΟΝ — *Stultitiæ Laus. Des. Erasmi Rot: Declamatio, Figuris Holbenianis adornata.* Basiliæ, MDCLXXVI. It has a cinque-cento frontispiece from a drawing by Holbein. There exist old English translations of the work, but some cuts are abominably travestied and others omitted—see "*Moriæ Encomium,*" or a *Panegyrick upon Folly.* London, sm. 8vo., 1709 (Woodward). This edition contains neither of the illustrations in question. They are however both tolerably rendered in the edition, without date, published by J. Barker, London, 12mo., and from this I have copied my cuts, which are accordingly not facsimiles.

† The exact words of the original here, are—Sed desino *παροιμιάζεσθαι*, ne videar Erasmi mei commentaria suppilasse—and this may be considered the proper source of Holbein's adaptation of this passage to Erasmus.

CHAP. IX.

"Epicuri de Grege Porcus."

is written in capitals ERASMUS. When the philosopher came to this illustration he is said to have exclaimed, "Ohe! Ohe! If Erasmus were still like this, he would certainly take a wife."* That the philosopher himself should be made to illustrate personally the contemptible condition of the man of wisdom, he may well have considered a little sharp and somewhat of a liberty on the part of his young painter acquaintance; and in a spirit of retaliation accordingly, half earnest, half humorous, he wrote the name of Holbein under a coarse and grotesque illustration of the low sensualism, indicated in the following quotation from Horace:—

"Me pinguem et nitidum, bene curata cute vises,
Cum ridere voles, Epicuri de grege porcum."†

HORACE, *Ep.* I., iv. 15.

* The original words are "Quam ad hunc locum perveniebat Erasmus, se pictum sic videns exclamavit, Ohe! Ohe! si Erasmus, adhuc talis esset, duceret profecto uxorem." Patin's *Moriæ Encomium.* Preface. I confess I do not quite see the point, unless the implied loneliness were to force him into marriage; or possibly his comparatively youthful appearance in the sketch.

† "My sleek skinn'd corps, as smooth as if I lye
'Mong th' fatted swine of Epicurus' sty."

"Epicuri de Grege Porcus."

This is one of the coarsest sketches in the book, but Erasmus had not far to go for it, it is on the page next to his own portrait. This porcine Epicurean is a gross, heavy, pot-bellied fellow with a huge mouth, sitting at a table which he is about to unburden of its good fare; he is at the moment in the act of draining a bottle into his mouth with his left hand, while his right arm is twined round the neck of a woman seated by his side.

And this *jeu d'esprit* Patin, and some others, have considered sufficient evidence that Erasmus intended to deliberately point to Holbein's character as that of a confirmed reckless sensualist. I am afraid they simply convict themselves of a very reckless disregard of all evidence generally, and of Christian fellow-feeling in particular. Holbein's repute is however safe enough, no sane man now-a-days would convict or judge him on such an indictment as this.

Patin himself certainly gives us no better justification than this anecdote, for the very gross picture he has drawn of the painter's general habits in private life: it seems strange that the question did not occur to Patin's mind how it was possible, that such a low sensualist could make and keep so many distinguished friends, or could attain to, and retain such excellence in his art. The more we inquire into the matter the more shocked we become at the scandalous levity of his biographers and commentators, who have ventured to perpetuate such an uncharitable picture of their neighbour, without producing the slightest justification—De mortuis nil nisi verum; and as my ambition is to give a true picture of Holbein's life as far as accessible materials enable me to do so, I have felt it imperative to reproduce these scandals in the shape of records, trusting that they may meet the inevitable fate which must eventually overtake all that is false.

Holbein's wife and children. 1525-6.

One of the most striking pictures in the Basel Museum, realistic and thoroughly life-like, is that of Holbein's wife and children. I say children because there are two in the picture, but one child only is spoken of (*Weib und Kind*) in a letter to

CHAP. IX.

Holbein's wife and children. 1525-6.

Holbein from the burgomaster of Basel in 1532. This circumstance is not difficult to explain. That Holbein's wife Elizabeth Schmid was a widow, and that she had when he married her certainly one son living, by her first husband, Franz Schmid, has been already mentioned. The picture is commonly called the painter's wife and children, but it most probably represents his wife Elizabeth, her son Franz Schmid, and his own son Philip, a child about or rather less than two years old; it is however difficult to judge of a baby's age in nature, and in a picture this difficulty is certainly very much increased.

The figures are of the natural size, are painted on paper attached to wood, the whole picture being about 2 ft. 6 in. high by 2 ft. wide.* The mother is a stoutish woman, between thirty and forty years of age and perhaps a good deal nearer forty than thirty, she must have been several years older than Holbein. She is seen nearly in full face, staring vacantly at something before her, and is in a low dress somewhat exposing a large full bosom: she has on a veil over her hair and forehead. She holds on her lap with her left arm the young child, which is stretching its arms out as babies are in the habit of doing when they see something they want, or some one they wish to go to; its expression is animated, and it seems to be quite suitably dressed. The right hand of the mother rests on the right shoulder of a handsome boy who is standing in front of her, showing his side face and looking towards his little brother: this boy may be eight or nine years old or even ten, not more; and I assume him to be Holbein's step-son, for if the picture were painted as early as I suppose, Holbein could not have been his father.

This picture does not indicate the slightest symptom of poverty, sickness, or wretchedness of any kind; the expression of the mother is certainly mysterious and unpleasant, and she has a slight cast in one of her eyes; she is in fact a plain coarse-looking middle-aged woman, and seems to have few

---

* Engraved in von Mechel's *Œuvre de Holbein*, &c. By B. Hübner, 1790.

Holbein's wife and children. 1525-6.

attractions for a painter's eye. The faces of the children however appear happy and cheerful enough. One peculiarity of the composition is that there is no real unity in it; the baby's is the only natural face in the group, the mother is in a reverie, and the handsome boy though looking towards his brother, is not looking at him, but over him. It is just possible that these three portraits were made at separate times and were only grouped afterwards, by pasting the three together on a panel, and then arranging the accessaries into a picture, as we now find it. The whole work is very effective, with quite the vital force of Titian, though without his practised mastery, but also without the least convention. It has little or none of that brownness which we meet with in several of the painter's portraits of this period. Yet as a mere picture, these portraits are I think inferior to the head of Amerbach in the same collection: the piece belonged to Amerbach, and is catalogued in his son's inventory.*

The later we defer the painting of these portraits, the nearer we bring the ages of Holbein and his wife together. Let 1525 be the date of the picture, 1523 may be considered the year of the baby's birth, and if we assume the bigger boy to be about eight years older than the baby we have 1514 or 1515 for the time of his birth. The baby might still be spoken of as a child, in 1532; but not the boy who would be then a full-grown lad, able to earn his livelihood, and help to support his mother too. The German writers call this child a little girl, but Holbein never had a daughter by his Basel wife. This general misconception is founded on an old error, communicated by A. Merian to von Mechel, where he says that in a family-tree of the Merians, printed in Regensburg, in 1727,†

* "Holbeins fraw und zwei kinder von im H. Holbein conterfehet uf papir mit ölfarben, uf holz gezogen." The individual names of Holbein's family were only discovered a few months ago, in the archives of Basel, by Herr His-Heusler. See the "*Beiträge*," &c., Vol. VIII. *Der Goldschmied Philipp Holbein, ein sohn Hans Holbeins des Jüngeren.* January, 1866. The picture was dated, but in cutting round the figures, apparently previous to pasting them on the panel, the last of the four figures of the date was cut off, and we have only the 152× remaining.

† See Hegner, *Hans Holbein*, &c., p. 115.

CHAP. IX.

Holbein's wife and children. 1525-6.

it is stated that Judith Weiss the wife of Rudolph Syf, born in 1597, was the granddaughter of the incomparable painter Hans Holbein. It is clear that, from the year of her birth, she was nothing of the kind, and if related to the painter, she must have been his great-granddaughter, that is the granddaughter of Philip Holbein. It must be evident, on the slightest consideration, that a lady born about the year 1523, could not have a daughter born in 1597; when any daughter of Holbein's wife must have been about sixty or sixty-five years of age.

That Holbein left his wife and child is certain, but whether they were in the full sense of the word forsaken is very questionable; he occasionally visited them and must have contributed at all times in some way to their support, or he could not have retained the good opinion of the magistracy of Basel, which he certainly never lost. The living apart from them in after years may have been the result of circumstances, as it was with Romney, who left his wife and children in Lancashire when he came up to London in 1762, and he did not return to reside with his wife until 1799; when he was an old man and wanted a nurse.

Holbein is said to have been driven from Basel by his wife's temper; this may or may not be true, and it may also be true that some disorderly conduct or neglect on his part may have tended to aggravate a natural infirmity of temper: yet of any positive misconduct on the painter's part there is no evidence whatever, and after all, he was but a young man when he left Basel. Dr. Patin does not evoke a single authority for any of his assertions, and the daughter merely repeats the father: however we have a tradition of a very definite character in its tendency, though of an indefinite shape, and it must rest in the mazes of mystery for the present. Though he took himself away, he left what property he possessed behind him and no doubt works of his own, which would contribute by their sale to the support of his family. We do not know that his wife was not a consenting party to his departure, trusting in his power to get work in such a great city as London, though

CHAP. IX.

Holbein's wife and children. 1525-6.

he may have exhausted the patronage of Basel: and further, we must assume that he left with the knowledge and consent of the town-council, and the wife herself may have had some occupation which rendered her partly independent of her husband. All the public or official patronage Holbein seems to have received from the town-council, during the last few years of his residence there, was a sum of 2 florins for painting a *shield* or two at Waldenburg, in 1525, and this money (2*l.* 10*s.*) he received only on the 3rd of March 1526 ! ! !* It is not strange that he left Basel, but rather wonderful that he stayed there so long.

There is certainly something terribly real in the vitality of this portrait of his wife ; the eyes are full of life but there is no happiness in them ; what is the true history of this woman, there is nothing apparently weak or silly about her ? Whence this frown of abstraction and look of deadened sympathies, which neither she nor Holbein have been able to suppress ? Does it arise simply from straitened means at home, or was she a jealous woman, or regretting the change of the past for the present husband ? Has she created a hell for herself out of her own wilfulness and impatience, or does her unhappiness arise from ill-usage or neglect on the part of Holbein ? We can never know, but there is a something in her countenance which disposes one to acquit the painter of being in any material degree the source of all the inward discontent this living picture represents : she is certainly not an attractive person. Charity suggests one other solution to the mystery. There is that difference between the ages of the beautiful boy and the infant in its mother's arms, which would easily admit of a third child whose place was between these two, but who had then gone to its other home, leaving only a hopeless regret in the bosom of the mother. Her family was incomplete, and the incompleteness would be all the more felt, when those that remained were closed around her for such a monumental purpose as their perpetuation in a picture. The effort

* His-Heusler. Woltmann, *Beilagen*, p. 373.

CHAP. IX.

Holbein's wife and children. 1525-6.

of bringing back to her mind the image of a lost child, would fully account for the peculiar expression of the mother in this portrait. However this is a mere conjecture, the interval between the ages is sufficiently accounted for if we assume the older child to be that of her first husband, the Franz Schmid who afterwards became guardian to Philip, after his mother's death, and the difference of eight or nine years in their ages will render the charge quite possible.

The two children might be Holbein's if we could assume the picture to have been painted just before his second visit to England in 1531; but both the style, and the remains of the date are against this, the three figures of the year—152 × all that now remain. It has much more of the easy freedom of his earlier works, than the precise manner of those he executed in England. I consider the age of the younger child quite precludes the notion that the picture was painted in 1529, for as Holbein left Basel in 1526 and did not return for three years, so young a child as this baby could not possibly have been his. And this further would give us the difficulty of accounting for two boys instead of one. Of this one, history has already given us a very good account.

Lais Corinthiaca. 1526.

The museum of Basel contains an interesting portrait bearing the date of the year 1526 assigned to Holbein, and though there is no doubt about the date, I think the authorship is very questionable. Of two very elaborately painted portraits of the same young woman, on one is carefully and conspicuously painted LAIS CORINTHIACA 1526, much more carefully finished than any writing I have ever seen on any picture by Holbein; and before her are lying some gold coins: in the other, a somewhat inferior picture, she is represented as Venus, with a little boy as Cupid, playing with an arrow. The portraits are half-length, the panels are about 12 in. high by 8 in. wide: the style of the painting is more Milanese, in colouring and in treatment, than anything else, exceedingly elaborate, cool in colour, dry in manner, and altogether unlike any other known work by our painter. In this case I have not the slightest faith in the Amerbach

Lais Corinthiaca. 1526.

inventory, and the entry in this list, compiled by Basil Amerbach about 1586, is the only authority for considering these portraits the work of Holbein; they are described as the portraits of *eine Offenburgin,* whether that means a lady of Offenburg or of the name of Offenburg,* I cannot say. The utmost however that this entry proves, is that Basil Amerbach, the son of the collector, was under the impression that they were by the hand of Holbein, but whether led by tradition, or by misconception, cannot now be determined. There is a drawing of this LAIS, washed pen and ink, which was formerly in the Fesch Collection, among the other Holbein drawings of the museum, where it is held as the original sketch for the picture, but it is still further from the hand of Holbein than the painting itself, of which it is a mere crude and imperfect copy, by an unpractised hand. Charles Patin in his list, calls this picture an Alsatian lady, and there is a story that the Lais the second portrait of the lady was the result of not a little malice on the part of the painter, whoever he may have been. It is this—the first portrait, that of the lady as "Venus with Cupid," was either not paid for at all, or so meanly estimated that the indignant artist forthwith revenged himself by painting the lady again, putting a few pieces of money before her and inscribing the picture LAIS CORINTHIACA, Lais of Corinth, as we find it. It certainly must be considered a wonderful piece of labour for so small a revenge, though not at all small the malignity that could conceive it and carry it out. I believe the explanation to be a pure invention, and anything but a felicitous one; if the painter considered that he had already thrown his labour away, it is strange that he should throw so much more after it.

The two portraits have a decided Milanese character, in the manner of the scholars of Leonardo da Vinci. A visit to Milan could not have had such a wonderful influence on

* The entry is as follows—*Item, zwei tafelin daruf eine Offenburgin conterfehet ist, uf eim geschrieben* LAIS CORINTHIACA, *die andere hat ein kindlin by sich. H. Holb. beide mit oelfarben, und in ghüssen* (frames). P. Vischer, *Kunstblatt,* 1838, p. 215. See also Woltmann's *Beilagen.*

CHAP. IX.

Lais Corinthiaca. 1526.

Holbein's taste as is shown in these portraits, or if such be allowed to be possible, it is just as remarkable that he should have laid this taste down again without leaving a trace behind. We have no account of Holbein's ever having visited Milan, but this is not an improbable thing for him to have done. Indeed Milan is enumerated among the places that Holbein would be permitted to visit, should he settle in Basel, in the letter or document given to him by the burgomaster of Basel in the year 1538.*

Among the Swiss masters of this time distinguished for delicacy of execution, as far as we can judge from pictures ascribed to them, were Hans Asper and Nicholas Manuel, called Deutsch, but to me the pictures have an Italian character.

The Meier Madonna.

I am induced also from various reasons, to conclude that the celebrated picture of "The Meier Family, adoring the Infant Christ, in the arms of the Virgin," commonly called the "Meyer Madonna," was painted before Holbein visited England. If the dates of so great a proportion of his more important works are deferred, as some have done, until after his English visit, it leaves us at a loss to conjecture how his later time at Basel was occupied. This picture, I speak of that example in the palace of Prince Charles of Hesse, in Darmstadt, is of his more finished early manner, with the elaborate drawing, and the rich colouring of the portrait of Boniface Amerbach. To assume that it was painted after his return to Basel in 1529, is omitting all consideration of the religious animosities engendered by the very general reaction against ecclesiastical tyranny and imposition which the energies of Luther had finally brought to an open issue with Romanism, and which had been thoroughly successful in Basel, in 1529. This picture though as rationally treated as such a subject could possibly be, is still as a composition quite within the forbidden province of Mariolatry, and would probably not have been tolerated at Basel immediately after the religious riots of that year.

---

* See Chapter XV.

The Meier of this picture is the Burgomaster Jacob Meier "zum Hasen," whom Holbein painted, with his wife, in 1516; but he is painted this second time with all the improved mastery that ten years' practice may be supposed to have produced. The museum contains among its Amerbach drawings, studies for three of the heads of this picture—the burgomaster himself, his wife, and daughter, and they are fine drawings in his own style well known in England, but not of that superb character of execution displayed by many of the "Windsor Drawings." The composition is sufficiently given in the accompanying outline: the figures are about two-thirds the scale of life.

CHAP. IX.

The Meier Madonna. 1526.

The centre of the picture is occupied by the Madonna, who is standing on a Turkey carpet, before, not in, a circular-topped niche, and she holds in her arms on her left side a smiling infant, who is reclining on her bosom, and stretching out his left hand to those below him. On her right are kneeling, on the same carpet, close to her, the burgomaster, and a son who holds a little boy standing naked before him; on the left of the Madonna kneel the wife, another woman (her mother?), and a daughter whose hair is very elaborately dressed and ornamented. The composition is skilful, the expression sympathetic, the drawing vigorous, elaborate, and true, the colouring deep and harmonious, with Holbein's characteristic brown tone of this time. The back-ground is a piece of Renaissance decoration, the hollow or apse of the niche is scollopped, by its side are two pilasters, just showing their capitals only.

In oil, on wood. The height of the panel to the top of the niche is—1·44 metres—one metre and forty-four centimetres, or about 4 ft. 8½ in.; to the horizontal part over the top of the pilasters—1·125 met.—or 3 ft. 8¼ in. and the width is—1·01 met.—or nearly 3 ft. 3½ in.

The picture seems at one time of its obscure wanderings to have belonged to some English possessor, for it has written on the back—"No. 82, Holy Family Portraits, A.D.;" it has also the arms of a Herr von Warberge and his wife.

CHAP. IX.

The Meier Madonna. 1526.

This picture was purchased in 1822 by Prince William of Prussia either from M. Delahante, a picture dealer in Paris, who seems to have resuscitated it, or from his brother-in-law, Signor Spontini, for a sum variously stated as 2500 and 2800 thalers = 420*l.*; and it was presented by him to his daughter the Princess Elizabeth, on her marriage with the Prince Charles of Hesse-Darmstadt in 1836.*

This picture is commonly held to be Holbein's master-piece, but the world has been forced to judge it from the inferior repetition or rather copy, in the Dresden Gallery, well known out of Germany through the fine lithograph made from it by Hanfstängl.

Now that I have had the opportunity (though a bad one, for the picture is disadvantageously hung) of inspecting this Darmstadt example, my impression that that in the Dresden Gallery was a copy is confirmed. It may have been copied about 1530, possibly by a pupil of the painter's, for some branch of the family, though I see no reason why it should not be of later origin. Under any circumstances it appears to me to be a copy, not a repetition or replica by Holbein himself; there are parts in it that Holbein can scarcely have painted. The differences in the two are great, in expression, in colouring, and in execution; there is much more character in the heads of the Virgin and of the child in her arms, and indeed in all the heads in the Darmstadt picture; its colouring is browner, and the details are everywhere more pronounced, especially in the head-dress of the daughter, and in the carpet: in fact it has the ordinary superiority of an original by a great master, over the copy by an inferior painter; the weakest part of the Dresden example being the head and neck of the Madonna and the expression of the child in her arms. The Madonna, in some attempt to beautify her, has been deprived of natural force, and weakly idealized, and the happy child of

* See the notice by Dr. A. Zahn in Naumann's *Archiv*, &c., XI., 1, 1865, from which my illustration is taken.

THE MEIER MADONNA.

P. 166.

The Meier Madonna. 1526.

the original, has, through incapacity more than anything else, been rendered so void of childlike expression, as to have been pronounced sick, or even dead, by some, though this in spite of its extended arm is absurd enough.

Further, the proportions of the back-ground details are changed in the copy; the Darmstadt picture has certainly a somewhat cramped or stumpy effect, the niche presses too closely on the head of the Virgin, and this defect has been remedied in the Dresden picture, the niche is raised 12 centimetres, or 4¾ in., and the pilaster caps with it, by which considerable space is gained about the heads of the kneeling figures. The proportions of the two pictures differ accordingly: the Dresden example is—from the base to the top of the horizontal edge over the pilasters 1·245 met. or 4 ft. 1 in.; to the top of the circular portion 1·59 met. or 5 ft. 2½ in.; the width is nearly the same in both—1·03 met. or about 3 ft. 3½ in. Of these two pictures that at Dresden is shown to the utmost advantage, while that at Darmstadt is seen to the utmost disadvantage.

The picture at Dresden has not the peculiar colouring of Holbein of this time, while that at Darmstadt is one of the best and most characteristically coloured of all his works; he did not improve in colouring in later years; it is seldom that we find both brilliancy and transparency in his portraits, such as is not uncommon in the works of Titian; but it is equally true that we seldom find brilliancy of colour and transparency of complexion in nature. A picture does not always gain in truth in the same proportion that it acquires an access of effect. Holbein seems to have never lost his power of seeing, or his appreciation of faithful accuracy over conventional effect. His heads may suffer when compared with the masterly effects of Rubens, Rembrandt, or Velazquez, but not more I believe than the *originals* themselves would suffer in diminished glory, if they could at will be compared with their own portraits by these painters. In looking at a portrait by Holbein, we are reminded of the person painted, not of the painter. Holbein certainly was "a man very excellent in making of physiog-

CHAP. IX.

The Meier Madonna. 1526.

nomies," as ambassador Hutton terms him: there was no slobbering in his work.*

As regards the history of these two pictures neither can be positively traced to Basel; they have indeed no history, but one of them, which belonged to Remigius Fesch, was purchased at Basel from the descendants of the Meyer family, for 100 gold pieces or crowns, by Lucas Iselin, who died in 1626, the time he does not state, but it was early in the seventeenth century, before 1610;† however it left Basel and was bought by Michael Le Blond, agent or minister of the court of Sweden at Amsterdam, but in what year is quite uncertain. Sandrart tells us that Le Blond, when he was in Amsterdam, about 1640, had already long before (therefore possibly about 1633),‡ parted with the picture for 3000 florins, much against his inclination, to one John Loessert, a rich accountant or banker of Amsterdam. This sale is also noticed by Patin, who says the price was 1000 Imperial pieces or thalers, about 150*l.* sterling; and he adds that Loessert again sold it for three

* *State Papers.* Henry VIII., 1849. Vol. 8, p. 18. See the quotation from Hutton's letter to Cromwell, dated Brussels, March 14th, 1538, in the XV.th chapter of this work.

† This Lucas Iselin was a Rathsherr or Councillor; can he have been also the Dr. Iselin of whom Van Mander complains, for not having furnished him with some information concerning Holbein? The picture was sold by Remigius Fesch, certainly before 1610, when he died. Fesch had inherited it indirectly from the Meiers; his third wife Rosa Irmi, was a daughter of Anna Meier, the kneeling girl in the picture. This is from a MS. of another Remigius Fesch, grandson of the former, in the Library at Basel, communicated to Dr. Woltmann by Herr His-Heusler. See *Holbein*, &c., p. 324. The title of the MS. is *Remigii Feschii humanae industriae Monumenta*, and it is dated 1628, but it was continued later. It is from this MS. apparently that Patin derived much of his account of Holbein's works. Most of the above facts are given in detail also from His-Heusler, by G. Jh. Fechner, in an essay entitled *Zur Deutungsfrage und geschichte der Holbein'schen Madonna.* Leipzig, 1866.

‡ Dieser Herr hat *lang forher*, auf inständiges bitten, dem buchhalter Johann Lössert, für 3,000 gulden verkauft, eine stehende Maria auf eine tafel gemahlt, mit dem Kindlein auf dem arm, unter der ein teppich, worauf etliche vor ihr knien, die nach dem leben contrafätet seyn. *Teutsche Academie*, 1675, *Mahlerey*, p. 252. Sandrart's words here seem to imply that he did not know the exact subject of the picture, as he has not named it. Patin and others say that Le Blond *bought* the picture in 1633; I believe it to be much nearer the truth that this was the year in which he sold it. Seven years would correspond with Sandrart's *long before.* Le Blond had acted as the Art agent of the Duke of Buckingham as early as 1625. Sainsbury's *Rubens*, p. 61.

The Meier Madonna. 1526.

times the money (3000 thalers therefore, or 450*l.*?) to Maria de' Medici, the exiled queen-mother of France, who was then residing in the Netherlands. Sandrart's account does not quite agree with this, as he gives 3000 florins as the price paid by Loessert to Le Blond; but it is easy to make a confusion of prices; the price is here of no consequence, but the sale of the picture to Maria de' Medici is important; and this is not mentioned only by Patin, but is positively recorded in the MS. of Remigius Fesch just referred to. The queen removed to Cologne, and there died in July 1642.

So far then this very unsatisfactory history leaves us with the picture among the effects of the queen at Cologne: we certainly lose it from this time. Many years took place between the sale of the picture by Le Blond, and the queen's death, so that her death did not throw the picture into the hands of the Loessert family; the queen's effects would most probably go to France, and this "Meyer Madonna" should accordingly turn up again in Paris. Yet notwithstanding all these circumstances, the next time we hear of the picture, it is in Venice, a hundred years after the death of Maria de' Medici, where it is called the "Family of Sir Thomas More," showing most decidedly a broken link in the tradition; but what is also curious is that this picture, then in the possession of the Delfini family, passed to them from a banker of the name of Avogadro, who procured it in Amsterdam, at the close of the seventeenth century, in lieu of a debt of 2000 sequins owing to him by the Loessert family, then bankrupt. So that notwithstanding the sale of the Basel picture to the queen-mother of France, this family still possessed a picture of precisely the same composition, but which had in the course of years been miscalled the "Family of Sir Thomas More." I can only account for this confusion by assuming that when in the possession of the original purchaser John Loessert, the picture was copied before it was sold to the queen-mother, or possibly for Le Blond himself, after he had so reluctantly parted with it, this copy passing later to the Loesserts; and that while the copy found its way to Venice as we have seen, the original found its

CHAP. IX.

The Meier Madonna. 1526.

way to Paris, and there lay in obscurity until it was discovered by the expert eye of M. Delahante, when it was sent to Germany for sale; and thus it eventually came into the possession of the royal family of Prussia. It is a matter of not uncommon occurrence for indifferent heads of families to allow younger branches to take away occasionally a family portrait, substituting a copy in the place of the original; and thus an original may be lost or despised, while the copy substituted for it is still treasured as an original; I know cases in point, and I believe the "Meyer Madonna" history is of a very similar nature, and in its result identical.

The precise time that this picture left Basel, is not known, but it is supposed to have been after the death of Lucas Iselin in 1626; this is of course quite immaterial to the subsequent history, but is an inquiry of some interest as regards the Earl of Arundel, the famous collector and admirer of the works of Holbein. From a letter written from the Hague, in June 1621, by Sir Dudley Carleton to Lord Arundel, we learn that there was a picture by Holbein at Amsterdam which the earl desired, but which Sir Dudley could not succeed in procuring. He says—"Having wayted lately on ye K. and Q. of Bohemia to Amsterdam, I there saw ye picture of Holben's yor L^p^ desires; but cannot yet obtayne it, though my indeavours wayte on it, as they still shall doe."*

There is certainly no special reason why the above extract should refer to the "Meyer Madonna," nor is there any very good reason why it should not, unless it can be shown that *both examples* were still in Basel in 1621; it cannot, however, be ascertained that even one of them was there at that time: Iselin's copy may have been sold in his own lifetime, though this does not agree with the tradition. Lord Arundel certainly never got the picture.

The only document we have respecting the alienation of this picture is a vague one, it is an entry in the Fesch

* See a fuller quotation from this letter in Ch. XV. It is published in Sainsbury's *Papers on Rubens*, p. 290.

The Meier Madonna. 1526.

manuscript referred to, and is the original source apparently of Patin's account. The words of the manuscript are :—

A°·163 × (year uncertain) suprad. pictor Le Blond hic a vidua et haeredibus Iselij ad S. Martinum, emit tabulam ligneam trium circiter ulnarum Basiliensium tum in altitud. tum longitud. in qua adumbratus praedictus Jac. Meierus Consul ex latere dextro una cum filiis, ex opposito uxor cum filiabus, omnes ad vivum depicti ad altare procumbentes, *unde habeo exempla filii et filiae in Belgio a Joh. Ludi pictore ex ipsa tabula depicta.* Solvit is Le Blond pro hac tabula 1000 imperiales et postea triplo majoris vendidit Mariae Mediceae Reginae Galliae, viduæ Regis Lud. 13. matri, dum in Belgio ageret, ubi et mortua. Quorsum pervenerit, incertum.

To the above entry he has added the following marginal note—Tabula haec fuit avi nostri Remigii Faeschii Consulis, unde Lucas Iselius eam impetravit pro legato Regis Galliar. uti ferebat, et persolvit pro ea centum coronatos aureos solares anno circ. 1606.*

From the above it is evident that the time of Le Blond's purchase is quite uncertain. Iselin's heirs had the picture in 1626, provided Iselin had not himself parted with it before. An interesting passage in the note is that about the painter John Ludi or Giovanni Lodi who copied Fesch's two figures of the group, when the picture was in the Netherlands: *may he not have also copied the whole picture*, at the same time? The reader will have observed that the measurements given by Fesch are inaccurate, and the description is also imperfect, the writer apparently had never seen it. As regards Giovanni Battista Lodi, he is spoken of by Antonio Campi as an excellent master, indeed he mentions his name with a few others as illustrating the *colmo della perfezione* to which the art had reached in his time. Lodi was born at Cremona about 1580, and in the church of SS. Egidio ed Omobuono in that city is an altar-piece painted by him in 1611, representing the "Virgin and Child in glory, with Saints Carlo and Antonio

* Fechner, *l. l.*, p. 33.

Abate below."* Lodi may have communicated to Fesch the fact of the sale of the picture to Maria de' Medici.

Just a hundred years, as I have observed, after the death of Maria de' Medici, we find the Dresden picture in Venice, under the name of the "Family of Sir Thomas More;" *and as such* it was then bought from Giovanni Delfino, by Count Algarotti, for Augustus III., Elector of Saxony. The purchase was completed on the 4th of September 1743; the price of the picture being 1000 sequins or 22,000 *livres de Venise*, but comprising various expenses, including a present to the painter Tiepolo, who assisted in the negotiation, the whole cost amounted to 28,024 Venetian *lire*.†

---

* See Zaist, *Pittori, &c., Cremonesi.* Vol. II., p. 45. Cremona, 1774.

† I am at a loss to suggest an equivalent sum in English money for this amount. We have the account in sequins and lire; the lira of Venice is given in Kelly's *Universal Cambist* as 2½*d.* English, which at 22 the sequin, would give only 4*s.* 7*d.* as the value of that gold coin, while it is commonly calculated at twice that amount. The price of the picture therefore may be estimated at either 300*l.* or 600*l.* Mr. Julius Hübner in his *Verzeichniss der Königlichen Gemälde Gallerie zu Dresden*, 1862, has adopted the higher estimate: he gives the whole account in detail, as follows:—

	Livres de Venise.
4 7br, 1743. Payé à Mrss Delfino pour le tableau de Holbein 1000 sequins, ou	22,000
„ Donné à Mr. Tiepolo, qui a été l'entremetteur du marché un présent en argenterie et chocolat et une canne avec une béquille d'ambre montée en or, valeur de 50 sequins, ou .	1,148
„ Donné a l'homme d'affaire de la casa Delfino	440
„ Donné aux domestiques de la casa Delfino	22
28 8br. Payé au Sieur Gai pour le quadre du tableau . .	330
15 9br. Payé à Giacomo Zandini pour la caisse du tableau 5 sequins	110
15 Janvier 1744. Payé à la boutique della Fama pour du velours vert pour la caisse du Holbein	188
do. Payé à la boutique de S. Filippo Neri pour du galon pour la meme caisse	66
15 Janvier. À Marco Manzini pour la façon de la dite caisse .	50
21 Janvier. Payé au serrurier pour feraille de la caisse du tableau de Holbein	50
10 Febrier. Payé au doreur Ant. Pompeo, &c.	980
3 Mars. À Mr. Platzer à compte de l'accord fait pour transporter les tableaux a Dresde (some other pictures were sent with it)	1,760
3 Mars. Payé à l'Erle (?) qui devoit conduire les dits tableaux 40 sequins	880
	S. S. 28,024

[The

The Meier Madonna. 1526.

The subject of this picture has been variously explained. Some have considered it a votive picture, dedicated in a private chapel, to commemorate the recovery of a sick child. Another refinement is, that the child in the arms of the Virgin, is the *soul of a deceased child*, to which I have no sentimental objection. I cannot however countenance the notion that the child is the *soul* of the woman kneeling next to the Virgin, who is supposed to have recently died. Others consider the composition as a mere ordinary devotional picture painted in veneration of the Madonna; and there is no good reason why it should be anything else than a portrait group of the Meier family combined with the religious sentiment which is implied by the introduction of the Virgin Mary and the Divine Infant. Its German explanations are numerous, voluminous, and tedious beyond endurance, and the opinions are of course diverse; if I were to follow them all I should very soon weary my reader; it is a case of *quot homines tot sententiae,* and one opinion is about as valuable as another. The official catalogue by Matthaei, published in 1833, and sold in the gallery for many years, describes the picture as follows:—"The family of Jacob Meyer, Burgomaster of Basel. The father is kneeling full of devotion, with his family, before the mother of the Lord, who stands in the middle of the picture, and holds in her arms an apparently deceased child of the family."* This somewhat absurd interpretation is now given up, and the present official account is—"Jacob Meyer, Burgomaster of Basel, kneels worshipping with his family before the Virgin Mary, who holds the infant Christ in her arms."† This if not the more refined is certainly the more obvious interpretation of a very simple subject.

The waggons left Venice with the pictures on the 6th of March 1744, accompanied by Algarotti's servant Zuane Zorzi, and the count himself received them at Dresden on the 10th of April following.

A somewhat similar account to the above, but on a much larger scale, had to be paid by the British Government when in 1857 it purchased the "Family of Darius before Alexander," by Paul Veronese, from the Pisani family in Venice.

* *Neues Sach-und Ortsverzeichniss der Königlich Sächsischen Gemälde Gallerie zu Dresden.* No. 546, p. 92.

† Hübner, *Verzeichniss,* &c, 1862. No. 1809, p. 386.

CHAP. IX.

The Meier Madonna. 1526.

Mr. Ruskin has pleaded for the sentimental rendering of the composition; he says, "The received tradition respecting the Holbein Madonna is beautiful; and I believe the interpretation to be true. A father and mother have prayed to her for the life of their sick child. She appears to them, her own Christ in her arms. She puts down her Christ beside them—takes their child into her arms instead—it lies down upon her bosom and stretches its hand to its father and mother, saying farewell."*

I think we might assume the baby in arms to be the soul of a deceased child of the family, without also inferring that the naked boy below represents the infant Christ; the two ideas have no necessary connection. A simpler solution would be that the child below is the sick child restored to health: from a broken left arm or otherwise, the Divine Child in the arms of the Virgin having taken the disease upon himself.

The idea of death and sickness connected with this work, not of any remote origin but first suggested by Ludwig Tieck, and Friedrich Schlegel, has arisen I imagine mainly from the imperfect execution of the head and countenance of the infant in the Virgin's arms; no such impression is conveyed by the Darmstadt picture, in which the expression is lively and cheerful.

Walpole has rather a curious passage concerning this very picture which he saw at Venice as the "Family of Sir Thomas More." Speaking of Holbein's various compositions of this subject, he says—"The fifth was in the palace of the Delfino family at Venice, where it was long on sale, the first price set, 1500*l.* When I saw it there in 1741, they had sunk it to 400*l.*, soon after which the present King of Poland bought it.

"It was evidently designed for a small altar-piece to a chapel; in the middle on a throne sits the Virgin and Child; on one side kneels an elderly gentleman with two sons, one of them a naked infant; opposite, kneeling, are his wife and daughters. The old man is not only unlike all representations of Sir Thomas

* *The Cornhill Magazine*, March 1860, p. 328.

The Meier Madonna. 1526.

More, but it is certain that he never had but one son.* For the colouring, it is beautiful beyond description, and the carnations have that enamelled bloom so peculiar to Holbein, who touched his works till not a touch remained discernible. A drawing of this picture by Bischop was brought over in 1723, from whence Vertue doubted both of the subject and the painter; but he never saw the original! By the description of the family of the Consul Mejer, mentioned above, I have no doubt but this is the very picture—Mejer and More are names not so unlike but that in process of time they may have been confounded, and that of More retained, as much better known."

* There is recorded a *bon mot* of Sir Thomas on the birth of his son: he had three daughters: his wife was impatient for a son; at last they had one, but not much above an idiot. "You have prayed so long for a boy," said the Chancellor, "that now we have got one who, I believe, will be a boy as long as he lives." This is given in Lewis's ed. of Roper's *Life of More*, 1731.

CHAPTER X.

Wood Engravings. The Dance of Death, and Bible Cuts.

Chap. X.

The Dance of Death at Basel. about 1450.

NGRAVING on wood has already been mentioned as one of the reputed accomplishments of Holbein, and as he has not only the credit of having designed the celebrated engraved Dance of Death commonly known as his, but till of late years has been considered also the painter of a series of pictures on the wall of the churchyard or burial-ground of the Dominicans at Basel, representing the same subject, I cannot altogether omit taking notice of this much-discussed topic. Not that any of these early Dances of Death really concern Holbein; there is no positive evidence that he had anything whatever to do with them, but it is just possible from the intrinsic merit and character of the designs themselves, in the engraved series especially referred to, which first appeared at Lyons in 1538, that Holbein is their author, and it is on this assumption, which is not without justification however, that this chapter finds a place in this volume; for it is neither my purpose nor my business to discuss here the origin or character of "Dances of Death" in general.*

* I refer those who are curious on this matter to the following works, among many, in which the subject is treated at considerable length. The Rev. J. F. Dibdin, *Bibliographical Decameron*. 3 vols., 8vo., 1817; F. Douce, *The Dance of Death exhibited in elegant engravings on wood; with a dissertation on the several representations of that subject, but more particularly on those ascribed to Macaber*

CHAP. X.

The Dance of Death at Basel. about 1450.

It seems that the old *Tod von Basel*, or "Dance of Death" of Basel was still in existence as late as 1805, and was habitually visited by travellers as a work by Holbein. It is however a much older work. Its origin is ascribed by Ochs,* to the plague which raged in that city between Easter and St. Martin's day, in the year 1439; when the famous Council of Basel was sitting. The pestilence travelled from Italy, and carried off before it left Basel about five thousand people, including many persons of position and distinction, killing as many as a hundred a day: ordinary habits were set aside, pits were dug near all the churches, and the dead bodies were buried promiscuously.

Something very similar had taken place more than a hundred years before; and there are in an old building at Basel, which was once a nunnery, but is now a salt warehouse, the remains of a "Dance of Death" dated 1312.†

After their deliverance, the council ordered commemorative

---

and Hans Holbein. 8vo. London, Pickering, 1833. U. Hegner, *Hans Holbein der Jüngere*. 8vo. Berlin, 1827, pp. 291-349. C. F. von Rumohr, *Hans Holbein der Jüngere in seinem Verhältniss zum Deutschen Formschnittwesen*. 8vo. Leipzig, 1836. W. A. Chatto, in the *Treatise on Wood Engraving, Historical and Practical. With upwards of three hundred illustrations engraved on wood by John Jackson*. Imp. 8vo. London, Charles Knight and Co., 1839.

There is little agreement in these accounts, but I believe the soundest views to be those of Dibdin, Hegner, and Chatto, who follows Hegner. Baron Rumohr maintains that Holbein was himself the wood engraver of the designs under discussion; I am sorry that in this instance I cannot agree with that sagacious writer. Douce does not even allow Holbein the credit of being the designer.

For wood engravings ascribed to Holbein as the designer see the list in J. D. Passavant's *Peintre Graveur*—Vol. III., pp. 353-421—where no less than 160 designs and sets of designs are enumerated. The completest account of the *Literature* of the "Dances of Death" is given in H. F. Massmann's *Literatur der Todtentänze*. 8vo. Leipzig, 1840. See also the *Essai Typographique et Bibliographique sur l'Histoire de la Gravure sur Bois. Par Ambroise Firmin Didot*. 8vo. Paris, 1863. The facsimiles of woodcuts, as they are called, are very much better given in the early work of Dr. Dibdin than in that of Jackson, some of whose Holbein reproductions are very poor; the few given in Dibdin's work are by Ebenezer Byfield and William Hughes, and are excellent.

* *Geschichte der Stadt Basel*. Vol. III., p. 279.

† The Basel Museum has some coloured copies from the remains of this old work, made in 1766 by Emanuel Büchel, who seems to have taken a special antiquarian interest in this matter of the Death Dances. Hegner, *Hans Holbein*, &c., p. 309.

CHAP. X.

The Dance of Death at Basel. about 1450.

paintings to be executed on the wall of the cemetery of the old Prediger-Kloster, or convent of the Predicants, in the suburb of St. John, showing, as had been similarly done before, the universal power and triumph of Death, that to him all ranks and grades were alike indifferent. Whatever indulgences the wealthy might purchase securing immunities after death, there was no such thing as an immunity from death itself.

The series consisted of about forty compositions, with life-sized figures, painted—or at least repaired—in oil. But the painter is not known, though one Hans Kluber has the credit of it; the exact date of the pictures is as little known as the painter's name; they were not completed of course till some years, and perhaps many, after the cessation of the pestilence. The first represented a Predicant, with nine listeners; the second a charnel-house, with skeletons playing drums and other instruments; then followed a series of five-and-thirty designs, in which Death appears inviting some one representative of a class, to the dance—the Pope, the Emperor, the Empress, the Cardinal, the Bishop, the Duke, the Duchess, the Count, the Abbot, the Knight, the Lawyer, the Councillor, the Chorister, the Doctor, the Nobleman, the Lady, the Merchant, the Abbess, the Cripple, the Hermit, the Youth, the Usurer, the Virgin, the Piper (Kiehepfeifer), the Herald, the Bailiff, the Judge (Blutvogd), the Fool, the Pedlar, the Blind, the Jew, the Heathen, male and female, the Cook, and the Peasant. Above and below each picture were four verses, emphasizing the moral in each case: below the Pope were the following lines—

Komm heiliger Vatter, werther Mann:
Ein vortanz musst ihr mit mir han;
Der *Ablass* euch nicht hilft davon,
Das zweyfach Creutz und dreyfach Cron.

Come, Holy Father, worthy man:
Now dance with me you must and can:
Indulgence boots not, nor renown,
Nor double Cross, nor triple Crown.

Such was the famous "Tod von Basel," neither original nor unique; nearly all the invited are very naturally resisting the invitation to the dance: the Pope was said to have been a portrait of Felix V. CHAP. X.

The Dance of Death at Basel, about 1450.

In 1520, or 1568, the date of the inscription being variously read, these paintings were restored by Hans Hugo Kluber, or Klauber, the original painter's son, who also added to the series, in one place—"Oekolampadius preaching the Gospel to the Pope, Emperor, and Cardinals," and himself and family carrying on the dance, in another.

The work was restored again in 1616, and a third and last time in 1703: in 1805, the wall was thrown down, to make way for improvements, and so the grim dance was finally broken up. The compositions are however preserved in a water-colour copy by Emanuel Büchel, now in the Museum of Basel, and in a series of copper plates engraved by Matthew Merian.*

The error which had attributed these wall-paintings to Holbein is easily accounted for; he appears to have certainly made a series of drawings of this subject, which was published, and acquired him a considerable renown even in his own life-time. Hence the "Dance of Death" of the famous Basel painter, which was in the hands of the multitude, not only of Germany but of other countries also, was almost of necessity confounded with the famous "Dance of Death" of Basel; especially by those who were not acquainted with both the painted and the engraved series. If Holbein's biographer had no more bewildering confusion than such as this is to combat his task would be a comparatively light one: the most difficult errors to refute are not those arising out of the misapprehensions of the ignorant, but those rashly promulgated through the conceit and vanity of the half informed.

Growing gradually abroad, in time the error was established at Basel itself. Holbein has also had the credit of painting

* *Todtentanz, wie derselbe in der löblichen und weitberühmten Stadt Basel zu sehen ist. Nach dem original in Kupfer gebracht, und herausgegeben durch Matth. Merian den Aeltern.* 4to. Frankfort, 1649. J. R. Füssli mentions a set of prints or cuts by Josias Denneker or De Necker of Augsburg made in 1544: this is possibly a confusion of the Basel, with the Holbein, Todtentantz, which last De Necker cut, in 1561.

CHAP. X.

The Dance of Death at Basel. about 1450.

the "Dance" of the Dominicans at Bern, which was the work of his contemporary Nicolaus Manuel, about eleven years older than Holbein; this has also perished in its original form but is preserved in copies.

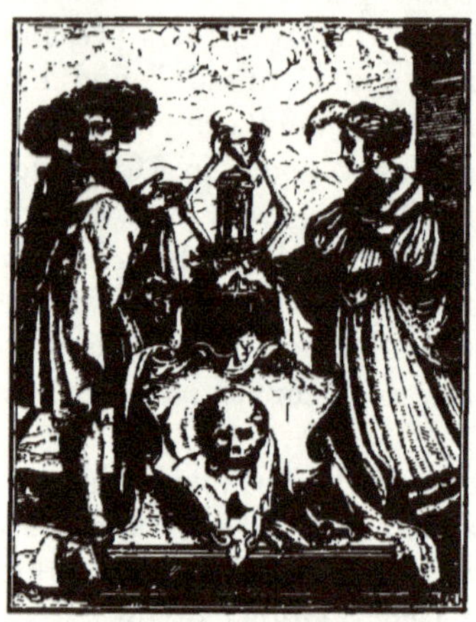

THE ARMS OF DEATH.

Holbein's Dance of Death. 1526.

Of Holbein's celebrated series representing this subject, there are some few sets of prints, which have been struck off on one side of the paper only; they are looked upon as the engraver's original proofs of the cuts, and are assumed to belong to a date as early as 1530; but this is all conjectural. They were apparently first published at Lyons, with French text in 1538.

The British Museum is in the possession of a complete set of forty-one proofs, with the exception of one—the Astrologer, No. 27, the place of which is supplied by a print, impressed on both sides of the paper: each subject is briefly described in old German. This set belonged formerly to Mr. Ottley. The veritable Dance of Death is comprised in thirty-seven designs; the first two of the series representing the Creation and the Fall, the cause of (spiritual) death; the last but one is the Judgment; and the last is the fanciful combination called "the Arms of Death;" it is engraved above.

Death appears as a skeleton, sometimes partly clothed, and

CHAP. X.

Holbein's Dance of Death.

1526.

occasionally naked; we see him first in the third design, "the expulsion from Paradise," where he is running before Adam and Eve, playing a guitar or lute; in other scenes he is represented with a drum, the bagpipes, a dulcimer, or a fiddle. On one occasion, when leading off the Abbot, he appears with mitre on his head and crozier in his hand; and he marches before the parson with bell and candle, vigorously ringing his bell. Occasionally his head is adorned with a wreath; in the thirteenth design, where he seizes the Duke, he is crowned with ivy. Some of his victims go quietly, some unconsciously, and others in vain resist, a few showing vigorous fight. Later editions have twelve and seventeen additional cuts, of which the most remarkable, in point of style, are seven groups of children, which, both for composition and drawing, would do honour even to Raphael; they are indeed completely in the taste of similar designs by the great Italian painter.

The evidence that this remarkable series of wood-cuts is from the original designs of Holbein is not conclusive, and this fact has accordingly been disputed. However some, as for instance Rumohr, have gone to the extent of asserting Holbein to have been not only the designer of the work, but its engraver also: this opinion, as already stated, I do not adopt. That Holbein was the author of the designs I cannot but believe; they bear in their vigour and dignity an internal evidence of his hand; the specimen engraving above is thoroughly Holbeinesque; it is quite in the style of the "Ambassadors" at Longford Castle: there is no other German artist known who could be reasonably substituted for Holbein. Further we have the evidence of a contemporary, and probably Holbein's friend, Nicholas Bourbon, a French poet, who was in England and thus speaks of the designs as Holbein's:—

> Dum Mortis Hansus pictor imaginem exprimit,
> Tanta arte mortem retulit, ut Mors vivere
> Videatur ipsa: et ipse se immortalibus
> Parem Diis fecerit operis hujus gloria.*

---

* Which is as much as to say that "Painter Hans has so artfully expressed the Image of Death, that very Death now seems a living being, and he by the glory of

CHAP. X.

Holbein's Dance of Death. 1526.

This certainly may have been written from common repute, though under the circumstances it is very unlikely; but at this early period common repute is very good repute indeed. And to the above may be added the significant fact, that two copies of this "Dance of Death" were preserved in the Amerbach cabinet at Basel, among the works after Holbein; and one of them may possibly have been placed there even by Holbein himself, a gift to his intimate friend Boniface Amerbach.

The following is the order of succession, under their old German titles of the original series, with the exception of the missing Astrologer:—

1. Die schöpffung aller ding.	The Creation of all things.
2. Adam Eva im Paradyss .	Adam and Eve in Paradise.
3. Ugstribung Ade Eve .	Expulsion of Adam and Eve.
4. Adam bawgt die Erden .	Adam tills the earth.
5. Gebeyn aller menschen .	Bones of all people.
6. Der Bapst . . .	The Pope.
7. Der Keyser . . .	The Emperor.
8. Der Künig . . .	The King.
9. Der Cardinal . .	The Cardinal.
10. Die Keyserinn . .	The Empress.
11. Die Küniginn . .	The Queen.
12. Der Bischoff . .	The Bishop.
13. Der Hertzog . .	The Duke.
14. Der Apt . . .	The Abbot.
15. Die Aptissinn . .	The Abbess.
16. Der Edelman . .	The Nobleman.
17. Der Thůmherr . .	The Canon.
18. Der Richter . . .	The Judge.
19. Der Fürspräch . .	The Advocate.

---

his work has made himself the compeer of the immortal Gods." See *Nic. Borbonii Vandoperani Nugarum Libri Octo.* 12mo. Basil, 1540. "De morte picta à Hanso pictore Nobili." Bourbon's reputed portrait is among the Windsor drawings, No. 30 of the first volume, in the original catalogue. And the poet himself thus celebrates the circumstance:—

Dum divina meos vultus mens exprimit Hansi,
Per tabulam docta praecipitante manu,
Ipse et ego interea sic uno carmine pinxi:
Hansus me pingens major Apelle fuit.

CHAP. X.

Holbein's Dance of Death. 1526.

20.	Der Ratssherr . .	The Councillor.
21.	Der Predicant . .	The Preacher.
22.	Der Pfarrherr . .	The Parson.
23.	Der Münch . . .	The Monk.
25.	Das Altweyb . .	The Old Woman.
26.	Der Artzet . . .	The Physician.
27.	. . . .	*The Astrologer.*
28.	Der Rychman . .	The Rich Man.
29.	Der Kauffman . .	The Merchant.
30.	Der Schiffman . .	The Navigator.
31.	Der Ritter . . .	The Knight.
32.	Der Groff . . .	The Count.
33.	Der Altman . . .	The Old Man.
34.	Die Greffinn . . .	The Countess.
35.	Die Edelfrau . .	The Lady.
36.	Die Hertzoginn . .	The Duchess.
37.	Der Krämer . . .	The Pedlar.
38.	Der Ackerman . .	The Ploughman.
39.	Dass Jung Kint . .	The Young Child.
40.	Dass Jüngst gericht .	The Last Judgment.
41.	Die Wapen dess Thotss .	The Arms of Death.

The cuts are ·065 of a metre high, by ·050 wide, or about 2½ in. by 2 in.; they are not all absolutely the same size: the engraving is exquisite, the lines being singularly fine and accurate, the character and expression very seldom suffering from the inexpertness of the engraver. The precision of line in some of the faces is wonderful, as in Adam's, in the Fall; the face of the Pope has a very fine expression produced by only a few touches; the King appears to be a sketch of Francis I., this may be assumed from the nose and from the sprinkling of fleurs-de-lys; the expression of alarm in the Abbot is very good, when too late he seems to have a suspicion that his life of sensual idleness and hypocrisy may after all turn out to have been but a fool's paradise: the Monk too is frightfully scared. The face of the woman seized by the robber, in the wood, among the additional cuts, is admirable in expression and remarkably well engraved.

Number 36 of the series, the Duchess, represents a woman sitting up in bed fully dressed, roused from her sleep by two

CHAP. X. — *Holbein's Dance of Death.* 1526.

skeletons, one of which is playing a fiddle, while the other is pulling the covering from the bed. On the lower part of the bedstead, in a small shield is the monogram HL which has given rise to much discussion, but is commonly assumed to represent the initials of the engraver; in the later editions and copies this monogram is mostly omitted.

The first edition known, appeared at Lyons in 1538, without name of either engraver or designer, under the following title:—

Les Simulachres & Historiées Faces
De La Mort, autant elegammēt pourtraictes
que artificiellement imaginées
a Lyon
MDXXXVIII.
Soubz l'escu de Coloigne.*

This was published by the brothers Melchior and Gaspar Trechsel; it contains a dedication to the abbess of the convent of St. Peter at Lyons, Madame Jehanne de Touszele, and has the forty-one cuts only, enumerated above. In 1542 two editions were published by John and Francis Frellon, one with French, and the other with Latin text. In 1545 editions appeared with fifty-three cuts, and in 1547 the number appears to have been increased to fifty-seven, though the title would imply that only twelve had been added to the original number. LES IMAGES DE LA MORT, *aux quelles sont adjoustées douze figures. Imprimé à Lyon à l'escu de Coloigne, par Jehan Frellon,* 1547.†

The designs comprised in the twelve additions commonly

* Images and storied aspects of Death, as elegantly drawn as they are skilfully conceived. At Lyons 1538. Under the sign of the Shield of Cologne. The title-page bears also a device used by the Frellons of a winged figure with three heads one male and two female, and an open book in front, containing the words ΓΝΩΘΥ ΣΕΑΥΤΟΝ, "know thyself," six letters in three lines being in each page. On the pedestal, upon which are various allegorical figures, are written the words USUS ME GENUIT. The publication was clearly designed more as an educational than an artistic production.

† The accountant-general, Mr. William Russell, has a copy of this edition; it is just possible that these extra cuts belong properly to the later edition issued in 1562, and that this is an exceptional example, as I do not find such an edition mentioned in the voluminous bibliography of this subject.

Holbein's Dance of Death. 1526.

announced are :—the Soldier ; the Gamesters ; the Drunkards ; the Old Buffoon ; the Robber ; the Blind Man ; the Waggoner ; the Lame Beggar ; the Infant with shield and arrow ; three Infants, one riding an arrow ; four Infant Bacchanals carrying a fifth in triumph ; and three Infants, one supporting a trophy of arms. These are the only additions in three issues of 1547.

The four others, making the additions amount to sixteen are :—a triumphal procession of children, with trophies ; Death taking away the young wife from the husband ; Death blowing a trumpet leading away the young husband ; and a group of children leading another mounted on horseback and carrying a standard. They are placed between the Robber and the Blind Man.

In 1562 the same publisher issued an edition with fifty-eight cuts :—*Les Images de la Mort, aux quelles sont adjoustées dix sept figures. Lyon, Chez Jean Frellon,* 1562, the seventeenth being a seventh group of children, with musical instruments. This number fifty-eight is never exceeded.

Of all the so-called original and early editions of this work one only was published at Basel :—*Icones Mortis, duodecim imaginibus praeter priores, &c. Basileae,* 1554. It was perhaps only got up at Lyons for a Basel publisher, as we see that the cuts were still in the hands of John Frellon in 1562.

An incomplete set of etchings of this "Dance," by Hollar, was published in Paris in 1651, and again by Douce in London in 1793. For a complete account of the various sets, original and copies, I must again refer the reader to the works quoted in the note to page 177.

In the original edition, in the dedication referred to, the writer regrets that the artist to whom we owe these beautiful designs had died without completing the series. The original words are, after a digression, p. 6 :—"Donc retournãt a noz figurées faces de Mort, tres grãdemẽt viẽt a regreter la mort de celluy, qui nous en a icy imaginé si elegãtes figures."

From the use of the word *imaginé* in the above quotation some have assumed that the designer was referred to, and that accordingly as Holbein was certainly not dead in 1538, he was

CHAP. X.

Holbein's Dance of Death.

1526.

conclusively proved to have not been the inventor or author of the series. The context however shows that the writer was really speaking of the engraver of the cuts, some of which, belonging originally to the series, as for instance the Waggoner, he regrets had been left in an unfinished state and could not then be published.

The finished cuts were the forty-one of which proofs of forty have been already noticed, as having German titles, and being preserved in the British Museum, and at Basel. As it has been shown that Holbein's title to the authorship of these designs is a very fair one, we may safely assume that the monogram H. L. in the thirty-sixth cut indicates the engraver. Now if we search for an engraver for whom these initials may pass, we find him as the engraver of another set of Holbein's designs, to which he has not contented himself with putting his initials, but has signed his name in full. This is the Todtentanz Alphabet preserved at Basel, also in the Print Room of the Dresden Gallery, and at Berlin, signed *Hanns Lützelburger, formschnider genant Franck.* A copy of this alphabet, in facsimile, published by Mr. R. Weigel of Leipzig, may be seen in the Print Room of the British Museum. And this Hans Lützelburger, wood engraver, called Franck, is assumed, not without justification, to have been the engraver of the "Dance of Death," and also of the best of the series known as Holbein's Bible cuts; likewise published at Lyons in 1538. Scarcely anything however, is known of Lützelburger; he was living in 1522,* but was possibly dead in 1538: he was certainly an exquisite wood engraver, if the cuts of the "Dance of Death" are his work.

There are four alphabets ascribed to him; that already mentioned, known as the "Little Dance of Death," in letters about an inch square, of which I have given three specimens; that of the "Dance of Peasants;" a third of the "Sports of Infants," somewhat smaller; and a fourth with ornaments,

* There is among the Utopia cuts, one of a battle in a wood, between clothed and naked men, and under it in a distinct tablet from a distinct block is the name and date—HANNS. LEUCZELLBURGER FURMSCHNIDER × 1.5.2.2.

consisting of twenty-three letters only. A proof sheet of these last, in the museum of Berlin, is signed and dated H. L. F. 1522. The designs of all these alphabets are accredited to Holbein.*

CHAP. X.

Holbein's Dance of Death. 1526.

Von Mechel has engraved a larger "Dance of Death," professedly from Holbein's original drawings, and of the same size, in forty-seven plates, published at Basel in 1780,† with French explanations. He borrowed these drawings from a Prince Gallizin, then Russian ambassador at Vienna; and what is remarkable, is, that nearly all such designs of the original set as have not the active image of Death at work in them, are wanting in the Gallizin series; for example the Creation, the skeleton house, the Last Judgment, the arms of Death, and the seven groups of children; as if they had no concern with the Dance.

The drawings which are pen and ink with washed shadows, have a somewhat remarkable pedigree, but as they really vary in many minor details from the old engraved cuts, they can scarcely have been the originals of those cuts. They are the kind of studies that some skilful artist might make for his own satisfaction and amusement from the cuts themselves. I have already related an anecdote from which we learn that Rubens made such studies, and he recommended Sandrart to do the same. The original drawings are said to have formed part of the rich Arundel collection of Holbein's works, and to have passed from that into the Low Countries where they became the property of Jan Bockhorst; they subsequently formed part of the celebrated Crozat collection, and were described by Mariette; at the Crozat sale in 1741 they were purchased by the Geheime-Rath Fleischmann of Strassburg, and from him they passed into the possession of Prince Gallizin, and they now form part of the Imperial collections at St. Petersburg.

Von Mechel however did not engrave from this original set,

* Passavant, *Peintre Graveur*, &c. Vol. III., p. 375; Rumohr, *Hans Holbein*, &c.

† *Oeuvre de Jean Holbein*, &c. In 6 parts, folio. Basel, 1780-92.

CHAP. X.

Holbein's Dance of Death. 1526.

but from copies made from them by a Swiss artist of the name of Rudolph Schellenberg.*

JOB ch. ii. v. 9 and 10.

Then said his wife unto him, "Dost thou still retain thine integrity? curse God, and die." But he said unto her, "Thou speakest as one of the foolish women speaketh. What? shall we receive good at the hand of God, and shall we not receive evil?"

Holbein's Bible cuts.

In the same year as the "Dance of Death," and under the same sign, appeared the Old Testament cuts:—HISTORIARUM VETERIS INSTRUMENTI ICONES AD VIVUM EXPRESSAE. *Unà cum brevi, sed quod fieri potuit, dilucida earundem expositione.* LUGDUNI, SUB SCUTO COLONIENSI. MDXXXVIII., with the same three-headed device in the centre of the page. The title is followed on the reverse with an address to the reader by Franciscus Frellaeus (Frellon), and then comes immediately the cut of the Creation, which with the three following are identical with the first four cuts of the Dance of Death. The others commencing with Noah's Ark (Archa Noï) are unequal, some few towards the end being engraved by a very unskilful hand, as those of Joel and Zacharias, especially; and the compositions are several of them formal and uninteresting from the very nature of their subjects; others and

* Hegner, *Hans Holbein*, &c., p. 323.

these not a few are exquisite designs, though perhaps on the whole they do not show the same spirit that we find in the Dance of Death; the subjects are of a more sober or solemn character. CHAP. X. *Holbein's Bible cuts.* 1526.

Among the fine compositions, the following are conspicuous:—Abraham receiving the three Angels; the Sacrifice of Isaac; the Burial of Joseph; the Brazen Serpent; the Death of Jeroboam's Son;* the Genealogy of Adam; Tobit become blind; Judith with the head of Holophernes; Job (engraved above); Daniel in the Lions' Den; Amos; and Jonas.

The plates vary somewhat in size, being about 3·3 in. wide, by 2·4 in. high; the Sacrifice of Abraham is 3·8 in. wide, by 2·4 in high. The number in the first edition should be ninety, and they have not the French verses beneath them which occur in later editions. The verses of Bourbon and Gilles Corrozet belong to the second edition, that of 1539; and it is in Nicholas Bourbon's address that we find these designs positively given to Holbein. In these lines Bourbon has paid his friend Holbein some extravagant compliments. He introduces us to the Homeric Hades and presents to us the shades of three great Greek painters, Apelles, Zeuxis, and Parrhasius:—

> Nuper in Elysio cum forte erraret Apelles
> Una aderat Zeuxis, Parrhasiusque comes.

Apelles lamenting the eclipse of their fame upon earth, exclaims

> Holbius est homini nomen, qui nomina nostra
> Obscura ex claris ac prope nulla facit.†

---

* Sir Joshua Reynolds appears to have adopted the bed scene of his "Death of Cardinal Beaufort" from this design.

† Chatto, in the *Treatise on Wood Engraving*, speaks of those lines as occurring in the first edition; he describes only the second edition assuming it to be the same as the first. I have a copy of the first before me, unhappily imperfect, which belongs to Mr. William Russell, and the differences between it and that of 1539 have been already pointed out. This work is extremely scarce—Jackson has engraved what is professedly a facsimile of the "Sacrifice of Abraham" in this Bible series, it is nothing of the kind, it is not only considerably smaller but is otherwise a wretched copy, done by some rude prentice-hand. As already noticed, very superior specimens are given in Dibdin's *Decameron*. The four cuts — Ezekiel xl.; Ezekiel xliii.;

CHAP. X.

Cranmer's Catechism. 1548.

While upon the subject of wood-cuts, it may be as well to say here all that I have to say upon the matter. The series of designs in Archbishop Cranmer's Catechism is commonly given to Holbein, but of the engravings of this work I am quite satisfied that he is wholly innocent, though one design by him and perhaps two, have found their way into it.

The title of the work is as follows: "Catechismus, that is to say a shorte instruction into Christian religion for the singular commoditie and profyte of childrē and yong people. Set forthe by the most reverende father in God, Thomas Archbyshop of Canterburie, primate of all Englande and Metropolitane. Gualterus Lynne excudebat, 1548."

The cut folio CCI. representing "Christ casting out a devil," has the signature HANS. HOLBEN. The engraving is sufficiently rough, but the composition is simple and good, and not unworthy of the great name it bears. Folio CL. has a cut of a "man at prayer," which is not so unquestionably good, though not without dramatic effect. On the floor near the praying monk is a book on the edges of which are two H's, but the first has lost its cross line. The other cuts of the work though not wanting in merits of composition are wretched as engravings. The circumstance of this work being published in 1548, has led some to infer that Holbein was then still living, but this kind of reasoning might be easily carried to the preposterous; we have only to affirm that no work of an artist can be published after his death, and we have attained it. The singular unskilfulness of the engravings themselves, should the designs belong to Holbein, sufficiently proclaim the fact that he must have been dead when they were executed and published.

The reason I have placed these various wood-cuts under the year 1526, so much before the time of their publication, is

Jonah i. ii. and iii.; and Habakkuk i.; which Chatto notices as additions in later editions are in the early volume before me; the last is the reverse of the Jonah which is one of the finest of the series for sentiment and execution. The edition of 1539 is in the British Museum. At Basel are some proofs printed on one side of the paper only.

Cranmer's Catechism. 1548.

simply that I assume all these designs for book illustration to have been made by Holbein while he was still at Basel. We have seen that some were engraved as early as 1522; and a German folio Bible, published by Christoff Froschauer at Zürich in 1531, contains copies of most of the Bible cuts.* The numerous cuts themselves must have occupied considerable time in their execution, and the drawings again, were most probably made some time before they were put into the engraver's hands. It is not at all likely that Holbein could have had leisure for such works in the first year of his sojourn in England, where he appears to have at once attained so great occupation in drawing and painting portraits, not to mention much other kind of work, that he can have had both little time and also but little inclination to enter into the speculations of foreign booksellers. On the contrary while at Basel he complained of lack of work, and had abundant leisure. His want of employment indeed is the only reason given by Erasmus, for his undertaking his journey to England.

* Hegner, *Hans Holbein*, &c., p. 342.

CHRIST CASTING OUT A DEVIL.

THE THIRD BOOK.

HOLBEIN IN ENGLAND.

CHAPTER XI.

THE PAINTER LEAVES BASEL, AND COMES TO ENGLAND, IN THE AUTUMN OF 1526, CARRYING A LETTER OF INTRODUCTION FROM ERASMUS TO SIR THOMAS MORE IN LONDON.

CHAP. XI.

The Painter leaves Basel. 1526-7.

SUCH, as far as can be now ascertained, was the career of Holbein before he settled among us. Before continuing the details of his progress, it will be well to come to a clear understanding of the landmarks from which we start, in an historical sense, as regards the great personages under whose influence his career in this country was directed.

Holbein probably arrived in England towards the close of the year 1526 or when the eighteenth year of the reign of Henry VIII. was advanced in its second semester, but the time is not certain. The plague was raging in Basel in the summer and autumn of this year, and this may have induced in some measure expedited Holbein's decision to leave the city for this country.

The king was yet living in peace with his first wife Catherine of Arragon, and Cardinal Wolsey, the butcher's son, whose cook dressed in satin velvet and gold, was still living at Whitehall (then York Place) as supreme minister of the realm.

CHAP. XI.

The Painter leaves Basel. 1526-7. 18th Henry VIII.

Henry VIII. was born on the 28th of June 1491, and acceded to the throne on the 22nd of April 1509; his wife Catherine, the daughter of Ferdinand and Isabella of Spain, and his brother's widow, was about eight years his senior, she was born in 1483.* Holbein was in his thirty-second year, in the prime of his manhood and at the zenith of his powers as an artist; Henry was in his thirty-sixth year, and Queen Catherine in her forty-fourth. Sir Thomas More, the painter's first patron in England, was in his forty-seventh year, he was not yet Lord High Chancellor but had been already made Treasurer of the Exchequer, Speaker of the House of Commons, and Chancellor of the Duchy of Lancaster, and was high in the king's favour.

To More we know that Holbein had access at once, and was kindly received, but it was years hence before he approached, or probably was even known to, the king personally, or any other of the exalted personages at the head of the state. Still the king can scarcely have remained altogether unacquainted with his works, as he may easily have seen some of them at Sir Thomas's, on the visits he occasionally paid him at his house in Chelsea: the king took great pleasure in passing a few quiet hours with his favourite councillor.

Contemporaries in England.

John Browne was at this time serjeant-painter to the king, an office he held for more than twenty years. He was appointed by patent dated at Eltham, on the 20th December, in the third year of Henry VIII. (1511), with an allowance of 2*d.* a day out of the issues of the lordship of Whitley, in Surrey, and four ells of cloth at Christmas, annually, of the

* In our chronological comparisons in this biography we have no less than four years to bear in mind—the natal years of the king, from the 28th of June; the regnal years of the king, from the 22nd of April; the old ecclesiastical and civic year, from the 25th of March; and the year of the calendar, from the 1st of January. The regnal and ecclesiastical are the important years.

CHAP. XI.

Contemporaries in England. 1526-7. 18th Henry VIII.

value of 6*s.* 8*d.* an ell, from the keeper of the great wardrobe.

He was elected an alderman of London on the 7th of May 1522. He made his will on the 17th of September 1532, and on the 21st of the same month, conveyed to his brother Paynter-stainers his house in Trinity Lane, which has from that time continued to be the London Painters' Hall. Dying soon after, he was buried in the church of St. Vedast, at the west end of Chepe, and his will was proved on the 2nd of December following.*

The principal painter in England in Holbein's time appears to have been LUKE HORNEBOLT of Ghent, if we may at all judge from the salary he received. I have already had occasion to refer to him as being in all probability the "Master Luke" through whom Holbein was led to take up miniature

* See J. G. Nichols, *Contemporaries and Successors of Holbein*, in the ARCHÆOLOGIA, Vol. XXXIX., where Browne's, and some other wills are given in full. Among the painters to whom Browne's house was consigned was a J. H.—John Hethe, the name probably we now write Heath. There was also a William Lucas among these painters, which I assume gives us another Master Lucas. On the former Mr. Nichols gives the following note:—

"JOHN HETHE, citizen and Paynter-stayner of London, was in the royal employment, and was very probably one of those engaged at Nonesuch (a palace of Henry VIII., near the village of Cheam in Surrey). By his will dated 1 August 1562, he bequeathed to his second son Lawrence '*all my moldes and molded worke that I served the King withall,*' and to Lancelot his elder son 'my frames, tentes, stoles, patrons, stones, mullers, with other necessaries belonging or appertaining to Payntour's crafte.' To each of his apprentices he left vjs. viijd., and a grinding-stone. (Prerog. Court of Canterb. Tashe 18.)

"The following items of this will are also remarkable:—'To the Company whereof I am free, to make them a recreation or banket ymmediatelye after my decease xxs. To the Knights of the Round Table (if I do it not in my lifetyme) xxs. to be spent at Myle End.' The latter were no doubt a volunteer company of bowmen. He desired his widow might 'have an honest room in my house, keeping herself sole and unmarried, and using herself after an honest maner with qyetness and love;' and he desired 'nothing in my hall to be moved, as tables, tresselles, stoles, portalles, virgynalls, hangynges, targettes, *pictures in tables*, so long as my said wife dwell in the house.' An account of John Hethe's funeral, after which the mourners were entertained 'with wine and figs, and good ale, and a great dinner,' will be found in Machyn's Diary, p. 32 (Camden Society's Publications); concluding with a statement that, as directed in the will, 'his company had xxs. to make merry withall at the tavern.' Two autograph signatures, *By me Joh'n Heth'*, are attached to the deed of feoffment of 1549;" by which the tenement nunc vulgariter dictum Paynter's Hall, was conveyed by Hethe and others to new Trustees of the Company.

painting.* Mr. Nichols, through the discovery of his will, has added materially to our information respecting this painter. We learn also from Guicciardini† that there were three painters of this family settled in England—the father Gerard, his son Luke, and his daughter Susanna. Gerard had in 1529 a monthly pay of 33*s.* 4*d.*; and he is said to have died here as court-painter to Philip and Mary, in 1558: thus surviving his son many years.

CHAP. XI.

Contemporaries in England.
1526-7.
18th Henry VIII.

The daughter Susannah is spoken of in very high terms as an illuminator, by Guicciardini, who notices her as Luke's sister; and there is a very interesting passage about her in Albert Dürer's *Diary*, on the occasion of his meeting her father at Antwerp in 1521. He says—"*Item, Maister Gerhart Illuminist hat ein Töchterlein, bey* 18 *jahr alt, die heist Susanna, die hat ein Plätlein illuminirt, ein Salvator, dafür hab ich geben* 1 *fl., ist ein gross wunder das ein Weibsbild also viel machen soll*"‡ From this extract we learn that she was born about 1503, and her brother will not have been either very much older or very much younger.‖ Like her father she is reported to have died in this country, in good circumstances at Worcester, as the wife of an English sculptor of the name of Whorstley, apparently her second husband.§

The time of their first visiting this country is uncertain, but Gerard buried a wife in Fulham church in 1529, and his

* Chap. I., p. 22, note.

† *Descrittione di tutti i Paesi Bassi, Altrimenti detti Germania Inferiore.* 3rd Ed., p. 129. The first edition was completed in 1566.

‡ "Item, Master Gerard Illuminator has a young daughter, about eighteen years of age, her name is Susanna; she had made a coloured drawing of our Saviour, for which I gave her a florin; it is wonderful that a female should be able to do such a work." "*Reliquien von Albrecht Dürer.*" Nurnberg, 1828, p. 133.

‖ Guicciardini speaks in high terms of this painter—"Luca Hurembout di Guanto, grandissimo pittore, et singulare nell' arte dell' alluminare." About his sister Susanna he is still more enthusiastic—"L' una fu Susanna Sorella di Luca Hurembout prenominato; la quale fu eccellente nella pittura, massime nel fare opere minutissime oltre ogni credere, et eccellentissima nell' alluminare, in tanto che il gran' Re Henrico ottavo con gran' doni & gran' provisione, la tiro in Inghilterra, dove visse molti anni in gran' favore, & gratia di tutta la corte, & ivi finalmente si mori ricca, & honorata."

§ Immerzeel, *De Levens en Werken der Hollandsche en Vlaamsche Kunstschilders*, &c. Amsterdam, 1842. He gives no authority for this.

CHAP. XI.

Contemporaries in England. 1526-7. 18th Henry VIII.

daughter Susanna had already found an English husband, Master Henry Parker, the king's bowman, and a yeoman of the robes.*

Luke had been made a denizen by patent dated 22 June 26 Hen. VIII. (1534),† is described as a native of Flanders, and was licensed to keep in his service four journeymen or covenant servants, born in parts beyond the sea, notwithstanding the statute to the contrary. By another patent dated the same day he was appointed painter to the king, and obtained a tenement and piece of ground in the parish of St. Margaret, Westminster.‡

Luke died in the month of May in 1544, as appears from a household-book in the possession of Sir Thomas Phillipps. He was paid his salary for the month of April, but in May is entered against his name :—

"*Item, for Lewke Hornebaude, paynter, wages nil. quia mortuus.*"

The following is Hornebolt's will, as published by Mr. Nichols in the ARCHÆOLOGIA, Vol. XXXIX.—Register Thirlby xxxviii :—

"In the name of God Amen. The yere of our Lorde God $m^{l}v^{c}$xliij, the raigne of our Soueraine Lorde Kinge Henrye the eight the xxxv yere of his most graciouse raigne. I Lucas Hornebolt, servante and painter unto the kinges majestie, hole of mynd, this do I ordeine and make my last will and testamente: First I bequeath my soule unto Allmightie God my Maker and my Saviour, and my body to be buryed where yt shall please my frendes in the parish of Saint Marteines in the Filde besides Charyngcrosse. All my gooddes moveable and unmoveable, my dettes paied, I will they shal be praysed and the value thereof to be devided in three equall porcions, and ij of these porcions with all the apparell and jewelles that belonged unto my wyffes

* Trevelyan Papers, i., 158. Quoted by Mr. Nichols.

† Mr. Nichols in the paper referred to, says 1524, which is probably a misprint for 1534.

‡ Patent 26 Hen. VIII., p. 2, m. (32), communicated by James Gardiner, Esq., to Notes and Queries, II. iv., 357. Nichols, ARCHÆOLOGIA, &c.

body I geve and bequeth unto Margaret my wyf, whome I make oone of myne executrices; the third porcion of my gooddes valued, my debtes payde, I geve and bequeth unto Jacomyne my doughter, whome I make th' other executrix. Item I wish that Richard Airell shal be my overseer, and he to have for his paines vj*s.* viij*d.* This will made the viij day of Decembre. Witnes Will'm Delahay and Robt. Spenser." The will was proved before Richard Lyell, LL.D. in the Consistory Court of Westminster, May 27th 1544, with administration to Margaret Hornebolt his relict.

CHAP. XI.

Contemporaries in England.
1526-7.
18th Henry VIII.

We may consider 1527, the nineteenth year of Henry VIII., and when he was first smitten by the charms of Anne Boleyn, as the first year of Holbein's activity in England; but there is no evidence that he approached the king, or any member of the royal family at this time, or even previously to his visit to Basel in 1529. When he returned from Basel and paid England a second visit, apparently in the end of the year 1531, Queen Catherine had already retired to the More in Hertfordshire, another palace that had belonged to Cardinal Wolsey. Though Holbein may have been presented to Henry VIII. in 1532, and even have painted his portrait as early as 1532 or 1533, he does not appear to have entered the king's service until some years later. When John Browne died in 1532, Andrew Wright succeeded him as serjeant-painter, and continued to hold that office during nearly the whole of Holbein's residence here. And though Wright died before Holbein (his will was proved by his widow on the 29th of May 1543) Holbein was not appointed Wright's successor. Whether such an appointment was beneath the reputation or position of our German painter, or above his reach, I will not venture to guess. Unless his burgher-ship of Basel interfered, the objection to him could not have been that he was a foreigner, for Anthony Toto, also a foreigner, succeeded to the dignity. Holbein may either have wanted court-influence, or possibly his reputation was not then what it has since become.

CHAP. XI.

Catherine of Arragon. 1526-7. 18th Henry VIII

It is difficult to prove a negative, but I conclude that Holbein never painted either Cardinal Wolsey or Queen Catherine of Arragon. The Cardinal died in November 1530, and there is certainly no known portrait of him by Holbein; that at Christ Church, Oxford, a small half-length with the hand in the act of benediction, is a coarse work that scarcely comes into the category of fine art: it bears on its frame the date 1526. Catherine's troubles commenced in 1527: Anne Boleyn was publicly acknowledged as the future queen in 1528; and Catherine of Arragon retired from the world a deserted wife, if not a broken-hearted woman in 1531. It is not very probable that she would have sent for the German painter in her retirement at the More. Even when Anne Boleyn was sharing royal state with her at Greenwich, her circumstances must have made her naturally withdraw from the outside world, but should it have been otherwise, any portrait of her at this time, must have shown us the countenance of an unhappy elderly or middle-aged lady considerably past forty years of age. No miniature or portrait of this queen by Holbein, could show us anything else, and the face must be a Spanish one too. If we can now get no nearer to the truth than common sense may take us, I think we may safely infer that Holbein never painted Catherine of Arragon.

Some of the portraits professedly hers, more especially miniatures, are clearly not hers. I could specify more than one miniature bearing her name, which represents a young pink-faced, pug-nosed, blue-eyed woman; which are certainly no more portraits of this Spanish queen than they are miniatures by Holbein. Most of these spurious designations are quite modern. Walpole had two so-called portraits by Holbein, of Queen Catherine, an oil picture, and a miniature which has been engraved by Harding, but they show nothing of the Spanish type.* There is a miniature in Her Majesty's

* Walpole, in his own "*Description of the Villa at Strawberry Hill,*" says, in describing the contents of the HOLBEIN CHAMBER—"Catherine of Arragon, first wife of Henry VIII., by Holbein: it was in the collection of Sir Robert Walpole,

collection, of a blue-eyed woman, 2¾ in. high by 2 in. wide, much of the same character, and which Mr. Fraser Tytler named Queen Catherine of Arragon, though it actually bore on its back, covered up at the time, the following very interesting inscription.*

CHAP. XI. *Catherine of Arragon.* 1526-7. 18th Henry VIII.

Anna Roper Thomæ Mori Filia
W Hollar pinxit post Holbeinium. 1652.

So that we have here ostensibly a miniature of one of More's daughters, by Hollar, after Holbein, arbitrarily transformed into Queen Catherine, almost in our own time. Anna should evidently be read or written *Mar.* for Margaret was Mrs. Roper's name. This is not the only instance of Margaret Roper figuring as Catherine of Arragon.

In the valuable collection of engraved portraits at Windsor, are several, according to their lettering, of this queen, of the same type as the picture in the National Portrait Gallery, representing a black or dark-eyed woman, with rather a straight nose, and holding a rose in her right hand: but none of the prints indicate the original source of the portrait.

There is one print by Vermeulen after Vanderwerff; another by R. White, and a smaller German print, without the engraver's name. They are all evidently from the same model, which is engraved likewise in Thane's "*British Autography.*" Some have the inscription: EFFIGIES CATHARINAE PRINCIPIS ARTHURI UXORIS HENRICO REGI NUPTAE. A drawing of this Queen in the same collection, made for George III. (6½ in. *h.* by 5½ in. *w.*), has much the same face as these prints, but is different in its costume; it is inscribed — CATHARINA HENRICI VIII. ANGLIAE REG. UX. CAROLI V. CAES. MATERTERA

---

and has been engraved among the '*Illustrious Heads.*'" He then adds, in a note, "Vertue thought it to be Catherine, Duchess of Bar, sister of Henry IV. of France; and so it probably is!" It was sold at the sale of 1842 for 31*l.* 11*s.* In his "*Anecdotes,*" &c., he gives us also the history of the miniature—"I have Catherine of Arragon, a miniature, exquisitely finished; a round on a blue ground. It was given to the Duke of Monmouth by Charles II. I bought it at the sale of the Lady Isabella Scott, daughter of the Duchess of Monmouth." It was sold at the sale of 1842 for 50*l.* 8*s.*

* Communicated to me by Mr. Woodward, her Majesty's librarian.

CHAP. XI.

Catherine of Arragon. 1526-7. 18th Henry VIII.

ANNO AET. XXX.; that is 1513–14, or four years after her accession. She is here by no means a young-looking woman, and is certainly quite unlike the "portrait of a woman with a monkey on her left arm," in the Duke of Buccleuch's collection at Montagu House, and engraved by Greatbach. A similar monkey is introduced into the picture of Sir Thomas More's family. We have a "woman holding a monkey," in the catalogue of Henry VIII.'s pictures, 1547:—No. 26, ITEM, a table with the picture of a womann having a monkey on her hande. The size is not given, but this *woman* was certainly not a queen.

Members and friends of Sir Thomas More's family, as drawn at this time by Holbein, for the family group, and independently, have supplied the materials for the portraits of several royal and noble dames; as is daily becoming more evident, by the appearance in exhibitions of known pictures and drawings under names which do not belong to them; some originals, some copies: the tradition has been broken, and identities have been subsequently invented; then by continuous copying and engraving one spurious generation succeeds another. It is to be hoped that extended publicity will gradually correct these anomalies.

Foreign Rivals in England.

Painters either British or foreign do not appear to have been very scarce in the time of Henry VIII.; the names of many are preserved; yet perhaps not much more than a very small percentage of those who earned a livelihood by painting of some kind—initial-letter writing, glass staining, heraldic painting, and so forth. I do not imagine however that the proportion equalled that of our own time: the population of England and Wales is now nearly five times what it was in the days of "Bluff King Hal." Such men as Holbein were of course scarce; he seems indeed to have almost obliterated the record of every contemporary, by the effect of his own subsequent transcendent reputation, though it is now quite certain that he had several rivals among his contemporaries, whose pretensions were little inferior to his own, if not quite on an equality. Such names

CHAP. XI.

Foreign Rivals in England. 1526-7. 18th Henry VIII.

as Mabuse, Lucas Hornebolt, Penni, Anthony Toto, Girolamo da Treviso, Van Cleef, and even William Stretes, show how far he was from having the field to himself or even without worthy rivals. Unfortunately what our own Englishmen were we do not know, but some of the respectable portraits of this period must undoubtedly have been their work.

Prices in England.

When Holbein came to England the average price of wheat was 6*s.* 8*d.* a quarter, about 9*s.* of our money, though 1527 was a famine* year. Beef and pork were a halfpenny a pound, mutton was three farthings; strong beer was a penny a gallon; good wine from three halfpence to twopence a bottle. There were few vegetables in those days; Holbein did not know what a potato is. They were fixed at these prices by the 3rd of the 24th of Henry VIII.† From other sources we find that here and in France‡ money was worth, on the whole, as regards mere prices of commodities, except wheat, nearly twenty times what it is now worth, and we must never forget this in the estimation of the value of the painter's pay or salary at this time. A penny then was certainly worth, as regards the ordinary necessaries of life, the present shilling, if a shilling was not of as much value in some cases even as a pound now. Money however has itself deteriorated in value,

* "In November, December, and January, 18th Henry VIII. (1526), fell such abundance of rain that thereof ensued great floods, which destroyed corn-fields, pastures, and beasts. Then was it dry till the 12th of April, and from that time it rained every day and night till the 3rd of June, whereby corn failed sore in the year following. In 1527 (19th Henry VIII.) such scarcity of bread was in London that many died for want thereof. The King sent to the city of his own provisions six hundred quarters. The bread-carts then coming from Stratford were met at the Mile End by a great number of citizens, so that the mayor and sheriffs were forced to go and rescue the same, and see them brought to the markets appointed, wheat then being at 30s. the quarter (of our money); but shortly after the merchants of the Steelyard brought from Danske (Danzig) such store of wheat and rye that it was better cheap at London than in any other part of the realm." *A true Relation of the most remarkable Dearths and Famines which have happened in this Realm since the coming in of William the Conqueror up to Michaelmas* 1745. 4to. 1748. Quoted by Jacob in his *Precious Metals*, &c. The German merchants of the Steelyard became afterwards Holbein's good friends, and he has left us some of their portraits.

† *Statutes of the Realm.* Quoted by Froude, *History of England*, Vol. I., ch. i.

‡ Deville, *Comptes de Depenses de la Construction du Chateau de Gaillon.* 4to. Paris, 1850.

CHAP. XI.

Prices in England.
1526-7.
18th Henry VIII.

and this deterioration has to be deducted from the enhancement price; the deterioration of the shilling from Henry's time to ours is 25 per cent.

In estimating the relative value of prices, we must consider therefore not only what money could procure, but what the metallic value of the money itself was—mere prices lead us into too high an appreciation of the rise. "The Norman pound," says Mr. Jacob, "was a troy pound weight of twelve ounces of silver, divided into twenty parts called shillings, and these again divided into twelve parts called either pennys or pennyweights. Thus the money of that period, taking the silver at 5*s.* per ounce, may be valued at three times the same denomination in the present day." From this time the shilling went on constantly changing in value. By Henry IV. a pound of silver was coined into thirty shillings, his shilling accordingly being equivalent to the present florin. Edward IV. reduced the value of the shilling still further by coining a pound into thirty-six and a-half of these pieces. Henry VIII. again reduced it, and in Holbein's time the shilling was worth about 1*s.* 4*d.* of our money, the pound being coined into forty-five shillings; and afterwards into forty-eight. In the sixth year of Edward VI. the pound made sixty shillings, and Queen Elizabeth finally reduced the shilling to about its present value, sixty-two to the pound; the pound sterling remaining twenty shillings throughout.*

Measuring Holbein's salary by the above test, we have 30*l.* or six hundred shillings at 1*s.* 4*d.* each, which is exactly 40*l.* of our money, and estimating the productive worth of silver at about twelve times that of the present day, his 30*li.* were to him nearly what a salary of 500*l.* is to the present civil servant; or calculating more strictly on the scale of the old shilling, and allowing 25 per cent. for deterioration in value, we may consider it the equivalent of quite 400*l.* of our money.†

* *An Historical Enquiry into the Production and Consumption of the Precious Metals.* By William Jacob, Esq., F.R.S. 2 vols. 8vo. London, 1831.

† The same rate of wages continued with little alteration throughout the reign of Henry VIII. "In the Hampton Court accounts for 28 Hen. VIII., even

CHAP. XI.

Prices in England. 1526-7. 18th Henry VIII.

Much has been said of the enormous wealth in the precious metals of Cardinal Wolsey, yet this was only comparative. What he possessed would be but an ordinary allowance for an English nobleman of the present day. Stow represents his silver plate as something fabulous, but in the inventory of his effects, preserved in Rymer's *Foedera* (p. 375) a very much more modest account is given; he possessed altogether 9,565 ounces, worth according to the money value of that day, 3*s.* 8*d.* per ounce. At the moderate rate of 5*s.* per ounce in our money, the total value would be about 2,400*l.* only.

Plate was the luxury of the rich; common people were obliged to be content with wood and pewter; the gentry however also used wooden cups. Mr. Eyston of East Hendred possesses the can commonly used by Sir Thomas More; it is a pint cup, with a lid and handle made of pieces of oak bound together by rings of silver, and narrower at the top than the bottom; it is still perfect. Ordinary houses at this time were of a very primitive character; they were commonly made of wooden frames filled in with mud and straw, with thatched roofs, the ground-floor being the flattened earth: even the wealthy had no carpets, they had to put up with clean rushes or straw or mats of the same material. The whole population of England and Wales in Henry VIII.'s time was about four millions only.

Henry VIII., whose court was considered the most magnificent in the world, did not spend 20,000*l.* a year; yet there was not that difference in the cost of articles of luxury that there was in the cost of articles of common consumption.

The salary of a parish priest not much before this date was

---

in the winter months superior carpenters are paid 8*d.*, 7*d.*, and 6*d.* a day; prentices, 6*d.*, 5*d.*, and 4*d.*; wire-drawers, 8*d.*; bricklayers, 6*d.*; prentices, 5*d.*; joiners, 7*d.*; prentices, 6*d.*, 5*d.*, and 4*d.*; plumbers, 7*d.*; scaffolders, 6*d.*; plasterers, 8*d.*; the servitors, 5*d.*; netmakers, 6*d.*; prentices in the King's closet, 10*d.*, 9*d.*, and 8*d.*; gardeners, 6*d.*; common labourers, 4*d.*, some 4½*d.*; chalk-diggers, 5*d.*; and the same for the summer months. Weeders in the King's new garden, all women, 3*d.* a day; but in another entry two women employed in weeding two days are paid 8*d.* each. The pheasant-keeper at Hampton Court had 2*s.* the week, and 4*d.* for his bed, with an extra allowance for seed, eggs, &c." Brewer's *Letters and Papers, Foreign and Domestic, of the Reign of Henry VIII.* 1862. Vol. I., p. cxii.

CHAP. XI.

Prices in England. 1526-7. 18th Henry VIII.

about five guineas a year, 5*l.* 6*s.* 8*d.*, rarely more; labourers, skilled and ordinary, received from 8*d.* to 3*d.* a day, accordingly; and even distinguished painters received only from one guinea and a half to five guineas for a picture; but the remuneration of the painter was quite capricious, and sometimes, compared with other payments, exceedingly high.* An

* Felix Summerly (Mr. Henry Cole, C.B.) in his Hampton Court Handbook. 12mo. 1852, has given some interesting notes on the wages of labour in Cardinal Wolsey's time, from original accounts preserved in the Public Record Office, respecting work done at Hampton Court. In note B, page 70, is the following:—"PAINTERS—The master at 12*d.* Three at 8*d.*; and one grinder of colours at 5*d.* the day." These were probably what we call house-painters.

In page 82 is a note respecting Anthony Toto—Toto dell' Nunziata, one of the King's painters, an Italian of whom very little is known; he must however have been a man of distinction afterwards, as in 1543 he succeeded Andrew Wright, as serjeant-painter to Henry VIII. By the assistance of Mr. Charles A. Cole, of the Record Office, I have found these and some other entries of interest—*Hampton Court Accounts*, Chapter House. Vol. C., 6, 12. Dispensing with the old orthography, we find the following entry, which belongs to the year 1530, the 22nd of Henry VIII. (page 106):—

"Painting of divers tables as ensueth: —To Antonye Tote, painter, for the painting of five tables standing in the King's library—First, one table of Joachim and St. Anne. Item, another table, how Adam delved in the ground. Item, the third table, how Adam was droven out of Paradise. Item, the fourth table, of the burying of our Lord. Item, the fifth table, being the last table, of the burying of our blessed Lady. The said Antonye, taking for the said five tables, by a bargain in great, 6*l.* 13*s.* 4*d.*" Toto appears to have been also a restorer of old pictures, from the following entry, in the same page:—"Item, to the said Antonye for sundry colours by him employed and spent upon the old painted tables in the King's privy closet, 13*s.* 4*d.*" On page 16 of the same volume, is "also paid to Antoyne Tote, painter, for the painting of four great tables—that is to say, one table of our (Lady) of Pity; another table of the four Evangelists; the third of the *Maundythe* (the feet-washing on Maundy Thursday?). The fourth (omitted). The said Antonye taking for the said tables, by a bargain with him made, by great—20*l.* soll." Here we have an able foreign painter executing by contract, large pictures at 5*l.* each: those above referred to, which he painted for 1*l.* 6*s.* 8*d.* each, must have been small pictures. Some of these works may possibly yet be recognised. As Antony Toto, according to an extract from the "Trevelyan Papers" given by Mr. Nichols in the *Notices* quoted (ARCHÆOLOGIA, Vol. XXXIX.), was in this year, 1530, already in receipt of a salary of 25*l.* a year from the King, it would appear from the above payments, that these royal salaries were honorary, or retaining fees for express duties, but not comprising payment for pictures; unless indeed the above-mentioned pictures were executed before the date of the warrant granting the pension. The following is the quotation:—"Item, paid to Anthony Toto and Bartholomew Penni, painters of Florence, upon several warrants being dated the 4th day of June, Anno xxij°, for their wages, after the rate of 25*li.* a year to every of them, to be paid unto them quarterly, &c., during the King's pleasure, 18*li.* 15*s.*" They had further an allowance for *livery*

Prices in England. 1526-7. 18th Henry VIII.

income of 20*l.* a year qualified a country gentleman to be a justice of the peace.* The price of land was in proportion. The father of Hugh Latimer, the great reformer of the church, was a solid English yeoman, of Thurcaston in Leicestershire. "He had no lands of his own," but he rented a farm "of four pounds by the year," on which "he tills so much as kept half a dozen men; he had walk for a hundred sheep, and meadow ground for thirty cows."† We find the salaries of painters varying from ten and twenty pounds to upwards of sixty pounds per annum, and these I assume to have been simply honorary or retaining fees; the painter's time may have been still at his own disposal, with the exception probably of some occasional work of ceremony and state heraldry; such as providing tabards for the heralds, for instance; or presenting the King with a painting on New Year's day; and even in that case a present was given in return. Holbein's was not one of the highest pays given; but as time advanced they seem to have slowly but gradually been increased. Edward VI. gave better pay than his father; Guillim Stretes, a Dutchman, and the painter I imagine of not a few "Holbeins," had a salary of 62*l.* 10*s.* from that King. But even in 1538 a female artist, Mrs. Lavinia Teerlinck, the daughter of Simon Benninck of Antwerp, the celebrated miniature painter, was in receipt of a higher salary than Holbein by 6*l.*: she became still more

—against the 8th November of this year, the 22nd of Henry VIII. (1530) is this entry—"To Anthony Toto and Bartholomew Penni, painters, for their livery coats, 45*s.*"

Painters were in receipt also of a daily wage, when employed. In the volume of the *Hampton Court Accounts*, quoted above, are the following entries:—

Page 110, 22nd Henry VIII.

"Painters new painting and gilding certain antique heads brought from Greenwich to Hanworth at the King's commandment, and new garnishing of the same.

Antonye Tote at xii*d.* the day.
Philyp Arkeman at x*d.* the day.
Lewes Williams at ix*d.* the day.
John Devynk at iij*d.* the day."

In another place—

"ALSO paid to Anthony Toto and John De la Mayn, the King's painters, for their wages, coming from London to Hanworth for to see the finishing and setting up of certain antique heads new painted and gilded, either of them by the space of three days at xii*d.* the day, for themselves and their horses —vis." Page 550. 24th Henry VIII. June.

* Froude's *History of England*, Introduction, Vol. I.

† Latimer's *Sermons*, p. 101. Quoted by Froude, Vol. II., p. 95.

CHAP. XI.

Social state of England. 1526-7. 18th Henry VIII.

distinguished as a miniature painter in the times of Mary and Elizabeth. If she deserved her great celebrity, it is just possible that some of the delicate miniatures ascribed to Holbein are the work of her hand.*

The years that Holbein resided in England constitute perhaps the most important and exciting period of our history; we are still reaping the harvests from the seeds of those days, social, spiritual, moral and physical. Priestcraft had filled the measure of its iniquities, and the worried flocks at length turned upon their destroyers, and avenged the slavery of ages. The influence of the great Wittemberg reformer was already felt in our island. Patrick Hamilton,† our protomartyr, had gone over to Germany to look on the arch-heretic with his own eyes; he spoke with Luther and with Melancthon, and returned to his country, here to spread the contagion of his perilous doctrines, dangerous indeed to the priests. So the bishops seized him, and early in 1527, in front of the old

---

* See Weale's *Beffroi*, Vol. II., which contains an account of Benninck and his daughter Liévine; her husband George Teerlinck was not an Englishman, but of the village of Blankenbergh, near Bruges. Simon Benninck settled in Bruges in 1518, and died there in 1561. Lavinia is noticed by Vasari—"Levina, figlia di maestro Simone da Bruggia suddetto, che dal detto Enrico d'Inghilterra fu maritata nobilmente, ed avuta in pregio dalla Reina Maria, siccome ancora (1566) è dalla Reina Lisabetta." Guicciardini also notices her, *writing in* 1566, he says—"Et di donne vive nomineremo quattro: la prima è Levina, figliaola di maestro Simone di Bruggia gia mentionato, la quale nel miniare come il padre è tanto felice & eccellente, che il prefato Henrico Re d'Inghilterra la volle con ogni premio haver' a ogni modo alla sua corte, ove fu poi maritata nobilmente, fu molto amata dalla Regina Maria, & hora è amarissima dalla Regina Elisabetta." Mr. J. G. Nichols gives the following details—"At Midsummer, 1547, *Maistris Leryn Terling paintrix*, was receiving quarterly wages of x*li*. (Trevelyan Papers, I., 195, 203, 205). In 1556 she presented to Queen Mary, as a New Year's gift, a small picture of the Trynitie (Progresses of Queen Elizabeth, Vol. I., p. 34). In 1558 (the 1st of Elizabeth) she presented *the Queen's picture finely painted upon a card*, which remained with Her Majesty, under the care of Mrs. Newton; and had in return *one casting bottell guilt*, weighing $2\frac{3}{4}$ oz. In 1561, on the like occasion, there was presented—*By Mrs. Levina Terling, the Queene's personne and other personages in a box finely painted.* This present was so much esteemed by the Queen that it remained *with her said Majestie, i.e.*, was retained in her own keeping. The paintrix received in return *one guilt salt with a cover*, weighing $5\frac{1}{2}$ oz. (Progresses of Queen Eliza., Vol. I., pp. 117, 126)." *Contempora ies and Successors of Holbein*, &c. ARCHÆOLOGIA, Vol. XXXIX.

† Nephew of the Earl of Arran, and titular Superior of Ferns.

College of St. Andrew's, they burnt him for *Lutheranism*, thus hurrying the consummation of their own destiny; from each drop of their young victim's blood sprung up a fresh heretic; the green blades of promise, as it were, bursting out from the barren soil.*

CHAP. XI.

Social state of England. 1526-7. 18th Henry VIII.

In this year 1527 too, a practicable breach was made also in the material defences of Rome; Giulio de' Medici as Clement VII., Pontifex Maximus, then sitting in the chair of St. Peter, was shut up in his own stronghold on the Tiber, by the orthodox forces of the most Christian King and Emperor. 1527 saw also the dawn of Henry's difficulties and troubles, and many were the marvellous incidents exhibited to Holbein in the career of his great patron; from the hanging of a monk or the suppression of a monastery to the crowning or beheading of queens, and the successful defiance of priestly curses and papal interdicts. Holbein could here witness the true Renaissance, not of art only, but of society, religion, and humanity. Our painter had the privilege of almost constant intercourse with nearly all the most prominent agents of this great revolution; there was scarcely a man or even a woman of great mark, of this drama of real life, of whom we have not some sketch or picture by Holbein; and we may depend upon it that we have, through the master-pencil of this Augsburg painter, more faithful portraits, truer effigies of the prominent men and women of Henry's time, than of those of any other period of our history, not excepting even the days of Vandyck or of Reynolds.

From Basel to London. 1526-7. 18th Henry VIII.

Such was the land of promise to which the humble painter of Basel hastened, with the letter of Erasmus in his pocket, as the key or talisman by which its treasures were to be made accessible to him. He was sufficiently justified in being sanguine in the promise held out to him in the answer of Sir Thomas More to Erasmus, in his letter of December 1525, which has been already quoted in the IXth Chapter.

Among the recently discovered documents concerning Hol-

---

* Froude, *History of England*, &c., Vol. IV., p. 58.

CHAP. XI.

From Basel to London. 1526-7. 18th Henry VIII.

bein, is a letter of the 4th of July 1526, written on the painter's behalf by Heinrich Meltinger then Burgomaster of Basel, to the Vicar of the Order of St. Anthony at Issenheim. The elder Holbein had painted an altar-piece for the convent of Issenheim, and had left a quantity of painting materials in the place, of considerable value, Holbein had several times asked for these things, for his father, and after the father's death, for himself as heir, but in vain. The things had been plundered or destroyed in the peasant riots of the time, and the Burgomaster of Basel now wrote, with a view to procuring for Holbein a just compensation for his loss.* Our painter had need of all the money he could collect, on the eve of such a journey as he now contemplated: we will trust he got his due.

He carried at the same time a letter to Peter Giles—Aegidius, chiefly known to the learned of his own world for his travels in Asia and in Africa, and for an account he published of Thrace and Constantinople, and known to our world, like a great many others, from the circumstance of having had his face painted by a very able painter, though Hans Holbein was not the man. The letter to Aegidius is dated August the 29th 1526, so that the journey was undertaken probably in the fine early autumn weather, good for any kind of travelling, but especially good for the pedestrian, and it is possible that Holbein's means did not admit of any very much more expensive method of passage. Rhine rafts and canal boats also afford an inexpensive mode of locomotion. Supposing that Holbein begged his way in a certain measure, he would have done only what was quite common among English university students three hundred years ago, or among German students even thirty years ago. He was doubtless encumbered with but little luggage, any strong man of ordinary common sense may easily carry all necessary change on his back, for a much longer journey than from Basel to London; and though Holbein no doubt had his sketching folio with him, it is very improbable that he bur-

* Woltmann, *Holbein, &c.*, *Beilagen*, p. 374.

dened himself with a portrait of Erasmus: we know that this was not necessary, as the portrait or specimen had been already sent in 1525.

Quintin Matsys the great master of Antwerp, was well known to Erasmus and had painted his portrait, as already assumed. It was natural that Holbein in passing through the great city of Antwerp should wish to see its renowned painter, but we have no record of their meeting. Erasmus in his letter to Aegidius mentions Quintin in an incidental manner only. He says:—"He who gives you this letter, is the man who painted me. I will not trouble you with his praises, though he is a distinguished artist. *If he should wish to see Quintin*, and you have not leisure yourself to introduce him, you can let your servant show him the house. Here the arts are torpid; he seeks England, in order to scrape together a few angels. Through him you can write what you like."*

It is just possible that Holbein arrived here in October 1526, but we have no positive evidence when he left Basel or when he arrived here; we know nothing whatever of any stay in Antwerp, or of any visit to Quintin Matsys; but we know that he did not paint the portrait of Aegidius at Longford Castle. Dr. Waagen's imaginary delay of Holbein in Antwerp on that ground therefore is dissipated; just as his theory about the pictures of "Lais Coronthiaca" and the "Venus," being painted on the same occasion, is also quite groundless. We know that Holbein was in England in 1527, because we have the portraits of Englishmen bearing that date.

The painter is said to have left Basel by stealth, or on the

---

* Qui has reddit, est is, qui me pinxit. Ejus commendatione te non gravabo, quanquam est insignis artifex. Si cupiet visere Quintinum, nec tibi vacabit, hominem adducere, poteris per famulum commonstrare domum. Hic frigent artes; petit Angliam, ut corradat aliquot Angelatos, per eum poteris quæ voles scribere.

An angel or angelet was an English gold coin worth latterly about half a sovereign, so called from the stamp of the archangel Michael on it. Its original value was that of the noble, 6s. 8*d*., which would be about its worth when Holbein came to England: it had on the reverse at this time "O crux ave spes unica." They commenced in Edward IV.'s reign and ceased with Charles I. See the *Penny Cyclopædia*, art. Angel.

CHAP. XI. *From Basel to London.* 1526-7. 18th Henry VIII.

plea that he would shortly return; to escape from his wife, says Patin, which I believe to be false; Erasmus gives a better reason in the letter quoted—want of work; and the painter was not only justified in trying a greater field, but showed his wisdom in doing so. The common story is that the then Earl of Arundel, passing through Basel, saw some of Holbein's paintings, and being capable of appreciating their worth, all the more from having just visited Italy, advised him to try his fortunes in England. As Erasmus was well acquainted with England, Holbein may have got the same advice from him also. This Earl of Arundel story, is based apparently on an application to Holbein of an anecdote which, we learn from Pliny, belongs originally to Apelles the renowned Greek painter, though the coincidence may of course have a genuine foundation.

Ptolemy Soter and Apelles, during the life of Alexander, were not on good terms: and when the painter was afterwards forced by bad weather to put into the port of Alexandria, during the reign of Ptolemy, in Egypt, some of the great painter's rivals, aware of the antipathy Ptolemy had to Apelles, induced the king's clown to invite the painter to sup with the king. He accordingly went, much to the surprise and indignation of Ptolemy, who angrily demanded by what authority he had ventured into his presence. Apelles, though unable to answer, unabashed, seized an extinguished coal from the hearth, and in an instant sketched a man's face upon the wall, in which Ptolemy, even from the first lines, immediately recognized his buffoon: the painter was thenceforth received into favour with the king.* With this story compare the following —When Sir Thomas More asked Holbein, who it was that advised him to visit England, he replied that he had forgotten his name, but seizing a piece of charcoal, with a ready hand sketched a face, when the Earl of Arundel was instantly recognized.

Holbein's Earl of Arundel was, not Henry as Walpole supposes, but William Fitzalan, the twenty-first earl who was born

* See my "*Epochs of Painting,*" 1864.

in 1484, succeeded to the title in 1524, and survived Holbein a few months: he died January 23rd, 1544.* According to our anecdote however, as Holbein delayed his visit some time, it was possibly Thomas Fitzalan the twentieth earl, who advised him to try his fortunes in England. As this story may be true, I have not suppressed it. Any how we in England are certainly indebted to the man, whoever he was, who was the cause of Holbein's settling amongst us.

CHAP. XI.

From Basel to London.
1526-7.
18th Henry VIII.

On his journey to us Holbein on this occasion, or perhaps later, passed through Strassburg, and under the plea of procuring work, visited the principal painter of the city, soliciting employment: the sequel is another stock anecdote in the history of art. Patin does not tell his story well, and whether Holbein went out of mere curiosity to have an interview with a distinguished painter, remaining himself unknown, or for any other purpose, such as creating curiosity about himself, we are left to guess; just as we are left to guess the name of the painter.

Holbein called the next day, when the master was out, and left his specimen in the picture of a fly which he painted on the forehead of an unfinished portrait then standing on the master's easel. The painter returned home, saw the fly on his picture and attempted to drive it away, in vain; his effort resulting only in astonishment, and admiration of his unknown visitor, whom he immediately sought out in the city, but Holbein had left and was already on his road to England.

We have a portrait in the National Gallery that would very well serve for the subject of such an anecdote as this — the portrait of a Swiss lady of the maiden name of Hofer, on whose large white cap a fly has rudely settled, and the illusion is not bad. This picture is ascribed, at hazard, to Sigmund Holbein, our painter's uncle; to fit it to this story we should ascribe it to HANS BALDUNG commonly called GRIEN, who was at this time the principal painter of the district, and was a little later finally domiciled at Strassburg.

---

* See Tierny's *Castle and Town of Arundel.*

CHAP. XI.

From Basel to London. 1526-7. 18th Henry VIII.

Holbein might well have a curiosity about this master as he then had a great reputation, and was the painter of the celebrated altar-piece in the cathedral of Freiburg in Breisgau, where are the two altar-wings by Holbein himself, noticed in the seventh chapter.

Hans Baldung's picture is still in good preservation; he was about twenty years older than Holbein, having been born about 1475, in Gmünd in Swabia. His altar-piece in the cathedral, representing the Crucifixion, is signed "JOANNES BALDUNG COG. GRIEN GAMUNDIANUS. DEO ET VIRTUTE AUSPICIBUS FACIEBAT." He was painting for the cathedral during the years 1513–16. Between 1533 and 1552 he held the office of court painter to the Bishop of Strassburg, and was settled in that city, where he died on the 10th of August 1552. It appears that his labours for the Chapter of Freiburg Cathedral were so extensive, that they could not afford payment down, but commuted the capital sum for an annuity, and it is only through this circumstance that we have accurate knowledge of the painter's death, which is recorded in the books of the cathedral as follows:—"1552 *uf Circumcisionis Domini. It.* 8 *pfund* 12 *schilling* 6 *pfenning dem Baldung maler zu Strassburg. Obiit Lorencii* Ao. 1552."*

Among the monograms given to Holbein is HB; why I cannot explain, he certainly never used it; and at Hampton Court, is a small panel 16 in. *h.* by 13 in. *w.*, numbered 1085, which is described in the catalogue as Holbein by himself. It is the half-length of a young man with a beard, in a black cap on which is a medal, he wears a black doublet and furred gown, with a gold chain and cross, on his neck, and a sword by his side: in his left hand he holds a glove; he has a ring on his forefinger, with yellow devices on a blue shield. This portrait is not by Holbein, nor does it represent Holbein; it bears the known monogram of Baldung, who was a famous portrait painter—HGB H and B. with G on the cross-bar of the H,

* J. Heller, *Kunstblatt*, 1846, p. 122.

and is dated A.D. 1539 : he sometimes used the simple H. B., for his name was Baldung not Grien, or Grün as it is commonly written. The picture is injured, and has been retouched; the upper part of the G has disappeared, but I have no doubt about the monogram having been originally similar to that of Hans Baldung called Grien, and possibly his.

CHAPTER XII.

Holbein as the Guest of Sir Thomas More at Chelsea, 1527–9.

Chap. XII.

Earliest English Portraits.
1527.
19th Henry VIII.

ITHER late in 1526 or early in 1527 it seems pretty certain that Holbein was received by Sir Thomas More at Chelsea; and in this chapter we have to review the labours and events of this first visit to England, the duration of which extended to between two and three years, a period that he might be absent from Basel without forfeiting his rights of citizenship, and a term for which a man might reasonably leave his family without being liable to the accusation of desertion of it; Holbein however no doubt had the required leave of absence from the town-council, at the head of which was some time during his absence his friend and patron Jacob Meier zum Hasen, of whose family we have the noble portraits at Darmstadt and at Dresden.

The painter as the guest and retainer of Sir Thomas More, who lived at Chelsea in a house built by himself, and where he had a small farm, would necessarily be circumscribed in his practice to the circle of Sir Thomas, which was however an extensive and a learned one. Many of More's friends are among the Windsor drawings. Archbishop Warham was intimate with Erasmus, as well as Sir Thomas More; and the king's astronomer Kratzer, was also in the same circle and intimate with More's friend Aegidius. Collet Dean of St. Paul's is another of More's friends whose reputed portrait is among these drawings, and it is an excellent one; but if the dean died in 1519, this must be a misnomer. Sir Thomas's house at Chelsea is supposed to be that now called Beaufort House; he had out-buildings, and a gallery a little way from his house. Sir Thomas was of course in affluent circumstances, though his landed property was but small. As a barrister he had made an income of above 400*l.* a year, which was then worth about 8000*l.* of the present time.*

CHAP. XII.

Earliest English Portraits.

1527. 19th Henry VIII.

The dated portraits of this period are not many, but we have a few very interesting ones:—that of Archbishop Warham, the stanch opponent of all church reform, and no doubt as good a hater of the Protestants as Sir Thomas himself; and that of Sir Henry Guildford, the Comptroller of the King's Household, whom I assume also to have been an intimate friend of Sir Thomas More: both have shaven faces, beards were not yet in fashion. These were high personages for the obscure young German painter to have as sitters, but they were of course procured through his patron's influence, not his own reputation, though Holbein proved himself quite worthy of the occasion, and did not allow his opportunities to be lost. Both these portraits are noble pictures; but Sir Henry Guildford's has now considerably suffered, and the archbishop's we have in duplicate, to say nothing of inferior copies.

The Windsor Drawings.

Of both the above portraits, there are drawings, or preparatory sketches, in the Windsor portfolios, which collection, perhaps the most valuable of all the Holbein treasures preserved to us, was apparently the gradual accumulation of the studies, made by the painter, for the various pictures he executed during his fourteen or fifteen years' practice as a portrait painter in this country; not that these drawings show

* See the original Memoir by William Roper; also the "*Life*," &c., by his grandson Thomas More, 8vo., London, 1726; and Arthur Cayley's *Memoirs of Sir Thomas More, with a new Translation of his Utopia*, &c. 2 vols. 4to. London, 1808.

CHAP. XII. — *The Windsor Drawings.* 1527. 19th Henry VIII.

us all or perhaps even half of the portraits he painted here, because we have several portraits of which there are no drawings, and in many cases it is evident that the picture is simply an adaptation or completion of the original paper or parchment study, by a little after-colouring and varnishing. Some of these drawings are much more advanced than others, being nearly or quite completed in body colours or crayons; such require but a coat of varnish to make them to all intents and purposes as effective and lasting as oil pictures.

It is evident that this system of drawing first from the life, in coloured chalks and charcoal, with occasional force touches put in with the pen or the hair pencil, was developed by Holbein before he came to England; there are several examples in the Basel Museum, as for instance the man's head with the large slouched hat, and the studies of heads for the "Meier Madonna" picture. His own portrait in the same collection, one of the Amerbach drawings, engraved at the beginning of this volume, is an example of a more finished specimen of this tempera or crayon drawing.

Among Holbein's earliest portraits in this country, is also certainly John Reskimer's of Murthyr, a Cornish gentleman, of which the original drawing is in the Windsor collection. This profile though showing completely Holbein's tone of colouring is not so palpably original as some other of his earlier works described: it is quite possibly a copy. However it is a fine picture; it represents a young man seen in profile, the regard turned to the spectator's left; he wears a small black cap, and has a long red beard; and what is somewhat uncommon at this time, the hands are admirably drawn. The back-ground is green, of a blueish tone, and is varied by some sprigs of vine, very skilfully put in. On oak, or possibly on paper or parchment attached to oak, 17½ inches *h.* by 12½ in. *w.*

Among the Windsor drawings, also, are several of Sir Thomas More's family, showing still more fully that the method of making such preparatory studies was a part of Holbein's already established practice, and not commenced here. For instance, we have of Sir Thomas's family, as they

LORD VAUX.

From the Drawing by Holbein at Windsor.

The Windsor Drawings. 1527. 19th Henry VIII.

appear in the large picture at Nostell Priory belonging to Mr. Charles Winn, apparently seven preliminary studies, on white paper, from which the heads in the picture seem to have been painted, and we know that these studies belong to the time of Holbein's first visit to this country, as the picture or composition in which they occur was certainly completed in 1529 before the painter's return to Basel.

The heads are: Sir John More, the father; Sir Thomas More; John More, the son of Sir Thomas; Anne Cresacre, afterwards the son's wife; Elizabeth Dancey, Sir Thomas's second daughter; Cicely Heron, the youngest daughter; and a cousin or relative named Margaret Gigs, afterwards Mrs. Clement. There is another something like Margaret Roper his eldest daughter, but this is doubtful. She is called Lady Henegham. The female head-dress was then so peculiar that the individual character very much suffers from it: the favourite covering seems to have been the diamond-shaped cap or hood, with a black veil or fall behind.

Archbishop Warham.

One of the first portraits of importance painted in this country, and a remarkable specimen of the painter's powers, is that of WILLIAM WARHAM, ARCHBISHOP OF CANTERBURY, a half-length, on panel, nearly full face, and showing both hands; a crucifix in his right hand, an open book near his left, and a brown damask curtain in the back-ground. This is a picture as well as a portrait; all the accessaries are excellent, and especially the jewelled crucifix, which is precise and accurate without being hard. We have two excellent examples of this picture:—that exhibited at Manchester in 1857, and now at Lambeth Palace,* and that in the Louvre. The two pictures are so very similar, that one may be a copy of the other, yet they have their differences. The Louvre example is much the more highly coloured and is painted with a thicker impasto; the

* There are two other repetitions of this portrait in Lambeth Palace, one of which, on wood, with a green curtain, has been lately repaired and put under glass; but both these examples seem to be very inferior copies, and will not compare either with that which was at the Manchester Exhibition, or that in the Louvre. I have carefully examined all. 32 in. high, by 26 wide.

CHAP. XII. *Archbishop Warham.* 1527. 19th Henry VIII.

Lambeth example is more carefully modelled, more dryly executed and grey in colour. As we cannot compare the two side by side it is difficult to come to a decided opinion, my inclinations lead towards the Lambeth picture as on the whole preferable, notwithstanding its less showy colouring. The Windsor drawing from which the head is painted is admirable, though now much rubbed and damaged. Both pictures are inscribed—*Anno Dm̄. MDXXVIJ. Etatis sue LXX.* That at Lambeth is said to have been presented to the archbishop by Holbein (more probably by Sir Thomas More). It was lost during the civil wars, but was recovered again, as was supposed, by Sir William Dugdale, who restored it to Lambeth in the time of Archbishop Sancroft.* "Archbishop Parker," says Walpole, "entailed this, and another of Erasmus, on his successors; they were stolen in the civil war, but Juxon repurchased the former." The history of the Louvre portrait is not known, but it belonged to Louis XIV. I instance this picture as an illustration that Holbein had the power of seeing what he looked at, and of perfectly transferring to his picture what he saw. *Suum cuique* might have been Holbein's motto; he gave every man his own, substituting nothing from himself, and this I imagine to be a very high quality. We have already seen, from many of his works enumerated, that he was a man of sufficient powers of imagination, but he was the master of his imagination, and kept it well under control: this too is a distinction. Too many painters, and especially portrait painters, are unable to quite see what they look at, and to borrow John Hutton's expressive word, only *slobber* what they see after all.

Sir Henry Guildford.

Another fine example for style and character, is the half-length of SIR HENRY GUILDFORD, BART., with the chamberlain's staff in his right hand, now in the Queen's closet in Windsor Castle.† It is very well modelled and very dignified in pose and expression, but is not in a fit state to judge of its colouring, which is not at all like that of the archbishop's portrait, in the

* Lysons and Brayley.

† On oak, 32 in. high by 26 wide.

Sir Henry Guildford. 1527. 19th Henry VIII.

Louvre; it is very dirty and much cracked. The back-ground is characteristic—a green curtain on brass rings and rod, drawn aside; and a green ground with some young vine branches or ivy twigs. He has introduced such branches in the back-grounds of many of his smaller portraits, painted in England. This portrait also is inscribed on a cartellino—*Anno D: MCCCCCXXVIJ. Etatis suae xlix.* There is an excellent portrait bearing this year's date, in the gallery at Dresden, representing a small half-length of a man, nearly full face, in a black furred cap and dark dress or gown edged with black velvet; his right hand rests on a box or table, in the left he holds a paper, inscribed 1527. The cut of the hair and the shaven face harmonize with other portraits of this time, indicating some Englishman; and at the same time aiding to justify the ascription of the picture to Holbein. It was in the Dresden Gallery as far back as 1722, having been purchased by Baron Rechenberg for the Elector Augustus II., King of Poland. On wood, about 15½ in. high, by 12 in. wide.

This gallery possesses three other small excellent portraits, on wood, ascribed to Holbein; but of uncertain persons and of uncertain time. They are all mentioned in the original old inventory of the year 1722, which was drawn up for the magnificent Augustus II.*

Sir Thomas More.

SIR THOMAS MORE'S was naturally one of the first of the portraits painted by Holbein in England. Passavant in his "*Kunstreise durch England und Belgien*" mentions a portrait of Sir Thomas More, with the date 1527, as being in the gallery at Brussels, and supposes it to be that which was in 1823 in Mr. Beckford's collection at Fonthill Abbey: he speaks of it as a life-sized bust portrait. The small freely executed portrait of a man, with a book in his hand, on a bright green ground, 9 in. high by 6½ in. wide, now in the gallery at Brussels, and

---

* See the catalogues. In that ascribed to Heineken or Lehninger, published in French in 1786, besides "Mr. Morett," are ten pictures under Holbein's name: in the catalogues of J. Hübner, 1862, they are reduced to seven. A very elaborate history of the Dresden pictures, as far as known, is given in Dr. Schäfer's *Königliche Gemälde-Gallerie zu Dresden.* 3 vols. 8vo. 1860.

CHAP. XII. — *Sir Thomas More.* 1527. 19th Henry VIII.

of which there is a print by Vorsterman, reversed, does not correspond with this description: nor does it agree with the portrait of Sir Thomas More. I observed no such date upon it, nor is a date mentioned in the new catalogue of that gallery by M. Edouard Fetis.* This picture is said to have come from the old collection of M. Jean Van den Wouvere. It corresponds no better with the description of Beckford's picture in his sale catalogue of 1823—"A Portrait of Sir Thomas More, with a medal at his girdle, bearing an inscription; a chateau and garden scene in the distance—*From Lord Lansdowne's Collection.*" In the Lansdowne catalogue, it is called simply a "Portrait by Hans Holbein," and it sold at the sale in 1806 for 24 guineas. The "Dog and dead Game" by Weenix, now in the National Gallery, was sold at the same sale for 56 guineas.

Mr. Huth has a fine life-sized portrait, a sitting half-length, dated 1527, and there are copies of it, but it is not free from retouches. I do not suppose that there is a portrait of Sir Thomas by Holbein of any other date than this of 1527: this is the portrait of the family picture. We have the same head in the same position everywhere; in the Windsor drawing, in the several portraits, and in the family sketch and in the large pictures.

I am acquainted with no other independent Holbein portrait of any of the More family but that of MARGARET ROPER, at Knole;† which whether by Holbein himself or a copy, is a genuine portrait, conspicuous for individuality: it is considerably rubbed and injured, and the hands, especially the left, have been very unskilfully repainted, but it is the same as that of Margaret in the family picture, and very superior to it as a portrait. On wood, 2 ft. 2 in. *h.* by 1 ft. 8 in. *w.* The date of this portrait would be probably 1529, judging from the

* *Catalogue Descriptif et Historique du Musée Royal de Belgique.* 2nd Ed. 1865.

† Contributed to the South Kensington Exhibition, in 1866, by the Countess of Delawarr, as Queen Catherine of Arragon. Walpole possessed a portrait of Margaret Roper, which was copied by Vertue from the family picture. From that at Nostell Priory, I presume.

sketch of the family picture, where the age, twenty-two, is given for that year.

Sir Thomas More. 1527. 19th Henry VIII.

Another portrait of the year 1527, ascribed to Holbein, is that belonging to the Queen, called DR. THOMAS LINACRE. Both the painter however and the subject of this picture must be questioned; the painting is more like that of Quintin Matsys than of Holbein, and Dr. Linacre died in 1524. The portrait is possibly a copy, but it is a good one; it is a small half-length in black cap and coat, a three-quarter face looking to the left, and showing the hands: in his right hand he holds a paper inscribed "*Anno* 1527." On wood 18 in. *h.* by 13 in. *w.*

Sir John Godsalve. 1528. 20th Henry VIII.

Of the year 1528, we have two well-known dated pictures; the small portraits of Sir Thomas and John Godsalve, on the same panel, in the gallery at Dresden; and the king's astronomer Kratzer, life-size, surrounded by his instruments, now in the Louvre.

Among the Windsor drawings, is the half-length of an apparently middle-aged man, finished in body colour, but now much rubbed, and it wants but a coat of varnish to give it the effect of an oil picture. This drawing is worthy of notice not only for its own excellence, which is great, but also as most probably showing us how Holbein prepared his portraits on parchment or paper which he afterwards attached to wood and finished as pictures. This drawing is inscribed "SIR JOHN GODSALVE," yet it appears at first sight to represent the person who is seated writing, in the picture in the Dresden Gallery, where we are led to infer by the writing that his name is Thomas Godsalve. The picture, among the fine examples of this period, is a small panel 20 in. high by 15 in. wide, and is described in the Dresden Catalogue as "Sir Thomas and John Godsalve;" the principal figure and older man in a cap is writing with a quill pen the words—*Thomas Godsalve de Norvico Etatis suae anno quadragesimo septo.* The date—*Anno Dm. MDXXVIIJ.*—is written on a cartellino, in the background over the head of the younger man. There is certainly a strong family likeness between the two men; the second or

CHAP. XII.

Sir John Godsalve. 1528. 20th Henry VIII.

John, the son, uncovered, is seated a little on the right and behind the other. If however the drawing represents this younger man it must have been taken after 1528, for there seems a considerable advance in age. Sir John Godsalve was knighted at the coronation of Edward VI.,* and became afterwards that king's Comptroller of the Mint. The fashion of his hair in drawing and picture is the same as that of Sir Henry Guildford; his face is shaven, but a small stubble beard is indicated in the drawing: there is no beard in the Dresden picture.

Nicolas Kratzer.

The other portrait of this date, that of NICOLAS KRATZER, the astronomer, a native of Munich, now in the Louvre, formerly in Holland House, is not among Holbein's happier pictures, the subject was apparently not a favourable one. The portrait is a half-length, with the face nearly in profile, turned towards his left. He is seated at a table on which are various instruments; in his left hand he holds a polyhedron with various geometrical figures drawn on its sides, and in his right he holds a pair of compasses. On the table is also a paper on which is written his name, and the date 1528—*Imago ad vivam effigiem expressa Nicolai Kratzeri*, &c. in his fortieth year; the rest of the inscription is confused and injured. Holbein's Latin is occasionally very queer, notwithstanding his learned friends: his inscriptions I imagine were not often revised.

Albert Dürer made a drawing of this Kratzer, in 1520, when he was in the Netherlands; at the same time I suppose, as when he made his drawing of Erasmus. Albert notices this in his "Diary," he says—"In Antwerp I took the portrait of Master Nicolas, an astronomer, who resides with the king in England, he was very useful to me; he is a German, a native of Munich." This is the person also of whom Van Mander relates, that when asked by Henry VIII. how it was that he spoke English so badly, replied—"Pardon, your

* Strype, quoted by Walpole. There is a fine photograph of the Windsor drawing by Thurston Thompson.

CHAP. XII. John Fisher. 1528. 20th Henry VIII.

Majesty, how can a man learn English in thirty years?" He can scarcely have been in England anything like twenty years when Holbein painted him.*

Both Sir Henry Guildford and the archbishop, died in 1532; the latter having first protested against all infringement of the powers of the pope, or the privileges of the church, as if it were some close club, and as though it were not enough to claim all spiritual patronage, but it must needs have the monopoly of material prosperity and patronage in this world too.† Happy man, he little imagined what was to come to his Holy Mother, and that his own passing away with a protest only, was an enviable exit, compared with the fate impending over his friends Sir Thomas More, and John Fisher, bishop of Rochester. The portrait of the last, a hard ascetic face, is in one of the Holbein portfolios at Windsor, and is among the most expressive drawings of the series: there is also a fine finished drawing of Fisher in the British Museum. The faces of Warham, More, and Fisher, are all hard and ascetic; but of the three the least hard is certainly the archbishop's: all three are said to have had faith in the "Holy Maid of Kent."

Sir Thomas More.

More had been all his life much of the fanatic, at one time designing to turn Franciscan monk; he even boasted of his hostility to the Protestant reformers. "He so hated this kind of men," he said, "that he would be the sorest enemy that they could have, if they would not repent."‡ Such was the spirit with which this learned man, admitted to have been kind and social when in the midst of his own family circle at Chelsea, took possession of the Great Seals, as Lord High Chancellor of England, in October 1529. No wonder that the *fires* were again lighted at Smithfield. "The crime of the offenders varied," says Mr. Froude;§ "sometimes it was a

---

* "Kratzer in 1550 erected the dial at Corpus Christi Coll., Oxford. *Brit. Topogr.* Vol. II., p. 159. In one of the office-books are entries of payment to him.

April, paid to Nicholas the Astronomer . . . . 11*l.*

Anno 23 (1532?) paid to ditto . . . . . . 5*l.* 4*s.* 0*d.*"

Note by Walpole.

† Froude's *History of England.* Vol. I., p. 370.

‡ More's *Life of More*, &c., p. 211.

§ *History of England.* Vol. II., p. 83.

CHAP. XII.

Sir Thomas More.

1528.
20th Henry VIII.

denial of the corporeal presence, more often it was a reflection too loud to be endured on the character and habits of the clergy; but whatever it was, the alternative lay only between abjuration, humiliating as ingenuity could make it, or a dreadful death." "With Wolsey," says the same writer, "heresy was an error—*with More it was a crime.*" The pious bishop of London at this time was the Dr. Stokesley whose assumed portrait is now at Windsor, and whose character, from Hall, I have already quoted.

More was more tolerant in theory than in practice; he allows liberty of religion in his "Utopia;" but this was before the troubles of the Reformation, and before his pet dogmas received their rude shocks. Opposition hardened him, his own way was dearer to him than his life, for he gave this up rather than admit the king to be supreme head on earth of the Church of England. He gained his victory over the King, who destroyed only his body, not his spirit, but for this victory he sacrificed his own family. His wife was driven from his house at Chelsea, and all his property was seized after his execution, on the 6th of July 1535. It is true, his wife was not the mother of his children; the king however settled 20*l.* a year on her; a sufficiently moderate pension for a chancellor's widow. The name of More's first wife, and the mother of his four children, was Jane Colte: the second was Alice Middleton, a widow when More married her. His favourite daughter Margaret Roper may be said to have carried his skull with her to her premature grave, for she got possession of it after its exposure, for a fortnight, on London Bridge. She was buried in the vault of the Ropers under St. Dunstan's Church at Canterbury; where the skull may still be seen.* Her husband had a house at Canterbury. She died in 1544, in the prime of life; having attained her thirty-seventh year only.†

* See Cayley's *Memoirs, &c.*; *The Gentleman's Magazine* for May 1837; and Lord Campbell's *Lives of the Lord Chancellors.* Vol. II.

† In 1528 Margaret Roper had the plague or sweating sickness, but recovered, as was supposed through her father's prayers. "The manner of its

Sir Thomas was of a middle stature, says his great-grandson More, well-proportioned, of a pale complexion; his hair of a brown colour, his eyes grey, his countenance mild and cheerful (a character hardly supported by his portraits); his voice not very musical, but clear and distinct; his constitution, which was good originally, was never impaired by his way of living, otherwise than by too much study.

CHAP. XII. *Sir Thomas More.* 1528. 20th Henry VIII.

In religion Sir Thomas was a papist of the ultramontane school. In piety he was a great formalist, certainly superstitious, and an ascetic in disposition, as is shown by his whole life. He wore a hair shirt next his skin. "A few days before his execution he gave one which he had been wearing to his daughter Margaret. She bequeathed it to her cousin Margaret Clement, an Augustinian nun at Louvain. There it remained till the French Revolution, and it is now carefully preserved as a relic in a convent established at Spilsburg, near Blandford."*

Such was the quality and character of Holbein's first patron in England, and perhaps the best he ever had. It is a pity we know of so few pictures painted by Holbein for Sir Thomas More, and that of those few perhaps not one moiety is preserved.

The execution of Sir Thomas More was one of the most to be deplored of Henry's reign, and is that perhaps which has done most injury to his reputation. It is accredited chiefly to the

seizure," says Dr. Friend, "was this: first it affected some particular part, attended with inward heat and burning, unquenchable thirst, restlessness, sickness at stomach and heart (though seldom vomiting), head-ache, delirium, then faintness, and excessive drowsiness; the pulse quick and vehement, and the breath short and labouring. None recovered under twenty-four hours. The only cure was to carry on the sweat, which was necessary for a long time: sleep to be avoided by all means." *History of Phisick.* Vol. II., p. 335. Lewis's *Life*, &c., p. 47. The disease was widely spread in that year. "In 1528," says Dr. Goodwin, "towards the end of *May*, the *sweating sickness* returned again, and overrun the whole kingdom, and not only the Term, but the Assizes, were adjourned, by Reason hereof; it destroyed many Persons of Distinction, insomuch that the King himself retired to *Tittinhanger*, a Place then belonging to the Abbot of *St. Albans*, where, with the Queen, and a very small Number of other Persons, he remained till the sickness was abated." *An Historical account of the Plague and other Pestilential Distempers*, &c. 8vo. London, 1743. P. 19.

* Lord Campbell, *l. l.*

CHAP. XII.
Sir Thomas More.
1528.
20th Henry VIII.

personal animosity of Anne Boleyn,* but except for the base servility of the chief law officers of the crown it would have been impossible. Indeed it is ascribed immediately to the perjury of Solicitor-General Rich, afterwards Lord Chancellor, and whose head by Holbein is also among the Windsor drawings. He bore witness not only that More would not accept the king's earthly supremacy, but that he also denied it; the latter part of his testimony is said to be false.

We have only to read carefully that noble monument of human industry and sagacity, James Anthony Froude's "History of England from the Fall of Wolsey to the Death of Elizabeth," to learn the debased state of society at this time. The church and the clergy as a body were sunk to the lowest depths of infamy, here as well as on the continent, and it required no less great an administrator than Henry VIII. to take the first steps towards the rescue of the nation from its vast slough of immorality and superstition. No wonder he became harder as he grew older; it was a rod of iron that he had to use, and his own personal experiences were sufficiently sad—to have had two such wives as Anne Boleyn and Catherine Howard; we search the pages of the novelist for sensations, Henry had them, with a vengeance, at his own door. It was truly a stirring time for our German painter, but the king seems to have been invariably kind to Holbein after he had once entered his service, which is to the credit of both the painter and the king.

The hideous condition of the church and its belongings was nothing new to Holbein, who was familiar with such a state of things at home, whether among the reformed or unreformed.

To show the danger at this period of any aspirations or expressions of liberty of thought, as regards the settled super-

* When the news of the execution was brought to Henry, who was at the time playing at draughts, in the presence of the queen, he said, turning his eyes upon her, "Thou art the cause of this man's death;" and rising immediately left the room, and shut himself up in his own chamber. Cayley's *Memoirs*, &c.

stitions of the time, I will repeat Mr. Froude's brief story* of the fate of four spirited but rash young men of Suffolk who wantonly *insulted*, or rather destroyed, a wonder-working rood or crucifix at Dovercourt, during or just before the chancellorship of Sir Thomas More.

CHAP. XII.

Rood at Dovercourt. 1528. 20th Henry VIII.

"This image was of such power that the door of the church in which it stood was open at all hours to all comers, and no human hand could close it. Dovercourt therefore became a place of great and lucrative pilgrimage, much resorted to by the neighbours on all occasions of difficulty.

"Now it happened that within the circuit of a few miles there lived four young men, to whom the virtues of the rood had become greatly questionable. If it could work miracles, it must be capable, so they thought, of protecting its own substance; and they agreed to apply a practical test which would determine the extent of its abilities. Accordingly, about the time of Bainham's† first imprisonment, Robert King of Dedham, Robert Debenham of East Bergholt, Nicholas Marsh of Dedham, and Robert Gardiner of Dedham, 'their consciences being burdened to see the honour of Almighty God so blasphemed by such an idol,' started off 'on a wondrous goodly night' in February, with hard frost and a clear full moon, ten miles across the wolds, to the church.

"The door was open, as the legend declared; but nothing daunted, they entered bravely, and lifting down the 'idol' from its shrine, with its coat and shoes, and the store of tapers which were kept for the services, they carried it on their shoulders for a quarter of a mile from the place where it had stood, 'without any resistance of the said idol.' There setting it on the ground, they struck a light, fastened the tapers to the body, and with the help of them, sacrilegiously burnt the

* *History of England*, &c. Vol. II., p. 92.

† James Bainham, a barrister, one of the victims of the learned More and the pious Stokesley, who was burnt at Smithfield, on the 20th of April 1532. His crime was that he said "if a Turk, a Jew, or a Saracen do trust in God, and keep his law, he is a good Christian man." More himself sent him to the rack, in the Tower. See Foxe's *Martyrs*.

CHAP. XII.

Rood at Dovercourt. 1528. 20th Henry VIII.

image down to a heap of ashes; the old dry wood 'blazing so brimly,' that it lighted them a full mile of their way home.*

"For this night's performance, which, if the devil is the father of lies, was a stroke of honest work against him and his family, the world rewarded these men after the usual fashion. One of them, Robert Gardiner, escaped the search which was made, and disappeared till better times; the remaining three were swinging in chains six months later, on the scene of their exploit. Their fate was perhaps inevitable. Men who dare to be the first in great movements are ever self-immolated victims."

No doubt it was better for them that their bones should be bleaching on their gibbets, than that they should be at the bidding of priests, "crawling at the feet of a wooden rood, and believing it to be God." And all this happened about the twentieth year of Henry VIII.

The More family. 1529. 21st Henry VIII.

In the known earlier male portraits by Holbein, a peculiar fashion of wearing the hair prevails; it is cropped straight across the forehead, and hangs down lower than the ears all round the rest of the head; and the faces are shaven. Of course a mere fashion is not without many exceptions, but this known prevailing custom may assist us in approximating the date of some portraits, the time of which is not known. Where we find pictures with polled or closely cropped heads and bearded faces, we may assume them to belong to a later date than that class just described. The fashion changed in 1535, when Henry VIII. ceased to shave, and condemned long hair in his own household.† The cut of the hair is a better index than the beard, or moustache, worn at pleasure; some wore beards with the long hair; and the portrait of Sir Richard Southwell at Florence, which was painted in 1536, is an example of the long hair with the shaven face, after 1535; the Duke of Norfolk's, painted in 1540, is another. The

* From a letter of Robert Gardiner: Foxe. Vol. IV., p. 706.

† 1535. "The 8th of May the king commanded all about his court to poll their heads, and to give them example, he caused his own head to bee polled, and from thenceforth his beard to bee notted and no more shaven." Stow's *Annals*. Ed. Howes, p. 570.

The More family. 1529. 21st Henry VIII.

fashion therefore though adopted by the king, is no rule, but is a very good aid notwithstanding; the examples far outbalance the exceptions. If the rule were to be applied to Henry VIII., we might infer that Holbein did not paint the king before 1535, which is likely enough, as the few Holbein portraits of him are bearded, and with the head polled or closely cropped. Though beards were worn among gentlemen before 1535, they were more common after; and though long hair was worn after 1535, it was much more general before.

Sir Henry Guildford, the two Godsalves, Sir John More, Sir Thomas More, and John More, have all the long hair, and are beardless: Nicholas Kratzer is also without a beard. All Sir Thomas's portraits by Holbein are beardless, yet in July in 1535 he wore a beard, having ceased to shave probably when sent to the Tower, and it was of such a character that at his execution he stayed the headsman, to put his beard aside that it might not be injured; remarking—"Pity that should be cut, that has not committed treason." The most genuine of the several portraits of More which I shall speak of more in detail presently, is no doubt the Windsor drawing, and this is still in good condition; it represents a shaven face, but with a slight indication of a moustache, rather more than three-quarters turned to his left, with clear penetrating grey eyes looking fixedly before them; and this head seems to be the basis of all the other portraits of Sir Thomas, though in the fine print engraved for the Knaptons by Houbraken, he has a decided moustache. In 1529 More was living with his second wife, a widow "of good years, and of no good favour or complexion;" with his three daughters and their three husbands; with his only son John and his betrothed, Anne Cresacre; with his own father also, and with Margaret Gigs his niece, or some more distant relative, who afterwards married Dr. Clement; to these we may add his secretary Harris, his fool and servant Pattison or Patenson; and perhaps for a time his painter. With the exception of the three sons-in-law and Holbein himself, all are introduced in the large family picture, still preserved in several examples, one of

CHAP. XII. *The More family.* 1529. 21st Henry VIII.

which I assume to be that noticed by Van Mander. In this example there is in the back-ground a twelfth figure, a man in a green gown reading a book, by a window, who is so modestly placed that he may be the painter, but this notion has never yet been mooted, and I admit it is not very likely that the painter should be so placed or so occupied. The total exclusion of the sons-in-law from the composition is worth notice; it is also remarkable that no child is introduced; Margaret had a son by this time. Erasmus, in a letter to his friend Faber bishop of Vienna, has left us a picture of this once happy family. You might there imagine yourself, he says, in the house of the Muses in another academy of Plato, but I do an injustice to More's house by comparing it with that society, which discussed morals it is true, but was engaged chiefly with philosophy and science. Sir Thomas's family was more a school for the exercise of the Christian religion and virtues. The leisure of all both male and female was devoted to the study of the liberal arts, though their chief attention was engaged on piety. No quarrelling, no disputing, no idleness was there: every one did his duty, with alacrity and affability. That there should have been unbroken peace in a family with such an arbitrary head over it, is not less remarkable than it is creditable to the family; we know that this peace lasted until that head was subjected to constraint by a still stronger head, and that it then fell to pieces. Sir Thomas could lead, but could not be led.

As it is impossible to give any detailed or accurate account of what Holbein did during this first visit to England, and as Sir Thomas More's guest, we may at once turn our attention to the one great work of this time—"The family of Sir Thomas More." This picture, a few other recorded portraits, and possibly the two compositions illustrating Riches and Poverty, executed for the house of the Hanse merchants here, exhaust the materials we have to consider as the results of Holbein's first sojourn among us. I feel that the catalogue is imperfect, but yet do not suppose that any portraits of Henry VIII. are among the omitted works.

The More family. 1529. 21st Henry VIII.

In October this year, 1529, More became Lord Chancellor, but Holbein had then already returned to Basel; certainly by August of that year; so that he was apparently never the guest of the Lord Chancellor, yet in the family picture, now at Nostell Priory, Sir Thomas is said by the Rev. Mr. Lewis to be represented in his Chancellor's robes and collar of SS., with a rose pendant before. That he has an SS. collar with portcullis and the double rose is certain, but his robe is the common furred gown of the time; the collar may belong to his dignity as a knight and councillor of the king,* or be a mere Lancastrian badge. As the very contrary is the case, as the father Sir John More is in a judge's robes, and as Sir Thomas is in a common gown, this circumstance is some evidence that the latter had not attained his highest dignity when the picture was painted: a fact which may be looked on as almost certain, as Holbein left England before Sir Thomas was made chancellor.

"For nothing," says Walpole, "has Holbein's name been oftener mentioned than for the picture of Sir Thomas More's family. Yet of six pieces extant on this subject, the two smaller are certainly copies, the three larger probably not painted by Holbein, and the sixth, though an original picture, most likely not of Sir Thomas and his family." This is certainly not a very satisfactory state of affairs, though Walpole has apparently exaggerated the embroilment for the sake of a little more point and effect in his antithesis, as was his wont.

Three or four of the pictures referred to may be easily disposed of; the last noticed, the reader is already aware, is the famous "Meier Madonna." Another, that once at Burford, in Oxfordshire, at the seat of Speaker Lenthall, is made up from the original composition, and later portraits of the family.

* In the sumptuary law of the 24th Henry VIII., c. 13, it is enacted "that no man unless he be a knight, after the said feast (Lady Day 1533), wear any collar of gold named a collar of S." Showing that there was no particular meaning in this ornament, though the double rose may signify the union of the two houses of York and Lancaster.

CHAP. XII. *The More family.* 1529. 21st Henry VIII.

The chief figures of Holbein's group are pushed to the right side of the picture, the spectator's left, and the space so obtained is filled in with portraits of the chancellor's grandson and wife and his great-grandsons. The left or more modern half consists of Sir Thomas's grandson Thomas More, with his wife Maria Scrope, and their two sons, both already grown up; the elder is the Thomas More who wrote the life of his great-grandfather, referred to above. The date of this composition is 1593; it contains altogether twelve figures: Margaret Clement and the step-mother are both omitted, as is also the secretary Harris, but the fool is inserted in the back-ground, raising or putting aside the curtain. A third example which may be dismissed, is Mr. Charles Sotheby's miniature copy of this Burford picture, ascribed to the hand of Peter Oliver.* There was also a large copy apparently of the Nostell Priory picture, at Barnborough in Yorkshire—the seat of the Cresacres, whose estates, through Anne Cresacre, fell to the Mores.

The first, or Burford example of these large pictures now belongs to Mr. Walter Strickland of Cokethorpe Park, Oxfordshire; the other, the Barnborough example, to Mr. Charles John Eyston of East Hendred, Berkshire; this last is much injured, and curtailed of its original dimensions. The following is the order of the figures in the Burford composition, which however as remarked, is neither Holbein's nor made up even purely of Holbein's materials; four of the figures having been introduced in 1593, fifty years after Holbein's death; as the attached ages and date show. Beginning at the spectator's left, we have in the first plane—Sir John More, Sir Thomas More, John More, Cicely Heron, Elizabeth Dancy, Margaret Roper, Thomas More, the son of John More just mentioned, and Maria Scrope, his wife. In the second plane—Anne Cresacre; and the two sons of Thomas More and Maria Scrope, great-grandsons of the Chancellor: in the extreme

* It is printed in Caldesi's *Photographic Historical Portrait Gallery.* Folio. Vol. I. 1864.

The More family. 1529. 21st Henry VIII.

back-ground is the fool Pattison. Of the above figures, Sir John, Sir Thomas, John, Cicely and Margaret, and the head of Anne Cresacre, are from Holbein's originals, so is the figure of Elizabeth Dancy, but from her change of position the lower part of her figure is concealed by her two sisters, sitting in front of her; in Holbein's drawing at Basel she stands by the side of her grandfather Sir John, and is seen in whole length.

There remain yet three to be considered, that described by Walpole as formerly at Heron in Essex, the seat of Sir John Tyrrel, but now I imagine in the possession of Lord Petre at Thorndon near Brentwood; the small pen-and-ink sketch in the museum at Basel, now dated 1530; and lastly the large picture at Nostell Priory near Wakefield, which is the same in composition as the Barnborough and Thorndon pictures. Of these compositions, in all, three different works, the Basel sketch is the only one at all identical with the example engraved by Von Mechel in 1794, in his "*Oeuvre de Jean Holbein*," &c.; he does not say where the original picture was, further than that it was in England, and he describes his print as the FAMILIA THOMAE MORI, ANGLIAE CANCELLARII. This, should it still exist, seems to be altogether the best composition, and to have more pretensions than any of the others to be the genuine family piece painted by Holbein himself, though I have not succeeded in finding any picture like it.

Engraved by Mechel.

On the extreme right of the composition, or the spectator's left, is the second daughter Elizabeth Dancy, standing; next to her is Margaret Gigs (afterwards Clement), pointing to a book in her left hand. Sir John More, judge, is next, seated on a bench, both his hands are seen, clasped together: Sir Thomas More is seated on the same bench by his side, on his left; both his hands are concealed in a muff or rather part of his gown. The son, John More, is next, standing leaning against the bench and reading in a small book which he holds in his hands: Patenson or Pattison the fool stands next to him. In front of Patenson is seated on a stool the youngest daughter Cecilia, the wife of Giles Heron; just before her a little to her

CHAP. XII.

The More family. 1529. 21st Henry VIII.

left, also seated on a stool, or perhaps on the floor, is the chancellor's favourite daughter Margaret Roper, holding an open book in both hands, but neither reading in it nor pointing with her left hand. Behind these two daughters, in the extreme left of the picture, seated in an arm-chair is Alice Lady More, Sir Thomas's second wife, the step-mother of his children; and in front of her is a small monkey, not very conspicuous.

In the back-ground, again commencing at the right of the picture or the spectator's left, is a buffet, on which is what has been described as a chamber organ, and on the same buffet in front are some vessels and other objects. Then follows a large curtain or wall-hanging, before which is suspended a clock; the two weights of the clock are seen, but no pendulum. Just under the clock stands Anne Cresacre: further on is a door-case and passage with the portion of a window. In the extreme left, behind Lady More, is a window, seen in perspective, but darkened, and in its recess stand a jug, a dish, some books, and a lighted candle. On the floor in front, in the centre of the fore-ground are a footstool and some books carelessly placed. In this picture therefore there are or were ten figures and a monkey. The print is 9½ in. high by 13¼ in. wide. The light comes entirely from the right, or spectator's left.

The Basel sketch, also engraved by Mechel, and of which there is a poor etching by Nicolas Cochin in the "*Tabellae Selectae*" of Caroline Patin, published in 1691, is almost identical in composition with that just described, but varies in some unimportant details. On the buffet, before the so-called organ, is a jug containing plants; and a lute is hung up against the curtain or wall-hanging; and in the window recess of the passage in the back-ground are standing two figures. The mother or Lady Alice appears to be kneeling before a desk, in the sketch; and over her is noted by Holbein *diese soll sitzen*, that is "this one shall be sitting," which she is in the later examples of the composition. The books and stool in the fore-ground are differently placed. This Basel sketch I take to be the cause of the common report that a copy of the picture was sent by Sir Thomas More to Erasmus at Basel. The alterations in it noticed are indeed so immaterial as regards the composition and general effect that they might possibly be the result of the painter's attempting to sketch the picture from memory, though I do not suppose this, as the likenesses are too accurate. The sketch at Basel and Mechel's print of it are dated 1530, but the date is omitted in Cochin's engraving. The size of this print is 10¾ in. high by 14¼ in. wide. Sir Thomas More's head is the centre of the composition in both.

CHAP. XII. *The More family.* 1529. 21st Henry VIII.

The best preserved of these family pieces is that of Nostell Priory near Wakefield in Yorkshire, which we will let the Rev. J. Lewis describe. In his time, in 1731, the picture was at Well Hall, the seat of the Ropers, at Eltham near Blackheath: a neat small engraving of this picture by Dean was published by Pickering in the *Bijou* for 1829. In this composition also the head of Sir Thomas is the centre of the picture.

"The room which is here represented seemed to me to be a large dining-room. At the upper end of it stands a chamber organ on a cupboard, with a curtain drawn before it. On each end of the cupboard, which is covered with a carpet of tapestry, stands a flowerpot of flowers, and on the cupboard are laid a lute, a base-viol, a pint pot or ewer covered in part with a cloth folded several times, and *Boetius de Consolatione Philosophiae*, with two other books upon it. By this cupboard stands a daughter of Sir Thomas More's, putting on her right-hand glove, and having under her arm a book bound in red Turkey leather and gilt, with this inscription round the outside of the cover *Epistolica Senecae.* Over her head is written *Elizabetha Dancea Thomae Mori Filia anno* 21.

"Behind her stands a woman holding a book open with both her hands, over whose head is written *Uxor Johannis Clements.**

"Next to Mrs. Dancy is Sir John More in his robes as one of the justices of the King's Bench, and by him Sir Thomas in his chancellor's

* "In the sketch of another of these family pieces, given us by the learned Dr. Knight, this lady is called *Margareta Gige* affinis, an. 22, which seems to intimate that this picture was drawn before that at Well Hall, though they were both done in the same year." [Her maiden name was Margaret Gigs.] In the Barnborough picture, now Mr. Eyston's, at East Hendred, the legend over this lady is—*Margareta Giga Mori Filiabus condiscipula et cognata.* A° 22.

CHAP. XII.

The More family.
1529.
21st
Henry VIII.

robes (?) and collar of SS. with a rose pendant before. They are both sitting on a sort of tressel or arm'd bench, one of the arms and legs, and one of the tassels of the cushion, appear on the left side of Sir Thomas. At the feet of Sir John lies a cur-dog, and at Sir Thomas's a Bologna shock. Over Sir John's head is written *Johannes Morus pater anno* 76. Over Sir Thomas's *Thomas Morus anno* 50. Between them behind stands the wife of John More, Sir Thomas's son, over whose head is written *Anna Crisacria Joannis Mori sponsa anno* 15. Behind Sir Thomas a little on his left hand stands his only son John More pictured with a very foolish aspect, and looking earnestly in a book which he holds open with both his hands. Over his head is written *Joannes Morus Thomae filius anno* 19.

"A little to the left of Sir Thomas are sitting on low stools his two daughters Cecilia and Margaret. Next him is Cecilia who has a book in her lap clasp'd. By her sits her sister Margaret who has likewise a book in her lap but wide open, in which is written *L. An. Senecæ—Oedipus—Fata si liceat mihi fingere arbitrio meo, temperem zephyro levi—* On Cecilia's petticoat is written *Cæcilia Herond Thomae Mori filia anno* 20, and on Margaret's *Margareta Ropera Thomae Mori filia anno* 22.

"Just by Mrs. Roper sits Sir Thomas's lady in an elbow-chair (?) holding a book open in her hands. About her neck she has a gold chain, with a cross hanging to it before. On her left hand is a monkey chained, and holding part of it with one paw and part of it with the other. Over her head is written *Uxor Thomae Mori anno* 57. Behind her is a large arched window in which is placed a flower-pot (a vase) of flowers and a couple of oranges. Behind the two ladies stands Sir Thomas's fool, who it seems was bereft of his judgment by distraction. He has his cap on, and in it are stuck a red and white rose, and on the brim of it is a shield with a red cross on it, and a sort of seal pendant. About his neck he wears a black string with a cross hanging before him, and his left thumb is stuck in a broad leathern girdle clasp'd about him. Over his head is written *Henricus Pattison Thomae servus.* At the entrance of the room, where Sir Thomas and his family are, stands a man in the portal who has in his left hand a roll of papers or parchments with two seals appendant, as if he was some way belonging to Sir Thomas as Lord Chancellor. Over his head is written *Joannes Heresius Thomae Mori famulus.* In another room at some distance is seen thro' the door-case a man standing at a large bow-window, with short black hair in an open sleev'd gown of a sea-green colour, and under it a garment of a blossom colour, holding a book open in his hands written or printed in the black letter, and reading very earnestly in it. About the middle of the room over against Sir Thomas, hangs a clock with strings and leaden weights without any case."*

The More family. 1529. 21st Henry VIII.

In Mr. Eyston's copy, a large piece has disappeared from the left side, probably through decay, or through fitting it into, or removing it from, a panel frame in which it was formerly placed, a portion is indeed wanting all round; and the proceedings of the repairer of the picture have been somewhat singular; instead of making good the injured parts, he has cut a certain breadth away in relining the picture and has painted out altogether what was then left of Lady Alice and her monkey, and of the more advanced of the two dogs. Through cutting this piece off the left end, the window and vase of flowers belonging to that side have entirely disappeared. With the exception of these changes and a few other unskilful repairs this picture is in the main identical with the Nostell Priory example, though very inferior to it. The variety in the inscription over the head of Margaret Gigs has been already noticed (in the note p. 235). The clock, which appears to have but one hand, points to a little before 11. On canvas, 7 ft. 8 in. *h.* by 9 ft. 9½ in. *w.* The Nostell Priory picture, also on canvas, is 8 ft. 3 in. *h.* by 11 ft. 6 in. *w.*, giving a difference of 7 inches in height, and nearly 20 inches in length.

The Thorndon picture likewise on canvas, is 8 ft. 3 in. *h.* by 11 ft. 2 in. *w.* It is in a better state than that at East Hendred, but appears to be also a copy of the Nostell Priory example, except that the little dog, called by Mr. Lewis a Bologna shock, is missing; the other dog, a kind of spaniel, is there: the clock indicates the same hour. Another difference is that Sir Thomas here wears a moustache. The cupboard is covered below by a cloth in square checques hanging before it; and Lady Alice is seated in a large scarlet arm-chair instead of on a stool: (?) on the floor are strewn rushes, but which are no

* See Roper's *Life and Death of Sir Thomas More, Knight, Lord High Chancellor of England, in the Reign of King Henry the VIIIth.* Edited by the Rev. J. Lewis. Small 8vo. London, 1731. P. 169.

CHAP. XII. *The More family.* 1529. 21st Henry VIII.

longer green: Sir Thomas has scarlet sleeves. Both these pictures are very coarsely painted.

To sum up a long story in a few words, we have three varieties of this More-family composition. The sketch at Basel, and Von Mechel's engraving, nearly identical, but of which I know no painting; the three very similar pictures though not absolutely identical, at Nostell Priory, Thorndon, and East Hendred; and lastly the more modern composition at Cokethorpe, and its miniature copy. The only one of the whole series that can be declared to be by the hand of Holbein is the small pen-and-ink sketch at Basel, in the museum there.

It is just possible that although Holbein drew all the separate portraits and sketched out his composition, that he never really painted the picture: the execution of which may have been suspended by his return to Basel, and never taken up again. These materials may have been afterwards worked into pictures, with some modifications, by other painters for the family. I do not know whether the following words of Margaret Roper, in a letter to Erasmus in November 1529, necessarily imply that the portraits in question were all on one piece — *Utriusque mei parentis nostrumque omnium effigiem depictam*—perhaps as effigiem, the accusative singular is used, *one piece* may be implied.

The Nostell Priory example is supposed to be that which belonged to Andries Van Loo in Van Mander's time, and after his death was bought by Mr. Roper, Sir Thomas's grandson, and placed at Well Hall, where Mr. Lewis saw it a century later; from the Ropers it passed to the present family of Winn, in Yorkshire, their representatives: it belonged to Sir Rowland Winn, in Walpole's time.*

* "This picture," says Walpole, "remained till of late years at Well Hall in Eltham, Kent, the mansion of the Ropers. That house being pulled down, it hung for some time in the king's house at Greenwich, soon after which, by the death of the last Roper, whose sole daughter married Mr. Henshaw, and left three daughters, the family picture, then valued at 300*l.* came between them, and Sir Rowland Wynne, who married one of them, bought the shares of the other two, and carried the picture into Yorkshire, where it now remains." *Anecdotes of Painting*, &c.

The More family. 1529. 21st Henry VIII.

Vertue, says Walpole, doubted the authenticity of this picture, not from the incompleteness of its finish, but because the heads are in different lights. I cannot, with Vertue, allow this to be a sufficient reason for doubting the picture: its want of finish is a much better. We know that Holbein was in the habit of painting from his drawings, and the drawings being made separately, and probably in different rooms and in different lights, the pictures would of necessity, from the painter's habit of strictly following his drawings, preserve their differences and individual character; besides two lights are possible in the room, coming from opposite directions; for in this picture the window is not darkened as in that engraved by Mechel. The fool is lighted from the window on his left, and this light extends, but with less force, to Sir Thomas; the father however next to him, and still further from the window, is lighted from the other side, from his right, from which a light is apparently coming strong enough to counteract that of the window on the left, though we do not see its source: the two women however next to Sir John having their backs to this supposed light from the right, are not affected by it, but receive a light on their faces, coming from the window opposite to them; and this is certainly inconsistent. The shadows of the faces are nowhere strong, and there is nothing offensive in this variety of lighting, which might not only be justified, but is exactly what we might expect from Holbein's practice. Even allowing the lighting therefore to violate a strict principle of unity, it is not such a peculiarity or defect as to condemn the picture as the work of a master, nor is it even absolutely an error, as it is in its principle quite consistent with ordinary circumstances, which may be seen at any time in a room lighted from different directions. A better reason for doubting its authenticity is a general flatness and want of mastery in its execution. All the hands with the exception of those of Cicely Heron are very poor; these are decidedly graceful.

It is quite probable that the picture may have been commenced though it was never thoroughly finished by Holbein, its completion having been interrupted, before his return to

CHAP. XII.

The More family.
1529.
21st
Henry VIII.

Basel, and no opportunity occurring afterwards to enable the painter to complete it. Some of the accessaries, as the dogs, are very poor. The left hand of Margaret Roper is very bad; and some of the faces are quite unworthy of Holbein. The floor is strewn with green rushes.

I can suggest two or three causes for this interruption; either Holbein's presentation to the king, or the fire which in August 1529 consumed a part of Sir Thomas More's house at Chelsea, and all his barns and the corn contained in them. This is a calamity which might well disturb the ordinary routine and occupations of a family. Before its reinstatement, if not already gone previous to the fire, Holbein must have returned to Switzerland: a third reason is the painter's compulsory return to Basel through the long expiration of his leave of absence as a citizen; being still bound by rights and duties there. When his house was burnt, Sir Thomas was staying with the king at Woodstock. A letter he wrote thence to his wife on the occasion is still preserved; it is dated the 3rd of September; the fire no doubt happened some days before; couriers were not very expeditious in those times, and a philosopher like Sir Thomas would not write immediately on the receipt of the news.

This was shortly before More was made Lord Chancellor, he was then in high favour with the king; he had just successfully carried out an important mission at Cambray, respecting negotiations for peace. As an illustration of the king's favour, may be related an anecdote told by his son-in-law Roper. "The king would on a sudden, come over to his house at Chelsea, and be merry with him, even dining with him without previous invitation or notice." After one of these dinners, when Henry was in an unusually benevolent mood, he walked with Sir Thomas, for about an hour in his garden, holding his arm round his neck. When the king was gone Roper congratulated his father-in-law on such an extraordinary mark of favour; as no man but Cardinal Wolsey had been so honoured before; with him Henry had once walked arm-in-arm. "I thank our Lord," replied Sir Thomas, "I find his grace my very good Lord indeed; and I believe he doth as singularly favour me as any subject within this realm. Howbeit, son Roper, I may tell thee I have no cause to be proud thereof; for if my head would win him a castle in France, it should not fail to go."

The More family.
1529.
21st Henry VIII.

It is necessary to be particular about the time of the fire at Chelsea, if we allow it to enter into the causes which brought Holbein's first visit to this country to its conclusion. I must mention therefore that on the 5th of this same month of September Holbein had already paid Erasmus a visit at Freiburg, where the latter was then residing; for the painter and this very family picture are the subject of remark in a letter from Erasmus to More, bearing that date. There is perhaps time enough for Holbein to have left England after the fire, and yet to have been in Freiburg on the 5th of September, but probabilities are much against this, and I believe his departure from this country arose from other causes, which will be considered in the next chapter. Some have imagined that Holbein carried over to Erasmus a copy of the picture; but Erasmus does not say so, and it is highly improbable that Holbein did anything of the kind, unless we accept the sketch as the copy. He spoke of and described the picture, and seems to have done more—either to have made a sketch of it from memory, or to have carried one with him from England, which I believe he did, and to have left this sketch with Erasmus. From this sketch, which is now in the museum of Basel, and which was engraved by Mechel in 1787, Erasmus could form a perfect notion of the picture itself and write about it as if he had seen it, as the sketch would make him quite familiar with the composition. "I have no words, my friend," he says, "to express the pleasure it gave me to see that whole family brought together before me, as the painter Holbein has represented it, so happily that I could have seen little more had I been present myself." All this might be as well said of the sketch in pen and ink as of a picture; and it is a fact that Erasmus does not speak of a picture, either to

CHAP. XII. — *The More family.* 1529. 21st Henry VIII.

the family or to any one else.* There is not, and never has been, any other "Family of Sir Thomas More" at Basel, than this small paper drawing; it has all the names and ages of each inserted, in Latin, and perhaps by Erasmus himself, though the surnames are sadly disguised by bad orthography and the attempt to Latinize them together. That the sketch itself is dated 1530 is nothing against this conclusion, for, as already remarked, the date is not reproduced in Cochin's engraving, though he has inserted the words *Holbein delin.* The ages further correspond with the year 1529, not 1530, so that we may conclude this date to have been added later, and after 1691, when Cochin's print was published.

Sir John More died in November 1530. Mechel's print has this date, it is inscribed *Johannes Holbein ad vivum delin: Londini* 1530. It is much better and larger than Cochin's, being the size of the sketch—14 in. high by nearly 20 in. wide.

This sketch however is not a sketch of the large Nostell Priory picture, though it may be of that engraved by Von Mechel, with just such minor alterations in it, as the imperfection of memory would be likely to occasion, or as might take place in carrying out the design. But it is just possible that the engraving of 1794 is nothing more than an elaboration from the sketch itself. The chief differences in the compositions are—that in the Nostell Priory picture Elizabeth Dancy and Margaret Clement have changed places; the hands of Sir John More are concealed; the figure of the secretary Harris is an addition; as are also the two dogs in the fore-ground; the monkey is altogether different; Lady More is sitting on a kind of camp folding-stool instead of an arm-chair (?); there is no lighted candle on the window-ledge; nor is there any lute hanging up; the foot-stool and the four books are omitted; and there

* His words are—"Utinam liceat adhuc semel in vita videre amicos mihi charissimos, quos in pictura Olpeinus exhibuit utcunque conspexi summa cum animi mei voluptate." Freiburg, 5th September, 1529, *Epist.* Lib. XXVI. Ep. 21. Again, in a letter to Margaret Roper, he says—"Pictor Olbeinus totam familiam istam adeo feliciter expressam mihi repraesentavit, ut si coram adfuissem non multo plus fuerim visurus." Ep. 50.

is a large addition to the flowers in the jugs or vases. The clock is also different.* The covering of the hands in Sir Thomas More's portraits by Holbein is noticed by Erasmus, who explains it by remarking that they were a little clumsy or rustic, and that Sir Thomas was in the habit of concealing them.

CHAP. XII. The More family. 1529. 21st Henry VIII.

The inscriptions on the sketch are:—1. *Elisabeta Dancea Thomae Mori filia, anno* 21. 2. *Margareta Giga Clemētis uxor Thome Mori filiabus condiscipula et cognata, anno* 22. 3. *Johannes Morus pater, anno* 76. 4. *Thomas Morus, anno* 50. 5. *Johannes Morus Thomae filius, anno* 19. 6. *Anna Grisacria Johannis Mori sponsa, anno* 15. 7. *Cecilia Herona Thome Mori filia, anno* 20. 8. *Magareta Ropera Thome Mori filia, anno* 22. 9. *Alicia Thomae Mori uxor, anno* 57; with the words "diese soll sitzen" above. 10. *Henricus Patensonus Thome Mori morio, anno* 40. And in the upper corner, on the spectator's left, is written in German character, near the hanging instrument, the following somewhat singular sentence—Klaficordi und ander seyte spill uf ein bretz—Clavicords and other stringed instruments on a board.

The following is Walpole's criticism on the Nostell Priory picture; after indorsing Vertue's objections to its authenticity. Vertue, he says, considered the picture, "but indifferent; on this I lay no more stress than I do on the case of that at Burford; but his observation that the lights and shades in different parts of the picture come from opposite sides is unanswerable, and demonstrate it no genuine picture of Holbein, unless that master had been a most ignorant dauber,† as he might sometimes be a careless painter. This absurdity Vertue accounts for, by supposing that Holbein quitted the chancellor's service for the king's, before he had drawn out the great picture, which however Sir Thomas always understood was to be executed; that Holbein's business increasing upon him, some other painter was employed to begin

* This clock is still preserved, and is now in the possession of Mr. Waterton of Walton Hall, Yorkshire.

† I have already remarked that I do not feel the force of this objection in the strong light that Walpole sees it.

CHAP. XII.

The More family. 1529. 21st Henry VIII.

the picture, and to which Holbein was to give the last touches; in short that inimitable perfection of flesh which characterizes his works. And this is the more probable, as Vertue observed that the faces and hands are left flat and unfinished, but the ornaments, jewels, &c., are extremely laboured. As the portraits of the family, in separate pieces, were already drawn by Holbein, the injudicious journeyman stuck them in as he found them, and never varied the lights,* which were disposed, as it was indifferent in single heads, some from the right, some from the left, but which make a ridiculous contradiction when transported into one piece."† The picture is without question unequal in its parts, some portions certainly being unworthy of Holbein, others though much better, still bear no trace of the great master's hand: the want of finish too is in parts apparent. The dogs are very bad, especially the foremost one; notwithstanding all this, however, there may be a genuine Holbein ground-work beneath.

The Windsor drawing, as observed, appears to be the original of all the portaits of More, in these family pictures and elsewhere; the position and expression are in all similar, and this drawing may possibly be the only portrait taken of him by Holbein actually from the life. Of this drawing Walpole remarks—"I do not know a single countenance into which any master has poured greater energy of expression than in the drawing of Sir Thomas More, at Kensington: it has a freedom, a boldness of thought, and acuteness of penetration that attest the sincerity of the resemblance. It is Sir Thomas More in the rigour of his sense, not in the sweetness of his pleasantry. Here he is the unblemished magistrate, not that amiable philosopher, whose humility neither power nor piety could elate, and whose mirth even martyrdom could not spoil. Here he is rather that single, cruel judge, whom one knows not how to hate, and who, in the vigour of abilities of knowledge, and good humour, persecuted others in defence

* The idea of a journeyman altering Holbein's lights, is rather a crude one for a professed art critic.

† *Anecdotes of Painting.* Vol. I., p. 92. Ed. 1849.

of superstitions that he himself had exposed; and who capable of disdaining life, at the price of his sincerity, yet thought that God was to be served by promoting an imposture; who triumphed over Henry and death, and sunk to be * * * the dupe, of the Holy Maid of Kent."

CHAP. XII.

Portraits of More.

1529.
21st Henry VIII.

Before leaving altogether Sir Thomas More's retreat at Chelsea, there is some account to be given of some other separate portraits of Sir Thomas and his family. The genuine portraits of Sir Thomas himself are not very numerous, though the variety of prints that bear his name, having no resemblance with each other, is something astonishing.* We have of course here to do only with Holbein's works, these are not numerous; except in the family picture all are bust portraits with little variation; some with a moustache and some without, and they mostly have the SS. chain on: the long beard spoken of in the story of his execution, was no doubt of prison growth. The Windsor drawing was clearly the study for the family picture, and has as surely supplied the model for all that followed it. In this drawing, taken before he was chancellor, not later than 1527, he is represented in the prime of life, with a very stern expression, and looking, as it were, into vacancy. The face in the family picture is nearly identical with this, but less stern in its expression; it was painted also probably in 1527, but not later than 1529, as Holbein's departure in the summer of this year, and the inscriptions by the various figures of the group, all testify; the ages of the whole family being reckoned from his year. I have already tried to account for the date 1530 being on the Basel sketch. We find this date again on another portrait of More, where it seems to have no right to be, unless as dating the copy. This is a large canvas picture of Sir Thomas and his father, at Hutton Hall, copied apparently from the two seated figures in the Nostell Priory group, with the addition of a coat of arms, and two original inscriptions. Over the head of the father, Judge More, is written—*Jo̅hes Morus Eques Auratus unus ex Judicibus Angliae. Aetatis* 77.

---

* See the Royal Collection at Windsor.

CHAP. XII.

Portraits of More.

1529. 21st Henry VIII.

1530: and over the son is *Thomas Morus filius et (hrs?) p̃dcti Joħis Mori: Eques Auratus Dõs Cancel: in Anglia. Aetatis* 50. 1530. It is quite possible, though not very probable, that the contradiction here shown is only apparent; both Sir John and Sir Thomas More may have still been in their respective seventy-seventh and fiftieth years when this copy was made; the same figures representing the age of Sir. Thomas in the spring of 1530 as had served for the summer of 1529: Sir John it appears had entered another year, he died in November 1530.

The original sketch of the portrait of Sir John More in this and the family picture is the head among the Windsor drawings, and it is one of the best preserved of them.

The most imposing of the portraits of Sir Thomas More, though it is not in a perfect state, is that already noticed as now in the possession of Mr. Henry Huth, formerly Mr. Farrer's. This is nearly identical with that in the family picture, except that both the hands are shown in Mr. Huth's; and it is painted with far more force. He is seated, in a black cap, and a black gown furred with sable, the sleeves of his coat being red; in his right hand he holds a folded piece of paper. The picture may be described as a half length; he shows a three-quarter face turned to the left. The eyes are dark grey, and the eyelid and the inside of the right eye have been injured and improperly repaired: the expression is harsh and even repulsive; it was painted in 1527, the figures M.D.XXVII. are in the lower right corner. In the back-ground is a green curtain. On oak, about 2 ft. 5 in. high, by 2 ft. wide. A similar portrait, on canvas, a copy, is in the possession of Mr. Charles J. Eyston, at East Hendred, Berkshire. The Marquis of Lothian possesses another copy of it. In Vanderdoort's catalogue of Charles I.'s pictures, is the following entry—No. 48, SIR THOMAS MORE, in a black cap and furred gown, with red sleeves. Wood, circular, 4 in. in diameter.

It is from the family picture of the Mores that we learn, that the portraits of nearly all its members are preserved among the Windsor drawings; and they are among the best of the series.* They are executed on plain white paper, before Holbein adopted that system, of questionable advantage, of spreading a *tempera* wash, in salmon colour as a priming, over his paper, as a preliminary operation to aid in the production of a flesh tint before commencing his drawing: the More drawings are also on larger paper than many of the others, being about 15 inches by 11.

CHAP. XII.

Portraits of More.

1529.
21st Henry VIII.

In the original catalogue found with these drawings, in Kensington Palace, the names of those represented are nearly all supplied, apparently from those written on the drawings, by Sir John Cheke, tutor to Edward VI., but these names are not always to be depended on; many of them are erroneous; for instance Elizabeth Dancy is called Lady Barkley; and Margaret Clement is misnamed Mother Jack, or Jackson, the nurse of Edward VI. If this Mrs. Jack, or Jackson is known by tradition to be among these drawings, she must be sought for among the yet unnamed female portraits of the series, of which there are eleven. That of the youngest daughter Cicely Heron is the anonymous portrait which was so admirably engraved in facsimile by F. C. Lewis, but which Chamberlaine would not make use of in his publication,† in case its superior excellence should have so overwhelmed the copies engraved by Bartolozzi, as to interfere with the sale of his work, which *professed* to be a series of facsimiles of the original drawings. It is much to be regretted that so many of these valuable drawings should have nearly perished. Their method is against their durability. They appear to be executed in charcoal, then tinted with red chalk, and finally strengthened with touches with the brush and Indian ink. Some are so worn by time and friction, that little more than the Indian-ink touches is preserved.

To return to the portraits of More; Henry VIII. possessed

* Their names are already given above, p. 217.

† Imitations of original Drawings by Hans Holbein, in the Collections of His Majesty, for the portraits of illustrious persons of the court of Henry VIII. With Biographical Tracts. By J. Chamberlaine, 83 plates. 2 vols., folio. London, 1792. See the catalogue of these drawings in the APPENDIX.

CHAP. XII.

Portraits of More.

1529.
21st Henry VIII.

one of which there is a curious story in Baldinucci,* that I have not come upon elsewhere. This picture, which he terms a stupendous portrait, Henry VIII. kept in an apartment together with those of some other eminent men. It happened that on the very day of the ex-chancellor's death (after the king had reproached her), the wicked Queen Anne Boleyn cast her eyes upon it, and seeing the expressive face of her enemy looking at her as if he were still living—she never forgave his refusal to be present at her wedding—she was seized with a feeling of either horror or remorse, and unable to endure the steady gaze and the reproaches of her own conscience, she threw open the window of the palace, and exclaiming "Oh me! the man seems to be still alive," flung the picture into the street: a passer-by picked it up and carried it away, and eventually it found a resting-place in Rome, where in Baldinucci's time it was still preserved in the Palazzo de' Crescenzi. The story I assume travelled to Rome with the picture.† We may apply an Italian saying to this anecdote—*se non e' vero, e ben trovato*—though it may not be true, it's not a bad story.

There is a good small portrait on panel of Sir Thomas More, in the Louvre, a three-quarter face turned to his left, which belonged to Louis XIV.; he wears his cap and furred robe and holds in his right hand a gold cross which hangs on a chain round his neck; in his left hand he holds a folded paper: it is 15½ in. high by about 12 in. wide. This Louvre picture may possibly be that with the eventful history in question. Francesco Scannelli, in his *Microcosmo della Pittura*, who wrote a generation earlier than Baldinucci, mentions, in an admirable passage concerning Holbein, a small portrait of extraordinary excellence, in the possession of Monsignor Campori, in Rome. It is of course impossible to identify a picture by such a description, as long as we cannot trace its passage from one possessor

* *Notizie dei Professori del Disegno da Cimabue in qua*, &c. Dec. IV., del Sec. IV. Giovanni Holbeen.

† I find no account of such a portrait in Rome now, nor do I know what this Palazzo de' Crescenzi, if it exist, may at present be called; the name is still preserved in one of the streets of Rome.

to another : for identity here we must assume that the picture passed from Monsignor Campori to the Crescenzi family, and from them to Louis XIV. Scannelli mentions two other portraits in the highest terms of commendation, one of which we can fortunately identify as the magnificent half-length known as "Mr. Morett," now in the gallery at Dresden. Indeed the whole passage of Scannelli is of that interest that it deserves to be quoted in full; even at the expense of a little anticipation as regards Mr. Morett, whose picture belongs certainly to the period of Holbein's second visit to England:—

Portraits of More.

1529. 21st Henry VIII.

"There was also lately among ultramontane painters a certain OLBENO, a highly qualified master, and in painting individual portraits verily stupendous. It is true in his execution there is something of that native hardness which belongs to his country in other respects; yet through his extreme diligence and truthful fidelity to nature, it shows a high degree of perfection. As we see, for example, in the already noticed gallery of H.S.H. the Duke of Modena, where there is a half-length portrait by him which in its exact imitation of nature is quite wonderful. A similar excellence is shown in the small portrait by the same master, now at Rome in the possession of Monsignor Campori. And again perhaps even still more excellent than any other picture by this artist is that at Verona in the gallery of Cortoni, also a half-length figure, a stupendous work, in everything complete."*

Hardness of manner.

Scannelli, observe, is not an indiscriminate eulogist; he felt something he was not accustomed to find combined with the highest excellence, yet even Leonardo da Vinci or Raphael and certainly other first-class Italian painters, are often quite as hard as Holbein: it is really the precision of nature which we find in Holbein, but without those embellishments or modifications which the consummate artist has often known how to apply to his work to harmonize it and subject it to a pleasing *general* effect which has a special charm in art. We

---

* *Il Microcosmo della Pittura*, DI FRANCESCO SCANNELLI *da Forli.* 4to. Cesena, 1657. L. II., p. 265.

CHAP. XII.

Hardness of manner.
1529.
21st Henry VIII.

look at nature with two eyes, we see accordingly no positive outline; we see indeed two outlines to everything we look at, one accordingly modifies the other, and the whole is softened in effect though sharp enough in reality. In a picture we see the same outline with each eye; exactly the opposite process therefore takes place, for while in viewing an object in the round we halve the cutting effect of the outline, in the flat we have a twofold impression of it, one from each eye. It is quite just therefore that the boundary lines of objects, and their parts should be subdued in painting; as in binocular vision there is no such thing as a cutting line in nature. Holbein though often, has *by no means always* neglected this refinement of the parts. He is indeed soft and general enough in his drawings, which are not minutely elaborated, but when he came to make out all the parts in the pictures he painted from these drawings, and probably often without nature to assist him, he fell into the fault of being over precise, or of elaborating a too positive expression of the minutiæ as mere component parts of what it was really his object to reproduce. I do not object to this precision and truth, a little distance modifies it, and it is certainly infinitely superior to that negligent handling which seems to have no other end than to produce a general effect, and is too often the mere cloak of incapacity; the "slobbering" of the infant artist who has commenced painting before he has learnt to make a proper use of his eyes.

Men are not always in a perfectly efficient state. The sort of mastery which we admire in Velazquez, is shown by Holbein occasionally, and certainly often in the little figures of his "Dance of Death," where by a few touches in the right place he has perfectly accomplished the desired expression. Velazquez, Rubens, Vandyck, Rembrandt, or Reynolds, the great masters of handling, could do no more; but how often both Rembrandt and Reynolds have missed the mark. A man who affects this style of execution should never miss the mark: he is the great master or nothing. Sir Joshua Reynolds in the group of views of the same child's face, in the National Gallery, called

"Heads of Angels" is the great master, because every touch is not only *what* it ought to be, but *where* it ought to be: in the large "Holy Family" close to it, he is nothing, or worse than nothing, a mere brush driver, there is scarcely a touch either what it ought to be, or where it ought to be.

Hardness of manner.
1529.
21st Henry VIII.

There can be no doubt about a certain "dryness" as Sir Joshua terms it about some of Holbein's portraits, more particularly of his English period, when I imagine he more frequently than formerly trusted to his own chalk sketch as his model, rather than to nature: yet there is no dryness whatever about the drawings themselves, the works he *did* execute from nature. There is none of this dryness in his best earlier works executed at Basel, which were apparently painted or completed directly from nature, as for example the portrait of Boniface Amerbach, or that of his own wife and children.

Sir Joshua in his "Notes" on some pictures at the Hague fully appreciates Holbein's fine colour, but seems to consider his dryness or hardness of manner somewhat fatal. Still considering the diversity of method in the manner of the two painters, his estimate of the German is a high one, though coming upon Holbein at once from the unsurpassable colouring and force of Rembrandt; a severe test to his simple portraiture.

Speaking of the fine picture of Henry's falconer, Cheseman, with a falcon on his fist, a bust, small life-size, now in the gallery of the Hague, Reynolds says*—"A portrait by Holbein; admirable for its truth and precision and extremely well coloured. The blue flat ground which is behind the head gives a general effect of dryness to the picture: had the ground been varied, and made to harmonize more with the figure, this portrait might have stood in competition with the works of the best portrait painters." On it he says is written "Henry Cheseman, 1533." This is inaccurate, and the ground is a kind of marine green not blue. All the catalogues of this

* *A Journey to Flanders and Holland in the year* 1781. Works, Vol. II.

CHAP. XII.

Hardness of manner.

1529.
21st
Henry VIII.

collection describe him as "Robert Cheseman;"* and the inscription is—ROBERTUS CHESEMAN. AETATES. SUÆ XLVIII. ANNO DM. MDXXXIII.

Though there may be a comparative dryness or positiveness in many of the portraits of Holbein I do not admit a want of harmony in them; a general truth implies a harmony; indistinctness and obscurity are not harmony. If every object is true in itself and as a component part true relatively to other component parts, it must be a harmony, and is in itself a living work of art. Whether such a work of art in painting can or ought to be thoroughly separated from, or made independent of its back-ground, is a fair question. In looking at an acquaintance, we certainly do not either look at or see the back-ground, but it is always there; we can look at it if we choose, and when we do we see something that has little or nothing to do with our acquaintance. In a painted portrait we must certainly have the ground, and doubtless the greatest masters have done well when they have so toned this ground into retirement, that we overlook it. In Holbein's grounds there are often two conventionalisms: he made them generally of a greenish hue, choosing this colour perhaps with the view of heightening the effect of the flesh tones, and he also very often wrote the person's name or date on this ground, in such case certainly treating it as if it were something utterly distinct from the portrait; a proceeding which true imitative art must reject. Still as Holbein has sometimes made his ground and his picture distinct, we may also judge them as two, and not require them to be a perfect harmony, we must look at the picture, separating it, in such cases from its ground, as we invariably separate it from its frame. Holbein's portraits themselves are always living harmonies. In his drawings where we have no back-grounds we feel this distinctly enough: many of these drawings are extremely free and yet accurately true, and as nearly perfect as the work of man can be.

Many men have given us fine effects, but few indeed have

* "Robert Cheseman, eenen valk op de vuist hebbende.",

worked like Holbein, and one should be sorry for the sake of a few more fine effects, to give up the living harmonies of this remarkable painter. We feel as if we had known or seen the men that Holbein has painted; he has reproduced nature, while your clever painters have only too often used nature as a mere means of showing their own cleverness.

CHAP. XII.

Hardness of manner.

1529.
21st
Henry VIII.

A SWISS LADY.

CHAPTER XIII.

Holbein visits Basel and Completes the Paintings of the Town-hall, but within two years returns again to England.

Chap. XIII.

He returns home.
1529-31.
22nd & 23rd
Henry VIII.

F Holbein's return to the city of his adoption in 1529 there can be no question, but the exact duration of the visit we do not know. He was still in Basel in October 1531, and was apparently much employed there: his chief work being the completion or continuation of the paintings of the council-hall of the new Rath-house.

As I have assumed Holbein to have been hitherto orderly in his proceedings, both in his coming and in his going, his return to Basel must be looked upon as a matter of necessity. That it was delayed so long was no doubt owing to the constant occupation which followed his introduction to, and the hearty reception he received from, Sir Thomas More. But in 1529 the painter's intercourse with the chancellor must have much diminished: in the summer of this year Sir Thomas took part in the negotiation of the peace of Cambray, and was absent for some time in the Netherlands, and after his return home he went to the king at Woodstock, as recorded.

After the completion (?) of the picture of the More family, Holbein may have felt himself at liberty to return home, in compliance possibly as much with his own wishes to rejoin his family as with the desire of the authorities of Basel, who were anxious for the return of a painter highly prized and honoured by the dignitaries of so great a prince as the King of England: his two years' leave of absence had certainly expired, and he was bound to return according to the laws of the municipality, unless by neglecting the duties of citizenship, he should forfeit its rights also. No citizen of Basel could enter the service of any foreign prince without the consent of the city; according to an order of the Great council, dated Saturday after St. Luke's day, in the year 1521. By this order it was illegal for any man, subject to the jurisdiction of Basel, either personally, or through any member of his family or any one belonging to him, to take or receive any pension or service money from any (foreign) prince, lord, or community whatever; and as I understand the order, all were liable to be put to the oath on this matter.*

CHAP. XIII. *He returns home.* 1529-31. 22nd & 23rd Henry VIII.

The condition of Basel held out but few inducements to the visit of an artist at this time. Religious dissensions had reached that pitch in 1529, that many of its principal residents had been forced to emigrate, and among these were Erasmus, the Burgomaster Meier zum Hasen, and some other of Holbein's friends and patrons. Erasmus gives a sad picture of the animosity of the reformers, incensed by the only too universal gross abuse of images by the Roman ecclesiastics, and accordingly the Iconoclasts showed as little discrimination in their throwing down, as the others had shown in their setting up.

Religious disturbances.

Erasmus, in a letter to his, and Albert Dürer's, friend Pirkhaimer, dated the 9th of May of this year, says, that there was not a statue left in its place, neither in the churches, nor in the vestibules, nor in the porches; not one even in the

* Sonnabend nach Lucæ 1521 wurde vom Grossen Rath eidlich verordnet: dass Niemand zu Stadt und Land künftig zu ewigen zeiten, weder durch sich selbst, sein weib oder hausgesind, noch niemand anders, keine pension noch dienstgeld von Keinem Fürsten, Herrn, Commun, noch niemand anderm bei seinem geschwornen Eide erwerben, haben, nehmen noch empfangen solle."—Ochs, *Geschichte der stadt Basel,* &c. Vol. V., p. 367. Quoted by Hegner.

CHAP. XIII.

Religious disturbances. 1529-31. 22nd & 23rd Henry VIII.

monasteries. The wall-paintings were all whitewashed over; what could be burnt was cast into the flames, and what not, was broken to pieces. Neither the intrinsic value, nor the merit, of a work of art was of any avail to save it.* The destruction was the more complete, because many were the destroyers of their own property, out of a spirit of fanatical reaction. Still something was saved, not a few having been removed or concealed; several however of Holbein's own works perished, though some were in a manner afterwards restored, as already related of the "Last Supper" in the Basel Museum.

Frescoes in the Rathhaus.

It was during this first return, in 1530, that Holbein completed the painting of the council-chamber, and for which he received the payments already given, during the summer and autumn of this year, amounting to 72 florins.† He received accordingly 60 florins each for the two first walls painted, and 72 for the third containing the two large frescoes, making 36 florins for a single composition, which was then in Basel a fair remuneration for a picture containing even thirty or forty figures. Holbein's figures were less than life-size.

On the 7th of October 1531 he received 14 florins as payment for some paintings of the two clocks of the Rhinthor—ornamental or storied dials?—"*von beden Uren am Rhinthor zmalen.*"

From these accounts it would appear that Holbein was absent from England in 1529, 1530, and part of 1531, over two years; there are certainly no traces of his presence in this country during that interval. He must have returned to England agreeably to the regulations of the town council, as appears from the Burgomaster Meier's kind letter of recal in 1532, quoted at the end of this chapter. When the council-chamber was once finished there seems to have been a total lack of worthy employment to detain him, satisfactorily to himself,

* "Statuarum nihil relictum est, nec in templis, nec in vestibulis, nec in porticibus, nec in monasteriis. Quicquid erat pictarum imaginum, calcea incrustura oblitum est; quod erat capax ignis in rogum conjectum est, quod secus frustulatim comminutum. Nec pretium nec ars impetravit, ut cuiquam omnino parceretur."

† His-Heusler, *Über Hans Holbein*, &c., p. 358.

from returning to his wealthy, commercial, and courtly patrons in England.

CHAP. XIII.

Back again in London. 1531. 23rd Henry VIII.

In the close of 1531 therefore when Holbein possibly revisited England, he must have located himself elsewhere than with Sir Thomas More, now Lord High Chancellor: some few years later he was settled in the parish of St. Andrew Undershaft. We know less how or when the painter came on his second visit, than we do concerning his first journey here. When he was introduced to the king is also unknown, though we have a little romance about the circumstances of the introduction, in the account of Van Mander. At an entertainment given by Sir Thomas More to the king, his majesty expressed great admiration for some pictures by Holbein, which the chancellor had designedly placed in the king's way, and of course like a loyal subject he offered these pictures to the king. Henry however inquired for the painter, and when informed that he was at his majesty's service, he declined Sir Thomas's gift; remarking that possessing the painter himself, he could have pictures at command.

I give this story as I find it: that Holbein was presented to the king, and entered his service is certain, but when these events took place there is no evidence to show, within a year or two. It is easy to add conjecture to conjecture, but failing facts even conjectures may sometimes be tolerable. It is possible that this introduction took place before Holbein returned to Basel, but if so it was followed by no immediate results; he did not enter into the king's service at that time, nor can he have had any hopes of so doing, or he would not have returned to Switzerland and remained away from England so long. Having once experienced the difference between a great capital and a small provincial town, Holbein can have had no patience to contentedly settle down in the latter, especially after his comparatively brilliant career in England. Having satisfied the demands of citizenship and exhausted the art demands of Basel, he would necessarily hanker after the land of his prosperity: there was nothing to keep him in Basel, but his family ties, and these we know were

CHAP. XIII.

Back again in London. 1531. 23rd Henry VIII.

not very strong. It is quite possible also that his wife should be content that her husband should reside where the better harvest was to be reaped, and his power of assisting her would be greater. There is nothing remarkable therefore in his releasing himself from Basel as soon as possible; and as he left his wife and family behind him, it was only prudent to depart with the sanction of the authorities of the city. But it would seem that on this occasion his leave of absence was for one year only, as he was recalled or desired to return in 1532, as will be shown presently: he did not however immediately comply, notwithstanding the flattering form in which the invitation was communicated to him.

Of the year 1531 we have no known works by Holbein, in England, miniatures or otherwise; even if known to the king at this time he was certainly not in his service. I am aware of several miniatures of an earlier date than this ascribed to Holbein, but independent of the absence of all corroboration of these pretensions, in the style of the drawings themselves, there are sufficient historical data to prove that several are certainly erroneously ascribed to him—some of these will be noticed in detail presently.

The Merchants of the Steelyard. 1532. 24th Henry VIII.

Of the year 1532 we have several dated portraits, but these are chiefly of Germans, apparently merchants settled here; and this would seem to show that Holbein had no special patronage to cause his return to England, no individual great patron to supply the place of Sir Thomas More. He might have felt himself quite justified in venturing his fortunes in London, on the mere strength of the reputation he had already acquired, by the many excellent works he had produced during his first visit; he had of course also made numerous acquaintances, and it is but natural that he should be more closely allied with his own countrymen, many of whom were settled in London, than with foreigners.

Among the portraits of this year ascribed to Holbein we have those of two German merchants, dated: George Gyzen, at Berlin; and the nameless member of the Stahlhof or Steelyard, at Windsor. The latter "a merchant, in a black cap, and

The Merchants of the Steelyard. 1532. 24th Henry VIII.

a knife in his hand, about to cut the seal of a letter," is said to have been presented by Sir Harry Vane to Charles I., but it does not bear that king's brand on the back, though such a portrait is mentioned as above in Vanderdoort's "Catalogue," No. 29, "a Whitehall piece," by Holbein, and it is valued in the inventory of the king's pictures at 100*l.*

It is the portrait of a youngish man with a brown beard, on an oak panel, 2 feet high by nearly 19 inches wide, the grain of the wood running transversely. He is dressed in a black furred surcoat, and is seated at a table, about to open a letter, by cutting its string with a knife; the address on the letter is not now legible, the only distinct word being *Stallhoff*; the first words may be *Dem Ersamen Heinrich*—showing that he was one of the Hanse merchants of the "Steelyard" in Thames Street. Lying on the table before him, is a piece of paper, on which he has written—*Anno Dm.* 1532 *am* (?) 26 *July. Aetatis suae* * * the age being defaced: near this paper are also some gold pieces, and a seal with a W for its device. The painting is somewhat dry and brown, being neither so rich nor transparent in colour as his earlier works, and shows the characteristic liny beard of Holbein's portraits: the background is of a raw umber hue, and has a shadow from the head cast upon it. The true colouring of this picture is somewhat obscured by dirt.

Georg Gyze

The superb portrait at Berlin is painted with a different palette, it is not more accurately executed than the Windsor picture, but is more delicate in its details, and much richer in colour; indeed it shows the highest Flemish finish, and is so delicate, so rich and clear in colour, as to unavoidably suggest a different hand from that which produced the other authentic works of our painter, of this time; though there may have been sufficient reasons for the extra care bestowed on this remarkable portrait, which is however unusually large for Holbein.

The picture is on oak, about 3 ft. 5 in. high by 3 ft. wide, and was formerly in the Solly Collection: the ground is green. The merchant, whose name is inscribed on the picture

CHAP. XIII. — *Georg Gyze.* 1532. 24th Henry VIII.

G. GYZE, which is said to be a Flemish name, is seated at a richly-covered table, in his office, about to open a letter, and is surrounded by every kind of accessary that could well be found in a merchant's counting-house, with the superfluous but agreeable embellishment of a glass of flowers exquisitely painted. He has on a red coat, and a black cap and overcoat. That so elaborate and perfect a work of art should not be inscribed with the name of the painter, is somewhat remarkable, and certainly to be regretted; the age of the subject and the year are given—*Anno Aetatis suae* XXXIIII. *Anno Dom.* 1532, and apparently his motto—*nulla sine merore voluptas.* Without going so far as to deny this picture to Holbein, I may be allowed to assert perhaps that there were certainly other painters living at the time who were also quite capable of producing such a work, some I have already noticed, as for example the Flemish Van Cleef, and others that I have mentioned. I give the reader the advantage of Mr. Ruskin's glowing description of the picture.*

"In the portrait of the Kaufmann George Gyzen, every accessary is perfect with a fine perfection: the carnations in the glass vase by his side—the ball of gold, chased with blue enamel, suspended on the wall—the books—the steelyard—the papers on the table, the seal-ring, with its quartered bearings—all intensely there, and there in beauty of which no one could have dreamed that even flowers or gold were capable, far less parchment or steel. But every change of shade is felt, every rich and rubied line of petal followed; every subdued gleam in the soft blue of the enamel and bending of the gold touched with a hand whose patience of regard creates rather than paints. The jewel itself was not so precious as the rays of enduring light which form it, beneath that errorless hand. The man himself what he was—not more; but to all conceivable proof of sight—in all aspect of life or thought—not less. He sits alone in his accustomed room, his common work laid out before him; he is conscious of no presence, assumes no

* *Cornhill Magazine*, March 1860, p. 326.

dignity, bears no sudden or superficial look of care or interest, lives only as he lived—but for ever.

CHAP. XIII.

Georg Gyze.
1532.
24th Henry VIII.

"It is inexhaustible. Every detail of it wins, retains, rewards, the attention with a continually-increasing sense of wonderfulness. It is also wholly true. So far as it reaches, it contains the absolute facts of colour, form, and character, rendered with an unaccusable faithfulness. * * What of this man and his house were visible to Holbein, are visible to us: * * if we care to know anything concerning them, great or small, so much as may by the eye be known is for ever knowable, reliable, indisputable."

The fact that this Gyzen was a London merchant is in favour of Holbein's authorship of the picture; but the address on a letter in his hand, does not contain the word Stahlhof, which we find on several other of the portraits of these German merchants; he may however have been a member of the company notwithstanding. On one of the letters he holds is distinctly written the following address—*Dem ersamen herrn Jerg Gyzen zu Lunden in engelant minem broder to henden.* To the honourable Herr George Gyzen in London, in England, my brother, to be delivered into his hands. His name was possibly Gyze, as in the picture, Gyzen being only the accusative case.

The portraits of Derick Born at Windsor, and of Geryck Tybis at Vienna, both bearing the date 1533, seem to be also of members of this same German society.

The Merchants of the Steelyard.

While speaking of portraits of the Hanse merchants of the Stahlhof or Steelyard, I take the opportunity of mentioning the two allegorical compositions of "Riches" and "Poverty," which Holbein executed for the Guild-hall of those merchants in Thames Street, probably in or about this year 1532, though there are no data from which their exact time can be fixed.

The pictures themselves which were in *tempera*, and of a large size, have apparently long since perished; the compositions however, are preserved to us in various drawings, including one possibly original sketch by Holbein himself, and now in the British Museum.

This privileged company of German merchants was dispersed

CHAP. XIII.

The Merchants of the Steelyard. 1532. 24th Henry VIII.

by Queen Elizabeth in 1598, and the Steelyard closed for some years; the two pictures were in 1617 * presented by the merchants' representative to Henry Prince of Wales, a known lover of the arts; and on that prince's premature death they appear to have passed into the possession of his brother, afterwards Charles I. They are said to have perished with other valuable works at Whitehall, in the fire which destroyed that palace in January 1698. Such is the conjecture of some; but as Felibien in his *Entretiens* on the Lives and Works of celebrated Painters, speaks of, and describes, these two pictures as seen by him in Paris, many years before that date,† I imagine it to be more probable that they shared the fate of the majority of King Charles's collections which were dispersed in Cromwell's time, and were sent abroad, and they may therefore possibly still be in existence. Further, Sandrart in his autobiography describes these two compositions, as seen by him in the "Long Gallery" at Arundel House—whether pictures or drawings he does not say; he notices them as the chief of Holbein's works belonging to the earl, and after them he describes three portraits by Holbein, as hanging in the same gallery :—Erasmus, Sir Thomas More, and a princess of Lorraine proposed to by Henry VIII. (Duchess of Milan ?). This was in 1627—they may have been presented to the earl by the king. It is under these circumstances very improbable that they were in Whitehall in 1697. These are the two compositions sketched by Zucchero in 1574, as recorded by Van Mander. He copied them, and those drawings came afterwards into the possession of Crozat. Vorsterman, jun., engraved prints from these drawings, or at least from the "Poverty;" Vertue never succeeded in finding a print of the "Riches." He discovered two drawings at Buckingham House,

* See Dr. Lappenberg's *Urkundliche Geschichte des Hansischen Stahlhofes zu London.* 4to. Hamburgh, 1851. § 7. Die gemaelde von Holbein, p. 82. They were given to the prince on the 22nd January, 1616-17. The house itself which occupied the site of the new station of the South Eastern Railway as far as Thames Street, was burnt in the great fire of 1666, but was afterwards rebuilt.

† Entretiens sur les vies et sur les Ouvrages des plus excellens peintres, &c. 2 vols. 4to. Paris, 1666.

Chap. XIII.

The Merchants of the Steelyard. 1532. 24th Henry VIII.

in black and white chalk, with coloured skies, which he assumed to be those made by Vorsterman for the purpose of engraving the compositions. Walpole however who afterwards purchased them did not agree with Vertue, but has conjectured that the "Triumph of Riches" was Vorsterman's, and the "Triumph of Poverty" Zucchero's.*

The British Museum possesses what is considered an original sketch of the "Riches" by Holbein himself; it is drawn with the pen and washed with Indian ink; is about 10 in. high by 22 wide; and by the side of it is now hanging† a curious old etching of a portion of it, but differing in many minute details, inscribed John Borg^st. Floret^o. 1561; it was executed in Antwerp: the artist appears to be unknown. On the same screen with these two are two large drawings with the pen, and washed with bistre, of the same compositions, by John Bischop, a Dutch artist who died in 1686. They may have been done from the originals after they were taken to Holland, before 1666. The "Triumph of Riches" measures about 13 in. high by 30 wide, that of "Poverty," about 13 in. high by 18 wide. They are in a good bold style and executed with great detail.

To judge from the above traces of these two great compositions, almost the only so-called historical works painted by Holbein in England, they were executed in a large style and bold manner, and displayed considerable resources of invention and composition. The subjects had reference to the pursuits of the Hanse merchants, the acquiring of Riches and the escaping from Poverty, though from their details one might imagine that Holbein considered poverty however repulsive to be less dangerous than riches.

"The Triumph of Riches."

The "Triumph of Plutus" was much the larger composition: the god is seated in a magnificent car, drawn by four white horses; he is enthroned on a high back seat, and is an

* They passed from the Strawberry Hill collection into that of Sir Charles Eastlake, who eventually bought them: they were sold at the sale in 1842 for 16*l*. 16*s*. They are engraved in Waagen's "Handbook of Painting," 1860

† On a screen in the King's Library, see Mr. Carpenter's "Guide to the Drawings and Prints exhibited to the Public, in the King's Library." 1865.

CHAP. XIII.

"The Triumph of Riches." 1532. 24th Henry VIII.

old man nearly bent double; his gold is spread before him. In front of him on a globe is seated blind Fortune scattering coins to some who are rushing forward for her favours. The charioteer is called *Ratio*; the four horses are named *Avaritia*, *Impostura*, *Usura*, and *Contractus*; the two off horses are ridden by *Liberalitas* and *Aequalitas*, while the two on the near side are led by *Bonafides* and *Justicia*; the reins are labelled *Nòtitia* and *Voluntas*: on either side is a crowd of followers, many are burdened by the weight of their purses or bags of gold, and all have historical names connected with riches, attached to them; the first is *Sichaeus*, among the last is *Cleopatra*, apparently the only woman among them. *Nemesis* is hovering in the clouds in the rear of the whole.

On this drawing are written two lines, on the evils attending wealth, said to have been furnished by Sir Thomas More :—

> Aurum blanditiae pater est natusque doloris
> Qui caret hoc moeret, qui tenet hic metuit.

The same lines were placed over the centre doorway of the Stahlhof building in Thames Street.

"The Triumph of Poverty."

Poverty or Penury, an old woman, over whom is the Greek word ΠΕΝΙΑ,* is drawn in a dilapidated waggon with a straw roof by two asses and two oxen; in the cart with her are *Industria*, *Usus*, and *Memoria* in front, and *Infortunium* behind; *Spes* is driving. The names of the asses are *Stupiditas* and *Ignavia*, and those of the oxen *Negligentia* and *Pigritia*; the animals are led by *Moderatio*, *Solicitudo*, *Diligentia*, and *Labor*: among the crowd of workmen and poor wretches escorting her are *Mendicitas* and *Miseria*.

On a tablet suspended to a tree, are the following lines, pointing out the instability of fortune and glory, and dwelling

---

* Sandrart in his description of these compositions as he saw them at Arundel House, calls this old woman HECALE (Hecate?) the name or word is Penia (Πενία) as given above, and means simply poverty or *penury*. There was no such goddess. I have never seen the name given in any account of these compositions, yet it is plain enough on the Museum drawing. Sandrart's HECALE is an enigma. Vorsterman's print has *Naenia*.

on the security and hopeful peace of poverty; also ascribed to Sir Thomas More:— CHAP. XIII.

"The Triumph of Poverty." 1532. 24th Henry VIII.

Mortalium jucunditas volucris et pendula
Movetur instar turbinis quem nix agit sedula.
Quid ergo confiditis in gloria?
Qui dives est penuriam formidat ignobilem,
Instabilis fati rotam semper timet mobilem
Degitque vitam prope fallibilem.
Qui pauper est nihil timet, nihil potest perdere
Sed spe bona lætus sedet, nam sperat acquirere,
Discitque virtute Deum Colere.

Recalled to Basel.

This is the place to notice Holbein's recal to Basel by the Burgomaster Jacob Meier (zum Hirschen, not he who is painted in the Meier altar-piece): the letter is dated Monday the 2nd of September 1532, and is as follows, commencing in the third person but continuing in the second:—

"To Master Hans Holbein the Painter, now in England.

"We Jacob Meier, Burgomaster and councillor of the city of Basel, send greeting herewith, and announce to our beloved burgess Hans Holbein, that it would give us great pleasure if you would return home again as speedily as possible. So will we, in order that you may be in a better condition to support your *wife and child*, at home, grant you an allowance of thirty pieces of money yearly, till something better can be done for you in accordance with our friendly desire towards you: this we wish you to be informed of to avoid future misunderstanding."*

* A literal translation of this letter being next to impossible if the sense of the English is to be preserved, I add the original:—

Meister Hansen Holbein dem Mahler, jetzt in England. Wir Jacob Meier Bürgermeister und Rath der Stadt Basel, entbieten hiemit unserm lieben Bürger, Hansen Holbein, unsern Gruss, und dabei zu vernehmen, dass es uns gefallen wollte, dass du dich zum förderlichtsten wieder anheim verfügest. So wollen wir, damit du desto besser bey haus bleiben, dein weib und kind ernähren mögest, dich des Jahrs mit dreyssig Stücken Geldes, bis wir dich besser versehen mögen, freundlich bedenken und versehen; (solches) haben wir dir, dich hienach wüsstest zu verhalten, nicht unangezeigt wollen lassen. Datum Montags 2 September 1532. Ochs, *Geschichte*, &c., V. 395; Hegner, *Hans Holbein*, &c., 242. His-Heusler quotes this letter in its original form; the words are the same though the spelling is very different.

CHAP. XIII.

Recalled to Basel.
1532.
24th
Henry VIII.

It is surmised that Holbein received this missive in the autumn while present with the court at Calais, but I have found no corroboration of the surmise, nor is there any evidence that he ever got it or ever visited Basel in consequence of its summons. Dr. Waagen records the fact as ascertained, quoting Hegner, who makes no such assertion, and he farther couples his statement with an extraordinary mistake both in the time and circumstances of the occasion. He says,* "This communication only reached the artist in 1533, on the occasion of the accompanying King Henry to the celebrated meeting with Francis I., called the *Field of the Cloth of Gold.*" The famous meeting referred to, as is well known, took place in June 1520; and the next meeting with which Dr. Waagen has confounded this interview, occurred in October 1532, when Anne Boleyn accompanied the king as Marchioness of Pembroke, and when it is quite possible that Holbein was present; he may accordingly have then received at Calais the kind summons of the Burgomaster of Basel.

Holbein's reported second visit to Basel is assumed (but not proved) to have taken place in the end of 1532 and in the beginning of 1533, he, instead of returning with the court to England, having prosecuted his journey to Switzerland, where the friendly feeling of the authorities towards him, enabled him apparently quickly to return to the country of his choice, and to a field of labour more in accordance with his great abilities, than could possibly be supplied by a small provincial town in Switzerland.† No doubt a proper provision was made for his wife and son Philip; the other of the two children left with the wife in 1526, Franz Schmid? having by this time attained to years enabling him probably to labour towards his own maintenance.

* *Handbook of Painting*, p. 198.

† There is a print by Hollar of a jeweller of the name of Hans; called Hans von Zürich, of which it is professed that the original by Holbein was painted in this year, in Switzerland. It is inscribed—*Hans von Zürch, Goltschmidt. Hans Holbein*, 1532. *W. Hollar fecit*, 1647, *ex collectione Arundeliana.* With a dedication by the publisher H. Vander Borcht, to Matthew Merian.

CHAPTER XIV.

Holbein presented to Henry VIII. Miniatures and other Portraits of the King and of the Royal Family.

E may perhaps admit, that there is some vague evidence or at least probability that Holbein was towards the end of the year 1532 known personally to Henry VIII., but there is nothing to prove that he was not known to him before this time; we may however assume for certain that he was not as yet in the king's service: but when was he presented?

Chap. XIV. *Presented to the king.* 1532-3. 25th Henry VIII.

From what has been said in the last chapter, about Holbein's visit to Basel, it is no longer very remarkable, that in the accounts of Sir Brian Tuke, Treasurer of the Chamber,* extending from the 1st of October, of the 20th of Henry VIII. (1528), to the 23rd of May, of the 23rd of Henry VIII. (1531), we should find no mention whatever of Holbein, though several other painters are noticed in those accounts. For a great part of the time Holbein was in Basel; and as to the rest it corroborates my opinion that Holbein had not been brought personally to the king's notice, before his return home after his lengthened sojourn with Sir Thomas More. I have already alluded to the story of his presentation having been

* Extracts in Trevelyan Papers. Part I. Edited for the Camden Society by J. P. Collier; referred to in Mr. Franks's paper in the Archæologia.

CHAP. XIV.

Presented to the king.
1532-3.
25th Henry VIII.

brought about by Sir Thomas More; this may or may not be true, but it is probable. The fact that More was no longer chancellor in the autumn of 1532, he having resigned the seals in May of that year, would perhaps favour the supposition that Holbein's presentation to the king may have taken place previously; but as there seems to be only this bare probability, I must, as I am endeavouring to write a history, not a romance, leave the matter as it stands, quite uncertain.

We have some fine portraits of this year, dated, by Holbein, but not one of the king. An early portrait of Henry VIII., compared with the mass of the ordinary half-lengths of him dispersed over the country, is in the gallery at Hampton Court. This is a good picture, but does not show the characteristic firm touch of our painter. It is a half-length; his hair is cropped close to his head, and he has a short beard, both are of a sandy colour; he is dressed in cloth of gold and fur, and wears a cap and white feather; in his hands is a scroll, with the following legend from the Gospel of St. Mark—MARCI—16. "ITE IN MŨDUM UNIVERSŨ ET PREDICATE EVANGELIUM OMNI CREATURE." Under the scroll is a red cushion; the ground is green. The picture is considerably rubbed, especially about the mouth and eyes; the mouth is badly repaired and the lights are gone from the eyes. The hands are well drawn but somewhat enamelled, after the fashion of Van Cleef. On oak, 2 ft. 4 in. *h.* by 1 ft. 10 in. *w.* It formed one of the collection of Charles I., and from a note on the back—"*Changed with my Lord Arundel,* 1624"—it appears to have been given to the king by the Earl of Arundel. Tradition did not give this portrait to Holbein, for Vanderdoort in his catalogue, ascribes it *either* to Holbein or Van Cleef: I am inclined to consider the latter the better name, but a still more suitable name is perhaps Girolamo da Treviso, for the head shows much of his handling.

After 1533, Holbein appears to have rarely dated his pictures, which is a misfortune. Certainly if painters had not only inscribed their works with their own names and dates, but also with the names of the parties represented, they would have saved posterity, immense labour, and endless conjecture, setting aside the positive benefits that might have accrued from such a practice. That many families might possibly under such circumstances have been deprived of their "imaginary ancestors," is but a light disadvantage for the general world, to be put into the other side of the scales. Let the present generation take warning, and attach the names of individuals to the backs of their photographs; if not, there is a chance of the class of "imaginary ancestors" attaining to the number of millions; they may be less valued however as they get cheaper.

CHAP. XIV.

Presented to the king.
1532-3.
25th Henry VIII.

Queen Anne Boleyn.

In November 1532, Anne Boleyn was privately married to Henry VIII.;* in June following, she was publicly crowned by Cranmer at Westminster, and on the 7th of September 1533 the Princess Elizabeth was born. I find no authentic portrait whatever, by Holbein, of either the mother or the daughter. Among the drawings at Windsor, is one of a young woman to which Anne Boleyn's name is attached (No. 18, Vol. II.), but no reliance can be placed on the designation.† There is a drawing inscribed *Lady Mary, after Queen* (No. 39, Vol. II.), which may possibly be authentic as far as age is concerned, but the countenance suggests doubt: the Lady Elizabeth can only have been drawn by Holbein as a child: this queen was just ten years old, at the time of the painter's death. In the Royal Collection is a reputed portrait of the PRINCESS ELIZABETH, in her sixteenth year, ascribed to Holbein: it is now in

* Froude, *History of England*, &c. Vol. I., p. 418. 3rd. Ed.

† The Berlin gallery has a small picture of a Queen Anne, about 14 inches by 11, which Dr. Waagen in his "Catalogue" has named Anne Boleyn, by Holbein. She is in a black cap and white feather, with her hands crossed before her; and the picture is inscribed—ANNA REGINA 1525. *Anno Aetatis*, 22. Rather an unhappy inscription for a picture of Anne Boleyn: of course the doctor repudiates the writing. The picture may be genuine, though that it has nothing to do with either Anne Boleyn or Holbein is perhaps the right explanation of the matter. A similar figure in hat and feather, with her hands crossed before her, but larger, on wood 33 in. *h.* by 23 in. *w.*, belonging to Sir Montague Cholmeley, was this year in the South Kensington Exhibition. It is inscribed — ANNA REGINA 1530. HB, but it is neither the picture of Anne Boleyn nor by Holbein.

CHAP. XIV.

Queen Anne Boleyn. 1532-3. 25th Henry VIII.

St. James's Palace. So long as the period of Holbein's death was deferred eleven years beyond its true date there was nothing impossible in the ascription. Vanderdoort has catalogued this portrait, as "a Whitehall piece by Holbein" representing "Queen Elizabeth when she was young, to the waist." This description is not accurate; the figure is quite to the knees.

The Princess Elizabeth.

To speak from the figure itself, I should judge its subject to have been certainly not more than thirteen years of age at most when the portrait was taken: she is standing, showing the face in full, in a pink damask gown, and a white satin and gold petticoat, with a head-dress of pearls, and many rich jewels about her person; she holds in her hands what appears to be now a *green* rather than a *blue* book; by her right side is placed sloping on a kind of desk, another book open, but in which no trace of print or manuscript remains; behind her is a thin transparent curtain; the back-ground is brown. Inscribed in the right upper corner—*Elizabetha Filia Rex Angliae.* On oak, 3 ft. 6 in. high by 2 ft. 7½ in. wide.

The Princess Mary.

Who the painter of this picture may have been, it is difficult to surmise: that it was not Holbein is certain; he was clearly the same as the painter of the Princess Mary's fine portrait, belonging to the Society of Antiquaries.* She is in a brown and yellow, or tawny brocaded dress, the sleeves being heavily furred at the elbows, and like the Princess Elizabeth, is loaded with rich jewels and pearls, exquisitely painted, and almost identical in pattern in both pictures. She stands with her hands crossed one over the other; in the back-ground is a red gold-fringed hanging showing the creases of the folds in squares. On oak, 3 ft. 4½ in. high by 2 ft. 6 in. wide. Signed in the lower right corner HFt with the obscure remains of a date by the side of the monogram, showing 54, which figures I

* Both pictures were hung this year, 1866, in the Portrait Exhibition at South Kensington; where also was exhibited the queen's picture of Edward VI., which is possibly by the same hand: it is inscribed—*Edwardus Sextus Rex Angliae.* It is a three-quarter length reaching to below the knees.

The Princess Mary. 1532-3. 25th Henry VIII.

imagine to be the second and third figures of the date rather than the third and fourth; at present nothing beyond these two figures is at all legible, and these are sufficiently obscure. The date may have been 1543–6; it is difficult to imagine that it was ever 1554, as clearly written below, for this cannot be the portrait of a woman thirty-eight years of age; the face is quite youthful, and may easily represent that of a woman under thirty.* The monogram is not identified with that of any known painter of this time; it is certainly not Lucas de Heere's; HE has been explained as his mark, though not satisfactorily, as H. E. HE is a monogram and when written by De Heere, if ever written by him, must be explained as L. H. F. *Lucas Heere Fecit:* we find this mark on the allegorical picture of Queen Elizabeth at Hampton Court, with the date 1569, and we find it also but in a different form, as H. E. I assume, on the so-called Sir Anthony Denny portrait, at Longford Castle, with the date 1550; and it is on a portrait of Henry VIII. at Trinity College, Cambridge, with the addition of the word *fecit*, showing that it cannot be De Heere's in this case.

The discovery of the painter of these two portraits is greatly to be desired; they are not the work of either a boy in his teens or of a lad of twenty. In 1546 when they may have been painted, De Heere, born in 1534, had only just entered his teens; Anthony More, born in 1525, was but young for such a work, supposing him to have been in this country at the time; otherwise as the pupil of Schoorel the style is such as he might be supposed to have adopted in the early part of his career: but the signature is certainly not his. Even interpreting the defaced date as 1554, Lucas de Heere cannot have been the painter, he was too young at the time, he did

* The date 1554, in rather modern-looking figures is very legibly written below the monogram; as a picture would not be twice dated, and I fancy I see the defaced date at the side, I take this to be the attempt of some one to interpret and restore the damaged date, and under the impression that the picture was of Queen Mary, not the princess, the 54 has perhaps been complemented accordingly, into 1554; I give this however as a mere conjecture. The monogram is not HF or HE, but HFt, though the small t to the naked eye looks like a mere blot.

CHAP. XIV.

The Princess Mary. 1532-3. 25th Henry VIII.

not visit this country until some few years later, and his style was not so elaborate. Hornebolt's style and signature are both unknown, but he was living in May 1544. If Hornebolt be suggested as the painter, we are driven to seek another name for the portrait called the Princess Elizabeth, which certainly represents a girl beyond her eleventh year, unless indeed that princess were remarkably precocious. An alternative is that it may not represent this princess; a conclusion that Walpole came to. HFt 1544, is quite a possible signature for Hornebolt.

Mr. Nichols in his Paper on Holbein's contemporaries, already referred to, has called attention to the fact that in the Privy Purse Expenses of the Princess Mary, occurs under the date of Nov. 1544, the following entry: "*Item, paied to one John that drue her grace in a table, V*[li.]" Sir Frederick Madden in his annotations to these accounts, remarks that there is a picture of Mary inscribed "LADI MARI DOUGHTER TO THE MOST VERTUOUS PRINCE KINGE HENRI THE EIGHT. THE AGE OF XXVIII. YERES. ANNO D'NI. 1544," of which an engraving was made by Thane in 1778. Neither of these pictures may have been by Hornebolt, but it is just possible that the former entry, if both do not refer to the same picture, may indicate the above-described portrait. At that time 5*l.* was a very large price to pay for a portrait, and the picture must have been an elaborate one.

If we consider that this group of the three children of Henry VIII., Edward VI., at Windsor, and the two princesses, was the work of one man at nearly the same time, we to a great extent limit the names of the painters to whom we might ascribe them: that the two princesses are by the same hand is certain, but that the prince is also by the same hand, admits of question, though the same drapery-painter may have been employed in all. The prince's portrait can scarcely have been executed before 1547 or even later; and at that time both Hornebolt and Girolamo da Treviso were long since dead; they both died in 1544. Van Cleef was living, and was quite capable of such work, but the monogram HF[t] certainly excludes

The Princess Mary. 1532-3. 25th Henry VIII.

him;* though it need not exclude Gerome, as this name was commonly written by painters in its Latin form with an H., and the signature in question might be interpreted as *Hieronymus Fecit.*†

The picture of the Princess Elizabeth was in the collection of Charles I., and is described by Vanderdoort as follows:—

65. A Whitehall piece by Holben.

> Item, the picture of Queen Elizabeth when she was young, to the waist, in a red habit, holding a blue book in both her hands, and another book lying upon the table. In a gilded wooden frame, painted on board. 5 ft. × 4 ft.

With the Court at Calais?

October 1532 is the period necessarily assigned for the painting of the several portraits of Francis I., and of some of the members of his court, which have been ascribed to Holbein: independent of the improbability of Holbein's having had any opportunity to paint such pictures during this interview between the two kings at Calais, this autumn, supposing him to have been present, which is not shown, the pictures themselves, by their style, contradict the ascriptions; there does not appear to be any picture of any member of the French court by Holbein. On the other hand these portraits are com-

* Ordinary accounts state that Van Cleef died in 1536, which I believe is an error for 1556. Van Mander dates this painter's ultimate insanity from his disappointment in finding that Anthony More's introduction of him to Philip II. of Spain when he came to this country to marry Queen Mary, resulted in nothing, as the Spanish prince had so high an opinion of the works of Titian, that he had no eye for those of the Fleming: this was in 1554. If the monogram had been IF[t], it might possibly have stood for *Justus Fecit.*

† We have a fine altar-piece by Girolamo da Treviso, in the National Gallery, "The Madonna and Child enthroned," with saints and angels, &c.; but this is signed IERONIMUS. TREVISIUS. P. The style is good, and the surface is of an enamelled character, not at all unlike the portrait of Henry VIII. just described. It is not known when the painter came to England, but if the cause of his coming here was, as is reported, his unsuccessful competition with Perino del Vaga at Genoa, it may have been even as early as 1530, when he was in his thirty-third year. Girolamo was born at Treviso in 1497, and was killed by a cannon ball in 1544, near Boulogne while acting as an engineer, in the service of Henry VIII. See Federici, *Memorie Trevigiane su le Opere di Disegno,* &c. 1803.

To return to the orthography of the name Gerome, the altar-piece in the National Gallery, by Girolamo dai Libri, is signed HIERONYMUS A LIBRIS. F.

CHAP. XIV.

With the Court at Calais.
1532-3.
25th Henry VIII.

pletely in the manner of Francis's own painter JEAN CLOUET, commonly called JEANNET, a Fleming settled in France, and married to a French wife, and who was painter and *varlet de chambre ordinaire* to Francis I., from 1518 to 1541.*

It is possible that some exchanges of pictures took place at these meetings. Caroline Patin speaks of such a possible exchange, Henry receiving from Francis a Madonna by Leonardo da Vinci, for some portraits by Holbein; I repeat this circumstance simply as a rumour that has already found circulation.

It is sufficiently remarkable, and says much for Holbein's reputation among the generations that immediately followed him, that he should have absorbed within the vortex of his fame, nearly all his own immediate rivals or contemporaries in England; but that also the principal of his contemporaries of a great foreign court that he is not known ever to have visited, should meet with the same fate, and not only in England but on the continent too, as at Florence, Antwerp, and elsewhere, is indeed extraordinary.

I allude to such works as the portraits of French personages at Hampton Court; Mr. Morrison's "Anne of Cleves;" the Earl of Dudley's Francis I., which appears to belong to FRANCOIS CLOUET, or the younger Jeannet; to the equestrian portrait of Francis I. at Florence; and the Francis II., as a little boy, now in the gallery at Antwerp.

The Battle of Spurs.

This is perhaps the place to say a few words about the pictures of the "Battaile of Spurs," the "Field of the Cloth of Gold," and other similar works at Hampton Court, there ascribed to Holbein. This species of painting, though not without cleverness, is mere pictorial mechanism: Holbein never produced anything of the kind, since the few of his earliest bread-and-cheese pictures painted at Basel; such as the school-

* Jeannet's wife was Jeanne Boucault of Tours, their son Francois succeeded to the rank and employment of his father in 1541; and the later works of this family of painters, four altogether, are the productions of Francois, who was also called Jeannet, and is commonly confounded with his father: he was still living in January 1571, but was already deceased in 1574. Le Cte de Laborde, *La Renaissance des Arts à la Cour de France.* Peinture. 1850-5.

master's sign, of the year 1516. These works belong to a much earlier time than Holbein's, and were doubtless the work of some such man as JOHN CRUST, a painter living in the earlier years of Henry VIII., concerning whom and his work, Mr. Cole has published an interesting extract from the exchequer records : Crust was possibly the painter of these very pictures.* Another of Henry's painters VINCENT VOLPE was employed on views and such work as this; he was in the receipt of a salary of 20*l.* a year, as late as 1530.†

CHAP. XIV.

The Battle of Spurs.

1532-3. 25th Henry VIII.

To this year belongs Holbein's most important work in England; the so-called "Ambassadors," at Longford Castle, near Salisbury; by no means the most delicate or refined, but the largest and that on which he has bestowed the most labour. The subject is doubtful, but it is supposed to represent SIR THOMAS WYATT, the poet and diplomatist, and some learned friend; the indicated age of the principal figure in the picture corresponds with that of Sir Thomas Wyatt, who was born in 1503.

The "Two Ambassadors."

1533.

* Exchequer volume, Chapter House, C. 5., 10. 6th Henry VIII.—1515.
"Payntors drawing the Towne of Bullon and grounde about the same—John Crust and his servant 13 days, at 12*d.* by the day.
Divers colours and stuff bought for the same:—

First, paid for 3 ells of lynen clothe	2s.
Item for half a pound of Vermeleon	5*d.*
— " " " Whitelede	1*d.*
— " " " Reade lede	1*d.*
— " " " Verdgreace	8*d.*
— " " " Spanysh brown	1*d.*
— " 1 quarter of orpiment	4*d.*
— " 1 lb. of yellow ocur	2*d.*
— " 1 qrt. of gume armonyck	4*d.*
— " 1 unce of flory	2*d.*
— " 1 unce sangwyn dracones	16*d.*
— " 1 qrt. of oyle	5*d.*
— " a botell of erth	1*d.*
— " for paper and brystyll	6*d.*
— " for 1 lb. glewe	4*d.*
— " for threde	1*d.*
— " 1 lb. of rooset	16*d.*
— " ½ lb. generall	6*d.*
— " 1 dossen pott for colors	6*d.*
— " a great pott of erth	1*d.*"

Summerley's *Hampton Court*, p. 82.

† Trevelyan Papers. I. 144-177; quoted by Mr. Nichols.

CHAP. XIV.

The "Two Ambassadors." 1533. 25th Henry VIII.

By the side of a double table, or "what-not" of two shelves, are standing two gentlemen; the one on the spectator's left is magnificently dressed, in a pink satin doublet, and a black jacket, over which is a black surcoat lined with ermine; he wears a black cap; and round his neck is a simple chain with a large badge of the archangel Michael, attached to it. On a gold dagger-hilt at his side, is written his age—ÆT. SVÆ 29: a magnificent green and gold tassel is hanging here. He is looking straight out of the picture.

The other man on the opposite side of the "what-not" has on a doctor's cap, and a brownish green figured morning gown; on the "what-not" by his side, on which he is leaning with his right arm holding a glove in his hand, is a book and on the edges of its leaves is written—*Aetatis suae* 25.

The upper shelf of the table is covered with a Turkey carpet, and on this shelf are a celestial globe, some sun-dials, and other scientific implements in great abundance. On the lower shelf are a terrestrial globe, a guitar, some musical pipes, an open music book with German words, and a book of calculations also with German words. Beneath the lower shelf, on the floor, is another guitar, in shadow; and in the fore-ground quite in front, is a singular object which looks like the bones of some fish. The whole of the back-ground is a green damask curtain. The floor of the room is parquetted, or paved with various coloured marbles in a simple geometrical pattern; and in one of the forms just below the lower edge of the ermined overcoat of the figure presumed to be Sir Thomas Wyatt, is the following legend:—

JOANNES
HOLBEIN
PINGEBAT

1533

In oil, on ten boards joined vertically, 6 ft. 9 in. high by 6 ft. 10 in. wide. It has been engraved by J. Pierron, and published in the "Le Brun Gallery."

The faces of this picture are somewhat hard, but finely

drawn; Sir Thomas's beard is well made out, with a few very fine lines: the hands are rather formal and are not perfectly modelled; there is a hardness throughout in the painting of the accessaries, but the execution is generally very perfect, though much of it must have been left to assistants, for the amount of labour altogether bestowed upon this picture is prodigious. Some of the details, as for instance the books, are exceedingly elaborate. Sir Thomas Wyatt's magnificent dress is admirably painted, and this figure has altogether a very grand and imposing effect. Unfortunately the picture is covered in many parts with a dirty spoilt varnish, which requires to be removed to restore it to its proper effect; it was doubtless once a brilliant picture. There are two sketches of Sir Thomas among the Windsor drawings. Holbein was distinguished for a portrait of Sir Thomas Wyatt; probably the above-described picture; for in some funeral lines on the poet who died in 1541 aged only thirty-eight, Leland, in a small quarto printed in London in 1542, entitled *Naeniae in Mortem Thomae Viati Equitis Incomparabilis, Joanne Lelando Antiquario autore*, Holbein is spoken of as the greatest in his art, for some such work.

The "Two Ambassadors." 1533. 25th Henry VIII.

Under a small woodcut, on the reverse of the title, is the following encomium on both painter and painted :—

In effigiem Thomae Viati.

Holbenus nitida pingendi Maximus arte
Effigiem expressit graphicè; sed Nullus Apelles
Exprimet ingenium felix animumque Viati.

Derick Born.

In a similar style to the last picture with the same cool brown flesh, is the fine portrait of a young man in the Queen's collection at Windsor—DERICK BORN—belonging to the same year. It is a small half-length of a handsome youth, dressed in black satin, with a white collar, embroidered with black thread. He is resting with his right elbow on a stone, and the left hand easily placed on the right wrist: on the forefinger of this hand is a gold signet ring, the device, a coat of arms. The back-ground is plain green, but is agreeably varied by some vine sprigs, the leaves of which, of a yellowish-brown

CHAP. XIV. — *Derick Born.* 1533. 25th Henry VIII.

tint, are nearly all foreshortened. Inscribed DER. BORN ETATIS SUÆ 23 ANNO 1533. On oak, 1 ft. 11½ in. high by 1 ft. 5¾ in. wide. On the back are the brands of King Charles I., and of William IV.

It has also the following lines highly complimentary to the painter, written on the lower edge of the panel, on a plinth or band, stating that the picture wants but a voice, to be mistaken for Derick himself:—

> DERICHUS SI VOCEM ADDAS IPSISSIMUS HIC SIT,
> HUNC DUBITES PICTOR FECERIT AN GENITOR.

I have already noticed the portrait of Henry VIII.'s falconer Robert Cheseman, now at the Hague, and painted in this year.

Geryck Tybis. The gallery of Vienna also possesses an excellent portrait of this date, of a man in a black cap and furred black gown, standing at a table sealing a letter; near him are a seal and some papers, on one of which is written—*Geryck Tybis zu London* 33 *Jahr alt.* 1533. On oak, 18 in. high by 13 wide. A portrait of similar style and the same size, but not so decidedly of the Holbein character, which however may arise from the few years' interval between their periods, is hung as a pendant to the Geryck Tybis; it represents a young man also in a cap and black furred gown, holding a partly open book in his right hand; and is inscribed ANNO DÑI 1541. AETATIS SUAE 28.

Amb. Fallen? The gallery at Brunswick possesses a fine portrait of this time of one of the merchants of the Stahlhof, in character similar to that of Geryck Tybis (No. 375). The portrait of a man in a black surcoat; with two letters and a glove in his hands; it is inscribed IN ALS GEDOLTIG. SIS ALTERS 32. ANNO 1533. Which signifies—In all things patient. In the thirty-second year of his age, 1533. In the letters in his hand are two very interesting addresses,* but the name is so imperfectly given that it can only be guessed at; it seems to be Fallen. On one is—*Dem Ersamen Festen* (?) *H* (errn)

* For which I have to thank Dr. Woltmann.

Fallenn zu Lund (on) *in Stalluff si dis* * * * * On the other is — *Dem Ersamen Hn. Amb. Falen zu Lūden in Stalhoff sy diesser briff:* "this letter is for the Honourable Herr Ambrose Falen at London in the Steelyard."

CHAP. XIV.

Sumptuary law.

1533. 25th Henry VIII.

It was on Lady Day 1533, that Henry's sumptuary law against the then prevailing extravagance of dress was to come into operation—it was entitled "An Acte for Reformacyon of Excesse of Apparayle." Though many restrictions are made, still abundance of latitude seems to have been left to the middle class, then comparatively a small and insignificant body.

As an illustration of the expense some must have gone to in their dress it will be sufficient to quote a single provision. None but the king or members of the royal family were henceforth to wear purple silk, or cloth of gold tissue, *except* dukes and marquises, and these might wear cloth of gold provided it did not cost more than 5*l.* the yard. To give an adequate notion of the expense of this luxury it will be sufficient to state, that a single yard of this cheaper sort of tissue cost the amount of just two months of Holbein's salary, or nearly the whole year's stipend of an ordinary parish priest. We weave silks at the present day still more costly, absolutely in amount of money, but not approaching the expense relatively, in value.

The Lord Chancellor was permitted to wear any velvet silk or satin, except purple, and any fur but black genet: this fur (wild cat) and lucern (lynx) appear to have been the most select and costly: ermine, and yellow sable seem to have been very generally worn, by the nobility, and by others abroad; in the statute referred to, sable was limited to the rank of a viscount. Satin and damask were commonly worn by the gentry; ordinary citizens, tradesmen, and servants were limited to the use of cloth, and instead of furs, lambs' wool.*

* The Harleian MS. in the British Museum, No. 1419; and the Augmentation Office volume 160 in the Record Office, show the wonderful wardrobe and amount of furniture, possessed by Henry VIII. Such an outfit as he possessed would cost many hundreds of thousands of pounds now-a-days.

CHAP. XIV.

Portraits of the king. 1533. 25th Henry VIII.

I find no certain portraits of the king at this time by Holbein. There is said to be a drawing of Henry by him, at Munich, in the Print-Room there, a head on paper, life-size, but the date is of course uncertain. Vanderdoort, in the catalogue published by Bathoe, mentions two miniatures ascribed to him;* even should Vanderdoort be right in his ascription of them to Holbein, it is next to impossible to identify them now. The Duke of Buccleuch possesses two at Montagu House; one a mere head 1¾ in. in diameter, on a blue ground; free but carefully touched in places, and it has a good general effect. The other, 2½ in. in diameter, also on a blue ground; the face is free, but retouched about the forehead: the general effect is good, but the right hand holding a ring is exceedingly ill drawn. Miniatures once genuine, may become so disfigured by repairs, often rendered indispensable, through wear and tear, and natural decay, as no longer to be identified with themselves in their uninjured state. Slight blemishes and spots are often immaterial, but when coarsely repaired their injury is magnified tenfold; but even such bungling repairs are not so mischievous as where merely injured parts have been replaced by new, as the hand for instance, which is worthless if ill drawn. We may regret a damaged hand in a fine miniature, but what is that compared with the introduction as a substitute, of a piece of clumsy patchwork that has neither nature nor art to recommend it? Such delicate things as miniatures, unless the most skilful hand can be secured, had better be left in their decayed state; we can often trace beauties through decay, but seldom through unskilful repairs.

I am not going to give a list of the miniatures of Henry VIII., but the Queen possesses four, ascribed to Holbein, apparently on no other grounds than that they are portraits of Henry VIII., which I think it desirable to notice. Three of these portraits

* The measurements given in this edition of King Charles's catalogue, seem to have been often added by Vertue, and they are not unfrequently wrong: he possibly included the frame sometimes in the dimensions of the picture.

appear to have been executed before Holbein came to England, and the fourth, after our painter's death. They are— CHAP. XIV.

Portraits of the king. 1533. 25th Henry VIII.

1. HENRY VIII., three-quarter face, turned to the left; on card, round, $1\frac{5}{6}$ in. in diameter; bright blue ground. Inscribed H. R. VIII. AN^O. ETATIS XXXV°., that is, in 1526. He has on a black cap with a feather; the beard is shaven entirely off, and the hair long light brown, hangs over and conceals the ears.

2. HENRY VIII., three-quarter face, turned to the left, on card, round, $1\frac{1}{2}$ in. in diameter; bright blue ground. Inscribed REX. HENRICVS. OCTAVVS. Nearly identical with that above described, except that the face is nowhere shaven; the age seems to be about the same. Both these miniatures are said to have belonged to Charles I., to whom they were given according to the tradition by Lord Suffolk. They are catalogued in a MS. by Vanderdoort at Windsor, but they are not in that catalogue ascribed to Holbein: they are numbered 48 and 49.

3. HENRY VIII., three-quarter face, turned to the left, oval $1\frac{9}{10}$ in. *h.* by $1\frac{7}{10}$ in. *w.*; on card; blue ground. The face is young and much the same in other respects as that first described, especially as regards the long hair, and the absence of beard. It is inscribed H. R. VIII. AN^O. XXXV., with H and K combined in a lover's knot, above; the K necessarily signifying Queen Katharine of Arragon, as the portrait is evidently not that of the king when advanced in years. The numerals I am forced to take to refer to the king's age, as in the first instance, not to his reign. The difference is material; while 1525–6 was the thirty-fifth of his age, the thirty-fifth of his reign was 1543–4; when he was very fat, cropped his hair, and had a grey beard. The interval is exactly that between Holbein's visit to this country and his death; he came to England in the thirty-sixth year of Henry's age, and died in the thirty-fifth of the king's reign. To judge from the inscription on the portrait of Sir Richard Southwell at Florence, Holbein would have written AN^O. H. VIII. XXXV., if he had intended to signify the regnal year. Mr. Magniac

CHAP. XIV.

Portraits of the king. 1533. 25th Henry VIII.

has a similar miniature to this; it was exhibited at South Kensington in 1865.

4. HENRY VIII., in oil on paper, attached to oak, round, 2⅝ in. in diameter; green ground. Inscribed—HENR. 8 REX. ANGL. ÆTA: S. 57. Full face, in hat and feather, with an ermine or some other white fur collar, close under the chin. The face, with scarcely any hair, and a thin beard, is the same type as that so familiar to us in the ordinary portraits of the king, as in the Yarborough picture; or in the somewhat later Kimbolton, Serlby, Warwick, and other similar portraits, all repetitions of the same head with a variety in the costume only, and belonging apparently to the last year of the king's reign, 1546. The age on the miniature is an error; Henry VIII. never entered his fifty-seventh year; having been born in 1491, he would have only completed his fifty-sixth year if he had survived until the 28th of June 1547.

On the back of this miniature is a small paper label on which is written in an old hand, and in faded ink, "*King Henry 8th*," and in a modern hand, and fresh ink, has been added "*by Holbein.*" Before the discovery of the date of Holbein's death, the error of ascribing to him portraits of Henry at the close of his life was not evident: it is now patent. Most false ascriptions must necessarily be the growth of time; but three fourths perhaps of the works attributed to Holbein, are so on no better grounds than the above miniature has been named.

As not one of the above four miniatures is by Holbein, the reader may ask, "By whom were they painted?" This is more than I have undertaken to say. I do not presume that Lucas Hornebolt had any hand in the water-colour drawings; the same objection holds with him as holds with Holbein; he was most probably not in England at the earlier period, and in 1546 he had been dead already two years. There was a painter in England, of great repute in 1546, who was quite capable of executing the oil miniature; this was Guillim Stretes, a Dutchman, to whom I shall have occasion to recur: in 1551 he was enjoying the high salary of 62*l.* 10*s.* a year, as painter to Edward VI. He acted, I believe, a very much more important part, among foreign artists in this country, than he has ever had the credit of doing. But an artist especially celebrated in miniatures and Holbein's contemporary was Lavinia Teerlinck, noticed in the eleventh chapter; surely some of the works by which she earned her renown must be preserved.

Chap. XIV.

Portraits of the king.
1533.
25th Henry VIII.

An exceedingly fine miniature, in every way excellent, with a coat of arms on a back-piece, German? was exhibited at South Kensington in 1865, by Mr. J. Heywood Hawkins, a small round, on card, with blue ground, the portrait of a lady, inscribed—*Anno Aetatis suae* 23. This, as every good miniature of the time, is ascribed to Holbein; why, it would be difficult to say, except that the prestige of Holbein's name is assumed to give value to everything ascribed to him. We have no *key* to Holbein's miniatures; there is not a single miniature in existence, that can be positively assigned to Holbein. We have only the vague assertion of Van Mander that he painted miniatures; there is no contemporary account of his drawings of this class, nor is there a single document proving the fact. The Queen's miniature of Lady Audley, if any, may be accredited to him, for it is identical with the drawing of that lady, in the Windsor series; this however is not proof of its authorship. If there had been no other good miniature painter of the time, then there might be some reason in giving all possible works to Holbein; but we happen to know that there were several good miniature painters of this time. This miniature, "Elizabeth wife of George Touchet, Lord Audley," is a round, $2\frac{1}{3}$ in. in diameter, with a blue ground, painted on the back of the two of hearts; it is good but damaged. Mr. Hawkins's "Lady" is finer than this "Lady Audley." Another miniature lent by Earl Spencer, similar in style, in the Kensington Exhibition of 1865, of remarkable excellence, is that numbered 950 in the catalogue—"Sir John Boling Hatton, and his mother;" signed, and dated, in gold letters L 1525. On a bright green ground. Can this L mean Lavinia? Both this miniature, and Mr. Hawkins's "Lady"

Lady Audley.

CHAP. XIV. — *Lady Audley.* 1533. 25th Henry VIII.

appear to be by the same hand. L. might also mean Luke, but Hornebolt was probably not in England in 1525, though we do not know that he was not.* 1525 may be too soon also for Lavinia Teerlinck.

In speaking of the Queen's miniatures I may mention here also that of Sir Henry Guildford, an oval, 3 in. *h.* by 2½ in. *w.* The face is fine, but young; it has a small delicate moustache; he is in a large grey cloak, edged with white fur, and has on a black cap, and he holds his sword with his left hand. If this miniature really represents Sir Henry Guildford, as a young man, how can it have been painted by Holbein? Sir Henry was one of Holbein's first sitters, and then, in 1527 he was nearly fifty years of age; he certainly appears his age in the fine Windsor portrait of him, though in the portfolio-drawing I should guess him to be somewhat younger.

The Dukes of Suffolk. 1534-5. 26th & 27th Henry VIII.

The Queen is also in possession of two miniatures of the two sons of the Duke of Suffolk, who both died of the plague or sweating sickness in 1551, which are ascribed, and perhaps justly to Holbein. They are particularly interesting as having their dates fixed—September the 6th 1535, and the 10th of March 1541:—HENRY BRANDON Duke of Suffolk, in a black cap with white feather, and a black coat with green sleeves, blond hair cropped all round; he is resting his left arm on a table, on which is written—ETATIS SVÆ 5. 6 SEPDEM. ANNO 1535. Blue ground, painted on the back of the ace or three of clubs. The other is his brother CHARLES BRANDON Duke of Suffolk, in a grey and red coat, with black cuffs; his shirt collar is embroidered with black thread round the outer edge: blue ground. On a tablet is inscribed—ANN 1541 ETATIS SVÆ 3. 10 MARCI. This is painted on the back of a king. Both are the same size—1$\frac{1}{12}$ of an inch in diameter; they are said to have been given to Charles I. by Sir Henry Vane, and both are entered as Holbein's work in Vanderdoort's

* This miniature is given in the official catalogue to Lucas de Heere, who was not born till nine years after it was painted. Sir John was father of Sir Christopher Hatton, Lord Chancellor in Queen Elizabeth's time.

catalogue. They are interesting drawings, freely, firmly, and yet elaborately executed.

CHAP. XIV.

Church dissensions.
1534-5.
26th & 27th Henry VIII.

If we may except the first of the Duke-of-Suffolk miniatures, as correctly named, I am not aware of any known work by Holbein of these years 1534 and 1535, nor is there any record of any journey by him: there appears to be no positive trace of him whatever, that can be assigned to these years; there is nothing that can even by inference be presumed to belong especially to this time; though there is no reason to suppose that he was then absent from London, or that he was less occupied with his ordinary pursuits at this time, than at any other.

The catastrophe of the More tragedy in July 1535 has been already traced in its chief features. John Fisher bishop of Rochester had suffered from the same cause a few weeks before his friend; and he had been made a cardinal by Pope Clement just before his death. In fact this distinction, considered as a species of papal defiance, is supposed to have expedited the old man's trial. I have already noted among the Holbein drawings, an admirable one of Fisher's remarkable face; of which the British Museum possesses a more finished example, apparently from the Windsor sketch.

Eliza Barton the famous nun of Kent and her monkish accomplices were executed at Tyburn on the 21st April 1534. In the same month Henry was excommunicated by Clement VII. (Giulio de' Medici), who thus gave the death-blow to the old superstition in England; the immediate result of the sentence was the abolition by the king of the pope's authority in this country, and he had himself proclaimed—under Christ supreme head of the church in his own dominions—*In Terra sub Christo supremum Ecclesiae Anglicanae et Hibernicae Caput.* So much for the *brutum fulmen* of his holiness of Rome.

A royal order was issued "that all manner of prayers, rubrics, canons of mass books, and all other books in the churches wherein the bishop of Rome was named, or his presumptuous and proud pomp and authority preferred, should

CHAP. XIV.

Church dissensions. 1534-5. 26th & 27th Henry VIII.

utterly be abolished, eradicated, and rased out, and his name and memory should be never more, except to his contumely and reproach, remembered; but perpetually be suppressed and obscured."*

In October of this year Clement VII. died, and was succeeded in the papacy by the Cardinal Alessandro Farnese as Paul III., who now prepared, but issued later, a far more terrible *Bull* against the king than his predecessor had pronounced:—"The king, with all who abetted him in his crimes, was pronounced accursed—cut off from the body of Christ, to perish. When he died, his body should lie without burial; his soul, blasted with anathema, should be cast into hell for ever. The lands of his subjects who remained faithful to him were laid under an interdict: their children were disinherited, their marriages illegal, their wills invalid; only by one condition could they escape their fate—by instant rebellion against the apostate prince. All officers of the crown were absolved from their oaths; all subjects, secular or ecclesiastic, from their allegiance. The entire nation under penalty of excommunication, was commanded no longer to acknowledge Henry as their sovereign. No true son of the church should hold intercourse with him or his adherents. They must neither trade with them, speak with them, nor give them food. The clergy leaving behind a few of their number to baptize the new-born infants, were to withdraw from the accursed land, and return no more till it had submitted."†

Thomas Cromwell. 1535. 27th Henry VIII.

Soon after More's death, a general visitation of the religious houses, was determined upon, under the direction of that "Hammer of the Monks" Thomas Cromwell, who had been Wolsey's secretary, and was now "viceregent of the king in all his ecclesiastical jurisdiction within the realm;" which visitation resulted in a few years, in the ever-memorable suppression of those dens of vice the monasteries. This famous minister became later one of Holbein's patrons, but I have not

---

* Royal Proclamation, June, 1534. See Froude, *History of England*, &c. Vol. II., p. 243.

† Froude, *l. l.* Vol. II., p. 417.

yet been fortunate enough to see any satisfactory portrait of Cromwell by Holbein, though many are ascribed to him: one would imagine that there must be some such picture of importance. The Lord Cromwell's portrait is one of the very few of Holbein's works mentioned by Van Mander, as already noticed in my first chapter. There is a head of him, a drawing, similar to those at Windsor, at Wilton; and Captain Ridgway, of Waterloo Place, London, possesses a capital head of him the reverse way, which appears genuine and in good condition; it is almost in profile; on wood, 12 in. square.

CHAP. XIV

Thomas Cromwell. 1535. 27th Henry VIII.

One also reputed to be and apparently Holbein's, but with the face almost entirely repainted, is in the possession of the Countess of Caledon. It is a sitting half-length showing the profile and bears signs of having been a well-modelled portrait; but Cromwell was evidently not a good subject for a picture. The various accessaries in this portrait, especially those on the table—the pen, book, and papers, &c.—have a decided Holbein character: the latter bears the following interesting inscription—*To our trusty and right wellbiloved Counsailler Thomas Cromwell, Maister of o^r Jewelhouse.* On wood, 2 ft. 6 in. *h.* by 2 ft. *w.* In the upper part of the picture is likewise the following inscription on a scroll, added perhaps after Cromwell's death:—

ET . BONUS . ET . PRUDENS . CHRISTI . REGISQUE . MINISTER.
CONSTANS . VIR . PROMPTUS . PECTORE . FRONTE . MANU.
VIX . IN AMICITIA . TALIS . VIX . NASCITUR . HEROS.
PLUS . PATRIE . FIDUS . PLUS . PIETATIS . AMANS.

There is a print of this picture, ascribed to Hollar, but it does not bear his name.

On the 7th of January 1536, Queen Catherine of Arragon died at Kimbolton, and was buried at Peterborough: the see of Peterborough was founded as a memorial of her. She wrote an affectionate letter to the king shortly before she died, and Henry could not restrain his tears while reading it.

Death of Queen Catherine. 1536. 28th Henry VIII.

On the 2nd of May following Queen Anne Boleyn was

CHAP. XIV.

Disgrace of Anne Boleyn. 1536. 28th Henry VIII.

arrested at Greenwich and committed to the Tower; on the 10th, true bills were found against her for adultery by the Grand Juries of Middlesex and of Kent; on the 15th, she was convicted and condemned; and after having been divorced she was on the 19th, beheaded on Tower Green. The five gentlemen condemned with her, had been executed on the 17th; namely George Boleyn Lord Rochfort, Henry Norris, William Brereton, Sir Francis Weston, and Mark Smeton.*

On the 20th of May, the day following the execution of Anne Boleyn, the king married Jane daughter of Sir John Seymour, in accordance with the expressed desire and to the great satisfaction of his Privy Council and the peers, indicating however an indecent haste which has very much injured his reputation with posterity.

"If we are to hold Anne Boleyn," says Mr. Froude, "entirely free from fault, we place not the king only, but the Privy Council, the judges, the Lords and Commons, and the two Houses of Convocation, in a position fatal to their honour and degrading to ordinary humanity." It is strange if not true that she should have acquired the reputation of having been the inveterate enemy of two of Henry's most distinguished councillors, Wolsey and More. The former spoke of her under the title of "the night-crow," as the person to whom he owed all which was most cruel in his treatment; as "the enemy that never slept, but studied, and continually imagined, both sleeping and waking, his utter destruction."†

Derick Berck.

At Petworth House, in the hall, is a portrait of another of the "Steelyard" merchants, DERICK BERCK, apparently by

* "Smeton was hanged; the others were beheaded. Smeton and Brereton acknowledged the justice of their sentence. Brereton said that if he had to die a thousand deaths, he deserved them all; and Brereton was the only one of the five whose guilt at the time was doubted. Norris died silent; Weston with a few general lamentations on the wickedness of his past life. None denied the crime for which they suffered; all but one were considered by the spectators to have confessed." Froude, *History of England*, &c. Vol. II., p. 522.

† Cavendish's *Life of Wolsey*, p. 316. Singer's edition, quoted by Froude, *History of England*, &c. Ch. 2. p. 188. 3rd Ed.

name; painted in this year. The record of the subject is preserved in a way not unusual with the painters of this age, and of which Holbein has left us several examples: namely that of letting his sitter hold a letter in his hand, with his own name and address upon it. This portrait is the half-length of an intelligent-looking man, dressed in black, and wearing his beard: the style of painting is similar to that of the Longford picture, and the Stahlhof merchant at Windsor. The hands are well drawn, and in the left he holds a letter with the following address, not perfectly legible:—*Dem ersam und fors'nn* (?) *Derick Berck to Londen uyt* (?) *Stahlhof* * * * *befall ds briff*—To the honourable and provident Derick Berck, in London, of the Steelyard, belongs this letter. On a table before him is lying a scrap of paper, on which is written *Olim meminisse juvabit*, and below is the date *Añ.* 1536, *Aeta:* 30. On oak, 20 in. high by 16 in. wide. Near this picture is a smaller portrait, similar in style, but inferior, showing a middle-aged man, three-quarter face; also holding a letter in his hand, dated 1537. The hands, more especially the right, are ill drawn. The picture is possibly genuine, but it may have suffered by time, and by restoration.

Derick Berck. 1536. 28th Henry VIII.

The English Bible.

In this year Henry VIII. ordered the Bible to be translated into English, and in the following year it was set up in the churches; a blessing we seem to owe indirectly to the king's irascible opponents, those two old bishops of Rome, Giulio de' Medici and Alessandro Farnese.

"From 1536," says Mr. Froude, "when the vicar-general's injunctions directed every parish priest to supply his church with a copy of the whole Bible, editions based all of them on the translation of Tyndal, followed each other in rapid succession. The bishops who had undertaken to supply a version satisfactory to Catholic orthodoxy, had still left their work untouched. The king would not be trifled with. The Bible, in some shape, his subjects should possess; and if unsupplied by the officials of the church, he would accept the services of volunteers whose heart was in their labours. Coverdale's edition was followed, in 1537, by Matthews's, 'printed with

The English Bible. 1536. 28th Henry VIII.

the king's most gracious license;'* and the same version, after being revised by the Archbishop of Canterbury, was reprinted in 1538, 1539, 1540, and 1541, under the name of 'the Great Bible,' or 'Cranmer's Bible.'"

The edition of 1539 had a large cut illustrating the title, which is ascribed to Holbein; it is 14 in. high by $9\frac{3}{8}$ in. wide, but is certainly not by Holbein; it is disfigured by the mannered draperies characteristic of the so-called German "little masters," and the drawing of the figures is about as contemptible as it well can be. Hans Brosamer, another H. B. who lived at Fulda between 1537 and 1554, was also a Bible illustrator; he furnished some designs on wood for the Lutheran Bible of 1558.

Henry VIII.

The Earl of Yarborough possesses what appears to be a genuine half-length portrait of the king, painted after 1535, when he "polled his head:" it is the best I have seen, of all the full faces; and it may be by Holbein. He is dressed in cloth of gold and ermine, with a black cap decorated with a white ostrich feather, hanging over the right; in his right hand he holds his gloves, the left is resting on his dagger tie. He wears a collar of jewels, and a chain supporting a large jewelled locket.

The eyes are grey, the beard is darker than in the Windsor portraits, and the head is of the same type as the Kimbolton, Windsor, and Warwick pictures, but seems somewhat younger. It has something of the Longford picture of the "Ambassadors" in its style of modelling. On wood, 3 ft. 2 in. high by 2 ft. 5 in. wide. There is a record that this portrait was presented by the king to Sir James Worsley, Knight, Governor of the Isle of Wight, after a visit to Appuldercombe. It was exhibited at the British Institution in 1850. I certainly know no other of the half-lengths of Henry VIII. that can be compared with this one.†

* "Matthews's name is supposed to have been fictitious. There is no real difference between his version and that of Coverdale." Froude, *History of England, &c.* Vol. IV., p. 290.

† Among portraits of the king were two curious works at Strawberry Hill, upon what authority I know not, but both ascribed to Holbein. One was a small whole length of Henry cut in

In this year, 1536, was painted the admirable portrait of SIR RICHARD SOUTHWELL, now in the Uffizi Gallery, Florence, and of which there are several copies. This portrait, one of the most characteristic of Holbein's works of its class, is remarkable for its striking individuality : its original sketch is among the Windsor drawings. The picture was finished on the 10th July 1536, and it shows perhaps a greater care in some of its parts than those bearing the dates 1532 and 1533. Sir Richard Southwell has been mentioned in relation to Sir Thomas More, he became later a person of more inportance; he was Master of Ordnance to Queen Elizabeth; when the portrait was taken he was in his thirty-third year only. Small half-length, sitting, a black-haired man, with his face closely shaven, and his hair cropped straight across the forehead ; three-quarter face looking to the left; his hands are resting on a table, the right being clasped over the left, and on the forefinger is a ring with a green stone. He has on a black cap, in which is an engraved red stone, a head, set in gold; a dark coat, showing four buttons against the shirt (these buttons are indicated in the Windsor sketch just as they are painted in the picture), and black satin sleeves. The shirt is white, tied at the neck, and with ruffles at the wrists; the hands are very finely painted. He wears also a plain gold chain, but this is not very conspicuous. The back-ground is a deep green, almost uniform, and it bears the following inscription, in letters of gold :—

CHAP. XIV.

Sir Richard Southwell.
1536.
28th Henry VIII.

On the right side of the head—X^o. IVLII. ANNO.
H. VIII. XXVIII°.
On the left side—ETATIS SVÆ
ANNO XXXIII°

On oak, about 19 in. high by 14 in. wide.

---

stone, formerly in the Arundel collection, and which belonged later to Lady Elizabeth Germayn; this was sold for 64 guineas at the sale of 1842: the other was a bust of the king in box-wood, with, instead of a George, a watch hanging about his neck; this fetched 38 guineas at the same sale. Both were bought by John Dent, Esq.

CHAP. XIV.

Sir Richard Southwell. 1536. 28th Henry VIII.

Inscribed on a silver tablet, on the frame:—*Effigies domini Ricardi Southwelli Equitis Aurati, Consiliarii privati Henrici VIII. Regis Angliae.**

An excellent copy is in the Louvre, brought from Germany in 1806; another copy, in the possession of Mr. H. E. Chetwynd Stapylton, was exhibited at South Kensington, in 1866; where also was shown a copy in my possession, on an Italian panel, about 22 in. by 17 in. sight measure, painted about 1835 by the Florentine artist MICHELI, who drowned himself in the Arno about 1850. He was celebrated for the excellence of his copies from pictures by the old masters at Florence.

Edward Seymour.

Among the smaller portraits by Holbein, those which may be classed as oil miniatures, is perhaps that at Sion House of Edward Seymour Earl of Hertford, Queen Jane Seymour's brother, and afterwards Duke of Somerset and Lord Protector. There is something of the handling of the Longford "Ambassadors" in this portrait; it is a small half-length on panel, and represents a middle-aged man, with an unusually long nose, and a long thin beard; he is in a dark cloak, with a black cap and dusky feathers, and holds hanging in his right hand an ornamented locket: the face is three-quarter turned to his right; the back-ground is a pale bluish green. On panel, 8½ in. high by 7 in. wide.

Somerset was a great friend to the Reformation; in 1547 he repealed the "Bloody Statute" which had been passed in 1539; but he managed to make several powerful enemies. He was accused and convicted of felony, for having compassed the death of the Duke of Northumberland and of the Marquis of Northampton, and was beheaded on Tower Hill on the 22nd of January 1552, to the great sorrow of the people of London, with whom he was so popular, that, after his execution, they dipped their handkerchiefs in his blood.†

* The frame bears also Holbein's name, the name of *Cosimo Secondo*, its possessor; and the arms of England with the date 1621. Engraved in outline, in the *Reale Galleria di Firenze Illustrata*, 1817.

† See Froude, *History of England*, &c. Vol. V.

Before proceeding with the biographical career of our painter, I may here notice a series of undated portraits, ascribed with more or less truth to Holbein, some of which may belong to this period; while others if his work were probably executed a little sooner. As they have no fixed place, they may as well be noticed here as elsewhere. They are the portraits of—Queen Jane Seymour; Sir Brian Tuke; Sir William Butts, his wife Lady Butts; Lady Rich; Dr. John Chambers or rather Chamber; and the grand half-length in the Dresden Gallery, known as "Mr. Morett," until lately ascribed to Leonardo da Vinci, though that it is a genuine work by Holbein, we may now rest satisfied. CHAP. XIV. *Undated portraits.* 1536. 28th Henry VIII.

The portrait in the Belvedere Gallery in Vienna, called QUEEN JANE SEYMOUR, finely painted, is nearly a half-length, on the small scale so often adopted by Holbein in his portraits. She is turned slightly to her right, showing almost the full face, and is dressed in red velvet, the sleeves being enriched with gold thread; she has pearls and rubies on her neck, and wears the peculiar diamond-shaped cap or hood, apparently the favourite female head-dress of the time, commonly with a black veil or fall attached behind: her hands are crossed before her. On oak, about 2 ft. high by 18 in. wide (No. 61). The "Queen Jane Seymour" in the collection at Knole, appears to be a copy of this picture at Vienna. The blue or grey eyes however do not harmonize with the apparently light hazel eyes of the Whitehall portrait of Van Leemput. *Jane Seymour.*

The portrait of DR. JOHN CHAMBER, physician to Henry VIII., in the same gallery, is likewise a good picture. It represents a very old man, in a doctor's cap and a black furred gown, showing a three-quarter face turned to the left: he holds his gloves in his hands. On wood, also about 2 ft. high by 18 in. wide (No. 62). This picture is virtually dated, as it is inscribed on the ground—ÆTATIS. SUE. 88; the doctor's age, if known, will give the year; the portrait is nearly identical with that in the Barber-Surgeons' picture, which was painted possibly in 1541, but perhaps later: it is *Dr. Chamber.*

CHAP. XIV. — *Dr. Chamber.* 1536. 28th Henry VIII.

the first of the three on the king's right hand, and is a fine old head.*

In the same room with these two portraits, is also a fine oil miniature ascribed to Holbein; the bust portrait of a young lady, richly dressed, with her hands crossed before her. She has on a red gown with a black surcoat over it, and wears a white and gold diamond-shaped hood, with the black fall behind: on her bosom is a gold brooch. On wood, 8 in. high by 6 in. wide (No. 27).

Sir Brian Tuke.

Among English portraits of this time may perhaps also be classed that of SIR BRIAN TUKE, whose accounts as Treasurer of the Chamber have already been referred to. According to Dr. Waagen, this portrait exists in duplicate, with only some slight variations: the English example was formerly at Corsham Court near Chippenham in Wiltshire. It is now in the possession of the Marquis of Westminster.† It is a small portrait of a man in black, with a gold chain and cross on his neck, and sleeves of gold stuff; in his left hand he holds a pair of gloves, and with the right points to a folded piece of paper on which are the following words from the Latin Vulgate of the Book of Job—*Nunquid non paucitas dierum meorum finietur brevi?* (rendered in the Douay version "*Shall not the fewness of my days be ended shortly?*" Job x. 20). On the green ground is the following inscription—BRIANUS TUKE, MILES. ANNO AETATIS SUAE LVII., with his motto *Droit et Avant,* below. Dr. Waagen assigns it the date 1529, and assumes it to represent the same person as the following portrait now in the Pinacothek at Munich, formerly at Schleissheim, and painted in the taste and manner of Von Melem. A man in black, with a gold chain round his neck, to which a crucifix is suspended; below is a piece of paper with the quotation from Job, as above, and a reference to the passage; but in the

* It was etched by Hollar in 1648—*D. J. Chambers, Anno Aetatis* 88, *Holbein pinxit,* 9 in. *h.* by 7 in. *w.* Chamber was a churchman as well as a physician, he died in 1549.

† It was bought for the marquis at Mr. R. Sanderson's sale at Christie's, in June 1848, for 74*l.* 11*s.* It is not among the pictures at Grosvenor Gate, and I have not seen it.

back-ground is a green curtain, from behind which a skeleton appears looking at the man before him, and with his right hand points to an hour-glass in his left; the sand of the glass being nearly run down. Signed IO. HOLPAIN. There is no other inscription; no name. This picture is not a bad one, but the signature is suspicious, as that of our painter; and the style does not proclaim it to be the work of Holbein. On wood, about 15 in. high by 20 in. wide.*

CHAP. XIV.

Sir Brian Tuke. 1536. 28th Henry VIII.

A couple of small pictures in this country, in the possession of Mr. W. H. Pole Carew, are of a more genuine character. These are a pair, on oak, about 18 in. by 14, a common size with Holbein; they represent SIR WILLIAM and LADY BUTTS: he was physician to Henry VIII., and died on the 17th September 1545. Butts is introduced by Shakespeare in his Henry VIII.,† and he is also one of those present, at the

Sir William and Lady Butts.

* The new Munich catalogue (1865), misled by the error in Dr. Waagen's *Handbuch der Deutschen und Niederländischen Malerschulen* (1862), has recorded the picture as the "Portrait of Sir Brian Tuke Miles." In the doctor's *Kunstwerke und Künstler in England* (1838) the name is given correctly as Sir Brian Tuke. Crivelli was from 1490 in the habit of adding MILES (Knight) to his signature, but Sir John, or the Cav. Giovanni Crivelli Miles, would have an odd appearance in a catalogue.

† (Act V., Sc. 2.) *Enter* DR. BUTTS.

CRANMER. So.

BUTTS. This is a piece of malice. I am glad I came this way so happily: the king shall understand it presently.

CRAN. (*aside.*) 'Tis Butts, the king's physician; as he pass'd along, how earnestly he cast his eyes upon me! Pray heaven he sound not my disgrace. For certain this is of purpose laid by some that hate me (God turn their hearts! I never sought their malice), to quench mine honour: they would shame to make me wait else at door; a fellow-counsellor, among boys, grooms, and lackeys. But their pleasures must be fulfilled, and I attend with patience.

Enter, at a window above, the KING and BUTTS.

BUTTS. I'll show your grace the strangest sight—

K. HEN. What's that, Butts?

BUTTS. I think your highness saw this many a day.

K. HEN. Body o' me, where is it?

BUTTS. There, my lord: the high promotion of his grace of Canterbury, who holds his state at door, 'mongst pursuivants, pages, and footboys.

K. HEN. Ha! 'Tis he, indeed: is this the honour they do one another? 'Tis well there's one above them yet. I had thought they had parted so much honesty among them (at least, good manners), as not thus to suffer a man of his place, and so near our favour, to dance attendance on their lordships' pleasures, and at the door too, like a post with packets. By holy Mary, Butts, there's knavery: let them alone, and draw the curtain close; we shall hear more anon.

The king sent Dr. Butts with a ring to Cardinal Wolsey; this ring, says Walpole, was a cameo on a ruby, of the king himself, which had been formerly given to him by the cardinal.

CHAP. XIV. — *Sir William and Lady Butts.* 1536. 28th Henry VIII.

ceremony of that king giving a charter to the Company of Barber-Surgeons, and now in their Hall in Monkwell Street; the doctor is a profile on the right of the picture on the king's right hand, immediately behind Dr. Chamber: the portrait is the same in both pictures.

The doctor is in this example, in profile, looking to the left; but the picture is much damaged, and coarsely and unskilfully repainted. The wife, in very much better condition, is a charming specimen of Holbein's manly simple style, and of his masterly skill in modelling after nature; the face is quite life-like.

Sir William is in a black cap, and black coat with sable edges, and a plain gold chain on his shoulders: in the once green back-ground is written ANNO ÆTATS SVE. LIX. Butts was possibly painted in 1541, for the group introduced into the composition commemorating the grant of a charter to the Barber-Surgeons. There is a fine old copy or replica of this picture in the National Portrait Gallery. The wife, a daughter of Mr. John Bacon, of Cambridgeshire, is nearly in full face looking a little to her right, she is also in black, with the peculiar diamond-shaped head-dress of the time, with the usual black veil or kerchief hanging down behind; she has on also a white partlet, with black embroidery on the collar, which is often seen in Holbein's portraits, very skilfully managed; and she wears a rose in front. Inscribed—ANNO ÆTATIS SVE. LVII. The back-grounds and inscriptions of both pictures have been badly repainted. Lady Butts is among the Windsor sketches. As is also the drawing of the following portrait, that of the wife of Lord Chancellor Rich, who succeeded Sir William Paulet as Lord Keeper of the Great Seal in 1547.

Lady Rich.

LADY RICH, bust portrait, nearly full face turned to right; a diamond-shaped hood, with a black velvet fall; and in an open black dress with white frill, and a gold medallion brooch pendant before; the figures on this brooch are exquisitely put in; blue back-ground. On wood, 17 in. by 13. A fine expressive portrait, with a thin rich carnation; and one of those examples which give us the very decided impression, that Holbein troubled his sitters as little as possible, and worked alone, relying on the accuracy of his observation, and a drawing made for the express purpose of painting from—a safe enough practice perhaps for Holbein, in an ordinary way, but even with such powers as his, a disadvantage. The left hand, partly seen below, is weak. This portrait was formerly at Croft Castle.* CHAP. XIV *Lady Rich.* 1536. 28th Henry VIII.

We now come to a very important picture, the so-called portrait of "Mr. Morett" in the Dresden Gallery. This is one of the completest of Holbein's portraits, and one of the finest of his works; it has until lately been attributed to Leonardo da Vinci, and the person represented has been and is a matter of dispute: it has been called Sir Thomas More, Lodovico il Moro, Mr. Morett, Count Moretta, and even Charles Brandon Duke of Suffolk; I have adhered to the name given to it in Hollar's print from the drawing, here photographed, formerly in the Arundel collection. That the picture itself was ever in the Arundel collection, seems to be shown, by one of the following letters, to be at best doubtful. Thomas Howard Lord Arundel, was apparently an indefatigable collector and seeker of Holbein's works; several letters showing this nobleman's general interest in works of art, are still preserved, and we have Holbein prominently mentioned in four of them: on the 17th of September 1619, he writes to Sir Dudley Carleton at the Hague †:— *"Mr. Morett.'*

"My Lord:

"I have received from your lordship a very fine basin of stone with an ewer *alla Antica,* for which I must give you very many thanks, and am sorry you remember me so much to your charge; *I hear likewise, by many ways how careful your lordship is to satisfy my foolish curiosity in inquiring for the pieces of Holbein.* For the other little things

* Contributed by Mr. Walter Moseley, of Buildwas Park, Wenlock, Shropshire, to the South Kensington "National Portrait Exhibition" in 1866, where it was however called "Queen Catherine of Arragon."

† He was English minister at the Dutch Court. See Sainsbury's *Original unpublished Papers, illustrative of the Life of Sir P. P. Rubens,* &c. 8vo. London, 1859, for these letters in their genuine form. Appendix Nos. XLIV., LIII., LV., and LVII.

CHAP. XIV. — "Mr. Morett." 1536. 28th Henry VIII.

which I entreated Sir Edward Cecil to inform himself of, I thought it unmannerly to distract your serious affairs with them, and besides, your lordship so apprehends all occasions to forerun my desires as I should rather wish to be able to deserve some of your old favours than load you with new troubles; so with my service to yourself and your worthy lady, and my best wishes, I ever rest, your lordship's most affectionate friend to command,

"T. ARUNDELL."*

Sir Dudley Carleton to Lord Arundel (Extract).

"*Hagh, June* $\frac{12}{22}$, 1621.

"Right Honourable my most singular good Lord:

"Having waited lately on the King and Queen of Bohemia to Amsterdam, *I there saw the picture of Holbein's your Lordship desires; but cannot yet obtain it,*† though my endeavours wait on it, as they still shall do.

"We have now a young man (Gerard Honthorst) growing into reputation in these parts who began with Bloomer (Abraham Bloemaert) of Utrecht where he dwells likewise, and hath been for some years at Rome and other parts of Italy to mend his art: which consisting much in Night-works, he desired of me an invention to my mind whereby to make trial of him in the which I might rest assured was no copy. I gave him Aeneas flying from the sack of Troy and in a posture *pariter cometique onerique timentem;* wherein how well he hath acquitted himself your Lordship will be best able to judge by the piece, which will be delivered your Lordship by this bearer, and which I will beseech you to accept as it is. It is without exception to the good will of the presenter what defect soever your Lordship shall observe in the skill of the painter.

* * * * *

"Your Lordship's most humble and most faithful servant,

"D. C."

"I do now send a picture at full-length, of the young Prince

---

* Thomas Howard Earl of Arundel and Surrey, K.G., of whom there is a magnificent portrait by Rubens, in the possession of the Earl of Warwick. A half-length in armour, the right hand leaning on his baton, on canvas 4 ft. 1 in. *h.* by 3 ft. 4 in. *w.* The Duke of Sutherland also has a fine half-length of this nobleman by Vandyck. He possessed, says his biographer Sir Edward Walker, p. 222, numerous paintings, "and of the most excellent masters, having more of that exquisite master Hans Holbein, than are in the world besides!"

† The "Meier Madonna" is possibly referred to, see the remarks in the ninth chapter, p. 170.

Frederick Henry (whom we have here at this present with the King and Queen) to His Majesty, which will be presented by my Lord of Buckingham. I shall gladly know your Lordship's opinion of the work, for the life and likeness, we all here think that Michel of Delph (Mirevelt) hath not been so happy in any other picture this many a day."

" *Mr. Morett.*" 1536. 28th Henry VIII.

Sir Isaac Wake to William Boswell (Extract).

" *Turin*, $\frac{\textit{November 26}}{\textit{December 6}}$, 1628.

"My dear Friend and Sweet Heart,

* * * * *

"The picture after which you do seem to inquire was made by Hans Holbein in the time of Henry VIII., and is of a *Count of Moretta.* My Lord of Arundel doth desire it, and if I can get it at any reasonable rate he must and shall have it. * * * * *

"Your faithful friend and servant,

"I. WAKE."

The Earl of Arundel to Sir Henry Vane (Extract).

" *Arundel House, April* 25, 1629.

"Good Mr. Cofferer,

* * * * *

"I must likewise give you very many thanks for your care concerning Bloome's (Bloemaert's) painting and *book of Holbein*, and the King protests against any meddling with it, at 600*l.*, which he says cost him but 200*l.* For the *drawings* I hoped to have had them for 30*l.*, but rather than fail, as I told you, I would go to 50*l.*, but never think of 100*l.*, nor 50*l.* offered without sure to have it; if he would let it come, upon security to send it back, I should be glad, if not, let it rest. * * *

"Your most faithful friend to command,

"ARUNDELL AND SURREY."

The foregoing extracts extend over a period of nearly ten years, from September 1619 to April 1629 inclusive, and in them we have mention of two pictures and a book of drawings, by Holbein. One of the pictures is clearly the Dresden portrait now under consideration, the other *may be* either the "Fountain of Life" now at Lisbon, or even the famous Meier altar-piece, which we are told by Sandrart was in Le Blond's possession in Amsterdam, and sold by him there long before Sandrart was in that city (about 1640); this might be years

CHAP. XIV.

"Mr. Morett." 1536. 28th Henry VIII.

after the date of Sir Dudley Carleton's letter; but we don't know when the picture first found its way to Holland. Yet should this conjecture be right, it is strange that the earl should have been outbidden by Le Blond in a matter of 150*l.* for such a picture, unless a total change of circumstances intervened and the purchase took place unknown to Lord Arundel.

What the "Book of Drawings" may have been, it is difficult to guess; scarcely the Windsor collection? for these, which did belong to the Earl of Arundel, were according to tradition given to him by the Earl of Pembroke.

MR. MORETT, the half-length of a man, showing the full face, in a black cap with a cameo, and splendidly dressed in black satin, silk, and taffeta, with a broad sable collar; the fore-sleeves cut and pulled with white. In his right hand he holds a glove; his left, gloved, rests on and holds the gilt sheath of a dagger, hanging by a chain to a waistband; white ruffles at his wrists. Round his neck hangs a simple gold chain, to which a locket is appended. In the back-ground is a green damask curtain. On wood, about 3 ft. 1 in. high by 2 ft. 6½ in. wide.

Splendid as this dress is there is nothing that a common burgher might not have worn, even after the sumptuary law passed by Henry VIII. in 1532. On this account I am inclined to look upon the portrait as that of a simple citizen, and nothing more: he has on no velvet, no purple, no cloth of gold.

The following is the history of this portrait of "Mr. Morett" or "Count Moretta," though the physiognomy is not Italian. He is called Thomas Morett, and whether Morett or Moretti, all accounts make him a distinguished jeweller in the service of Henry VIII.; he was accordingly the friend and fellow-labourer of the painter, and Holbein seems certainly to have done his work *con amore.* The first positive knowledge we have of the picture is that it formed part of the collection of the Duke of Modena. We see from the letter of Sir Isaac Wake, written at Turin in 1628, that the picture was then

"*Mr. Morett.*" 1536. 28th Henry VIII.

known, and appears to have been in the market; Sir Isaac there declares that the earl should have it if a reasonable sum could buy it. From 100*l.* to 200*l.* would at that time have been a reasonable sum, but I conclude that the earl never did get the picture, though he had the original drawing; and in the following century we find it in the ducal collection at Modena, into which it certainly passed as an acknowledged work by Holbein. I have already quoted the passage from Scannelli's *Microcosmo*, which notices Holbein—*Olbeno*—and particularly mentions a "wonderful" half-length portrait by him in this gallery: this was in 1657.

Some later *custode*, perhaps, at a loss to know who Thomas Morett might be, conjectured that it could be only Thomas Morus, the painter's great patron; and so Morett became Morus: a few years or so later still, it seems to have been as puzzling to understand who this Morus in a princely dress, can have been, and the name was again transformed into Moro; this was at least intelligible to a northern Italian, and what Moro so distinguished as Lodovico Sforza Il Moro, notwithstanding the complexion is rather ruddy than dark? but if Lodovico Sforza, the portrait must clearly have been painted by Leonardo da Vinci; in some catalogues he is Francesco Sforza; and so the matter stood in 1746, when the Modena Gallery was transported to Dresden, and so it remained for one hundred years later. Rumohr, the most intelligent of German critics, had already from pure feeling pronounced it a work by Holbein, but what was mere opinion against tradition?* However the connoisseurs of the Saxon capital and of Germany were not a little shocked when Herr von Quandt in 1846, setting aside mere guess-work, published an article in the *Kunstblatt* showing that this famous picture was neither of Lodovico il Moro, nor by Leonardo da Vinci, but simply the portrait of a jeweller employed by Henry VIII., and certainly

* Director Matthäi, in his catalogue which I bought in the gallery in 1835, casually mentions in a note that some critics had lately ascribed the picture to Holbein, but otherwise it remains as absolutely ascribed to Da Vinci, as in the earlier books.

CHAP. XIV.
"Mr. Morett." 1536. 28th Henry VIII.

painted by the master of the "Meier Madonna." His position was much supported by his accompanying the essay with a copy of Hollar's engraving from the drawing of "Mr. Morett," then (1647) in the Arundel collection; though as this etching and the picture are really not much alike, his inference was considered to be still doubtful, and the final restitution was not made to Holbein until the year 1860, when the original drawing itself by Holbein had been purchased for the Saxon government by Mr. Gruner after Mr. Woodburn's sale in London, in June, of that year.* It now hangs by the side of the picture, and the Moro-da-Vinci myth has become a matter of history. I know no work by Leonardo da Vinci that will bear comparison with it. The drawing itself, for force and truth is quite unsurpassed; it shows what can be accomplished by the point, without the aid of colour, when guided by a hand that obeys with the minutest mechanical precision, the control of an eye that nothing can escape, or the balance of a judgment by which nothing is too minute to be measured.

* See the new catalogue by Julius Hübner, Dresden, 1862, 2nd Ed. It is reported at Dresden that the late king Frederich August, there not being any Leonardo in the gallery, objected to the change of name, and the consequent exclusion of the great Florentine from his gallery: the restitution therefore could not take place till after that king's death. The drawing was sold for 43*l*. Mr. Gruner paid 50 guineas for it (352 thalers 26 ngr.). Hollar's etching, 4 in. in diameter, is inscribed "Mr. MORETT." *W. Hollar fecit, ex Collectione Arundeliana. A° 1647. 31 Dece.* It is a poor work, quite unworthy of the drawing, of which our photograph gives an adequate rendering.

CHAPTER XV.

Holbein a Servant of the King's Majesty.

ITH the year 1537 we enter, at last, a period in which we have many fixed dates and facts respecting Holbein in England, satisfactorily demonstrating his residence in London and showing his connection with the court of Henry VIII. We do not know of any payments which were made to him, as in the king's service, in 1537, these occur first in the accounts of the next year; but this date of 1537 is very important as being that of the great picture of Henry VIII., so much praised and copied, which was in the Privy Chamber in the Palace at Westminster at Whitehall, or what had been commonly known as York House, the palace surrendered by Cardinal Wolsey to the king.

Royal Portraits at Whitehall.

1537. 29th Henry VIII.

The accounts referred to are contained in a Book of Payments of the Royal Household, from February 1538—29th Henry VIII. to midsummer 1541—33rd Henry VIII.; they were formerly in the Library of the Royal Society, but are now in the British Museum.*

The first payment made to Holbein is that of a quarter's salary 7*l.* 10*s.* on Lady Day, March 25th, 1538; and as this is

* Arundel M.S. 97. The items relating to Holbein have been already published in part by several, but completely by Mr. Franks in his paper on the "Discovery of Holbein's Will," in the 39th vol. of the Archæologia, 1863.

CHAP. XV.

Royal Portraits at Whitehall.
1537.
29th Henry VIII.

not entered as an advance, it was for the preceding quarter, showing that the painter was in the king's service at the commencement of the year 1538, and therefore probably also in 1537 and even earlier: the accounts of these years are not preserved. We may feel pretty certain that Holbein was a "servant of the King's Majesty" in the year 1537; it was in this year that the great Whitehall picture was painted, representing Henry, his father, and the two queens, Elizabeth of York and Jane Seymour.

We have already learnt something from Van Mander concerning the fine figure of Henry VIII., painted by Holbein on the wall of the Privy Chamber in this palace, and which in his time, 1604, was still in perfect preservation. He says that the king, as he stood there, majestic in his splendour, was so life-like, that the spectator felt abashed, annihilated, in his presence. Though the picture perished in the fire which consumed that palace in January 1698, we can fortunately still judge of its size and effect, and of the composition too, from the large cartoon of the right-hand half, containing the king and his father, now in the possession of the Duke of Devonshire at Hardwick Hall; and from the small copy of the finished picture, showing also the two queens on the opposite side, by Remée, or Remigius van Leemput, made in 1667 for Charles II., and now at Hampton Court;* for this copy, says Walpole, Van Leemput received 150*l.*, which seems a very large sum, for that time. Walpole goes on to say, "Holbein's original drawing of the two kings is in the collection of the Duke of Devonshire. It is in black chalk, heightened with Indian ink, and as large as life; now at Chatsworth. The architecture of this picture is very rich, and parts of it in a good style." It appears to be done with a brush in distemper, in black and white, not in chalk; it is very elaborate, but drawn in a firm vigorous manner; the boundary lines however are harshly defined, like those of a fresco cartoon, a fact no doubt owing to

---

* Engraved by Vertue. Both cartoon and picture were exhibited this year, 1866, at South Kensington, in the National Portrait Exhibition.

Chap. XV.

Royal Portraits at Whitehall.

1537.

29th Henry VIII.

the drawing's being made, not for effect, but to be traced for transferring to the wall; the outline has been pricked all over, showing that the drawing has been traced or pricked from for pouncing, and in the effort to plainly define the outline, the anatomical delicacy of modelling, in the legs, has been damaged or neglected; the calves are rather baggy than muscular. Parts of the drawing are evidently by an assistant, but parts are free and exquisite, as for instance the ornamental details, the cinque-cento arabesques, &c., which probably Walpole refers to as the "good parts" of the architecture of the picture. The figure of the king is full life-size, but looks even colossal; the breadth of shoulder however is much exaggerated, being full three feet, no dress could account for such a breadth, and the right shoulder is quite thrown out of its place. The cartoon is about two squares, measuring nearly 9 ft. in height by 4 ft. 6 in. in width. The king was proud of his proportions and of his legs especially; this we learn from the correspondence of Piero Pasqualigo a Venetian ambassador-extraordinary who visited this country in April 1515.

To stand with arms akimbo and legs apart seems to have been a favourite attitude with him when on his feet. Pasqualigo tells the following anecdote in a letter dated the 3rd of May 1515, when the king was just upon twenty-four years of age:—His Majesty came into our arbour, and addressing me in French, said, "Talk with me awhile! The King of France, is he as tall as I am?" I told him there was little difference. He continued, "Is he as stout?" I said he was not; and he then inquired, "What sort of legs has he?" I replied, "Spare." Whereupon he turned aside the front of his doublet, and slapping his thigh with his hand, said, "Look here! I have also a good calf to show."*

* *Four years at the Court of Henry VIII. Selections of Despatches of Sebastian Giustinian.* London, 2 vols., 8vo. 1854. Vol. I., p. 91. The following is the original Venetian patois:—"La maiesta Regia vēne a ritrovarne nel nostro: et volta cosi a me disse in Frācese: parla un poco cō mi: el re di Frāza ello si grādo di psona como mi: Io li dissi che lera pocha differētia: disse ello si grosso, dissi clī nō: disse che gābe ha lo, dissi sotile: et alhora el si averse il saio davāti e metēdosi la mā ala coxa, disse guarda qua, io ho pur bona gāba sotto." (B. M. c. zz. g. 7.)

CHAP. XV.

Royal Portraits at Whitehall. 1537. 29th Henry VIII.

The cartoon is not identical with Van Leemput's copy, and it accordingly shows that some changes were made during the progress of the original picture. Henry's face in the cartoon is turned slightly to his left, towards his queen, Jane Seymour, who occupies a corresponding place with him, on the other side of the composition; in the copy his face is seen in full; the dress is also different, both doublet and surcoat; the right hand is differently treated; and in the small shield in the grotesque cinque-cento frieze in the back-ground, the lover's knot in the cartoon, uniting an H. and a J., has given place to the word ANNO in the picture. The head of Henry VII. also is somewhat indifferent and inferior in the picture. Although the cartoon was evidently prepared for the monumental work in Whitehall, the picture was as evidently not painted from it. The lower inscription on Van Leemput's copy distinctly tells us that it was reduced from the large Whitehall picture, by the commands of Charles II., in 1667; in it therefore we have the exact character of the greater work.

The composition is sufficiently formal, it was purely an heroic iconic monumental work, comprising not only the two heroes, but their wives also, and especially commemorating his father's pacification of the country after the terrible war of the Roses, and his own victory over the papacy, and the restoration of religion. In the centre is the face of what appears to be a high marble pedestal, on the top of which are placed two cushions; on the floor below, which is of different elevations, is carelessly thrown a Turkey carpet, which runs behind the pedestal, and is ruffled up by the interruption; the back-ground is a rich piece of Renaissance decoration in various coloured marbles, with pilasters, niches, and frieze. On the right hand of the pedestal, on the first step, stands the king, in the well-known attitude described, a glove in his right hand, and his left resting on his dagger, gold hilted, and in a gold and blue velvet sheath; his doublet is brown, richly jewelled and cut; his gown, furred, is red, and brocaded with gold thread; his flat bonnet is ornamented with pearls and a white feather. Opposite to Henry on the other side of the pedestal is the

Royal Portraits at Whitehall. 1537. 29th Henry VIII.

small figure of his queen, Jane Seymour, a woman with a light brown or hazel eye, but a very aquiline nose, and this is the only portrait of the queen that can be depended on; it is a key that should solve the riddle, or a sword to cut the knot, of other portraits reputed to be hers. Her dress seems to be tawny and gold, with full ermine sleeves, and she wears necklaces of pearls; she holds her hands before her, clasped; and a little white dog is reposing on the long skirt of her dress. On a still higher step, and nearly behind Henry VIII. and his queen, are Henry VII. and Queen Elizabeth of York; the king is leaning with his left arm on the cushion on the pedestal, and holds a glove in his left hand; while he adjusts his gown with his right: the head is nearly full face, is much the same as in the bust of this king ascribed to Torregiano, but it is very inferior in dignity and effect to the head in the cartoon. Elizabeth of York stands with her arms crossed, and holding up her dress with her right hand. In the two cartouches or shields in the frieze is the date of the original painting, ANNO 1537. And on the face of the pedestal is the following inscription, and glorification of the two kings, father and son*:—

Si juvat heroum claras vidisse figuras,
  Specta has, majores nulla tabella tulit.
Certamen magnum, lis, questio magna, pater ne
  Filius an vincat, vicit uterque quidem.
Iste suos hostes, patriaeque incendia saepe
  Sustulit, et pacem civibus usque dedit.
Filius, ad majora quidem prognatus, ab aris
  Submovet indignos substituitque probos.
Certae virtuti Paparum audacia cessit,
  Henrico Octavo sceptra gerente manu.

* Which seems to mean this—If there is any satisfaction in seeing the illustrious countenances of great men, look at these, no picture ever bore more noble. The great contest, the strife—it has been a question whether the father or the son were the superior—both are equally victors. He overcame his enemies, suppressed insurrections in the country, and restored peace to his subjects. The son, born to still greater things, removed the rogues from the altars and put honest men in their places. To his great virtue the audacity of the popes yielded. With the sceptre in the hand of Henry VIII. religion was restored, and the doctrines of God began to be held in due reverence.

CHAP. XV.

Royal Portraits at Whitehall. 1537, 29th Henry VIII.

Reddita religio est, isto regnante Deique
Dogmata cœperunt esse in honore suo.

Then follows the painter's signature, on a plynth below :—

PROTOTYPUM JUSTAE MAGNITUDINIS IPSO OPERE TECTORIO, FECIT HOLBENIUS JUBENTE HENRICO VIII. ECTYPUM A RÉMIGIO VAN LEEMPUT BREVIORI TABELLA DESCRIBI VOLUIT CAROLUS II. M. B. F. E. H. R.
A°. DM. MDCLXVII.

It is therefore to Charles II.'s anxiety to possess a smaller picture of this composition, that we owe the preservation of one of Holbein's most important and interesting designs: whether any more of the cartoon is in existence, is not known; but the figure of the king himself we have in life-sized copies, with some alterations in the accessaries, as in the really magnificent portrait of the king in the carved chamber at Petworth House; and in the much coarser example belonging to Mr. Danby Seymour, which with the exception of the curtain, substituted in the place of a portion of the pedestal and the figure of Henry VII., appears to be an exact copy of the portrait of Henry VIII. in this Whitehall picture. There is also a full-sized copy of the figure of the king at St. Bartholomew's Hospital, with another variation of the back-ground and floor: Henry VIII. reconstituted this hospital in 1544: it had been condemned with the rest, at the general dissolution of the religious corporations.* There were doubtless many copies, both large and small made of this popular portrait: Lord Spencer has a small bust portrait of the king, which is nearly identical with the cartoon; and there is another, on copper, formerly at Lee Priory, but now in the National Portrait Gallery, of the same size, and much the same in all respects, as Lord Spencer's, but not in such good condition. The

* St. Bartholomew's possesses also one of the ordinary half-lengths of the king, of the Kimbolton and Warwick type, inscribed ANNO Dñi 1544, ÆTATIS SVÆ 55. The date perhaps commemorates the reincorporation of the hospital; the age is wrong by two years. The portrait is of course ascribed to Holbein; the dress is skilfully enough painted, but the face is inferior.

dimensions of the original, or Holbein's prototype of the natural size, on the wall, was apparently about nine feet square. Van Leemput's copy, on canvas is 3 ft. 3 in. high by 3 ft. wide. Mr. Danby Seymour's picture, on wood, is 7 ft. 8 in. high by 4 ft. 5 in. wide.*

Chap. XV. *Royal Portraits at Whitehall.* 1537. 29th Henry VIII.

There seems to have been some attempt made to clean the two heads in the cartoon, and Henry VIII.'s face is nearly washed out.

Birth of Prince Edward.

On the 12th of October of this year, Prince Edward was born at Hampton Court, to the great joy of the nation; but within the fortnight this great blessing was followed by the irreparable calamity of the death of Queen Jane, who through some neglect of her attendants, in the midst of well-doing, took cold, and died on the 24th of the month, and Henry VIII. was again a widower; and the Privy Council as usual, immediately urged upon him the necessity of undertaking a fresh marriage.

Death of Queen Jane.

The Duchess of Milan.

In this year Paul III. published his great *Bull* against the king; the substance of it has been already given. Henry had opened negotiations of marriage with the emperor for the hand

* There is an entry in Pepys' "Diary" respecting the gallery at Whitehall, which is not easy to understand; he says—"Augt. 28, 1668 With much difficulty, by candle-light, walked over the matted gallery [at Whitehall], as it is now with the mats and boards all taken up, so that we walked over the rafters. But strange to see how hard matter the plaister of Paris is, that is there taken up, as hard as stone! And pity to see *Holben's work in the ceiling blotted on, and only whited over!*" Vol. IV., p. 12, 13. Ed. 1854. What work can this have been, and what is the sense of the words in italics; should "only" be read *all?* Or can it be that Holbein decorated the ceiling of the gallery at Whitehall? He has the credit of having designed the ceiling of St. James's Chapel. The Whitehall ceiling was probably in relief, and picked out with colour; and Pepys was perhaps lamenting that instead of restoring it, it was messed and merely whited over: *only* would then be the correct word. The ceiling of St. James's Chapel is a curious work, a panelled Renaissance design, and tastefully coloured. It was repaired in 1836 by Sir R. Smirke; the general ground is blue; the panellings are defined by ribs of wood gilt; there are also ornaments in foliage, painted green; and there are many coats of arms emblazoned in their proper colours. A small running open ornament, cast in lead, enriches the under sides of the ribs. The date 1540 occurs in several places, and various short inscriptions are scattered about, as—Henricus Rex 8—H and A, for Henry and Anne of Cleves, with a lover's knot between them; also VIVAT REX—DIEV ET MON DROIT, &c. A view of the ceiling is given in Richardson's *Architectural Remains of the Reigns of Elizabeth and James 1st.* Folio. London, 1838. Pl. 12.

CHAP. XV.

The Duchess of Milan. 1538. 30th Henry VIII.

of his niece, Christina Duchess of Milan, and the young widow of Francesco Sforza.

Everything seemed to proceed smoothly until the month of October, when a coolness on the part of the emperor became apparent, said to have been brought about by the hostility of the pope, who had been incensed beyond endurance, by the formal destruction in this month of October of the shrine of Thomas à Becket in Canterbury Cathedral; the formal *Bull* was promulgated, and the King of England was, in theory, deposed by the bishop of Rome.

In January 1539 the negotiations for the marriage were finally broken off, not by the lady herself, but by the emperor. The documents show no unwillingness on the lady's part, and there was no good reason why there should be any unwillingness: the execution of a faithless wife, was nothing to make an honest woman tremble, though one conscious of her own want of rectitude might well feel nervous under the circumstances. The following reply put by Walpole into the mouth of the Duchess of Milan is by Sandrart reported of the Princess of Lorraine, meaning the same lady; she was afterwards Duchess of Lorraine. One story has doubtless as much truth in it as the other; both are from the same source, some spurious fabrications of a later time, or the duchess herself may have made some such observation in later years. "After the death of Jane Seymour," says Walpole, "Holbein was sent to Flanders to draw the picture of the Duchess Dowager of Milan, widow of Francis Sforza, whom Charles V. had recommended to Henry for a fourth wife, but afterwards changing his mind, prevented him from marrying. Among the Harleian MSS. there is a letter from Sir Thomas Wyatt to the king, congratulating his majesty on his escape, as the duchess's chastity was a little equivocal. If it was, considering Henry's temper, I am apt to think that the duchess had the greater escape. It was about the same time that it is said she herself sent the king word, '*that she had but one head; if she had two, one of them should be at his majesty's service.*'"

Fortunately among the very few documents relating to

The Duchess of Milan. 1538. 30th Henry VIII.

Holbein, we have among the State Papers of Henry VIII. a very interesting letter to Cromwell, from John Hutton, the English minister at the court of the regent of the Netherlands, at Brussels, which gives us a detailed account of Holbein's interview with the duchess, on the occasion of his visit to Brussels for the purpose of painting her portrait, in March 1538, pending the above-mentioned marriage negotiations.

The following is an extract from this letter, which throws also some light on the marriage negotiations,—Mr. Haunce or Hanns being our painter; surnames were then of little account; our painter was probably much better known as Mr. Hanns than as Holbein.

(No. 488). *Hutton to Cromwell, 14th March,* 1538.

"My most bounden duty remembered unto your good Lordship. Pleaseth the same to be advertised, that the 10th of this present month, in the evening, arrived here your Lordship's servant Philip Hobbie, accompanied with a servant of the King's Majesty's named Mr. Haunce, by which Philip I received your Lordship's letter, bearing date at St. James's the second day of this present. The effect whereof apperceived, having the day before sent one of my servants towards your Lordship with a picture of the Duchess of Milan, I thought it very necessary to stay the same, for that in my opinion it was not so perfect as the cause required, neither as the said Mr. Haunce could make it. Upon which determination I despatched another of my servants, in post, to return the same, which your Lordship shall receive by this bearer. The next morning after the arrival of your Lordship's said servant I did address myself unto the Lady Regent, declaring unto Her, that the night past there arrived at my lodging a servant of your Lordship's, with one other of the King's Majesty's; by which your Lordship's servant I had received commission to certify Her Grace that the Emperor's ambassadors, resident with the King's Majesty my master, had made earnest overture unto your Lordship for a marriage to be treated, betwixt the Majesty of my said master, and the Duchess Grace of Milan. To the which albeit your Lordship was of no less good inclination for the furtherance of the same, than the said ambassadors were, yet your Lordship thought it not expedient to be broken unto the King's Highness, without having some further occasion ministered for the opening of the same.

"And for as much as your Lordship had heard great commendation of the form, beauty, wisdom, and other virtuous qualities the which God

CHAP. XV.

The Duchess of Milan.
1538.
30th Henry VIII.

had endowed the said Duchess with, you could perceive no mean more meet for the advancement of the same, than to procure her perfect picture; for which your Lordship had sent, in company of your said servant, a man very excellent in making of physiognomies; so that your Lordship's desire was that your said servant might in most humblest wise salute the Duchess's Grace, requiring that her pleasure might be to appoint the time and place, where the said painter might accomplish his charge.

"The Regent, when I began to declare this foresaid purpose, stood upon her feet; but after she had a little inkling to what effect the same would come, she did sit down, not moving, till I had finished all that I had to say, and then answered as followeth: 'I thank you for your good news. This is not the first report that I have had of the good inclination that the Lord Cromwell hath to the Emperor's affairs, for recompense whereof I trust he shall not find us ingrate. And as to his desire in this behalf, it shall gladly be accomplished.' Then I said, 'Madam, I have yet further commission, which is to certify the same unto the Duchess's Grace.' Her answer was, that she would go to Council, and when the Duchess came to her oratory, I might (have) very good opportunity to talk with her. With that the Regent departed towards the council chamber, and I tarried the Duchess's coming; who being come to her oratory, where as remained no more but two of her ladies, I certified Her Grace the whole effect of your Lordship's commission concerning Philip Hobbie, whom, when Her Grace would give audience, would more amply certify your Lordship's pleasure. She made answer that, if ever it should lie on her power, the good will of your Lordship showed towards her, which she in no part had deserved, should not remain unrecompensed; and that as to your said request it was not to be denied, albeit that she, being there with the Queen her aunt, thought it not meet to make any grant thereunto without her consent, which she would move to obtain at the first convenient leisure, that she might have with the Queen concerning the same. Commanding to be called unto her one, named the Lord Benedict Court, who next unto M. de Correra is chief about her; who being come, she said unto him, 'Go with the ambassador and entertain a gentleman that is at his lodging, and know where you shall find him at such time as I shall send you for him.' This done, we took our leave of Her Grace, and came to my lodging, where the said Lord saluted Philip Hobbie, communing together in the Italian tongue a certain space, and then took his leave to repair again to the court; which I perceiving, required him to take the portion with us at dinner, which he promised to do; but after being otherwise minded, he sent us word that he could not come, but would see us after dinner; which appointment he kept. For at two of the clock in the afternoon he came for Philip to come speak with the Duchess his mistress: who can make relation to your Lordship more at large what passed at that time.

Chap. XV.

The Duchess of Milan.

1538.

30th Henry VIII.

"The next day following, at one of the clock in the afternoon, the said Lord Benedict came for Mr. Haunce, who having but three hours' space hath showed himself to be master of that science, for it is very perfect; the other is but slobbered in comparison to it, as by the sight of both, your Lordship shall well apperceive. The same night Philip took his leave of the Duchess. * * * *

"From Brussels this 14th day of March, by the hand of your Lordship's most bounden,

"John Hutton."

(Superscribed.)

"To the right honourable and his singular good Lord,
My Lord Privy Seal. In haste, haste, post haste."

This three hours' sketch has been suggested to be the small panel with the head and hands of the duchess, now at Windsor. She is very plainly dressed in black, and sits with her hands crossed before her; she has rather a demure look, but when animated the countenance was possibly very handsome. The head is vigorously painted and very natural; it shows however no complete finish, which if the picture referred to, is exactly what one would expect; but it lacks also the mastery one would expect to find in a free sketch by Holbein. The hands are inferior, but they appear to have been partly repainted; the back-ground has also been entirely repainted. On wood, 17 in. high by 13 in. wide. This picture is supposed also to have been the original from which the full-length portrait of the duchess, now at Arundel Castle, was painted; but of this larger work, more presently. There is nothing in Hutton's letter to show that Holbein did anything more during the three hours he was with the duchess than make a chalk drawing similar to those at Windsor; and one of them, well finished, might be spoken of with all and more than the enthusiasm bestowed upon it by the delighted ambassador. The Windsor sketch scarcely justifies the commendation, and in its present state, looks much more like a clever study from the Arundel picture, than its pattern: anyhow the distance

CHAP. XV.

The Duchess of Milan.

1538. 30th Henry VIII.

between them is immense, but this does not prove much, for a very inferior master to Holbein could elaborate a magical effect from a mere rough sketch, provided this possessed the real germs of truth in it.

Payments of the Household.

Holbein's name occurs five times in Sir Brian Tuke's account of payments of the "Royal Household" for this year; in the following entries the *pound* represents 1*l.* 6*s.* 8*d.* and the *shilling* 1*s.* 4*d.**

Lady Day, Anno xxix.:—Item for Hans Holben, paynter, vii.li. xs.

Midsummer, Anno xxx.:—Item for Hans Holbyn, paynter, for one hole yere's annuitie advaunced to him beforehand the same yere, to be accomptedde from o^r^ Ladye dey last past, the somme of xxx.li.

Michaelmas, A^o.^ xxx.: —Item for Hans Holbyn, paynter, wages—nihil^a^ quid solutum per warrantum.

(Holbein was at this time in Basel.)

December, A^o.^ xxx.:—Item payde to Hans Holbyn, one of the Kingis paynters, by the Kingis commaundement, certefyed by my Lorde pryviseales lettre, x.li. for his costis and chargis at this tyme sent aboute certeyn his Gracis affares into the parties of high Burgony, by way of his Graces rewarde, x.li.

Christmas, A^o.^ xxx.:—Item for Hans Holbyn, payntir Nihil.

The first entry records the payment of one quarter's salary, at the rate of 30*l.* a year, due on the 25th March, 1538; the second records the whole year's salary of 30*l.* paid at midsummer, partly only in advance; it reached to the 25th March 1539. The third entry tells why Holbein had nothing then to receive, which is made clear by the advance in midsummer. These are all most important records as regards Holbein, but the last of the four entries is the most interesting, at this moment. It records the payment of 10*l.* for travelling expenses in upper Burgundy, which we may perhaps assume to be for his visit to Brussels, to paint the duchess; and it includes apparently a second 10*l.*, either as a payment for the

* See the remarks on the relative values of money in the twelfth chapter.

portrait, or as simply a mark of the king's favour: this is however not at all clear, the double entry may refer to the same x.*l.* One would certainly have imagined that the expenses which were incurred in March, would have been refunded before December; and it is quite possible that the journey referred to was for another matter. In the summer of 1538 Holbein was again in Basel, and there for the last time. As he received payment at the midsummer quarter, after his visit to Brussels, and yet was in the course of the summer and autumn in Basel, it shows that he made two journeys from England in this year. This evidence is given by Hegner, who quotes a letter written in September, by Rudolph Gualter in Basel, to Antistes Bullinger in Zurich. He says, "Hans Holbein came to Basel recently from England, and he gives such a glowing account of the happy condition of that kingdom, that after a few weeks' stay he means to go back again."* He appears to have returned to England towards the end of October. The fifth entry of *Nihil* against his name, occurs simply because he had been paid his salary in advance.

CHAP. XV.

Payments of the Household. 1538. 30th Henry VIII.

Visits Basel for the last time.

Holbein must have visited Basel for the purpose of procuring further leave to remain in England; this he obtained, but it was not at all willingly granted by the council, who wished much to have him in Basel, as we learn from an important document from the Burgomaster Jacob Meier (zum Hirschen) dated the 16th October of this year, in which he makes a final effort to persuade our painter to settle in Basel.

This agreement or contract† is curious and interesting; the following is its complete substance: I cannot give quite a literal translation of it, nor is it needed:—"We Jacob Meier Burgomaster, and the council of the city of Basel, send greeting, and make known by this letter, that we from the special good will we bear to our honourable and beloved

* "Venit nuper Basileam ex Anglia Joannes Holbein, adeo felicem ejus regni statum praedicans, qui aliquot septimanis exactis rursum eo migraturus est." Hegner, *Hans Holbein der Jüngere*, p. 246.

† It is endorsed "Master Hans Holbein the Painter's Pension"—*Meyster Hannsen Holbeins des Malers bestallung.*

CHAP. XV.

Visits Basel for the last time.

1538.

30th Henry VIII.

citizen Hans Holbein the painter, because his art has acquired him a great reputation among painters, also that he may be useful to us in our city, in architecture and other matters that he well understands, and undertake likewise any work in painting that we may require to be done, and for which he shall be properly paid, do hereby promise and order, that for the whole term of his life, whether he be sound or sick, he shall receive the annual service pension of fifty florins, to be paid quarterly.

"Further, as the said Hans Holbein has now for some time been in the service of His Majesty the King of England, and as by his occupations he may not easily be able to withdraw himself from that service, so we give him two years' grace from the date of this letter, to remain in England, and to procure a gracious permission to depart, and during these two years, his wife, residing with us, shall receive forty florins a year, ten florins being paid to her every quarter, to commence from this coming Christmas. On the condition that Hans Holbein shall within the two years specified take his leave of England and settle here in Basel among us, and his pension of fifty florins the year shall begin from the day he arrives. And as we well understand that the art and work of the said Holbein, is of that high character, that it should not be thrown away on old walls and houses; we, notwithstanding our annual allowance, permit him, as he cannot be always worthily employed by us, solely on account of his great art and handicraft, to work for foreign kings, princes, lords, and cities, and to receive and take payments from them; we permit him once, twice, or even three times in the year, with our sanction, not at all without, to visit France, England, Milan or the Netherlands, and to carry such works of art as he may here produce to those countries for sale, but he is on no account to remain in foreign parts, but to transact his business and to return immediately home again, and hold himself at our service, in accordance with his vow and undertaking. And so when the oft-mentioned Holbein shall by the will of God have paid the debt of nature, and have departed this life of troubles, then shall this pension and service money cease, and this warrant be considered of no effect, we and our successors shall be absolved from all further responsibility. This letter and all its conditions have we openly and honourably under our responsibility communicated to the oft-named Holbein and with our city official seal appended to it, given it to him in his own hands, on Wednesday this 16th day of October, in the year XXXVIII."*

CHAP. XV. *Visits Basel for the last time.* 1538. 30th Henry VIII.

Solicited to settle in Basel.

This document, so creditable to Holbein, in which the very laws of his state are set aside in his favour, failed in its effect; he never returned to Basel, though it may have been his intention to do so. His wife is mentioned in it, and to secure some provision for her may have been an inducement for his acceptance of it, as well as the unavoidable uncertainty which hangs about the future, notwithstanding the satisfactory state of affairs in the current moment. We must not forget that the wife had now a grown-up son of her own to whom she might look for some support. Holbein's son is not mentioned in the agreement, from which I infer that he took charge of him from the time of the drawing up of the document itself. Holbein under all circumstances would have found it difficult to forsake the English capital for such a place as Basel, but all at once and just upon the expiration of the two years' grace allowed, his uncle Sigmund died, and bequeathed him all his property in Bern; this was at latest in November 1540. The property appears to have been taken possession of by Franz Schmid, on behalf of his mother, Holbein's wife, in January 1541. Philip was at that time already provided for; he was at that time living in Paris apprenticed to a goldsmith there, and was then a lad of about eighteen years of age. His wife's circumstances therefore having wholly changed, he felt no longer bound on her account to fulfil his conditional engagement, and he remained in England; there really was nothing material or moral to urge him to Basel.

Such a document as that we have just read is not the kind

* First published by Hegner, in 1827, and again given by His-Heusler in 1866, in the paper already referred to, in the original old orthography.

CHAP. XV.

Solicited to settle in Basel.

1538. 30th Henry VIII.

of letter that town-councils are in the habit of giving to disorderly drunken spendthrifts, and if the acquaintance and affection of such men as Amerbach, Frobenius, Erasmus, Sir Thomas More, or Henry VIII., or of such women as Margaret Roper, is not enough to set aside the scandalous gossip of an exiled French accoucheur and his daughter, this deliberate and exceptionally honourable record certainly might do so with all sensible people. Holbein's habits were doubtless censurable in some respects, but it is not for us to judge; we are not acquainted with all the circumstances, and should temper our inferences, in our ignorance, with charity. Amerbach was the only one of his former intimate friends who was still living in 1538; Erasmus had been then dead about two years.

One of the most interesting discoveries of Herr His-Heusler, is that of the letter of the Burgomaster Adelberg Meyer, to Jacob David in Paris, dated the 19th of November 1545, making known the fact of Philip Holbein having been placed by his father about 1539 with his fellow-townsman Jacob David, a jeweller settled in Paris. I have therefore no hesitation in assuming that when Holbein returned from Basel in the late autumn of 1538, he brought away with him his son Philip, then a boy of about fourteen years of age, and returning through Paris placed him with this Jacob David,* no doubt an old acquaintance and friend, and had him brought up to the

* This is certain, the burgomaster complains that though Philip Holbein had served honourably the whole six years for which his deceased father had placed him with David, that the latter would not give him his discharge and enable him to return home, or enter on his *wanderjahre*. Six years and more, from November 1545, will take us back to the beginning of 1539 or even to the end of 1538, when Holbein may have visited Paris.

The letter runs—"Wir Adelberg Meiger Burgermeister, und Rath der Stadt Basel embietend dir Jacoben David unsern grutz, und darby zuwüssen, das uns glouplich angelangt, das du Philippen Holbein, auch dem unsern, über und wider, *das er dir seine sechs jar, die er dir von wylundt Hansen Holbein seligen, seinem vater, unserm Burger versprochen gsin, eerlich und redlich ussgedient.* Yetzt, so er seiner gelegenheit nach, von dir scheiden und zuwandlen begert, seines eerlichen und redlichen dienens, wie du aber vor Gott, und aller erbarkeit schuldig bist, kein abschied geben wollst," &c., &c. * * * Datum donstag den XIX. tag Novemb. A° XLV.

jeweller's art, in which he became afterwards a successful master. Holbein therefore is exonerated from the accusation of any neglect of his son, however matters may stand with his wife, and whether the fault were more on his side than hers is yet a question to be decided. Holbein narrowly escaped the plague, a second time in Basel. "In 1539, there was a plague at Basil, as Platerus informs us, which continued after some remission 'till the following year, when the summer was excessively hot. There were several eminent persons died of it."*

CHAP. XV.

Solicited to settle in Basel.

1538.

30th Henry VIII.

After 1537 Holbein seems to have been in such favour with the king that he had apartments or at least a painting room in the palace at Westminster (Whitehall). I have already referred to the anecdote told by Van Mander about the misadventure with an inquisitive nobleman. The burden of the story is this: the painter was engaged on the picture of some lady for the king, there is no occasion to assume that any lady was actually sitting to him at the time, he may have been painting her portrait from some drawing of his own, as was certainly his wont, or he may have been completing the picture and touching on the accessaries: let us suppose that he was engaged on the full-length portrait of the Duchess of Milan, from the now-renowned sketch made at Brussels in March, and that the king was anxious for the picture, and did not wish it to be exposed to vulgar eyes. While thus engaged a certain earl, one of the noblemen of the court, visited his studio, and finding the door locked knocked for admission; the painter excused himself, and informed his lordship that he was engaged and could not be then disturbed, but requested him to come some other time. Such a refusal from a low painting fellow was not to be borne, and the nobleman made a great noise at the door, threatening to break it open if he were not immediately admitted. This was too much for the patience of the sturdy German, and opening the door, he unceremoniously thrust the obtrusive courtier headlong down the

The Painter and the Peer.

* Dr. Goodwin, *An Historical Account of the Plague*, &c. 1743.

CHAP. XV.

The Painter and the Peer.
1538.
30th Henry VIII.

stairs which led to it, hurting him seriously. Holbein just heard his adversary's exclamation of "Oh, Lord! have mercy upon me!" fastened his door again, and then, not knowing whether his man were dead or alive, made his escape through one of the windows of his room, and hastily sought out the apartment of the king. He approached him with tremblings, fell on his knees, at once soliciting his pardon for a great offence that he had committed against his majesty, without however relating the details or the catastrophe of the encounter, though Henry had asked for an explanation; the king however consented, provided Holbein gave him an honest account of what had happened. When Henry heard the details of the story he somewhat repented him of his too hasty compliance; however he told the painter not to go away, but to wait in one of the adjoining rooms. Shortly afterwards the peer arrived, carried in a chair, smarting with indignation under the affront that he had received, and gave his version of the occurrence, omitting all mention of the cause of the insult, mixing up much that was false with a little that was true, and demanding an adequate punishment for the offender. But seeing that the king, who felt how unjust the nobleman's story was, seemed to make very light of the matter, he imprudently lost his temper, and threatened to take the law into his own hands. This was too much for Henry, who becoming angry on his part, exclaimed, "Now you have no longer to deal with Holbein but with me, the king! do you think this man is of so little consideration with us? I tell you, my lord, that out of seven peasants, I can, if I please, any day, make seven earls; but out of seven earls I could not make one such artist as Hans Holbein." The earl beseeched his pardon, and as he took his departure, the king warned him, that if he ventured by himself or through others to offer any violence whatever to Holbein, he should consider it as an offence against his own royal person.

A full-length portrait of the Duchess of Milan was one of the pictures in the king's possession at his death, and is most probably that now at Arundel Castle: it is thus described in

Duchess of Milan.
1538.
30th Henry VIII.

in the king's catalogue:—"12. Item, a greate table with the picture of the Duchyes of Myllayne, being her whole stature." Van Mander remarks that Federigo Zucchero when in England in 1574, had been much struck with the full-length portrait of a certain countess, dressed in black satin, at the Earl of Pembroke's, by Holbein, and said that he had never seen so fine a portrait in Rome.

This portrait is exactly similar in pose to the small picture of the duchess already described, except that it is a whole length instead of a bust; the hands even though very differently executed are in the same position. It is on wood, about 5 ft. 10 in. high by 2 ft. 8 in. wide, and bears in a cartellino or label the following inscription:—*Christine daughter to Christierne K. of Deñark, Duches of Lorragne and hered. Dutches of Milan.*"* The writing is however excessively rubbed, and I could not satisfy myself as to every letter of the legend. It is on a fictitious piece of paper attached to the dark blue sea-green ground, near her left shoulder, by four dabs of sealing-wax; if the back-ground therefore means anything it means a wall; this treatment is simple enough, but not in the least offensive.

Though this portrait is strictly an iconic figure, it is a stupendous picture, and may be compared with "Mr. Morett" in the Dresden Gallery. We have few young ladies painted by Holbein, and but for this picture could scarcely form a sound opinion on his capability of portraying female beauty in its prime; but this picture shows us that he could do anything. I know no portrait that I can compare with it for simplicity and grandeur combined; both paint and painter are forgotten in looking at a work like this; you see only the incarnate spirit, and feel its very sphere; I cannot say as much of any portrait by Titian or by Vandyck; before their works you cannot forget the painter. "Lady Butts" is

* Mariette, *Abecedario*, Vol. II., p. 366. Paris, 1853-4, says—"Je serois tenté de croire que le portrait de cette princesse, qui, en 1585, se trouvoit à Milan entre les mains du president Don Ant. Londonio, et dont il y a une gravure faite par Augustin Carrache, dans *l'Histoire de Cremone* d'Ant. Campo, étoit celui qu'avoit peint Holbein; l'habillement tient beaucoup de sa manière." It is not the same.

CHAP. XV.

Duchess of Milan. 1538. 30th Henry VIII.

admirable as an old lady, but this duchess is still more admirable as a young one. Well might Zucchero say that he had never seen anything like it in Rome. I know of no portrait whatever that has the sphere of vitality so positively expressed; and then though the woman is really not beautiful, the expression is fascinating in the highest degree. The rich brown eyes, with the yellow ring immediately round the pupil, seem to admit you to the secrets of her thoughts, and the full pouting cherry lips irresistibly command admiration. The beauty of this exquisite portrait is indeed beyond ordinary powers of description.

She stands nearly upright, but with a slight stoop forward, looking full at the spectator; she has on a black satin gown, and over that a long black spencer lined with yellow sable; on her head is a black hood concealing the upper half of her forehead; around her neck and wrists are small white frills, with a black line on the outer edges; she holds a long light glove in her two hands, which brings them close together before her, and on the third finger of the left hand is a ring set with a large ruby; she seems not to know what to do with her hands, and is fidgeting with her glove. There is no other ornament about her. The ground she stands on is a buff, something the colour of a clean wooden floor, and this contrasts finely with the dark uniform back-ground. The figure seems to be the natural size: the face from the edge of the hood to the tip of the chin is exactly 5¾ inches. This is surely one of the most precious pictures in the world. But it is not in a perfect state; the face as well as the inscription has been rubbed, and there are some unskilful repairs about it, especially on the shaded portion of the forehead over the right eyebrow, and all down the shaded side of the nose.

Prince Edward. 1539. 31st Henry VIII.

In the roll of New Year's gifts, for the 30th Henry VIII., that is for January 1539, there is mentioned as Holbein's gift, the portrait of Prince Edward as a child. *By Hanse Holbyne, a table of the picture of the Prince's Grace.* In return for which the king's present to Holbein is also entered:—*To Hanse*

*Holbyne, paynter, a gilt cruse with a cover (Cornelis) weighing x. oz. 1 quarter.** There happen to be two portraits of the prince as a child which may be considered to correspond in a great measure with this description, though we must not forget, that at the beginning of this year the prince was not two years old. Holbein died before the prince attained his sixth year. It is clear therefore that Holbein can only have painted him as a child. Mr. Nichols, in the *Paper* referred to, remarks, "I am aware of three pictures only that bear this test,—those belonging to the King of Hanover, the Earl of Yarborough,† and the Duke of Northumberland; the two former, which are nearly identical, representing the royal child at half-length with a rattle, the third representing him standing, and about two years of age. These three may be regarded as unquestionably works of Holbein. There are also his three drawings of the prince in the royal portfolio at Windsor: the first taken from Edward in infancy, the second at the age of four or five, and the third in profile, apparently still older—though certainly not much so, if by Holbein."

CHAP. XV.

Prince Edward.

1539.

31st Henry VIII.

Mr. Nichols is probably correct in his conclusions, but I have not seen the picture formerly in the Georgen Garten at Herrnhausen, but now in the Welfen or Guelphian Museum, Hanover, and therefore have no opinion to give as regards the respective merits of the two portraits, which he terms nearly identical, but I should not be astonished to find, if a proper comparison could be made, that Lord Yarborough's portrait is a copy of that in Germany, from some few peculiarities in its execution, from some defects in the right hand, and a certain want of transparency, or a mealyness in the colouring, that are not entirely consistent with Holbein's practice.

Lord Yarborough's is a charming little picture. It is a half-length, showing the full face, with a little hair combed straight over his forehead; he is resting on a stone with his left arm

* Cornelis, says Mr. Franks, is evidently the king's goldsmith CORNELIUS HAYES, who is often mentioned in the Privy Purse expenses and in the Household accounts.

† Photographed very successfully by Caldesi and Co., in the volume on the Manchester Exhibition. It has also been engraved by Hollar.

CHAP. XV.

Prince Edward. 1539. 31st Henry VIII.

holding a gold rattle in this hand, the right hand he is extending before him, which, making allowance for some little redundancy of markings, is very pretty. The child is dressed in crimson velvet and gold, with full sleeves of cloth of gold, and white ruffles at his wrists; his bonnet covering a closely fitting white-edged cap, is also of crimson velvet with ornaments in gold, and plumed with a white ostrich feather. The background is a bluish green. On wood, about 22 in. high by 17 in. wide. On the stone on which his arm rests are the following eight idle complimentary lines to the father, by Sir Richard Morysine :—

Parvule patrissa, patriae virtutis et haeres
  Esto, nihil majus maximus orbis habet.
Gnatum vix possunt coelum et natura dedisse
  Hujus quem patris, victus honoret honos.
Aequato tantum, tanti tu facta parentis.
  Vota hominum vix quo progrediantur habent.
Vincito, vicisti quot reges priscus adorat
  Orbis, nec te qui vincere possit, erit.*

This picture was formerly in the Arundel collection, at Stafford House, where it was sold in 1720 ; it was subsequently in that of Sir Richard Worsley, at Appuldercombe, Isle of Wight, now the property of the Earl of Yarborough.

A sketch of this head is among the Holbein drawings at Windsor. And Charles I. had a copy of the picture by Peter Oliver, signed P. O., and inscribed—*Edwardus Princeps Filius Henrici Octavi Regis Angliae.*†

* Little one! imitate your father, and be the heir of his virtue, the world contains nothing greater—Heaven and Nature could scarcely give a son whose glory should surpass that of such a father. You only equal the acts of your parent, the wishes of men cannot go beyond this. Surpass him, and you have surpassed all the kings the world ever worshipped, and none will ever surpass you.

† Charles I.'s copy of this portrait by Oliver, is thus described by Vanderdoort:—

22. Item, the picture of King Edward VI. in his infancy, in a red cap with a white feather, and a red coat laced with gold, and golden cloth sleeves, holding in his left hand a round golden rattle, and with his right hand in some action; by a green table, whereupon is written in white and black letters. Being in a black shutting frame. *Painted upon the wrong light.* 4⅜ in. × 2 in.

Copied by Peter Oliver after Hans Holben, whereof my Lord Arundel has the principal limning.

Hollar's print is inscribed—*Wenceslaus Hollar fecit, ex Collectione Arundeliana. A°* 1650.

The Duke of Northumberland's full-length of the child, at Sion House, shows a still brighter expression of face, and appears somewhat younger; the probability is therefore in favour of this picture being the "New Year's Gift" referred to. The head is wrapped in a white-edged striped skull-cap, and a little hair hangs carelessly over the forehead, much the same as in the other portrait, but more freely executed; over this close cap is an ordinary cap, red, with a dark feather in it. On his neck is seen the little white shirt or petticoat, and there are also small white frills at the wrists; his jacket is of cloth of gold with a lined pattern over it, of this the arms only are seen, for he wears also a loose frock covering all but the arms, which are passed through a cut in the sleeves, the latter hanging empty by his sides. This frock is crimson embroidered with stripes in gold, and tied round his waist with a red band; his little thick-soled broad-toed shoes are visible, and he is standing on a green velvet cloth edged with gold, which is thrown carelessly over an ornamented stone tablet, containing the same verses that I have already given from Lord Yarborough's picture. The back-ground is a dark green curtain. On panel, 4 ft. 3 in. high by 2 ft. 5 in. wide, sight measure.

This portrait is considerably rubbed, and is slightly re-painted, even over the face, which has been a little *freshened.* It is very thinly painted, distinctly showing the preliminary drawing, apparently with chalk, in almost every part, the little dark lines being free to carelessness. The hands are a little extended, but have nothing in them; we see the back of the left hand, and this is childlike and beautiful, both in form and colour. On the slab or tablet is written *Edwardus Princeps*, on one corner, and on the other *Filius Henrici* 8, but this part of the inscription is almost entirely obliterated; the first two words though much rubbed are still quite legible.*

* Mariette, *Abecedario*, p. 366, has a curious note respecting a portrait of Edward VI., which in some degree corresponds with the above portrait, it was of about the same size, but he says nothing of a Latin inscription, and he calls it a *toile*—"Le portrait du Prince Edouard, fils du Henry VIII., à l'age de

CHAP. XV.

Prince Edward. 1539. 31st Henry VIII.

The very interesting portrait of the prince, when already king, at Petworth, we now know cannot have been painted by Holbein. Though somewhat hard it is a beautiful picture, and if we knew something positive about the paintings of William Stretes, some opinion as to his probable authorship of the portrait, might be reasonably pronounced; but as we know almost nothing of his works, any conjecture is a mere speculation. The portrait is a very elaborately painted full-length of the young king, seated on his throne, with a magnificent canopy over his head; the little monarch however seems to be rather leaning against, than comfortably seated on, the chair of state. The figure is of the natural size; the portrait was taken in the king's tenth year; it represents in every sense a fine face: both the expression and the features are beautiful. The picture is on canvas, and is inscribed in a cartellino, on the spectator's right—*Anno Dominj* 1547. *Anno Aetatis suae* 10. Stretes was at this time the king's painter: that this picture is more minutely finished than some others suggested in this volume to be the works of the same master, does not militate against the ascription in this case, as it is quite possible that the painter felt the occasion to be one which demanded the utmost care and skill that he could bestow upon his work.

Further payments.

The following are the entries, for this year, in the treasurer's accounts against Holbein:—

Lady Day, A°. xxx.—Item, for Hans Holbyn, paynter—Nihil quia prius per warrantum.

Midsummer, A°. xxxi.—Item, for Hans Holbyn, paynter, vij.li. x.s.

---

trois ou quatre ans, peint en détrempe sur une toile, écrue, vers l'année 1540, étoit à Paris, chez M. Crozat, chi l'estimoit un ouvrage d'Holbein; le Prince y est représenté debout en jaquette et bonnet d'enfant, et ce qui ne laisse aucun lieu de douter que ce ne soit le même tableau indiqué dans le présent inventaire, c'est qu'on y voit aussi un rideau, et que la toile n'est proprement que teinte tant les couleurs qui ont été appliquées dessus ont peu d'éppaisseur. M. le Baron de Thiers, heritier des tableaux de M. Crozat, son oncle, ne s'en souciant pas, le fit exposer en vente en 1751, et le tableau fut vendu à vil prix." The *Inventory* referred to is that of Henry VIII.'s pictures.

CHAP. XV.

July, A°. xxxi.—Item, to Mr. Richard Bearde, one of the gromes of the Kingis privichambre, and Hans Holbyn, paynter, by like lettre sent into the parties of High Almayne upon certain his gracis affaires, for the costes and chardgis of them bothe, xl.li. And to Hans Holben, for the preparation of such thingis as he is appoynted to carie with him, xiij.li. vi.s. viii.d.—in alle the somme of liij.li. vi.s. viij.d.

Further payments. 1539. 31st Henry VIII.

September, A°. xxxi.—Item, paide by the Kingis Highnesse commaundement certefied by my lorde privyseales lettres to Hans Holbenne, paynter, in the advauncement of his whole yeres wagis beforehande, aftre the rate of xxx.li. by yere, which yeres advauncement is to be accompted from this present Michaelmas, and shall ende ultimo Septembris next commynge, the somme of xxx.li.

Michaelmas, A°. xxxi.—Item, for Hans Holbyn, paynter, vij.li. x.s.

Christmas, A°. xxxi.—Item, Hans Holbyn, paynter, vij.li. x.s.

On the 25th March 1539, Holbein had necessarily no arrears of salary to receive, and he had been paid a whole year's allowance in advance on the 25th March preceding. It is difficult to explain these payments in advance, unless we suppose that the excuse of foreign travel, and accordingly absence from town at the times of payment, may have been admitted as a sufficient reason: at all events it shows that Holbein was in high favour at the court, and need not imply that he was very poor. He must have received sums of money for his works from other employers, if not from the king. There is no single entry anywhere showing the price Holbein received for any work executed for the king; it is just possible that his salary was considered to cover any commissions he may have received for work on the king's account. His pay however did not include travelling expenses, for of these charges we have important and interesting entries, and of, at that time, very considerable sums.

Travelling expenses.

In midsummer this year, he received his usual quarterly salary; and in July we find the considerable payment of 53*l*. 6*s*. 8*d*. for his own and his companion's Mr. Richard Bearde's expenses, incurred on a journey to the north of Germany, in

CHAP. XV.

Travelling expenses. 1539. 31st Henry VIII.

the Rhine country; and of this sum 13*l.* 6*s.* 8*d.* seems to have been for the apparatus for professional purposes, I suppose, which it was thought necessary that he should take with him. Such treatment as this was something to contrast very powerfully with the modest retaining pension of four or five guineas a year offered by the town-council of Basel. Jacob Meier (zum Hirschen) and his fellow-councillors should have been a little more liberal, and they might then possibly have secured the great painter's services in permanency. The expenses referred to are enough for the present day, and unless the cost of locomotion was excessive, must have been more than sufficient at that time when living was so comparatively inexpensive.

Holbein seems to have moved about considerably; in the summer of 1538 we found him in Basel; and in the summer of 1539 we find him in the duchy of Cleves, engaged by Cromwell or by the king, to paint the portrait of the Lady Anne, daughter of the Duke of Cleves, a German Protestant prince, pending the negotiation of a marriage between Henry VIII. and that princess, in furtherance of the Protestant alliance. The popular belief is that Holbein succeeded only too well; for partly on the strength of this portrait the king is said to have consented to the proposed marriage; which proved after all only another disastrous ceremony; for he found that he could not live with her, and she finally settled quietly at Richmond in the enjoyment of the rank of a princess, and a pension of 3000*l.* a year. She arrived in England on the 27th of December this year, was married at Greenwich on the 6th of January, 1540, but the marriage was never consummated, and she was divorced, with her own consent, on the 12th of July following. She died in 1557, surviving Henry only ten years.

Anne of Cleves.

This marriage involves an interesting episode in the life of our painter, out of which posterity has elaborated a romance, upon however a very slight foundation in fact. Bishop Burnet appears to be the author of the modern version of the story; at least I can trace no foundation for it any further back. He says, speaking of Anne of Cleves—"Hans Holbin having taken her picture, sent it over to the king. But in that he bestowed the common compliment of his art somewhat too liberally on a lady that was in a fair way to be queen the king liked the picture better than the original, when he had the occasion afterwards to compare them." * Instead of the promised beauty, says the bishop, they brought him over a "Flanders mare." There is nothing about a Flanders mare either in Stow's "Annals," or in Strype's "Ecclesiastical Memorials."

CHAP. XV

Anne of Cleves.
1539.
31st Henry VIII.

To say that the king's great minister Cromwell, lost his head, because our painter, departing from his ordinary truthfulness, made a beautiful picture of a plain lady, is both false and absurd; Cromwell fell for far other reasons, for which I must refer the reader to Mr. Froude's great work. In the first place did Holbein ever make her beautiful? In the second *did the king see* the portrait, or miniature, whatever it may have been—I believe it to have been one of his ordinary drawings—before he consented to the marriage? Henry can never have been so weak as to make a promise of marriage, on the mere sight of a portrait. Walpole, following Burnet, has written—"Holbein was next despatched by Cromwell to draw the Lady Anne of Cleve, and by practising the common flattery of his profession, *was the immediate cause of the destruction of that great subject*, and of the disgrace that fell on the princess herself. He drew so favourable a likeness, that Henry was content to wed her; but when he found her so inferior to the miniature, the storm which really should have been directed at the painter, burst on the minister; and Cromwell lost his head, because Anne was a *Flanders mare*, not a Venus, as Holbein had represented her." Here common sense and truth are both sacrificed for the sake of an antithesis.

This Venus that Walpole speaks of is not to be found, but there are several reputed portraits of the princess, ascribed to Holbein, some of which may be genuine, as the miniature in the

---

* *History of the Reformation*, Vol. I., Part I., p. 543; see also No. XVIII. among the Records, in the second part of this volume.

CHAP. XV.

Anne of Cleves.
1539.
31st Henry VIII.

possession of Colonel Meyrick, formerly Mr. Barrett's of Lee,* and the fine small half-length in the Louvre.

The Louvre portrait is a beautiful picture, but not of a beautiful woman, nor of a very stout one either: it represents an agreeable homely face, nothing more, and is no doubt a faithful picture of the person represented. She is standing, showing the front face, and with her hands crossed before her; much in the same position and with much the same demure look that we find in the portrait of the Duchess of Milan. She has on the ordinary cap or bonnet of the time, made of cloth of gold, and enriched with pearls and other stones; her dress is of crimson velvet braided with gold thread, and enriched with pearls: she wears a rich necklace, and has rings on her fingers and thumb. On parchment attached to canvas, about 2 ft. 2 in. high by 1 ft. 7 in. wide.

The fact of this picture being on parchment, induces me to look upon it (assuming it to be Anne of Cleves) as that taken by Holbein during the negotiations for the marriage: and though it may suggest a woman less coarse in feature and less swarthy in complexion than Anne is said to have been, it certainly represents no Venus; the nose especially, seems broad and flat.†

Walpole referring to the recorded miniature in question, speaks of it with some hesitation as possibly that now in the possession of Colonel Meyrick of Goodrich Court; he says, "This very picture, as is supposed, was in the possession of Mr. Barrett of Kent, whose collection was sold a few years ago, but the family reserved this and some other curiosities. The print

* Exhibited at Manchester in 1857.

† A head of "Anne of Cleves," in oil on panel, oval, about 3 in. *h.* by 2¼ in. *w.*, and signed H. H., dirty and injured, was exhibited by the Earl of Derby at South Kensington in 1865: the face is much the same as that of the Louvre picture. Houbraken in 1739, engraved the "Anne of Cleves" which was in the collection of Th. Barrett, Esq. (now Colonel Meyrick's.) 7 in. *h.* by 6 in. *w.* And Hollar has engraved a print similar to the Louvre picture, but reversed; 9¼ in. *h.* by 7 in. *w.* It is inscribed—*Anna Clivensis, Henrici VIII. Regis Angliae Uxor IIIIta. H. Holbein pinxit. Wenceslaus Hollar fecit aqua forti, ex Collectione Arundeliana, A.* 1648. Can this Louvre portrait have been the Arundel picture? This, and no miniature, I should imagine to have been the famous portrait about which so much has been written.

among the illustrious heads is taken from it, and so far justifies the king, that he certainly was not nice, if from that picture he concluded her handsome enough. It has so little beauty, that I should doubt of its being the very portrait in question—it rather seems to have been drawn after Holbein saw a little with the king's eyes.

CHAP. XV. *Anne of Cleves.* 1539. 31st Henry VIII.

"I have seen that picture in the cabinet of the present Mr. Barrett of Lee, and think it the most exquisitely perfect of all Holbein's works, as well as in the highest preservation. The print gives a very inadequate idea of it, and none of her Flemish fairness. It is preserved in *the ivory box in which it came over* (?), and which represents a rose, so delicately carved as to be worthy of the jewel it contains."*

The remark about the "carved ivory box" is inconsistent with his previous doubt of its being "the very portrait in question." Several of the miniatures of Charles I. were in carved ivory boxes, and Colonel Meyrick possesses a miniature of Henry VIII. in a similar ivory box. No such miniature is mentioned in the inventory of Henry VIII., or in Vanderdoort's catalogue of Charles I.'s collection.

Holbein only went to Germany on this business of the portrait in July; the payment was an advance; the entry mentions a round sum as allowed for the travelling expenses, 20*l.* each, and then the fixed charge of 13*l.* 6*s.* 8*d.* as the cost of the articles or for the preparation of the apparatus that the painter "*is appointed to carry with him.*" We find however from a letter of the Earl of Hertford (afterwards the Lord Protector Somerset) to Cromwell, dated the 17th of July, that the consent of the lady's brother, the Duke of Cleves, and of her mother, had then already been gained.†

The first notice of the portrait itself is in a letter to the king, from Dr. Nicholas Wotton, resident at Cleves, and engaged in the negotiations; dated from the castle of Duren on the

* Walpole's *Anecdotes*, &c. Note, p. 72. Ed. 1849.

† He writes from Wollfall, that he was "glad of the good resolution of the Duke of Cleves, his mother and Council." Ellis, *Original Letters.* First Series, Vol. II., p. 119.

CHAP. XV. — *Anne of Cleves.* — 1539. 31st Henry VIII.

11th of August following. He is speaking of the Lady Anne, and writes—"Her wit is so good that no doubt she will in a short space learn the English tongue, whensoever she putteth her mind to it. I could never hear that she is inclined to the good cheer of this country, and marvel it were if she should, seeing that her brother, in whom yet it were somewhat more tolerable, doth so well abstain from it. *Your Graces servante Hanze Albein hath taken th' effigies of my Ladye Anne and the Ladye Amelye, and hath expressyd theyr imaiges verye lyvelye.* * * * *

"Written at Duren the XIth day of August A°. Dnī. 1539."*

From the dates of the payment in question, and this letter together, we may perhaps safely assume that these portraits—drawings or pictures?—were taken in August, not before: nowhere is there any talk about any miniature. Indeed there is not anywhere throughout the whole transactions relating to this marriage, any allusion to any portrait by Holbein, true or false. Stow speaks vaguely of the misrepresentations of pictures and reports, but singularly enough this word *pictures* does not occur in the deposition of the Lord Admiral Russel, to which he refers. Stow makes the admiral put the following words as coming from the king—"Alas! whom shall men trust? I promise you I see no such thing in her as hath been showed me of her, *either by pictures or report*, and am ashamed that men have praised her as they have done." Lord Russell's own deposition is this—"How like you this woman? do you think her so fair and of such beauty as report hath been made unto me of her? I pray you tell me truth." Whereunto the said lord admiral answered, that he took her not for fair, but to be of a brown complexion. And the king's highness said, "Alas! whom should men trust? I promise you," saith he, "I see no such thing in her as hath been showed me of her, and am ashamed *that men hath praised her as they have done*, and I like her not." The remark about "pictures"

* Ellis, *l. l.*, p. 122. The portrait of the sister, the Lady Amelia, is not known, but may still be in existence, either as a drawing or an oil picture.

is Stow's interpolation.* Sir Anthony Brown, another of the deponents in the case respecting the divorce, does refer to pictures, but quite vaguely; he says "by pictures and advertisements." †

CHAP. XV. *Anne of Cleves.* 1539. 31st Henry VIII.

Stow makes a great feature of pictures in general, which seems rather absurd, in his report of the negotiations for the marriage. He says, "Some went over by the king, some by the Lord Cromwell, and some went voluntary, to view the Lady Anne of Cleave, and to negotiate her marriage with the king. All which *either by letters, speech, or both*, made very large and liberal reports in praise of her singular feature, matchless beauty, and princely perfections, and for proof thereof *presented the king with sundry of her pictures*, which the bringers ever affirmed to have been truly made, without flattery." Such is the gallery of portraits, that has been imagined out of the foundation of Holbein's single drawing. Stow however makes no mention of Holbein.

Let us hear the king himself; we have his original declaration in his own hand.‡ "Now to the matter I say and affirm, that when the first communication was had with me for the marriage of the Lady Anne of Cleves, I was glad to hearken to it, trusting to have some assured friend by it; I much doubting that time, both the emperor, France, and the bishop of Rome; and also because I *heard* so much both of her excellent beauty and virtuous conditions.

* * * * *

"I liked her so ill, and so far contrary to that she was *praised*, that I was woe that ever she came into England." We have further an interesting deposition from Sir Anthony Brown, who returning with the king in his barge from Rochester to Greenwich, relates that his highness spoke "these words very sadly and pensively, '*I see nothing in this woman as men report of her, and I mervail that wise men would make such report as they have done.*' With which words the

* Stow, *Annals.* Ed. Howes, p. 576. Compare Strype's *Memorials*, No. CXIV., Vol. I., Part II., p. 452.

† Strype, *l. l.*

‡ Burnet's *Reformation*, Records XVIII. Vol. I., Part II., p. 307.

CHAP. XV.

Anne of Cleves.
1539.
31st Henry VIII.

said Sir Anthony was abashed, fearing lest anything should be objected to my Lord of Southampton his brother, for that he had written to her praise."

Nowhere is there any allusion to any peccant miniature. When Henry VIII. returned to Greenwich, from the first interview at Rochester, Cromwell, who had been nervously waiting his arrival, asked him "How he liked the Lady Anne?" "Nothing so well as she was *spoken* of; if I had known as much before as I know now, she should never have come into the realm. But what remedy?"*

Cromwell to whom the blame, if to anybody, was due, at first shrunk from his responsibility, and accused Lord Southampton of raising false hopes by his letters from Calais, in which he had spoken of the "great *report* of her notable virtues and of her excellent beauty, such as he well perceived to be no less than was reported." The earl however repudiated all responsibility in the matter. He had been sent to bring the queen into England, and it was not his place to "dispraise her appearance." The matter being so far gone, he had supposed it to be his duty to make the best of it.†

It is somewhat strange that it should not occur to any one to blame the painter, or his deceiving miniature, if they were the cause of all this disappointment and mutual recrimination. I am satisfied that the whole story about Holbein's "professional flattery" and its fatal consequences is a mere fiction, and Walpole has pushed the matter to the verge of extravagance for the sake of an idle witticism. If Henry had thought that Holbein had misled him into such a dilemma, we should have known something of it; the painter would certainly not have escaped retribution. There is no evidence even that Cromwell suffered from Henry's disappointment, or that this was the cause that he in vain appealed to the king for mercy. It was after this fourth marriage (in April 1540), that Cromwell was created Earl of Essex. The charges against him were many,

---

* Burnet's *Collectanea*, p. 109. Quoted by Froude, Vol. III., p. 456.

† Strype's *Memorials*; see also Froude, *History of England*, Vol. III., p. 467.

and his enemies were legion. He was beheaded for high treason on the 28th of July 1540, having enjoyed his new dignity a little more than three months.* Chap. XV. *Anne of Cleves.* 1539. 31st Henry VIII.

The whole affair of his fourth marriage is an irretrievable disaster to Henry's reputation; not that it brought any wickedness to the surface, but as exhibiting him deplorably weak and wilful at the same time. And such was his wonderful ill-luck in his marriages, that his next choice resulted only in another catastrophe.

The fifth and sixth payments of this year seem to be irregular and inconsistent with the fourth, which as an advance for the whole year from September 1539 to September 1540, renders inexplicable the second of the two quarters' payments for Michaelmas and Christmas of the same year. The advance in September as such cannot have covered the Michaelmas quarter, but it certainly did that from Michaelmas to Christmas: the last quarter was clearly paid twice, if the entry is to be depended on. The circumstance is a singular one; accounts it appears were not very well kept in those times; though it might I suppose be possible even now for a government servant, to receive his salary twice in some establishment, not liable to the commissioners of audit. Holbein however was in the king's, not in the government, service, and was paid under the authority of the Lord Privy Seal.

Pursuing the accounts for the following year, 1540, we find the same irregularity continued, for two more quarters, as follows:—

Lady Day, A°. xxxi.:—Item, for Hans Holben, paynter, vii.li. x.s. *The last payments.* 1540. 32nd Henry VIII.

* "For eight years," says Mr. Froude, "his influence had been supreme with the king — supreme in parliament — supreme in convocation; the nation in the ferment of revolution was absolutely controlled by him; and he has left the print of his individual genius stamped indelibly, while the metal was at white heat, into the constitution of the country. Wave after wave has rolled over his work. Romanism flowed back over it under Mary. Puritanism, under another even grander Cromwell, overwhelmed it. But Romanism ebbed again, and Puritanism is dead, and the polity of the Church of England remains as it was left by its creator."—*History of England.* Vol. III., p. 351.

CHAP. XV.

The last payments. 1540. 32nd Henry VIII.

Midsummer, A°. xxxii.:—Item, for Hans Holben, paynter, vii.li. x.s.

September, A°. xxxii.:—Item, paide to Hans Holbyn, the Kingis paynter, in advauncement of his wagis for one half yere beforehande, the same half yere accompted and reconned fromme Michaelmas last paste, the somme of xv.li.

Following this advance we have the proper entries:—

Michaelmas, A°. xxxii.:—Item, for Hans Holbyn, paynter, nihil, quia prius per warrantum.

Christmas, A°. xxxii.:—Item, for Hans Holbyn, paynter, wages nihil, quia prius per warrantum.

With the next three payments, there is unhappily an end to these very interesting accounts:—

March, A°. xxxii.:—Item, paied to Hans Holben, the Kingis paynter, in advauncement of his half yeres wages before hande, after the rate of xxx.li. by yere, which half yere is accompted to beginne primo Aprilis A°. xxxij. domini Regis nunc, and shall ende ultimo Septembris then next ensuynge, the somme of xv.li.

Lady Day, A°. xxxii.:—1541, *Item for Hans Holben, paynter, wages, nil, quia praemanibus.*

Midsummer, A°. xxxiij.:—Item, for Hans Holbyn, paynter, nihil, quia prius.

Henry Earl of Surrey.

Among the greatest enemies of Cromwell were Gardiner bishop of Winchester and the Howards; and for a time the influence of the Howards with the king, was, through Henry VIII.'s fifth marriage, paramount. Our Holbein gallery comprises, according to common rumour, several portraits of at least three of this family: Thomas Howard the third duke, his son Henry Earl of Surrey, and his niece Catherine, daughter of Lord Edmund Howard, who, on the 8th of August of this year became Queen of England. "Uppon a notable appearance of honour, cleanness, and maidenly behaviour in Mistress Catherine Howard," writes the Privy Council to Sir

Catherine Howard.

William Paget,* "His highness was finally contented to honour that lady with his marriage, thinking in his old days,† after sundry troubles of mind which had happened to him by marriage, to have obtained such a jewel for womanhood and very perfect love towards him as should not only have been to his quietness, but also have brought forth the desired fruits of marriage."‡

CHAP. XV.

Catherine Howard. 1540. 32nd Henry VIII.

Perhaps never was an ill-fated husband more disappointed. I am acquainted with no authenticated portrait of this queen by Holbein; though there is a head to which her name has been given among the Windsor drawings. Of the duke there is one important portrait, which we have in duplicate, either copied, or repeated by Holbein; but of the earl it is questionable whether there exists any picture by Holbein, though his head also is supposed to be among the Windsor drawings. There is a bust portrait of him at Arundel Castle, in cap and feather, and holding a red carnation in his left hand, but it shows no trace of Holbein's art. The large full length of him at Knole, which has been ascribed to Holbein is certainly not by that painter: it is distinctly dated 1546, the earl's twenty-ninth year.

Guillim Stretes.

This is a picture that we have some grounds for ascribing to GUILLIM STRETES, King Edward's painter already mentioned, and if justly so, this almost unknown artist was quite worthy of his position. Of this portrait there is a repetition or copy at Arundel Castle, but with important variations in the accessaries; indeed the only resemblance is in the figure of the earl himself: the inscription is the same in both, except that SUAE is written SUE in the Arundel picture:—ANNO DNI. 1546 ÆTATIS SVÆ 29.

* This was in 1543, when Sir William was knighted. There is more than one reputed portrait of this nobleman, as Baron Paget, ascribed to Holbein; but Sir William or Mr. Paget was only thirty-seven years old when Holbein died, and he was created a baron by Edward VI., in 1550 only, when Holbein had been dead already seven years. There can be no portrait of the first Lord Paget by Holbein except as a young man; it is therefore very doubtful whether he comes at all into the Holbein gallery.

† The king was only fifty-two in these *old days*.

‡ Froude, *History of England*, &c. Vol. IV., p. 107. *Acts of the Privy Council*. Vol. VII., p. 352.

CHAP. XV.

Guillim Stretes.

1540.
32nd Henry VIII.

Strype notices two portraits of Edward VI., by Guillim Stretes; he says that Stretes received "fifty marks for recompense of three tables" made by him, "whereof two were the pictures of his highness, sent to Sir Thomas Hoby, and Sir John Mason (ambassadors abroad), the third a picture of the late Earl of Surrey, attainted, and by the council's commandment fetched from the said Guillim's house."* The mark was worth two nobles, or about 13*s*. 4*d*. Fifty marks therefore would be equivalent to 25*l*.; the price of each portrait was accordingly, about 11*l*. of our money, not an inconsiderable sum at that time.

The question is whether either of these two portraits of the Earl of Surrey was that fetched from the painter's house, at the time of the trial.

The Knole example appears to me a very superior work to the other; it is somewhat careless in parts, but shows many unmistakeable signs of mastery about it, and was not unnaturally ascribed to the great master of the period and place, unknown to have been already dead at the time.

The earl, a slight figure, is standing in the open air, near an archway, the arch being seen in part, with a piece of landscape in the distance. He is dressed in a brown doublet or jerkin, figured with light arabesques, and in very light hose, with the Garter round his left knee; and he rests his right arm on a broken pillar, holding his gloves in his hand. On the base of the pillar is the motto SAT SUPEREST: the picture is on canvas, and is 6 ft. 9 in. high by 4 ft. 3 in. wide. In a niche, in the right-hand upper corner of the picture is a little boy or *amorino* holding a red shield, with three lions, passant, and a label above; the arms of Thomas de Brotherton, son of Edward I., and Earl of Norfolk. This same device, three lions with a label above, constitutes the present *second quartering* of the arms of the Dukes of Norfolk; and without the label, occupies the first and fourth quarters of the royal arms. It was for altering his shield,

* *Memorials, &c.* Vol. II., p. 494. Quoted by Walpole.

Guillim Stretes.

1540. 32nd Henry VIII.

when the king was ill, in November 1546, and assuming the quarterings of the heir apparent to the throne, and he did this in spite of the inhibition of the heralds, that he was attainted for high treason, and beheaded in January 1547.*

If this was done in the Knole portrait, the shield has been altered since. The Arundel picture, in my opinion an inferior work, is also on canvas, and is about 7 feet square. The figure of the earl is almost lost in a mass of arabesque rubbish, which constitutes a kind of frame around him, arched just over his head; and over the crown of the arch is a large H; on the face of the arch, following the curve is the inscription already noticed, containing the date and age of the earl; and on either side is a figure holding a shield: that on his right bearing the Brotherton arms, that on his left, the arms of France and England combined, the fleur-de-lis in the first and fourth quarters and the lions in the second and third. Neither of the portraits therefore contains anything treasonable in it at present, as regards the assumption of the quarterings of the heir apparent, or that could make it an object of importance to the Privy Council. That the Knole picture is not by Holbein, is certain, that it is by Stretes is simply a conjecture, but in some measure justified by the painter's position, and by the record in Strype. It was certainly not painted by Girolamo da Treviso; it is not only not in his style, he had been already dead two years in 1546.

Stretes was probably the painter of the Bridewell picture of Edward VI., transferring that palace to London; as the

* Froude, in his *History of England*, &c., Vol. IV., p. 521, gives a document on this subject with corrections, in italics, by the hand of the king himself; it is taken from the *State Papers*, Vol. I., p. 891. Among the considerations mooted, is the following:—"If a man coming *of the collateral line to the heir* of the crown, who ought *not* to bear the arms of England *but on* the second quarter, with the difference of their ancestry, do presume to change his right place, and bear them on the first quarter, leaving out the true difference of the ancestry, and in the lieu thereof uses *the very place* only of the heir apparent, *how this man's intent is to be judged, and whether this* impute any danger, peril, or slander to the title of the prince, and how it weigheth in our laws?"

CHAP. XV.

Guillim Stretes. 1540. 32nd Henry VIII.

picture originally was, not as it is now. I imagine him also to have possibly been the painter of the so-called Holbein portrait of the "First Lord Delawarr," now in Mr. Holford's collection at Dorchester House, which is much after Holbein's time. It is a three-quarter length, full face, well painted, on panel, 5 ft. high by 2 ft. 7 in. wide. He was doubtless the painter of other existing portraits of Edward VI. than those above mentioned: that at Petworth has been already spoken of in connection with his name.

State of morals.

A few days after Cromwell's execution, the Duke of Norfolk met one of the departed minister's servants, a man who held an office in the exchequer, and who had married a nun:—"I know ye well enough," said the duke, "by God's body sacred it will never out of my heart as long as I live." The man by way of deprecating the duke's wrath, quoted Scripture. "I never read the Scripture," returned the conservative duke, "nor never will read it; it was merry in England afore the new learning came up; yea, I would all things were as hath been in times past." The time, in the graphic words of Mr. Froude, "when the world went smoothly with the church. When there was neither law nor order, when the strong trampled on the weak, and the ruling powers of the church were happy in their adulteries, and there was no justice but to the strong." When "the bishops and abbots ate, and drank, and sinned, and married their children, and believed their houses would continue for ever."*

As Holbein has been hardly judged upon little or no evidence, and as the question of his moral conduct must be yet again considered, it is right and necessary to give some notion of the general state of morals at this time in England; and as we will not assume that the priests were through the immunities of the "benefit of clergy," as a matter of course, worse than any other class of men, we may take their condition as a sample only of the general morals of the time. Cardinal

---

* MS. *State Paper Office, Domestic.* Papers endorsed Lascelles and Smithwick. See Froude, Vol. IV., p. 106, and Vol. IV., p. 58.

CHAP. XV.

State of morals.

1540. 32nd Henry VIII.

Wolsey indeed had complained to Pope Clement, that the priests, both secular and regular, were in the habit of committing crimes which, had they not been in "holy orders," would have infallibly involved the penalty of death; yet they were not only not degraded, but escaped with complete impunity. "Brothels were kept in London for the especial use of priests; the 'confessional' was abused in the most open and abominable manner. Cases occurred of the same frightful profanity in the service of the mass, which at Rome startled Luther into Protestantism; and acts of incest between nuns and monks were too frequently exposed to allow us to regard the detected instances as exceptions."

An exposure in the parish church, too common a thing to attract notice, and a fine of *six and eightpence* was held sufficient penalty for what the church stigmatized as a mortal sin. The system had certainly the advantage of being profitable to somebody. Even this, however, was severe punishment compared with the sentence passed upon a "priest who confessed to incest with the prioress of Kilbourn. The offender was condemned to bear a cross in a procession in his parish church, and was excused his remaining guilt for *three shillings and fourpence.*" This fining system was cleverly extended into a principle of licencing, and such as were disposed, clergy and laity, provided themselves with official permits for fornication and adultery at their pleasure. "There be knights," says an old document, "and divers gentlemen in the diocese of Chester who do keep concubines, and do yearly compound with the officials for a small sum, without monition to leave their naughty living."* In another report Mr. Froude found—"The names of such persons as be permitted to live in adultery and fornication for money," in the diocese of Hereford. The last comprises four vicars, four parsons, one dean, one priest, and ten knights or baronets, besides many others.†

What is most shocking in the matter above given, is not

* *Adam Bekenshaw to Cromwell.*

† *State Paper Office, MS. Tanner,* 105. Froude, *History of England,* &c. Vol. I., p. 199, &c. 3rd Ed.

State of morals.
1540.
32nd Henry VIII.

that men should live in adultery, which disorderly men will do at all times, but that a *professedly* Christian church should, for the sake of a few shillings, thus infamously authorize and licence the grossest immorality, and openly set at nought the laws both of God and man. The suppression of the monastic orders, whose religion was systematic hypocrisy, whose business was an organized uselessness, and whose pastime was a callous self-indulgence in general, was perhaps the greatest of all the great services Henry VIII. conferred upon his kingdom; and his very able minister Cromwell, though far from being immaculate himself, more especially as regards the love of power and the love of possession, deserves our lasting gratitude for the energetic manner in which, by the Divine permission, he carried out to the end the wishes and designs of his earthly master. His countenance certainly does not convey a good impression, judging from the head in the possession of Captain Ridgway; the eyes seem cunning and selfish, and the jaw is decidedly sensual; but there is vigour in abundance everywhere.

The Duke of Norfolk.

THOMAS HOWARD THIRD DUKE OF NORFOLK, born in 1473, was Lord High Admiral of England, and also a distinguished soldier; he was at the battle of Flodden: he had been likewise Lord Lieutenant of Ireland, and was successful in his administration of that government. He succeeded to the dukedom in 1524, and in 1539–40, when Holbein painted him, held the offices of Lord High Treasurer, Earl Marshal, and Lord Chamberlain. Yet this accumulation of honours only made his fall the more disastrous: he was arrested and attainted with his son for high treason, in 1546; and like him, would have perished on the scaffold, had not the king's death opportunely for the father intervened just before the time appointed for his execution. The duke remained however a prisoner in the Tower during Edward VI.'s reign, and was not let out until 1553 in the first year of Queen Mary; but it was only a release from his prison to his grave: he died in 1554 at the advanced age of eighty-one.

There are several portraits of this nobleman ascribed to

Holbein, of which one original is I think at Arundel Castle; the majority are certainly copies. One of the best examples is that in the Queen's closet, at Windsor Castle; this is a half-length on oak, or possibly, to judge from some singular raised cracks in it, on paper attached to oak, 2 ft. 7½ in. *h.* by 2 ft. *w.* It is branded on the back W R 43. It is the same as the Arundel portrait.

CHAP. XV.

The Duke of Norfolk.

1540.
32nd Henry VIII

He is in a red coat, and surcoat of the same colour lined with ermine, and wears a white collar embroidered with black; nearly full face turned slightly to the right, and the beard is completely shaven. He is decorated with the collar of the Garter, and the badge of St. George; in one hand he holds the gold stick or baton as Earl Marshal, and in the other the white staff of the Lord Chamberlain. The back-ground is plain dark green, and in the upper part of it is the inscription:—THOMAS DVKE OFF NORFOLK MARSHALL AND TRESVRER OFF INGLONDE THE LXVI. YERE OF HIS AGE. Which fixes the period of the painting at about the date 1540. The carnation of this picture, especially in the Windsor example, is unusually red for Holbein, but the modelling is excellent.

This portrait of the duke with that of the Earl of Surrey when in his twenty-fifth year are both introduced as hanging on the wall of the room, in a picture on copper, from a sketch left by Vandyck, of the family of Thomas Earl of Arundel, by Ph. Fruytiers of Antwerp; it has been engraved by Vertue. A drawing on vellum of the same composition was exhibited by Lord Stafford at South Kensington in 1866, inscribed—"*An. Vandyke inv. Ph. Fruytiers fecit*, 1642."

The inscriptions on the two portraits are very distinct—THOMAS HOWARD DUKE OFF NORFOLK MARSHALL AND TRESURER OF INGLONDE THE LXVI. YERE OF HIS AGE.—HENRY HOWARD ERLE OF SURRY ANNO AETATIS SUÆ 25. The picture of the duke is still to be seen at Arundel Castle; the earl's I have not met with. The duplicate or very careful copy of the duke's at Windsor Castle, had the same inscription but it has been defaced. That at Arundel is a masculine

CHAP. XV.

The Duke of Norfolk. 1540. 32nd Henry VIII.

expressive portrait, but seems to have been somewhat re painted about the face; it is however full of vigour and individuality and is quite worthy of Holbein's pencil: both are excellent pictures.

There is another half-length of the duke, to the knees, at Norfolk House, St. James's Square, but this is not by Holbein, it may have been made up from a portrait of Holbein's, but about a hundred years after his time, perhaps for the famous Thomas Earl of Arundel, the great collector and admirer of Holbein's works. The two staves, gold and white, are not held in the same attitude as in the Arundel and Windsor pictures; in the two latter they are nearly vertical and parallel, in the third they are held nearly at right angles. The duke in this picture seems a much younger man than sixty-six: he is dressed in a black cap, and red vest, with yellow sable about the neck, on which is an embroidered shirt collar, and he wears the collar and badge of St. George: his overcoat is lined with ermine; the sleeves are open but are tied close to his arms. On the back-ground, a bluish green, are some twigs of vine, and on the right of the picture is a Corinthian pilaster, on the base of which is written—*Thomas Duke of Norfolk, Lord High Treasurer and Earl Marshal of England & cet:* on wood, arched at the top—4 ft. high by 3 ft. wide.

St. Andrew Undershaft. 1541. 33rd Henry VIII.

In a Subsidy Roll for the city of London, dated the 24th of October of this year, 1541, is the following interesting matter concerning Holbein:—

"Aldgate Warde

* * * *

The Parisshe of Saint Andrewe Undershafte

* * * * * * *

Straungers

Bernadyne Buttessey, xxx.*li.* . . . . xxx.*s.*

Hanns Holbene in fee, xxx.*li.* . . . . iij.*li.*"

Here on the same income Holbein is taxed to exactly twice

CHAP. XV.

St. Andrew Undershaft. 1541. 33rd Henry VIII.

the amount Buttessey had to pay; which is explained by the fact that on these subsidies it was usual to tax "lands, fees, and annuities" at double the rate of goods.* The last payment to Holbein recorded in the accounts of the Treasurer of the Household was for midsummer of this year, *A° xxxiij.—Item, for Hans Holbyn, paynter, nihil quia prius.* The value of the above extract from the Subsidy Roll is that it fixes the residence of our painter, near the end of his life in the parish of St. Andrew Undershaft, which is of the utmost importance as enabling us to identify him as the veritable testator of the will to be considered presently; as it is contrary to common sense and probabilities that there should be living in the same parish, two strangers or foreigners of the name of Hans Holbein, both receiving salaries of 30*l.* a year.

The fact of Holbein's residing in the parish of St. Andrew Undershaft gives us a special interest in this city parish, of which the church is still preserved, as it escaped destruction in the great fire of 1666. We have in Stow a circumstantial account of the origin of the designation of this parish, and as I assume everything associated with Holbein's name to have a special interest with the reader, I here repeat it. The church of St. Andrew the Apostle was called *St. Andrew Undershaft* "because that of old time, every year (on May Day in the morning) it was used that an high or long shaft, or May Pole, was set up there, in the midst of the street, before the south door of the said church. Which shaft when it was set on end, and fixed in the ground was higher than the church steeple.

"This shaft was not raised at any time since evil May Day

* Franks, *Discovery of the Will of Hans Holbein*, &c. Where the author acknowledges his obligations to Mr. W. Nelson of the Record Office, who furnished him also with the following extract from an indenture of a Subsidy Roll, for the city of London, made the 4th day of April, 35th Henry VIII.:—

"Coleman Street Warde, St. Margarettesparysshe.

Mr. Sadler, alderman, in goodes mcc.*li.* .... xl.*li.*

* * * * * * * *

Hugh Holbeine iij.*li.*.......... vj.*d.*"

From the sum at which this Hugh Holbein was assessed he was probably an Englishman.

CHAP. XV.

St. Andrew Undershaft. 1541. 33rd Henry VIII.

(so called of an insurrection made by Prentices and other young persons against aliens, in the year 1517), but the said shaft was laid along over the doors and under the Pentises (pent-houses) of one row of houses, and Alley gate, called of the shaft, *Shaft Alley.* It was there, I say, hanged on iron hooks many years, till the third of King Edward VI. (1549), that one Sir Stephen, curate of St. Catherine Christ's Church, preaching at St. Paul's Cross, said there that this shaft was made an idol by naming the church of St. Andrew.

"I heard his sermon at Paul's Cross, and I saw the effect that followed: for in the afternoon of that present Sunday, the neighbours, over whose doors the said shaft had lain, after they had dined, to make themselves strong, gathered more help, and with great labour raising the shaft from the hooks (whereon it had rested two and thirty years) they sawed it in pieces, every man taking for his share, so much as had lain over his door and stall, the length of his house, and they of the alley, divided amongst them so much as had laid over their alley gate. Thus was the Idol (as the poor man termed it) mangled and after burned."*

The evidence that Holbein resided at one time in the parish of St. Andrew Undershaft, is satisfactory and conclusive. Vertue was under the impression that he lived in the Duke of Norfolk's house, in the Priory of Christchurch, near Aldgate, known as Duke's Place, but it seems that the Priory did not pass into the Duke of Norfolk's possession until 1558; Holbein's patron, therefore, the third duke, never possessed it,

* "*A Survey of the Cities of London and Westminster.*" Folio. London, 1720.

This church stands in the north-west corner of Aldgate Ward, and is nearly obscured by the houses in Leadenhall Street; it was built in 1520-32, by Sir Stephen Jennings, Lord Mayor of London in 1508, assisted by the parishioners, but chiefly at the charge of William Fitz-William, Esq., Sheriff of London in 1506, and afterwards one of Henry VIII.'s council. This famous May-pole must have indeed been a long one if it, as recorded, out-topped the steeple of the church, which including its turret is 91 ft. high. Stow was buried in this church, and has a painted terra-cotta monument in it, inscribed—OBIIT AETATIS ANNO 80, DIE 5 APRILIS 1605. See Stow, *l. l.*, and *London, Westminster and Southwark*, by D. Hughson, LL.D., Vol. II., p. 162.

as he had been then dead four years. Walpole indeed speaks of Holbein having some time lived on London Bridge, but I know not on what authority: he says, "The father of Lord Treasurer Oxford, passing over London Bridge, was caught in a shower, and stepping into a goldsmith's shop for shelter, he found there a picture of Holbein (who had lived in that house) and his family. He offered the goldsmith 100*l.* for it, who consented to let him have it, but desired first to show it to some persons. Immediately after happened the fire of London, and the picture was destroyed." That Lord Oxford's father found a picture on London Bridge in 1666 is possible, but that it was of Holbein and his family, is I believe purely imaginary: between 1543 and 1666 is a long time for such a picture by Holbein to have remained in the same house, and in spite of the diligent search of Thomas Earl of Arundel, for his works. Besides what could a picture of Holbein's family consist of? Dallaway, in a note to Walpole, enumerating various works ascribed to the painter, has the following:— "Holbein, his wife, four boys, and a girl (*sm*), Mereworth Castle, Kent;" and he surmises this to be either a repetition of that or the identical family picture, found by Lord Oxford's father, and quotes the following remarks on it by Gilpin:— "As a whole, it has no effect; but the heads are excellent. They are not painted in the common flat style of Holbein, but with a round, firm, glowing pencil, and yet exact imitation of nature is preserved—the boys are very innocent, beautiful characters." The description might almost do for the Earl of Morley's "Family of Bolingbroke," by Vandyck, which contains just seven half-length figures; though it contains a female short and a male too many. Certainly Holbein never had any such family: it must be comprised in the list of the painter's mythic works.

CHAP. XV.

St. Andrew Undershaft. 1541. 33rd Henry VIII.

There are two small portraits ascribed to Holbein bearing the date of this year, the so-called Sir Anthony Denny at Longford Castle, a small round, a bust; and the portrait of a young man, in the gallery at Vienna, already described as the pendant to that of Geryck Tybis, painted in 1533.

Sir Anthony Denny.

CHAP. XV.

Sir Anthony Denny. 1541. 33rd Henry VIII.

The Longford Castle picture is scarcely by Holbein, though it may be a copy of some work by him, neither is it a portrait of Sir Anthony Denny. It is described as an oil miniature, it is on oak, and is 4 inches in diameter; and is inscribed in gold capitals on a green ground—ANNO 1541 ETATIS SVÆ 29. As Sir Anthony was born in 1500-1, some other personage must be sought for this picture, which from a Dutch legend on the back seems to have been named in Holland—a paper label pasted on behind has the following:—"*Antoine Denny, een der Lords van de Bedcamer, en executeurs van het Testament van Koning Hendrik de* 8 *van Engelandt, &c.*" *Ric. Baker.* It represents a bearded man, in a black-brimmed cap and gown, with a plain gold chain twice round his neck.*

The Barber-Surgeons.

To this year also possibly belongs the Barber-Surgeons' picture of Henry granting a charter to the corporation. The Barbers and Surgeons of London originally constituting one company, had been separated, but were again in the 32nd of Henry VIII. combined into a single society, and it was the ceremony of presenting them with a new charter which is commemorated by Holbein's picture, now in their hall in Monkwell Street: in 1745 they were again separated, and the Surgeons constituted a distinct company, and had a hall in the Old Bailey. The date of this picture is not known, but it was necessarily in or after 1541, and as Holbein's life did not extend much beyond this time, there is some probability in the report alluded to by Van Mander, namely, that the painter died without completing the picture. Besides the king's, a seated full-length, crowned, and with the sword of state in his right hand, it contains also portraits of eighteen members of the guild, three kneeling on the right hand of the king, and fifteen on the other; and among them are conspicuous our friends Butts and Chamber, on the right; the head of the latter is effective and good, though the portraits generally are unsatisfactory; but Warden Aylef's, the second on the left, is

* It is engraved as such in Lodge's Portraits, &c.

especially good. The rest are indifferent, either owing to the fact of their having been some of them perhaps entirely repainted, or possibly having never had a touch of Holbein's in them.* The king is placed very stiffly, and the face, much repainted, is that we are familiar with in the many ordinary half-lengths of the king representing him in the last years of his life. The composition is anything but graceful, and there is not an entire hand in the whole piece: the king's hands are good, though slight and sketchy. The principle of the composition is somewhat Egyptian, for the king is made about twice the size of the other figures, though they are in front of him.

We have an interesting notice of this picture in Pepys' Diary,† where against the date August the 29th, 1668, that is two years after the great fire, he notes—"At noon, comes by appointment Harris to dine with me; and after dinner, he and I to Chirurgeons' Hall, where they are building it new, very fine; and there to see their theatre, which stood all the fire, and, which was our business, their great picture of Holbein's, thinking to have bought it, by the help of Mr. Pierce, for a little money. I did think to give 200*l.* for it, it being said to be worth 1000*l.*; but it is so spoiled that I have no mind to it, and is not a pleasant though a good picture."

Pepys is very candid about his motive for buying the picture;—because it was said to be worth 1000*l.*, he was willing to give 200*l.* for it, not that he wanted the picture for its own sake; however he did not like it, and he declined the speculation. When we consider the worth of money at that time, the estimated value seems an enormous one; Pepys' own

* There is a large engraving of this picture by B. Baron, but reversed; the names of the members of the guild are written in a most offensive manner over the face of the picture, which is a piece of barbarism, that belongs, I imagine, to a period long subsequent to the time of Holbein. These names are:—J. Alsop; W. Butts; J. Chamber; T. Vycary (the master of the guild, who is receiving the charter from the left hand of the king); J. Aylef; N. Symson; E. Harman; J. Monforde; J. Pen; M. Alcoke; R. Fercis; X. Samon; and W. Tylly; five of the second row are without names.

The *Illustrated London News* gave an effective cut of this picture, by Henry Linton, in 1856.

† Vol. IV., p. 13. Ed. 1854.

CHAP. XV. *The Barber-Surgeons.* 1541-2. 33rd Henry VIII.

price was not an inconsiderable sum. The picture is on oak, on vertical boards, about 6 ft. *h.* by 10 ft. 3 in. *w.* The College of Surgeons possesses an old but smaller indifferent copy of it, on paper attached to canvas; J. Alsop on the extreme right is omitted; and in the place of a tablet with a Latin inscription, which disfigures the Barber-Surgeons' picture, is a window, showing the old tower of St. Bride's, indicating, accordingly, the palace of Bridewell as the place of the ceremony.

There can be no question of the genuineness of this picture in its foundations, but in its present state it is not remarkable that it should cause discussions. I am disposed to believe that Holbein never did finish the picture, and from the great inferiority of the second series of heads, on the left hand of the king, I think that these must have been added later; there is no trace of Holbein's hand in them; and the fact of five of them being without names is also suggestive of the assumption, that these five were not even members of the guild when the picture was painted. Two of this back-ground group are named—X. Samon and W. Tilly; these therefore may have been Holbein's contemporaries though not introduced by him into the picture. It is not to be supposed that the king sat to Holbein for this portrait; it is the stock portrait of the time; the king is not looking at the master, Vycary, to whom he is handing the charter, but straight before him. The composition is a mere portrait piece, got up for the sake of the portraits. In the whole group of nineteen only five besides the king wear their beards—Aylef, Symson, Harman, Alcoke and Fereis. Monforde's, the fifth from the king, is a very expressive face, considerably repainted, but full of character. The three on the right—Chamber, Butts, and Alsop, are perhaps so separately placed as physicians to the king. The independent portraits of Butts and Chamber have been already described (pp. 293–5).

The first notice we have of this work is of the year 1618, when James I. wrote to the company for a copy of the picture; the following is the king's letter :—

"To our Trustie and Welbeloved ye Companie of Barber-Surgeons of London.

CHAP. XV.

The Barber-Surgeons.
1541-2.
33rd
Henry VIII.

"James R.

"Trustie and welbeloved we greete you well.

"Whereas we are informed, there is a table of Painting in your Hall whereon is the Picture of our Predecessor of famous memorie K. Henry the 8th, together w^h diverse of y^r Companie, w^h being both like him and well done Wee are desirous to have copyed, wherfore o^r pleasure is that you presently deliver it unto this Bearer our welbeloved Servant Sr Lionell Cranfield Knight—one of our Maisters of Requests whome wee gave commaundes to receave it of you and to see it w^h all expedition copied and redelivered safely: and so Wee bid you farewell. Given at our Court at Newmarket the 13th day of Januarie 1617" (1618).*

In this letter, it will be observed, Holbein's name is not mentioned; the portrait of the king was important, but its painter was of little or no account. It may be asked what has become of this copy—my answer is that I assume it to be the picture now at the College of Surgeons. This copy has been called the original cartoon, and there is a report that both belonged to the Barber-Surgeons before the separation of the latter in 1745, and that these then took away their picture to their new hall, but this is not so. The copy in Lincoln's Inn Fields was formerly in the possession of Desenfans, and at his sale in 1786 was purchased by the Surgeons' Company for fifty guineas. The circumstance of the window being in the Surgeons' picture, in the place of the tablet with the long complimentary Latin inscription† in the Barbers' picture, I

* The original letter is in the possession of the Barbers' Company.

† The inscription is as follows:—

Henrico octavo Opt. Max. Regi Angliae Franciae et Hiberniae Fidei Defensori ac Anglicanae Hibernicaeq. Ecclesiae proximo a Christo Supremo Capiti Societas Chirurgorum communibus votis Hac consecrat.

[Tristior

CHAP. XV.

The Barber-Surgeons. 1541-2. 33rd Henry VIII.

can only explain, that on some occasion when it was restored, perhaps after the Fire of London in 1666, when from what Pepys says, it may have got injured, this tablet, and the inscription, which seems to refer to the plague* and to the reform of religion, were then introduced, while the copy having been made many years before gives us the picture, in this respect, in its original state. The Surgeons' Company also, a few years after they bought their picture had recourse to a cleaner, and they put it into the hands of a man of the name of Lloyd, who in 1789, sent them in a bill of 400*l.* for the job; this exorbitant charge the council refused to pay, but offered 50 guineas as a fair remuneration, which the cleaner, having thought better of his demand, eventually accepted, in October of that year.

Queen Catherine Howard.

The beginning of the year 1542 witnessed another of those deplorable tragedies associated with the unfortunate marriages of Henry VIII. It was discovered that Catherine Howard had before her marriage freely encouraged the advances of no less than two lovers; her cousin Francis Derham, and one Mannock, a person employed in the household of the Duchess of Norfolk. Both these men confessed to a familiar intercourse with the queen before her marriage: she had further, with a fatal blindness, taken Derham into her service after she became

---

Tristior Anglorum pestis violaverat orbem,
Infestans animos corporibusque sedens;
Hanc Deus insignem cladem miseratus ab alto,
Te Medici munus jussit obire boni.
Lumen Evangelii fulvis circumvolat alis,
Pharmacon adfectis mentibus illud erit;
Consilioq. tuo celebrant monumenta Galeni,
Et celeri morbus pelliter omnis ope.
Nos igitur supplex medicorum turba tuorum
Hanc tibi sacramus religione domum;
Muneris et memores quo nos Henrice beâsti,
Imperio optamus maxima quæque tuo.

* There were six plagues in London, in the reign of Henry VIII., but the worst was that of 1543, so that if this plague be meant, the allusion, supposing the inscription to have been part of the original work of the painter, is an anachronism, for Holbein fell a victim to the plague of 1543.

Queen. She did not deny her culpability before her marriage, which was well known to the Duchess of Norfolk and others of her family, and yet they allowed the king's marriage to proceed. This previous misconduct turned out however, to be but a slight misdemeanor compared with what followed her marriage. She had, both at home and on journeys, received into her chamber at night, the king having a separate apartment, one of her gentlemen, named Thomas Culpeper; Lady Rochfort keeping guard on such occasions to prevent a surprise. "No reasonable doubt could be entertained, that the king had a second time suffered the worst injury which a wife could inflict upon him, that a second adultery, a second act of high treason, must be exposed and punished."* The queen and Lady Rochfort were confined in Sion House, pending a parliamentary inquiry. Derham and Culpeper were tried at Guildhall on the 1st of December 1541, pleaded guilty, and were hanged at Tyburn twelve days afterwards. A bill of attainder against Catherine Howard and Lady Rochfort was read for the first time on the 21st of January following, and for a second and third time on the 7th and 8th of February. On the 11th the bill was passed. The Commons were invited to the Upper House. The Duke of Suffolk in the name of the committee who had waited upon Catherine, declared that she had confessed the crime which she had committed against God, the king, and the English nation; that she implored God's forgiveness and only entreated that her faults might not be imputed to her family."* On Monday the 13th the two women were beheaded, on the same spot where the queen's cousin Ann Boleyn had suffered for her crimes. Both Catherine's uncle the Duke of Norfolk, and her cousin the Earl of Surrey, were present at the execution.

CHAP. XV.

Queen Catherine Howard.

1541-2.

33rd Henry VIII.

The Queen has among her miniatures at Windsor, one well executed, said to be "Catherine Howard by Holbein," she has some rich jewels on her neck; it is a circle $2\frac{1}{3}$ in. in diameter, has a blue back-ground, and is painted on the back

* Froude, *History of England*, &c. Vol. IV., Ch. 19.

CHAP. XV.

of the eight of diamonds: there is a print of it by Hollar. One of the anonymous ladies among the Windsor drawings, has also been designated Catherine Howard.

Henry marries his sixth wife. 1543. 35th Henry VIII.

Eighteen months after this last catastrophe Holbein witnessed a fifth royal marriage. He had seen two queens divorced, and two executed for adultery. Henry's sixth wife but fifth choice was the beautiful Catherine Parr, who had been already twice married; she was when the king selected her, the widow of Lord Latimer; and she was of the Protestant or reform party, to which the king himself, considering his sanction of the six articles of the bishop of Winchester's "Bloody Statute" can scarcely be said to have belonged, doctrinally, notwithstanding his energetic correction and suppression of so many church scandals and abuses. The Lady Latimer became Queen of England on the 10th of July 1543, and the king seems at last to have found the companion he desired, and to have spent the short remainder of his life in at least domestic peace.

The family of the king.

The names of Catherine Howard and Catherine Parr, both occur in catalogues of picture collections in association with Holbein's name, but I have no description to give of any authentic portrait of either of these queens.

There is a very remarkable picture at Hampton Court of Henry VIII. and his family, which is now vulgarly attributed to Holbein, though this was not the case in former years. This piece, a large fancy composition, is on *canvas,* 6 ft. *h.* by 10 ft. *w.;* it was formerly in the palace at Whitehall, and formed also one of the collection of Charles I. It is catalogued by Vanderdoort as "A Whitehall piece on *Board,*" but he does not ascribe it to Holbein, which he certainly would have done if there had been any tradition of the kind.

He thus describes the picture—"Item, a long piece painted with gold, where King Henry VIII. sits with his queen, and his son Prince Edward, on the right side, and his two daughters Queen Mary and Queen Elizabeth, standing at each side, and a fool at the left side, in the door with a jackanapes on his shoulder, and on the other side a waiting woman. Little

Chap. XV.

The family of the king.

1543.
35th
Henry VIII.

intire figures." This is certainly not a genuine picture, but is made up without discretion from various original materials or portraits, some of which may possibly have been by Holbein. The picture is not badly painted, indeed the architectural accessaries are executed with great skill, and are evidently the work of a painter whose business it was specially to execute such accessaries and probably costume generally. It is just possible that Lucas de Heere may have got up this picture for Queen Mary or even Queen Elizabeth herself. To judge from the size of Prince Edward, the time of the picture is intended to present the king at the close of his life, in 1547; for the prince is a boy about nine years old; but to be consistent, Mary should be thirty years of age, and Elizabeth in her fourteenth year, whereas the difference in their ages is so far disregarded that the authorities at Hampton Court have not known which was which, and have labelled the taller girl Elizabeth, and put Mary's name to what is really the portrait of a child. The queen, seated on the left hand of the king, is labelled on the frame "Jane Seymour," while the name should clearly be "Catherine Parr," the only queen who knew Edward as a boy of the age represented. The two figures in the garden behind, but seen through two doorways, are called William Somers and his wife.*

If this picture had been composed in the ordinary way, from nature, the inconsistencies it betrays could not have existed; I take it therefore for granted, that it is an arbitrary posthumous portrait, more than usually abounding in the inaccuracies of such fabrications. The queen ought to be, and is, possibly, Catherine Parr, for though the portrait has something of the features of Jane Seymour, it has not her

* As regards "Will Somers," Henry's jester, there is at Hampton Court a picture of "A man looking through a window," described as "Somers by Holbein." A comparison of this head with portraits of Somers will show that it is no more a portrait of the king's jester than it is a picture by the king's painter. Among a volume of old catalogues in the British Museum, is a MS. list of the pictures at Windsor Castle, without date. This "Peeping Tom" it seems was then in the "store-room" of the castle, and is entered in the inventory as "A fool looking out at a window" by the "Spanish Labradore."

CHAP. XV. — *Miniatures and drawings.* 1543. 35th Henry VIII.

eyes, as we find them in Van Leemput's copy of the Whitehall picture.

Of Holbein's pictures I have no further account to give. Except in some few cases of unusual importance I have limited my descriptions to authenticated or evidently genuine works. About miniatures I have had very little to say; not that there are not abundance of such works professed by their owners to be the work of Holbein; but as this belief is really the only reason for the ascription, I have felt no call to examine them in detail.

At the South Kensington Exhibition in 1865, there were twenty-three miniatures and drawings ascribed to our painter; of these I have incidentally noticed Nos. 652—"Henry VIII." marked H. R. VIII. Ano. XXXV; 1810—"Anne of Cleves," signed H. H.; 2082—"Henry VIII.;" and 2627—"A Lady," marked *Anno Aetatis suae* 23.* Among the others the following may be mentioned as fine examples of miniature painting, whoever the authors may have been—No. 1146—"Alicia, wife of Sir Thomas More," belonging to Mr. J. Heywood Hawkins, on card, with a bright blue ground; oval, about 3 in. high by 2 in. wide. No. 1603—"Thomas Lord Seymour of Sudeley," on vellum, with a bright blue ground, circular, about 1¾ in. in diameter, exhibited by the Duke of Buccleuch. No. 1645—"Lady Jane Seymour," a small round, with a bright blue ground, belonging to Mr. C. Sackville Bale, inscribed A°N XXV. No. 2093—"Portrait of a gentleman, in a furred dress," with a red moustache; a small oval, with an ultramarine ground, belonging to the Earl of Shaftesbury: and the "Earl and Countess of Kildare," Nos. 1029, 1011, in oil, on panel, about 8 in. high by 6 in. wide, each, contributed by Lord Boston.

I have already explained that I have made no special study of the drawings ascribed to Holbein, though many are noticed in this volume: a catalogue of the Windsor series of portraits

* See pp. 281-3.

Miniatures and drawings. 1543. 35th Henry VIII.

will be found in the Appendix. The question is not, who *has* a drawing by Holbein, but rather *who has not*, among collectors? The Archduke Albrecht, at Vienna, has the credit of possessing several; as has also the Duke of Devonshire, at Chatsworth. There is a collection also of pen-and-ink sketches ascribed to him at Worcester College, Oxford. The accountant-general, Mr. William Russell, has some very spirited small studies of heads; three remarkable sketches, on a piece of grey grounded paper which belonged formerly to Sir Uvedale Price, who bought them at the sale of Meyer the miniature painter, in 1790. The heads are, two of them, shaven, three-quarters of an inch from chin to crown; the third, with a beard, is about an inch and a quarter in length: the ground tint does good service, the modelling of the faces being made by a few touches in body colour, in pink and brown. On the back of this piece of paper is a pen-and-ink landscape, with buildings. Mr. Russell has also the pen drawing or tracing ascribed to Holbein, which belonged to Sir Thomas Lawrence, representing a numerous group of carefully drawn minute figures, a heavenly host, with the Lord above, in the centre, and the apostles below; the design for the upper portion of a large Gothic window, of five lights: the subject is supposed to be from the ACTS of the Apostles, i. 10–11: "And while they looked stedfastly toward heaven as he went up, behold two men stood by them in white apparel; which also said, Ye men of Galilee why stand ye gazing up into heaven? This same Jesus which is taken up from you into heaven shall so come in like manner as ye have seen him go into heaven."

Drawings in the Museum.

The British Museum affords a fine choice in the various departments of figure drawing, ornamental modelling, and architectural design. The "Passion" series of seven drawings, and the sketches for and from the Stahlhof compositions have been already described. Among other remarkable drawings by Holbein in the museum are the following six:—

1. The "Descent of the Holy Ghost;" a bold sketch with the pen, and tinted with Indian ink: from the Lawrence collec-

CHAP. XV.

Drawings in the Museum.
1543.
35th Henry VIII.

tion.—The Queen possesses a fine drawing, in sepia, heightened with blue and gold, at Windsor, in a more delicate style than this, representing "The Queen of Sheba;" it is engraved by Hollar. 2. A "Woman seated with four children;" and 3. "Five Musicians in a Gallery;" both outlined with the pen, and washed with Indian ink, and formerly in the Cosway and Utterson collections. 4. A "Cinque-cento design for a gold cup, or vase," of extremely beautiful scrolled details, and richly set with cameos and jewels; this was executed for Henry VIII., apparently about 1536–7, as it bears the motto of Jane Seymour—*Bound to obey and serve*—together with the initials of the king and the queen. This drawing belonged to Beckford; there is another of the same cup or vase, in the Bodleian Library, at Oxford; it is about 14 inches high. There is no better *cinque-cento* ornament than this: it is in the same taste as, but perhaps, purer than, the best work of Benvenuto Cellini, Holbein's contemporary, but his junior by five years. Cellini was in Paris in June 1537, and on other occasions afterwards, but does not appear to have ever visited this country. Holbein may have met with some of Cellini's work in France in 1538–9, but he cannot have seen much of it, and must have formed his own style quite independently of the Florentine artist; though if he ever visited Milan, which is possible, he might have seen fine cinque-cento work there. Cellini survived Holbein nearly twenty-seven years; he died at Florence on the 15th of January 1570, but his autobiography reaches only to 1562.

5. Another fine ornamental drawing with the pen and washed with Indian ink is the "Design for a clock," for Sir Anthony Denny; the two boys* surmounting this design are very beautiful, in a true Raphaelesque style; there is also a separate study for these two boys, taken from the Sloane volume of sketches. This clock was executed and presented in 1544 (? for 1545) by Sir Anthony, as a New Year's gift to

* Engraved for this volume.

THE JANE SEYMOUR CUP.

P. 358.

Henry VIII.; this fact is recorded on the drawing itself, which at one time belonged to Mariette, and was afterwards in the collection of Horace Walpole at Strawberry Hill. Mariette has left us his own description of it: he says—"Je possède aussi un fort beau dessein d'une horloge de sable, qui, suivant une inscription latine qu'on y lit, a été fait pour être présentée à Henry VIII., le premier jour de l'an 1545, par Antoine Deny, son chambellan. Le trait en est à la plume, et d'une netteté qui feroit soupçonner, au premier aspect, qu'il a été gravé; les ombres sont données avec un lavis d'encre de la chine. C'est ainsi que sont exécutés tous les desseins de Holbein qui me sont passés par les mains, et voici une copie fidèle de l'inscription: *Strena facta pro Anthony Deny camerario Regis quod initio novi anni* 1545 *Regi dedit.*"* At the sale at Strawberry Hill in 1842, this drawing was sold for 6*l.* 16*s.* 8*d.* only.

Chap. XV. Drawings in the Museum. 1543. 35th Henry VIII.

6. Walpole possessed likewise the remarkable pen-and-ink design, washed with colour, now in the museum, for a chimney-piece, in a rich Renaissance taste; which from the royal arms on it, was also probably designed for Henry VIII. It belonged to Jonathan Richardson, and was sold for thirty-two guineas at the Strawberry Hill sale, in 1842. Walpole suggests that it is possibly that mentioned by Peacham, as made for the new palace at Bridewell.

Architectural designs.

This elaborate drawing, which was lately bought for the nation for 100*l.*, is in a style consistent with Holbein's taste throughout the whole of his career; this is what cannot be said for the old Whitehall gateway ascribed to him, and which is engraved in the *Antiquities of Westminster;* or for the Wilton portico. The last is a plain Italian design of a double row of columns Ionic below and Corinthian above, displaying neither taste, nor knowledge of the style: the medallion figures inserted in the upper part appear from their costume to belong to a later time than Holbein's. As for the Whitehall gate it was a mongrel of Gothic and Renaissance quite unworthy of

* Notes to Walpole, *Abecedario*, &c. Vol. II., p. 370.

CHAP. XV.

Architectural designs.

1543.

35th

Henry VIII.

Holbein, and I should imagine an impossible design for him: it was similar in general character to the gate of St. James's Palace, at the bottom of St. James's Street.*

* "One cannot but lament," says Walpole, "that a noble monument of his genius has lately been demolished, the gateway at Whitehall, *supposed to have been erected for the entry of Charles V.;*" but that was a mistake: the emperor was here in 1521; Holbein did not arrive at soonest till five years after. A view of this gateway is given by Smith twice in his *Westminster*, but the two views do not agree. One, plate 34, is a general view of the old palace of Whitehall, copied from a rare print by Israel Silvestre:—*Veuë et Perspective du Palais du Roy d'Angleterre a Londres qui s'appelle Whitehall.* Silvestre died in 1691. The other, plate 35, is a print of the gate, by J. Brock, from an engraving by Vertue, published in 1725; but the two do not agree: see J. T. Smith's *Antiquities of Westminster; the Old Palace, St. Stephen's Chapel,* &c. 4to. London, 1807. Supplement, 1808. There is also a vignette of it in my edition of Walpole's *Anecdotes*, &c., p. 114. Ed. 1849.

CHAPTER XVI.

THE LAST STAGE.

EARLY deaths are fortunately not of very frequent occurrence in the annals of great painters, yet, some of the very foremost have been cut off in mid-career; as John van Eyck, Masaccio, Giorgione, Correggio, Raphael, Fra Bartolomeo, Andrea del Sarto, Annibal Carracci, Vandyck, Paul Potter and Le Sueur; to this list must be added the name of our painter. When we last heard of Holbein he was engaged in painting the portraits of the Barber-Surgeons who were received by the king at Bridewell; we next meet with him, on the day of his hastily preparing his will on the 7th of October, 1543, his forty-eighth year, when the plague, for the sixth time in Henry's reign, was raging in London.

CHAP. XVI.

Death of pestilence. 1543. 35th Henry VIII.

We have no account of this plague; the disease seems to have been an event of such common occurrence, that the chroniclers have contented themselves with simply mentioning it. Hall in his "Chronicle"* says, "In this yeare" xxxv[th] Henry VIII., "was in London a great death of the Pestilence, and therefore Mychelmas Tearme was adjourned to Saynt Albons, and there was kepte to the ende." In Stow's

---

* *The Union of the two Noble and Illustrate Families of Lancastre and Yorke, &c.* 4to. 1548. P. 257.

CHAP. XVI.

Death of pestilence. 1543. 35th Henry VIII.

"Annals"* we have—"In the meane space, to wit, on the 28 of July, Anthony Parson, Robert Testwood, and Henry Filmer, were brendt at Windsore. And a great death of pestilence was at London, and therfore Michaelmas terme was adjourned to St. Albons."

We have in modern times some experience of the kind of panic which afflicts a city under a visitation of cholera, but this perhaps can convey no notion of the state induced in the "good old times" in a city visited by that more terrible scourge, the medieval plague. I have myself had tolerable experience of a cholera panic, having been shut up many weeks in Rome when that disease was raging there in the summer of 1837. Of the nine English that were left in the city two perished; and altogether fifteen persons with whom I was more or less acquainted, fell victims to it. De Foe has drawn us a terrible picture of London during the plague of 1665; and later writers, with more or less success have attempted to realize its horrors to our minds; but nowhere is so vivid a representation given as in the simple diary of Pichatty de Croissainte who lived through the horrors of the plague of Marseilles, in 1720.†

It was the sensation created by this plague which probably led to the publication ascribed to De Foe, which first appeared in 1722; but as the work is possibly only a clever novel, it will not answer my purpose to quote it. We have however some authentic facts concerning the plague of 1665, from the account of William Boghurst, an apothecary of St. Giles's.

Boghurst in his account of this pestilence, says—"The wind blowing westward so long together (from before Christmas until July), was the cause the plague began first at the west end of the city, as at St. Giles's, and St. Martin's Westminster.

* *The Annales, or Generall Chronicle of England.* Fol. London, 1615. P. 585.

† *A Brief* JOURNAL *of what passed in the city of* MARSEILLES *while it was afflicted with the* PLAGUE, *in the year* 1720. 12mo. London, 1721.

‡ It is among the Sloane MSS. in the British Museum, *Λοιμογραφία*, &c. See some extracts in E. W. Brayley's edition of the "*Journal of the Plague Year*"—1665, published in the "Family Library" in 1835.

Death of pestilence. 1543. 35th Henry VIII.

Afterwards, it gradually insinuated and crept down Holborn and the Strand, and then into the city, and at last to the east end of the suburbs: so that it was half a year at the west end of the city before the east end and Stepney were infected, which was about the middle of July. Southwark, being the south suburb, was infected almost as soon as the west end.

"One friend growing melancholy for another was one main cause of its going through a family, especially when they were shut up, which bred a sad apprehension and consternation on their spirits; especially being shut up in dark cellars.

"Those that die of the plague die a very easy death generally: first, because it was speedy; secondly, because they died without convulsions. They did but of a sudden fetch their breath a little thick and short, and were presently gone, just as you squeeze wind out of a bladder. So that I have heard some say, 'How much am I bound to God, who takes me away by such an easy death.'

"If I had time, I staid by them to see them die, and see the manner of their death, and closed up their mouth and eyes; for they died with their mouth and eyes very much open and staring."

He says he commonly dressed forty sores in a day, and seems to have considered courage and cheerfulness among the best armour against the disease.

The following abstracts from Pichatty de Croissainte's Diary, may possibly realize a parallel to some of the frightful scenes which must have been witnessed by Holbein in the last summer of his life:—

July—"It rends the heart to behold on the pavement so many wretched mothers, who have lying by their sides the dead bodies of their children, whom they have seen expire, without being able to give them any relief; and so many poor infants still hanging at the breasts of their mothers, who died holding

CHAP. XVI.

Death of pestilence.

1543.
35th Henry VIII.

them in their arms, sucking in the rest of that venom which will soon put them into the same condition."

"Those one meets in the streets, are generally livid and drooping, as if their souls had begun to part from their bodies; or whom the violence of the distemper has made delirious; who, wandering about, they know not whither, as long as they can keep on their legs, some drop through weakness, and, unable to get up again expire on the spot; some writhed into strange postures, denoting the torturing venom which has struck them to the heart; others are agitated by such disorders of mind, that they cut their own throats, or leap into the sea, or throw themselves out of the windows, to put an end to their misery," pp. 36–37.

"Every night adds a thousand dead; and now none of the slaves are left to work, they are all dead, or sick of the distemper.

"As soon as one person in a house is seized with the distemper, that person becomes an object of horror and affright to the nearest relations. They take at first the barbarous resolution, either to drive him out of the house, or to fly and desert it themselves, and to leave him alone without assistance or relief, abandoned to hunger, thirst, and all that can render death the more tormenting.

"Thus wives treat their husbands, and husbands their wives, children their parents, and parents their children."

August—"Men are become only shadows, those who are seen well one day, are in the carts the next; and what is unaccountable, those who have shut themselves up most securely in their own houses, and are the most careful to take in nothing without the most exact precautions, are attacked there by the plague, which creeps in nobody knows how," p. 41.

September—"Above 2000 dead bodies were lying putrefying in the streets of Marseilles at the same time."

Such are the consequences of an indolent love of self, a systematic neglect of cleanliness, and an antipathy to fresh air. We have at last learnt somewhat better to keep our houses in order.*

CHAP. XVI.

Death of pestilence. 1543. 35th Henry VIII.

When a man dies in such a confusion as is indicated by the above extracts, posterity may well be at a loss to ascertain where he was buried. Speaking of St. Catherine Cree Church, Strype, in his additions to Stow's "Survey,"† observes—"I have been told that Hans Holben, the great and inimitable painter in King Henry VIII.'s time, was buried in this church; and that the Earl of Arundel, the great patron of learning and arts, would have set up a monument to his memory here, had he but known whereabouts the corps lay."

It was the plague of 1543 that carried off our painter. There is no distinct record of this fact; but we have it recorded that he died of the plague, and as by the fortunate discovery of his Will by Mr. Black, we have the approximate date of his death, we may now rest satisfied that it was the epidemic of this year that he fell a victim to.

As some corroboration of the identity of our painter and the testator of the Will in question, it is certain that there are no accounts of Holbein after this time. In reply to the inquiries of Mr. Franks, Mr. Joseph Burtt of the Record Office, writes as follows:—"I have gone through all the Wardrobe and Household matter here, subsequent to the 32nd of Henry VIII., and nearly the whole of the Exchequer matter, without

---

* The *Bills of Mortality* give us no accounts of the victims of the plague of 1543, as these records commence only half a century later, with the year 1593. The following are the numbers of those who died of the disease in London, on five subsequent occasions of its occurrence:—

In 1593, 11,503;	largest weekly number,	983,	week ending	August 4th.
„ 1603, 30,561;	„ „	3035,	„	Sept. 1st.
„ 1625, 35,403;	„ „	4463,	„	Aug. 18th.
„ 1636, 10,400;	„ „	928,	„	Sept. 29th.
„ 1665, 68,596;	„ „	7165,	„	Sept. 19th.

See Dr. Heberden, *Observations on the Increase, &c., of the Plague.* 4to. London, 1801.

† *A Survey of the Cities of London and Westminster.* Fol. London, 1720. P. 64.

CHAP. XVI.

Death of pestilence. 1543. 35th Henry VIII.

finding Holbein's name at all. These accounts are probably imperfect; and as to those of the Exchequer, it is difficult to say at that period where a certain kind of entry should be found. I looked also to the accounts of the Exchequer just anterior to the usual date of the death of Holbein, and I was unable to find his name."

I have given (at page 23) independent evidence showing that Holbein was already dead on the 19th of November, 1545.

THE WILL OF HANS HOLBEIN.

IN the name of God the father, sonne, and holy gohooste, I, JOHN̄ HOLBEINE, servaunte to the Kynges Magestye, make this my Testamente and last will, to wyt, that all my goodes shalbe sold and also my horse, and I will that my debtes be payd, to wete, fyrst to Mr. Anthony, the Kynges servaunte, of Grenwiche, y^e^ of summe of ten poundes thurtene shyllynges and sewyne pence sterlinge. And more over I will that he shalbe contented for all other thynges betwene hym and me. Item, I do owe unto Mr. John of Anwarpe, goldsmythe, sexe poundes sterling, which I will also shalbe payd unto him with the fyrste. Item, I bequeythe for the kynpyng* of my two Chylder wich be at nurse, for every monethe sewyn shyllynges and sex pence sterlynge. In wytnes, I have sealed and sealed this my testament the vijth day of Octaber, in the yere of o^{r} Lorde God M^{l}vCxliij. Wytnes, Anthoney Snecher, armerer, Mr. John of Anwarpe, goldsmythe before sayd, Olrycke Obynger, merchaunte, and Harry Maynert, painter.

* Keeping.

XXIX° die Mensis Novembris anno Domini predict. Johannes Anwarpe executor nominat. in testamento sive ultima voluntate Johannis alias Hans Holbein nuper parochie sancti Andree Undershafte defuncti comparuit coram Magistro Johanne Croke, &c. Commissario generali ac renunciavit omni executioni hujusmodi testamenti quam renunciationem dominus admisit deinde commisit administracionem bonorum dicti defuncti, prenominato Johanni Anwarpe in forma juris jurato et per ipsum admissa pariter et accepta. Salvo jure cujuscunque. Dat &c.

CHAP. XVI.

His will. 1543. 35th Henry VIII.

Holbene.—XXIX^NO die Mensis predicti commissa fuit administracio bonorum Johannis alias Hans Holbeñ parochie sancti Andrei Undershaft nuper abintestato defuncti Johanni Anwarpe in forma juris jurato ac per ipsum admissa pariter et acceptata. Salvo jure cujus cumque. Dicto die mens. &c.*

From the above document we learn for certain that HANS HOLBEIN, a servant of the king's majesty, who resided in the parish of St. Andrew Undershaft, and was in the enjoyment of a salary of 30*l.* a year, died between the 7th of October and the 29th of November 1543, and there is sufficient coincidence so far, to satisfy us that this Hans Holbein can have been no other than our painter: to suppose that there may have been *two Hans Holbeins, in the king's service receiving* 30*l.* *a year, and living in the same parish*, is surely courting the marvellous.†

* Found in the Registry of the Wills of the Commissary of London, preserved in St. Paul's Cathedral, in the book called BEVERLEY, folio 116. See *Discovery of the Will of Hans Holbein, &c.*, by A. W. Franks, in the 39th volume of the ARCHÆOLOGIA.

† Notwithstanding the above striking coincidences, which one would have imagined could lead to but one conclusion, we find the following passage in Mr. Samuel Redgrave's *Introductory Notice* to the catalogue of the EXHIBITION OF NATIONAL PORTRAITS, held at the South Kensington Museum, in 1866:— "The date of Holbein's death has become an important consideration in determining by whom many very fine portraits of this period were painted. It had been almost universally stated to have taken place in 1554, when in 1862 (1861) a will was discovered, which is concluded to be Holbein's. This will would prove his death to have happened in 1543, a date which has been supported by many collateral facts very learnedly brought to bear upon the question. There is yet, we venture to think, just sufficient absence of absolute proof of the identity of the testator with the painter to allow of that further examination of a question of so great interest which the present collection very opportunely offers." I offer Mr. Redgrave and any others to whom he may have communicated his doubts, the additional independent evidence of Holbein's early death, given in page 23 of this volume, and where I have also suggested the source of the old erroneous date of 1554.

CHAP. XVI.

His will. 1543. 35th Henry VIII.

One passage in the will is of peculiar interest:—Item, *I bequeath for the keeping of my two children which be at nurse, for every month 7s. 6d. sterling.* These children must have been quite young, and of course were not offspring of his Basel wife. We know that she was alive in 1541, but was already deceased in November 1545; she may have been dead even some time before the date of this will. It is quite possible that Holbein may have been a widower and have again married in England, but I think it is more probable that the children were illegitimate, both from our painter's circumstances, and the habits of those times; and also as there is no reference made to a wife in the will. This is however not a necessary conclusion, as the second wife may have been previously carried off by the plague. We are bound to give Holbein the benefit of every doubt, and the case I have suggested is not only possible but reasonable; still the probability is against it, as in the sixteenth century marriage was by no means the matter of course to a decent life, that it is commonly held to be in the present day. This irregular connection, even should it have been such, in one sense might be accredited to Holbein's advantage, as the state of pellicacy is infinitely superior, morally, physically, and socially, to the disorderly promiscuous intercourse habitual with the more dissipated and profligate.

The charge of 3*s.* 9*d.* a month for the maintenance of a child, a little more than a penny a day, seems a moderate allowance, yet when we consider the relative value of money, it must be pronounced enough.

As regards the form of the will itself, Mr. Franks observes, "It is not impossible that the haste and confusion occasioned by the pestilence may account for several apparently careless expressions in the will, and acts of administration. No executor is named in the will, although in the first administration act John of Anwarpe is spoken of as such. I am however indebted to the kindness of a legal friend for some remarks on these points:—

"Though the two official acts which follow the copy of the will may

His will. 1543. 35th Henry VIII.

at first appear inconsistent both with the will and also with each other; yet, if we suppose that John of Anwarpe was considered to have been appointed executor by implication (which the law allowed), much of the seeming inconsistency will disappear. The object of the renunciation may have been either to obviate some doubt which existed as to whether John of Anwarpe was so made executor (for the language is hardly strong enough), or to avoid certain liabilities that would have affected him as executor, but not as administrator. Formerly a person was said to have died intestate, not only when he left no will, but also when he left a will, and appointed no executor, or appointed executors, and they all renounced. In this administration act the testator is accordingly said to have died intestate. The word *abintestato* should, I presume, have been *ab intestato*. *Abintestatus* was not common for intestate; the more usual Latin term was *intestatus*, or *ab intestato*, as may be seen in Lynwode's Provinciale (Tabula, s. v.). Carpentier gives *abintestatus* as used in France. *Ab intestato* was in use in this country as late as the reign of Elizabeth (See West's Symboleography, s. 650).

"The great difficulty in these official acts is how John of Anwarpe could have been executor and Mr. Anthony not. If the latter had been executor also, and died before the testator, that should and in all probability would have been mentioned. However, if he were Anthony the king's servant, he is known to have survived the testator. The second of the two official acts is almost a repetition of the first, and both are dated on the same day. Such an administration in modern times would have been called an administration *cum testamento annexo*."

It would be interesting to know something of the lives and conditions of the four witnesses mentioned in this will, as we may assume them to have been the painter's more intimate friends. Mr. Franks in the Paper already referred to, has not failed to find some information respecting them.

JOHANNES ANWARPE, or JOHN OF ANTWERP, was a goldsmith. In the State Papers of Henry VIII. (vol. i., p. 892), is a report to the king, of bills stamped during the month of January, of the 38th Henry VIII.—1547, in which occurs the following item: "4. A warraunt to S[r] Edmunde Pekham, Treasurer of the Myntes, to deliver to John Andewarpe and Peter Richardson, goldesmythes, to be by theim employed to your Majestie's use, 80 oz. of crowne golde, of the value of 47*s.* the oz., amounting to 188*l.*"

CHAP. XVI.

His will. 1543. 35th Henry VIII.

Other evidence of his condition and relation to the court, is afforded by the account of the Privy Purse expenses of the Princess Mary,* where among the entries for March, 1537, is—"Item, payed for goldsmythes workes for my ladies grace to Johan of Andwarpe, iiij.*li.* xvij.*s.* vij.*d.*" And in the accounts of Sir Brian Tuke, under the date of April, A° XXXI. (1539), is the following—"Item, paide to John of Andwarpe by the kingis commaundment, certified by my lord priviseales lettre for the charges in causinge certain the kingis lettres of importance to be convayed with all diligence to Christopher Mounte and Thomas Pannell, his grace's servauntes and orateurs in Jarmayne, the somme of 1*s.*"

"As to ANTHONY SNECHER, armourer," says Mr. Franks, "his name shows him to have been a foreigner, perhaps one of the 'Almayne armourers' at Greenwich, whose monthly salaries are entered (but without any names) in the Royal Household books; his occupation might have brought him into contact with Holbein the painter, who made several designs for ornamental weapons, which are preserved among his drawings in the British Museum." In the Sloane MS.

Respecting HARRY MAYNERT, painter, no particulars have been ascertained. He was also possibly a German. A John Maynard is mentioned by Walpole as one of two painters who were employed under Torreggiano, on the tomb of Henry VII., at Westminster.

Of OLRYCKE OBYNGER, merchant, there is also no account: this name likewise appears to be German.

The Mr. Anthony to whom Holbein owed 10*l.* 13*s.* 7*d.* has been conjectured to have been Anthony Anthony of the Ordnance Department; and also Anthony Toto, who was at the time sergeant-painter to the king. Of the former are the following notices:—In the Privy Purse expenses of Henry VIII. is this entry against the 10th September 1531—"Paied to Anthony Anthony, for a clocke in a case of golde, x.*li.* x.*s.*" And in the Pepys Library at Cambridge are two rolls, written

* Ed. Sir F. Madden, p. 20.

on vellum, with illustrations and embellishments in gold, entitled *A Declaration of the Royal Navy of England, composed by Anthony Anthony, one of the officers of the Ordnance, and by him presented to King Henry VIII. An. Regni* 38 *Dñi* 1546, &c. A drawing in one of the rolls, represents the great ship Harry Grace à Dieu; it is engraved in the sixth volume of the Archæologia.* *His will.* 1543. 35th Henry VIII.

PHILIP HOLBEIN.

Philip Holbein. Of Holbein's son Philip, something has already been said. Little indeed is known about him; he was born at Basel about the year 1523, and at his father's death he was living in Paris, as the apprentice of the jeweller Jacob David, also a native of Basel, and with whom Philip had been placed by his father, apparently early in the year 1539. What else we know or may surmise of him, is from a petition addressed in 1611 to the Emperor Matthias by another Philip Holbein, imperial court-jeweller, and a citizen of Augsburg, then in the twenty-eighth year *of his life or service*,† and accordingly, if the former, most probably our painter's great-grandson, but possibly even his grandson, as Holbein's Philip was not more than sixty years old when this younger Philip was born. The petition was for a confirmation and augmentation of arms, which was granted in the following year, on October the 1st, 1612. He speaks of his family as having been originally of the canton of Uri in Switzerland, which is probably a mere conjecture, from the similarity of the Holbein with the Uri arms —a black bull's head on a gold field, with a ring in the nose, but without the star between the horns, which is seen on the Holbein shield, as still preserved in the Painter's Hall at Basel. This Philip Holbein was settled in Vienna from the

* A. W. Franks, *Discovery of the Will of Hans Holbein*, &c.

† "Ich für meine Person aber nun in die acht und zwanzig Jahre," &c. His-Heusler, *Beiträge*, *l. l.*, p. 380. The petition was first published by Hegner, in his *Hans Holbein Der Jüngere*, p. 31, but goes no further than the words quoted. Hegner found it among the papers of Mechel.

CHAP. XVI.

John and Jane Holbein. 1543. 35th Henry VIII.

year 1600; and his descendants were still living in Vienna in Hegner's time;* and there are Holbeins still living in England.

There were however Holbeins in this country even before the arrival of our painter, as shown by the two wills by two well-to-do persons of this name, a man and wife, which were communicated by Mr. W. H. Hart, at the meeting of the Society of Antiquaries, for April the 16th, 1863. They are preserved, in copies, in the registry of the Archidiaconal Court of Canterbury. There is no evidence that the John and Jane Holbein in question were either of foreign extraction or in any way connected with our painter; we may safely infer the contrary, as he is not mentioned in the wills, though he had been already seven years in this country, at their date, 1534, when he must have been well known in England.

Of these two wills, Mr. Hart observes :—

"The first is that of John Holbein of Folkestone, dated August the 21st, 1534; he directs his body to be buried in the church of Folkestone, 'comyng within the churche yn the ile beside the churche dore unto Ihus Chapell.'

"'Item, I bequeith unto the coveryng and makyng of a newe fonte to be made within the parishe churche of Folkestone, xlvj.*s.* viij.*d.*'

"This will was proved on the 16th of October following, so that the date of the testator's death is with certainty reduced to the intermediate period.

"The ancient font is still in existence in Folkestone church. It has an octagonal bowl with carved sides, on some of which are shields, but they are unfortunately all so defaced that no traces of what was once carved thereon can now be detected. The Tudor rose, however, still remains on one of the sides. The style of the font is somewhat earlier than the date of the will.

---

* *l. l.*, p. 34.

John and Jane Holbein 1543. 35th Henry VIII.

" The next will is that of the widow Jane* Holbein, dated the 25th November, 1534, wherein she desires to be buried in Folkestone church, near her husband John Holbein. This will was proved on the 16th of January following.

" This John Holbein had been resident at Folkestone for some period before his death; for one Hamon Dunkyn, by his will dated April the 6th, 1528, makes certain bequests to John Holbein of Folkestone, and gives him the custody of his son. Holbein is also made one of the executors."

* Mr. Hart's paper says *Jane*, but in the will of the husband the name *Anne* occurs throughout as that of the wife, while on the other hand the wife in her will describes herself as "I Jane Holbeine." Either the woman must have had both names, or there is some misreading here. She appears, from her will, to have been the widow of Robert Quylter before she married John Holbein.

APPENDIX.

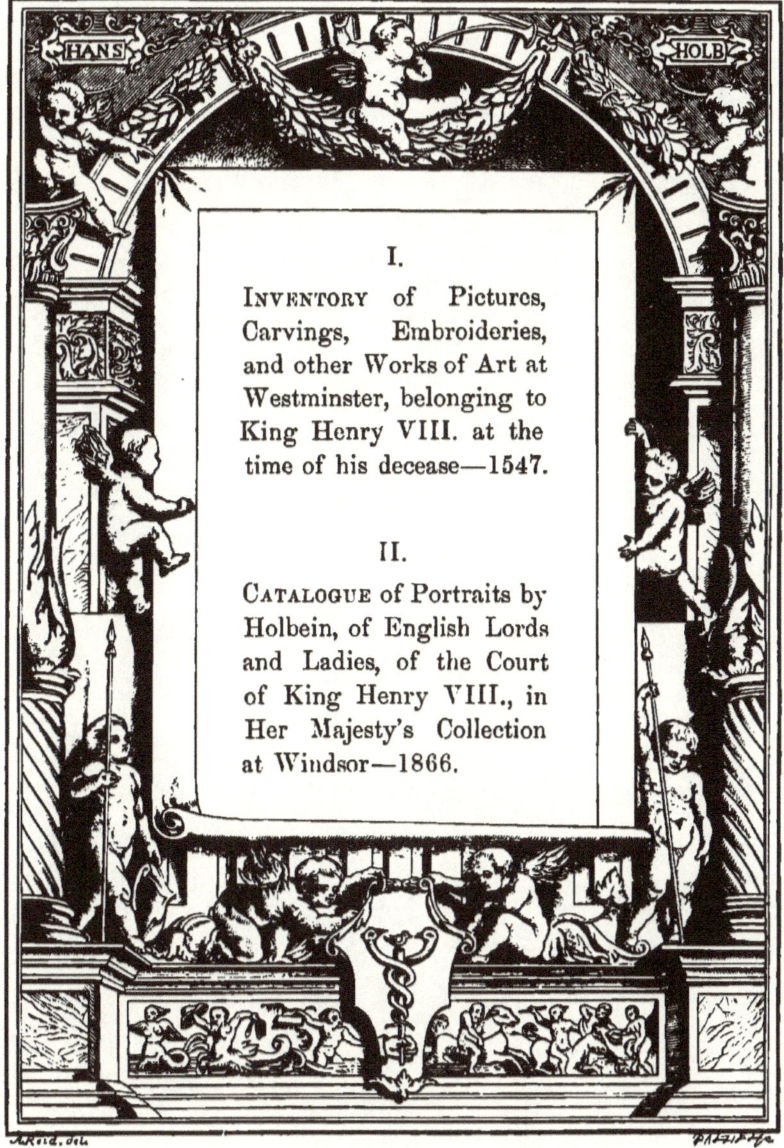

I.

Inventory of Pictures, Carvings, Embroideries, and other Works of Art at Westminster, belonging to King Henry VIII. at the time of his decease—1547.

II.

Catalogue of Portraits by Holbein, of English Lords and Ladies, of the Court of King Henry VIII., in Her Majesty's Collection at Windsor—1866.

APPENDIX I.

INVENTORY OF PICTURES, &c., IN THE PALACE OF WHITEHALL, IN THE YEAR 1547.

In the BRITISH MUSEUM, and at the RECORD OFFICE, are some manuscript volumes of great interest, containing an Inventory of the Furniture, and contents of the Wardrobes which belonged to Henry VIII., in his several palaces, up to the time of his death. This important document is thus described—" Inventory of our late Sovereign Lord King Henry the Eight, containing his Guarderobes, Household Stuff, and other Implements; made by virtue of a Commission under the great seal of England, bearing date at Westminster, the xiij. day of September in the first year of the reign of our Sovereign Lord King Edward the Sixth." Among the vast mass of objects described are many works of art, comprising a considerable Collection of Pictures, at Westminster, among which must certainly have been several by the hand of Holbein: in no case however is the name of the artist given, an omission which detracts enormously from the interest and value of the Inventory as a Fine Art Catalogue.

These volumes are — one, bound in two parts, in the Museum, belonging to the Harleian Manuscripts—No. 1419, A and B; and one among the Public Records—No. 160, of the Miscellaneous Volumes of the Augmentation Office. The latter is the earlier volume, the portion containing the Inventory of Works of Art (page 52 d) was written in the XXXIVth of Henry VIII., 1542, during Holbein's life-time. It is dated the 24th day of April of that year, and this volume bears on the first page the autograph of the king—" Henry Rex," thus:—

The Harleian MS., five years later, dates from the 1st of Edward VI.—1547. The part of the Inventory that more particularly concerns us in this place, is that commencing at p. 119, describing the Pictures and other works of art in the king's palace at Westminster, the old "York Place," or "Whitehall," as it was named after Wolsey's fall; the palace for which Holbein is said to have made a new gateway for Henry VIII. This collection at Westminster was under the charge of Sir Anthony Denny; but it by no means constitutes all the works of the kind which belonged to Henry; there were pictures, especially portraits, and other works, at Hampton Court, Greenwich, and at other royal palaces; some few are mentioned in the volumes cited, but the Westminster or Whitehall collection, in the charge of Sir Anthony Denny, appears to have been beyond comparison the most extensive: it was the king's special art-collection. The great majority of pictures elsewhere had, as far as may be judged by the descriptions, their counterparts at Westminster.

The following catalogue of this collection I have transcribed from the Harleian MS., which is a little more comprehensive than the Augmentation Office list, comprising further acquisitions made during the last years of the king's life. It was my intention to print the catalogue *verbatim et literatim*, but as I found on comparison that there was no fixed orthography for the various names and things mentioned, but that each transcriber wrote as it pleased him, and even varied the spelling of the same words in different pages, I give the list according to our own orthography, except occasionally where obsolete or archaic words occur. As my business is not with philology, the old spelling may, I assume, be safely dispensed with.

The publication of this catalogue may possibly lead to the identification of many more of the pictures included in it, several of which are doubtless still at Hampton Court and Windsor; some are well known. I have added the numbers and the notes in the margin, for the convenience of reference.

INVENTORY.

TUFF AND IMPLEMENTS AT WESTMINSTER, IN THE CHARGE OF SIR ANTHONY DENNY, KNIGHT, KEEPER OF THE HOUSE.

Tables with Pictures.

1. **Item,** one table having in it the five wounds, embroidered upon black satin. *Embroidery.*

2. **Item,** one table with a picture of Saint Jerome pointing upon a dead man's head. *Picture.*

3. **Item,** a table with the picture of a naked woman, holding a table with a scripture in it in th' one hand, and a bracelet upon th' other arm at the upper part thereof. *Picture.*

4. **Item,** a table of the decollation of St. John the Baptist. *Picture.*

5. **Item,** a table with the picture of a woman playing upon a lute, and an old man holding a glass in th' one hand, and a dead man's head in th' other hand. *Picture.*

6. **Item,** a table with the picture of a woman playing upon a lute, with a book before her, and a little pot with lilies springing out thereof. *Picture.*

7. **Item,** a table with the pictures of Saint Michael and Saint George, being in harness holding a streamer. *Picture.*

Portrait. 8. **Item,** a table with the picture of the French king, having a doublet of crimson colour, and a gown garnished with knots made like pearls.

Portrait. 9. **Item,** a table with the picture of the French Queen Elenora, in the Spanish array, and a cap on her head, with an orange in her hand.

Portraits. 10. **Item,** a table with the picture of the three children of the King of Denmark. With a curtain of white and yellow sarcenet *paned* together.*

Picture. 11. **Item,** a table with the picture of the hangman holding St. John's head in his hand, and a woman holding a dish to receive it. With a curtain of yellow and white sarcenet *paned* together.

Portrait. 12. **Item,** a great table with the picture of the Duchess of Milan, being her whole stature.†

Embroidery. 13. **Item,** a table with the picture of St. George on horseback, embroidered with Venice gold and silver.

Picture. 14. **Item,** a table with the picture of a naked woman sitting upon a rock of stone, with a scripture over her head.

Picture. 15. **Item,** a table of the naked truth, with the works of the bishop of Rome set forth in it.

Portraits. 16. **Item,** a table with the pictures of th' old Emperor, th' Emperor that now is, and Ferdinand. With a curtain, &c.

Picture. 17. **Item,** a table with the picture of our Lady holding our Lord taken down from the cross, in her arms. With a curtain, &c.

Portrait. 18. **Item,** a table with the picture of the lady Margaret the Duchess of Savoy. With a curtain, &c.

Picture. 19. **Item,** a table with th' history of *Filius Prodigus.*‡

Embroidery. 20. **Item,** a table with the picture of a woman holding the *Ver-*

---

* That is, a striped curtain hanging before the picture: very many of the king's collection were so protected. This group of portraits is now at Hampton Court, and is ascribed to Mabuse. See the description of it on page 85.

† Apparently the splendid portrait now at Arundel Castle, by Holbein.

‡ A picture of this subject, ascribed to Holbein, is in the Liverpool Institution.

*nacle** in her hands, embroidered with Venice gold and silver.

21. **Item,** a table with the picture of Mary Magdalen, with a cup standing by her, and a yellow flower in her hand. *Picture.*

22. **Item,** another less table with the picture of Mary Magdalen looking on her book, the box standing before her. *Picture.*

23. **Item,** a table with the picture of an old man dallying with women, and a pheasant cock hanging by the bill. *Picture.*

24. **Item,** one great table with the feast of Ahasuerus the King, and Vaschre the Queen. *Picture.*

25. **Item,** a table with the Nativity of our Lord.† *Picture.*

26. **Item,** a table with the picture of a woman having a monkey on her hand. With a curtain, &c.‡ *Picture.*

27. **Item,** a table with the picture of Frederick, Duke of Saxony. With a curtain, &c. *Portrait.*

28. **Item,** a table with the picture of Philip, Archduke of Austria. With a curtain, &c. *Portrait.*

29. **Item,** a table with a picture of Elizabeth of Austria, Queen of Denmark. With a curtain, &c.§ *Portrait.*

30. **Item,** a table with the picture of the Queen of Hungary, being Regent of Flanders. *Portrait.*

31. **Item,** a table with the picture of our Lady, and Christ sucking, and Joseph looking on a book. With a curtain, &c. *Holy Family.*

32. **Item,** a table with the picture of Prince Arthur. *Portrait.*

33. **Item,** a table with the picture of our Lord appearing to Mary Magdalen.‖ *Picture.*

34. **Item,** a table with the picture of a woman holding an unicorn in her lap. *Picture.*

---

* The Sancta Veronica.

† The words "with a cover of wood to the same," are added in the Augmentation Office Volume. The interval of five years between the making of the two lists seems to have involved changes in the number of the collection, and in the condition of the works themselves.

‡ The Duke of Buccleuch possesses a miniature of a "Woman holding a monkey," and in the portrait, so-called, of Queen Margaret Tudor, at Hampton Court, inscribed, *Aetatis suæ*, 26, the lady is carrying a monkey (a marmoset) on her hands.

§ The Augmentation Office Volume says—Elizabeth Queen of Austria.

‖ There is such a picture now at Hampton Court, ascribed to Holbein.

Sculpture? 35. **Item**, a table of alabaster with the picture of St. John the Evangelist.

Picture. 36. **Item**, a table with th' history of *Christiana Patiencia.*

Enamel. 37. **Item**, a folding table of the Passion, enamelled, set in leather, gilt.*

Embroidery. 38. **Item**, a table of the salutation of our Lady, embroidered with Venice gold and silk. With a curtain of red sarcenet.

Embroidery. 39. **Item**, a table of our Lady and St. Anne, with their husbands and kindred, embroidered with Venice gold and silk.

Picture. 40. **Item**, a table of the three kings of Cologne saluting our Lord.

Picture. 41. **Item**, a table with the picture of our Lord. With a curtain, &c.

Portrait. 42. **Item**, a table with the picture of King Henry the Seventh. With a curtain, &c.

Portrait. 43. **Item**, a table with the picture of Queen Elizabeth.† With a curtain, &c.

Portrait. 44. **Item**, a table with two folding leaves with the picture of King Henry th' Eight,‡ being young, wearing his hair, with a *flowre* of silver upon the lock.

Portraits, a diptych. 45. **Item**, a table like a book, with the pictures of King Henry th' Eight and Queen Jane.

Portrait. 46. **Item**, a table with the picture of the King's Majesty. With a curtain, &c.§

Portrait. 47. **Item**, another table with the whole stature of the King's Majesty, stained upon cloth. With a curtain of green sarcenet.‖

Portrait. 48. **Item**, a table with the picture of King Henry the Seventh's

---

* "Set in gilt leather."—Aug^n. Off. Vol.

† Elizabeth Woodville.

‡ In the Aug^n. Off. Vol. he is called "The King, his Majesty," being still living.

§ The Aug^n. Off. Vol. has "the picture of my Lord Prince's Grace," as Henry was then living.

‖ This is a full-length portrait on canvas, of Edward VI. when a child; because painted before 1542. I have already referred to such a portrait, as described by Mariette (p. 325, note). The Aug^n. Off. Vol. notices this work as a picture of "My Lord Prince his Grace." The Duke of Northumberland's portrait corresponding with the description is on wood.

mother, being Countess of Richmond. With a curtain of yellow and white sarcenet *paned* together.

49. **Item,** a table with the picture of King Henry the V.th. With a curtain, &c. *Portrait.*

50. **Item,** a table with the picture of King Henry the VI.th. With a curtain, &c. *Portrait.*

51. **Item,** a table with the picture of Queen Elizabeth, King Edward's wife. *Portrait.*

52. **Item,** a table with the picture of King Edward the iiij.th. With a curtain, &c. *Portrait.*

53. **Item,** a folding table with the pictures of the King of Castile's children. *Portraits.*

54. **Item,** a table of the Passion, of cloth of gold, embroidered and garnished with small pearls, lacking in sundry places.* With a curtain, &c. *Embroidery*

55. **Item,** a little round table with the picture of Mary Magdalen, sitting by her bed's side. With a curtain, &c. *Picture.*

56. **Item,** a table with the picture of Lucretia Romana, in a gown like crimson velvet, with green foresleeves, cut. *Picture.*

57. **Item,** a table with the picture of Lucretia Romana, being all naked, having like a *cipress* about her. *Picture.*

58. **Item,** a table with pictures of our Lady, our Lord sleeping on her breast, and a tree at our Lady's back. With a curtain, &c. *Virgin and Child.*

59. **Item,** a table of russet and black of the parable of the xviii.th chapter of Matthew, raised with liquid gold and silver. *Mosaic, or marquetry?*

60. **Item,** a table of walnut-tree with the picture of St. George on horseback, raised with liquid gold and silver. *Carving?*

61. **Item,** a table of the burial of our Lord, all of sundry woods joined together. *Marquetry or wood mosaic.*

62. **Item,** a table of walnut-tree of King Midas and Misery,† raised with liquid gold and silver. *Carving?*

63. **Item,** a table with the pictures of our Lady and our Lord in her arms. *Virgin and Child.*

---

* The Augm. Off. Vol. has also the words "and ix. counterfeit rubies, and ii. counterfeit turquoises."

† Calumny?

Allegorical portrait. 64. **Item,** a table with the picture of King Henry th' Eight* standing upon a mitre with three crowns, having a serpent with seven heads coming out of it, and having a sword in his hand, wherein is written VERBUM DEI.

Embroidery. 65. **Item,** a table with the picture of St. George on horseback, of cloth of gold tissued with silver. With a curtain, &c.

Carved triptych. 66. **Item,** a table with two folding leaves, of the Nativity of our Lord, wrought in bone.

Carved triptych. 67. **Item,** a table with two folding leaves of Lucretia Romana, wrought in alabaster.

Embossment. 68. **Item,** Item, a table of the Salutation of our Lady, embossed upon black velvet, garnished with sundry stones counterfeit, and pearls, sundry stones lacking. The frame being of black ebony garnished with silver, and lacking in sundry places both leaves and scrolls; and having upon the top thereof, the Father in the sun-beams, of silver and gilt, with an angel on either side, of silver, and above all a little cup with a cover of silver, and gilt with a *ceelor* and *testor* of yellow and white sarcenet *paned* together, and fringed with yellow and white silk, with a curtain to it of the same sarcenet.

Virgin and Child. 69. **Item,** a table with the picture of our Lady, and our Lord sleeping upon her breast.

Sculpture. 70. **Item,** a table with the picture of our Lady holding our Lord in her arms with divers angels and children of alabaster; our Lady standing in a tabernacle of wood, gilt with burnished gold, the ground thereof being of purple velvet. With a curtain, &c.

Portraits. 71. **Item,** a table with the pictures of the French King, the Queen his wife, and the fool standing behind him. With a curtain, &c.

Picture. 72. **Item,** a table with two folding leaves, with the picture of our Lady holding our Lord in her arms, with cherries in his hand.

Portrait. 73. **Item,** a table with the picture of a woman having like a bracelet on her arm, and like two pearls hanging at her ears.

---

* "The King's Highness," in the Aug. Off. Vol.

74. **Item,** a table with the picture of Lucretia Romana wrapped in a gown like sad tawny velvet. With a curtain, &c. *Picture.*

75. **Item,** a little table with the picture of the Queen of Castile. *Portrait.*

76. **Item,** a table with the picture of Lewis the French King. With a curtain, &c. *Portrait.*

77. **Item,** a little round table with the picture of the French King when he was young. *Portrait.*

78. **Item,** a table with the picture of one having long hair, being crowned, and having a robe like cloth of gold, and the fur being white. With a curtain, &c. *Portrait.*

79. **Item,** four tables of parchment set in frames of wood, with figures in them, and in every of them a manor place: viz., in one of them is written *Hampton Court,* in another *Amboyse,* in another *Cognac,* and in another *Sandit*(?). *Drawings?*

80. **Item,** a table with the picture of a young man, having like three brooches and a row of pearls upon his cap, and like a chain of stone and pearls about his neck, with a *bawdrike** about his shoulders, to hang his sword by. With a curtain, &c. *Portrait.*

81. **Item,** two great tables of black slate, to write upon, set in wood coloured like box. *Two slates.*

82. **Item,** a table with the picture of King Richard the Third. With a curtain, &c. *Portrait.*

83. **Item,** a table with the picture of Barcele the Countess of Corve.† With a curtain, &c. *Portrait.*

84. **Item,** a table with the picture of Charles th' Eight, French King. With a curtain, &c. *Portrait.*

85. **Item,** a great table with the picture of our Lady, with a book in her one hand, and our Lord in her other arm, and Joseph standing by. With a curtain, &c. *Holy Family.*

86. **Item,** a table with a picture of the Duke of Bourbon. With a curtain, &c. *Portrait.*

87. **Item,** three tables with the pictures of our Lord, embroidered *Embroidery.*

---

* Baldrick.

† Corne, or Carew?

upon cloth of gold; two of them with borders of crimson velvet, and th' other with a border of black velvet.

Embroidery. 88. **Item,** a table with the picture of our Lady, embroidered upon cloth of gold, with a border of crimson velvet.

Embroidery. 89. **Item,** a table of our Lord bearing his cross, embroidered with Venice gold and silk, with a border of black velvet.

Embroidery. 90. **Item,** a table with Pilate bringing forth our Lord, scourged, before the people, embroidered upon cloth of gold, with a border of black velvet.

Embroidery. 91. **Item,** a table embroidered with threads of Venice gold, upon flat gold, with the Holy Ghost, and the five wounds.

Embroidery. 92. **Item,** a table of embroidery, with the pictures of our Lady, and our Lord in her arms, and St. Anne; garnished in sundry places with small seed pearls, many of them being lost.

Embroidery. 93. **Item,** a table of embroidery, of Venice gold, silver, and silk; with the picture of our Lady holding our Lord in her arms.

Virgin and Child. 94. **Item,** a table with the picture of our Lady holding our Lord at her breast, her robe being red.

Picture. 95. **Item,** a table of the picture of St. Jerome holding death's head in his hand, and a lion lying by him.

Glass-painting. 96. **Item,** a table of the decollation of St. John Baptist painted upon glass; the borders thereof gilt with burnished gold.

Portrait. 97. **Item,** a table with the picture of King Henry the VIII., then being young.

Portrait. 98. **Item,** a table with a picture of Prince Arthur, wearing like a red cap with a brooch upon it, and a collar of red and white roses.*

Portrait. 99. **Item,** a table with the picture of th' Emperor, his doublet being cut, and a rosemary branch in his hand.

Triptych. 100. **Item,** a table with two folding leaves having in th' one of the leaves, the birth of Christ; in the middle, the three Kings of Cologne; and th' other leaf, our Lady giving our Lord suck.

---

* Now in the Royal Collection at Windsor; lately identified by Mr. George Scharf.

101. **Item**, a table with the picture of one being in black, with this scripture—GLORIFICAMUS TE SANCTA DEI GENETRIX. *Portrait.*

102. **Item**, a little table with the picture of Charles Duke of Burgundy. With a curtain, &c. *Portrait.*

103. **Item**, a table with the picture of Isabel Queen of Castile. With a curtain, &c. *Portrait.*

104. **Item**, a table with the picture of a woman in a French hood with a gown like cloth of gold, and blue foresleeves. With a curtain, &c. *Portrait.*

105. **Item**, a table with the picture of our Lady, holding our Lord in her lap; and a pomegrannte in her hand; with an angel playing upon a lute, and Joseph standing by. With a curtain, &c. *Holy Family.*

106. **Item**, a table of the seven sorrows of our Lady; embroidered. *Embroidery.*

107. **Item**, a table with the picture of a woman, her head and her neck bare, her garment cut and pulled out with white. With a curtain, &c. *Portrait.*

108. **Item**, a table with the picture of John Archduke of Austria. With a curtain, &c. *Portrait.*

109. **Item**, a table with a picture having a black cap with a brooch and a collar of scallop shells. With a curtain, &c. *Portrait.*

110. **Item**, a table with the picture of Philip Duke of Burgundy. With a curtain, &c. *Portrait.*

111. **Item**, a table with the picture of a woman having a tire upon her head like a mitre. With a curtain, &c. *Portrait.*

112. **Item**, a table with the picture of Julius Cæsar. With a curtain, &c. *Portrait.*

113. **Item**, a table with the picture of Philip Duke, the Hardy. With a curtain, &c. *Portrait.*

114. **Item**, a table with the picture of Charles the Great, Emperor. With a curtain, &c. *Portrait.*

115. **Item**, a table of the Salutation of our Lady, embroidered upon black satin, with two pillars and an arch, of crimson satin, embroidered with Venice gold, and in the top of the same, on each side, an angel. *Embroidery.*

116. **Item**, a table of embroidery with the picture of our Lady, and *Embroidery.*

our Lord in her arms, with a pear in her hand, and a dish of fruit standing by her.

Portrait. 117. **Item,** a table with the picture of Frederick the Third, Emperor, with a coif on his head. With a curtain, &c.

Pictures. 118. **Item,** two tables with the pictures of Lucretia Romana in red robes and lawn sleeves.

Pictures. 119. **Item,** two tables with the pictures of Mary Magdalen in red robes like damask, and a box in their hands.

Virgin and Child. 120. **Item,** a table with a picture of our Lady, and our Lord sleeping in her arms.

Ecce Homo. 121. **Item,** a little square table with the picture of our Lord crowned with thorn, his arms bound: stained upon cloth.

Embroidery. 122. **Item,** a table of embroidery with the picture of our Lady, and Christ sucking on her breast.

Embroidery. 123. **Item,** a little square table of embroidery, with the picture of our Lord crowned with thorn, and a reed in his hand.

Picture. 124. **Item,** a table with the picture of Lucretia Romana with th' history of the same.

Picture. 125. **Item,** a table with the picture of Adam and Eve.

Picture. 126. **Item,** a table with the picture of St. George, his spear being broken, and his sword in his hand.

Salvator Mundi. 127. **Item,** a table with the picture of our Saviour blessing with his one hand and holding th' other hand upon the world.

Virgin and Child. 128. **Item,** a table with the picture of our Lady, holding our Lord in her arms ready to suck.

Embroidery. 129. **Item,** a table of embroidery with the picture of our Lady holding our Lord sucking in her arms, and a daisy in his hand; with this scripture—O MATER DEI MEMENTO MEI.

Portrait. 130. **Item,** a table with the picture of the Duke of Sabaudie.* With a curtain, &c.

Portrait. 131. **Item,** a table with the picture of Duke John. With a curtain, &c.

Embroidery. 132. **Item,** a table with the picture of our Lord and our Lady, holding th' arms of the Passion, embroidered with Venice gold on black velvet. With a curtain, &c.

---

* Savoy.

133. **Item,** a table with the picture of a woman in a French hood, in a gown like cloth of gold, the sleeves turned up with white, and powdered with black. With a curtain, &c. *Portrait*

134. **Item,** a table with the picture of James King of Scotts, with a hawk on his fist. With a curtain, &c. *Portrait.*

135. **Item,** a table with the picture of Ferdinand King of Arragon. *Portrait.*

136. **Item,** a table of mother-of-pearl in roundells, of the birth and Passion of Christ, garnished with glasses instead of stones, and pinnacles of wood, gilt. With two curtains of green sarcenet. *Mother-of-pearl.*

137. **Item,** a table of two folding leaves of mother-of-pearl in squares, containing the birth and passion of Christ, and both laws. *Mother-of-pearl.*

138. **Item,** a table with the picture of the Duchess of Milan.* *Portrait.*

139. **Item,** a table with two folding leaves, having in th' one leaf the Salutation of our Lady, in the middle, the three Kings of Cologne saluting our Lord, and in th' other leaf our Lady giving our Lord suck. *Triptych.*

140. **Item,** a little table with a picture of the wife of the Lord of Fiennes. With a curtain, &c. *Portrait.*

141. **Item,** a table of the siege of Pavia.† With a curtain, &c. *Picture.*

142. **Item,** a table with two folding leaves, with the picture of our Lady, and our Lord sitting on her lap, and playing with her book. *Picture.*

143. **Item,** a table with the picture of St. George, sitting and holding his helmet on his lap, and his streamer in his hand. *Picture.*

144. **Item,** a table with the picture of our Lady, and our Lord being dead in her lap; embroidered with Venice gold and silk upon green velvet. *Embroidery.*

145. **Item,** a table with the picture of a woman called *Michaell*, with a red rose in th' one hand, and laying th' other hand upon a dog's back. *Portrait.*

---

* Possibly the small bust portrait of the duchess, now at Windsor, and described in page 313.

† Now at Hampton Court.

Picture. 146. **Item,** a table with the name of JHESUS, and the iiij. evangelists stained upon single sarcenet.

Portrait. 147. **Item,** a table with the picture of John Frederick Duke of Saxony. Stained upon linen cloth, being his whole stature.

Picture. 148. **Item,** a table with th' history of Orpheus, with sundry strange beasts and monsters; stained upon cloth.

Triptych. 149. **Item,** a table with two folding leaves of Christ taken down from the cross.

Portrait. 150. **Item,** a table with the picture of the whole stature of the King's Majesty,* in a gown like crimson satin, furred with lucernes. With a curtain of white sarcenet.

Portrait. 151. **Item,** a table with the picture of the Lady Elizabeth her grace, with a book in her hand, her gown like crimson cloth of gold, with works.†

Picture. 152. **Item,** a table painted and gilt with th' history of David and Goliath.

153. **Item,** a large table painted with sundry images of white and black upon *tike*,‡ nailed upon board.

Stained Cloths.§

Portrait. 154. **Item,** stained cloth with the picture of Charles th' Emperor.

Portrait. 155. **Item,** a stained cloth with the picture of the Prince of Orange.

---

* Edward VI., painted when he was prince. This and the three following were added after 1542, as they are not included in the Aug^n Off. Vol.

† This is apparently the picture of the princess now at St. James's Palace, and described on page 270. If we may come to this conclusion, it almost confirms my suggestion that the picture was painted in 1546. It is not mentioned in the Augmentation Office Volume, for the satisfactory reason that it cannot have been painted in 1542; its being comprised in this Inventory shows that it was not painted later than 1546, and that the princess was accordingly not more than in her thirteenth year when the portrait was taken.

‡ Ticken.

§ Though stained cloths or canvas pictures are here placed separately, we have already come upon several canvas pictures among the panel pieces; as No. 47, a portrait of Prince Edward; No. 121, an "Ecce Homo;" No. 147, a portrait of John Frederick Duke of Saxony; No. 148, a picture of "Orpheus;" and No. 153, a picture with figures in chiaroscuro.

156. **Item,** a stained cloth with men and women sitting at a banquet, and Death coming in making them all afraid, and one standing with a sword to keep him out at the door. *Picture.*

157. **Item,** a stained cloth with sundry men and women sitting at a banquet, in a wood, and a crimson cloth hanged betwixt the *croches* of two trees to shadow them; and a woman on horseback with footmen running by her. *Picture.*

158. **Item,** a stained cloth with Phœbus riding in his cart, in the air, with th' history of him. *Picture.*

159. **Item,** a stained cloth with th' history of Judith. *Picture.*

160. **Item,** a stained cloth with the picture of Solyman the Turk, being his whole stature. *Portrait.*

161. **Item,** th' history of King Asa of the breaking and casting down of the altars, with the idols; stained upon *tike.* *Picture.*

162. **Item,** th' history of Judith striking off Holophernes' head; painted upon *tike.* *Picture.*

163. **Item,** th' history of David striking off Goliath's head; painted upon *tike* and nailed upon a frame of wood. *Picture.*

164. **Item,** a painted cloth with the Triumph called the hurling of the canes, set in a frame of wood, walnut-tree colour. *Picture.*

Pictures.*

165. **Item,** a picture of a woman made of earth, with a carnation robe knit with a knot on the left shoulder, and bare headed, with her hair rolled up with a white lace.

166. **Item,** a picture of Moses made of earth; set in a box of wood.

167. **Item,** a picture of a woman made of earth, with a coif of orange colour upon her head; set in a box of wood.

168. **Item,** a picture of a woman made of earth, in a purple garment, with a garland of green leaves about her head.†

* Pictures. The Augmentation Office Volume has "Pictures of Earth," which signifies probably painted terracottas.

† "Set in a box of wood," Augⁿ· Off. Vol. All the other pieces were originally in boxes of wood, according to the older inventory, but in 1547, many of the boxes appear to have been missing.

169. **Item,** a picture of a woman made of earth in a robe of ash colour, and her hair trussed behind her ears.

170. **Item,** a picture of a Morian* boy made of earth, with a garment of white and blue.

171. **Item,** a picture of a woman made of earth, her garment being crimson, her head tired after Flanders fashion.

172. **Item,** a picture of a woman made of earth, with a carnation garment after the English attire, and bare headed with her hair rolled up with a white lace; set in a box of wood.

173. **Item,** a picture of a woman made of earth, in a green garment, with a garland of green leaves about her head.

174. **Item,** a picture of St. John's head in a dish of earth.

175. **Item,** a picture of Balthasar one of the Kings of Cologne, the head being of black *tuche*,† set in a brass, gilt, with a coronet on his head, of copper and gilt.

176. **Item,** a picture of a woman, with a child in her arms sucking, and another at her foot all of black *towche*, partly gilt, set upon a foot of wood and alabaster.

177. **Item,** a picture of a Morian boy, in a garment of blue and white.

178. **Item,** a picture of another Morian boy, in a garment of yellow and blue, with a red cap.

The end of the Inventory of the charge of Sir Anthony Denny at Whitehall.

---

* Moorish or Black.

† Towche, in the Aug^{n} Off. Vol.

APPENDIX II.

Catalogue of Portraits by Holbein, of English Lords and Ladies, of the Court of King Henry VIII., in Her Majesty's Collection at Windsor.

HAVE had frequent occasion to mention the Windsor portfolios, containing a fine series of original portrait sketches with crayons by Holbein. These drawings seem to have been in perhaps all cases preliminary studies for portraits, and of most of them portraits may have been painted; though it is remarkable how few can now be identified. There probably never were pictures of all; some have no doubt perished, a few may have gone abroad, others have been so much painted over as to be no longer recognizable; and several possibly are hanging safe in their dirt and obscurity in provincial mansions in England. The majority of the sketches are named, but many both male and female are left anonymous. *Lords and Ladies of the Court of Henry VIII.*

If the drawings were not originally described by Holbein, it is difficult to see how the names can be generally relied on; they are certainly false in some instances, and may be so in many. The names as originally given are preserved in the Chamberlaine prints after these drawings engraved by Bartolozzi,* and I have adhered to them in

* *Imitations of Original Drawings, &c.* 2 vols. folio, 1792–1800. These imitations are very free, and are certainly far from being fac-similes; they are much too uniform in character and finish. The historical notices are by Edmund Lodge, Lancaster Herald; and the few biographical facts recorded in the following summary notice of the collection, are from these memoirs. A list of the portraits is given also in the volume published by Bathoe, containing the Catalogue of the Collection of James II. 4to. London, 1758.

These drawings, as interesting historically as artistically, are at present arranged in four portfolios, having been lately remounted, under the direction of Mr. Woodward, the Queen's Librarian, on large white mounts, with raised fronts to protect them from being rubbed, in accordance with the wishes of His Royal Highness the late Prince Consort, and they have greatly gained in effect by the change. The smaller drawings are put two or more together, on the same mount.

Lords and Ladies of the Court of Henry VIII.

the accompanying catalogue of the drawings, as they were originally placed in the two volumes or portfolios in which they were arranged for George III. Queen Caroline, who discovered them, had had them framed and glazed, and they were hung for some years in Kensington Palace; hence they are sometimes called the Kensington Drawings.

They seem to have been executed with charcoal, and black and red chalk, the eyes, hair and beards, being commonly drawn in their proper colours; and it is remarkable how blue eyes prevail. Many are strengthened with the brush and indian ink, more especially in the outlines; but sometimes the whole face is modelled with great delicacy with the brush. Some of the beards are superbly put in. It is the more delicate shading and colouring with the crayons that has been worn away by time, hence the brush lines, of a more permanent nature, yet no doubt in perfect harmony originally, are left in many instances isolated and accordingly harsh: where they were more delicate, their effect is still nearly perfect.

Walpole gives the following history of these drawings:—"At present an invaluable treasure of the works of this master is preserved in one of our palaces. Soon after the accession of the late king, Queen Caroline found in a bureau at Kensington, a noble collection of Holbein's original drawings for the portraits of some of the chief personages of the court of Henry VIII. How they came there is quite unknown. They did belong to Charles I., who changed them with William Earl of Pembroke, for a St. George by Raphael, now at Paris. Lord Pembroke gave them to the Earl of Arundel."

Here the link is broken; but Dallaway thought they were purchased for the Crown, at the sale of Henry Duke of Norfolk, in 1686.

Walpole continues:—"There are eighty-nine of them, a few of which are duplicates:* a great part are exceedingly fine, and in one respect preferable to his finished pictures, as they are drawn in a bold and free manner: and though they have little more than the outline, being drawn with chalk upon paper stained of a flesh colour,† and scarce shaded at all, there is a strength and vivacity in them equal to the most perfect portraits."

"After Holbein's death," he adds, "they had been sold into France." And they then passed into the possession of a Mons. de Liancourt, from whom it appears, they were purchased for Charles I.

"Some have been rubbed and others traced over with a pen on the

---

* I find only two duplicates, Sir Thomas Wyatt and its copy.

† Not all. Some are on plain paper; most are on a tempera ground or priming of flesh colour, and others on what may be called a ground of salmon colour.

Lords and Ladies of the Court of Henry VIII.

outlines by some unskilful hand (?). In an old inventory belonging to the family of Lumley, mention was made of such a book in that family, with a remarkable note, that it had belonged to Edward VI., and that the names of the persons were written on them by Sir John Cheke. Most of the drawings at Kensington have names in an old hand; and the probability of their being written by a minister of the court who so well knew the persons represented, is an addition to their value."

Sir John Cheke as Holbein's contemporary may fairly have known the majority of the persons represented: he was professor of Greek at Cambridge, and one of the tutors of Edward VI. when prince, and he may have named them when in the prince's possession: Sir John died in 1557.* The tradition that these drawings belonged to Edward VI. must modify the report that they were sold into France after Holbein's death, as the prince survived the painter ten years. Allowing that Sir John Cheke may have known the greater number, it is certain that he did not know them all; he has omitted to name fourteen—nine ladies and five gentlemen: he must have been doubtful of about at least as many, and it is therefore quite probable that some ten or a dozen even are misnamed. A single picture—the "More family," has furnished us with the identities of three. In a few instances we have a repetition of the same name to portraits which apparently represent different persons; and we have also once or twice the same person represented at different ages.

That the drawings belonged once to the Earl of Arundel, we have recorded by a contemporary authority, in an interesting manuscript on *Miniature painting*, ascribed to Nicholas Hilliard.† Whoever the writer may have been, he had a high opinion of our painter. In a paragraph on the painting of shadows (p. 8) he says—"The black must be deepened with ivory black, and if in working in the heightenings and light-reflections, you will mingle with your ordinary black a little lake and indigo, or rather a little litmus instead of indigo, you will find your

* Cheke was a Protestant or Anglican, but after the death of Edward his life fell on evil days: under the apostolic fatherly government of my Lord Cardinal Pole, the blood-thirsty legate, he was recommended to return to the bosom of the church, and as he had only the alternative of recanting or burning, he recanted and died of a broken heart. He was the author of an essay *De Superstitione*, which he inscribed to Henry VIII.

† The manuscript is in the British Museum, No. 6000 MSS. *Harl.*, and on the fly-leaf is written "of Limning by Hilliard;" it is entitled "*An exact & Compendious discours concerning the Art of Miniatura or Limning*," &c. I should doubt its being by Hilliard, as "old Mr. Hilliard" is one of the painters mentioned in it; this is however not conclusive, and the book may have been written before 1619, the year of Hilliard's death.

Lords and Ladies of the Court of Henry VIII. black to render a rare and admirable reflection like to that of the well-dyed satin, especially if your lights be strong and hard; the manner whereof if you please to see imitably expressed, you will find abundantly for your content in the gallery of my most noble Lord the Earl of Arundell Earl Marshal of England, and done by the incomparable pencil of that rare master Hans Holebin, who in all his different and various manners of painting, either in oil, distemper, limning, or crayon, it seems was so general and absolute an artist, as never to imitate any man, or ever was worthily imitated by any."

It is in the chapter on the making of crayons (p. 15 d) that the writer notices the Windsor drawings. Speaking of their use, he says:—"I shall not need to insist upon the particulars of this manner of working; it shall suffice if you please to view of a book of pictures by the life, by the incomparable Hans Holbein servant to King Henry the Eighth. They are the pictures of most of the English lords and ladies then living, and *were the patterns* whereby that excellent painter made his pictures in oil by; they are all done in this latter manner of *crayons* I speak of, and though many of them be miserably spoiled by the injury of time and the ignorance of some who formerly have had the keeping of the book, yet you will find in those ruinous remains an admirable hand, and a rare manner of working in few lines and no labour in expressing of the life and likeness, many times equal to his own, and ever excelling other men's oil pictures. The book hath been long a wanderer, but is now happily fallen into the hands of my noble lord the Earl Marshal."*

Norgate, in speaking of crayon-painting, also refers to these drawings; he says—"A better way was used by Holbein, by priming a large paper with a carnation or complexion of flesh colour, whereby he made pictures by the life, of many great lords and ladies of his time, with black and red chalk, with other flesh colours, made up hard and dry, like small pencil sticks. Of this kind was an excellent book, while it remained in the hands of the most noble Earl of Arundel and Surrey. But I hear it has been a great traveller, and wherever now, he hath got his errata, or (which is as good) hath met with an index expurgatorius, and is made worse with mending."†

* This passage has been quoted by Dallaway, but incorrectly, and he has further added some words at the end which render the last paragraph inconsistent and almost valueless as historical evidence, as he has made it appear to have been written after the death of the Earl of Arundel, which is opposed to the sense of the last words quoted.

† Rawlinson MSS. No. 336, in the Bodleian Library, Oxford—"*A Treatise on Miniature or the Arte of Limning*" by Edward Norgate; quoted by Dallaway, in Walpole's *Anecdotes*, &c. Vol. I., p. 84. Ed. 1849.

Lords and Ladies of the Court of Henry VIII.

As regards the tracing and mending, above mentioned, by unskilful hands, I think there may be a question; I doubt it. Most, if not all, of the hard lines objected to are certainly by Holbein himself; few of the drawings were ever quite finished, and some parts have been drawn in with greater force and detail than others. Occasionally by the sides, small details of costume-patterns are put in, perhaps not with a pen, but with a hair-pencil, though some pens might not mark more clearly than a brush: the drawings have also many directions as regards colours and materials of costume written on them, exactly with the same kind of touch, with the pen or hair-pencil, as the harder lines in the faces are put in with. In some drawings the eyebrows as well as the beards are finished with these pen or pencil touches; and in most cases it is clear that the lines in the faces are hard and inharmonious now simply from the circumstances of the finer details being worn off by the constant friction of centuries, and thus leaving disagreeably prominent what was once as certainly in perfect harmony with the surroundings.*

---

* Walpole himself possessed, framed and glazed, in his *Holbein Chamber*, thirty-four of these drawings traced on oil paper by Vertue and Müntz, when they were preserved in Queen Caroline's closet at Kensington: and he thus describes them in his description of the Strawberry Hill Villa:—

1. Sir Thomas More.
2. Lord Vaux (by Müntz).
3. Lady Henningham.
4. William Parr, Marquis of Northampton, brother of Queen Catherine.
5. A Lady unknown.
6. Ditto.
7. Sir Nicholas Poins.
8. Catherine Willoughby, fourth wife of Charles Brandon, Duke of Suffolk.
9. Henry Howard, Earl of Surrey, the poet.
10. Nicholas Cratzer, astronomer to Henry VIII. (This name does not occur in the old catalogue.)
11. Edward Clinton, Earl of Lincoln, Lord High Admiral of England.
12. Doctor Colet, Dean of St. Paul's (?).
13. Sir Thomas Elyot, the author.
14. Henry Howard, Earl of Surrey, younger than the preceding.
15. A Gentleman unknown.
16. William Fitzwilliam, Earl of Southampton.
17. Edward Stanley, Earl of Derby.
18. Bourbonius, a French poet.
19. Fisher, Bishop of Rochester. Richardson the painter had another of these, which was engraved among the "Illustrious Heads."
20. Thomas Boleyn, Earl of Ormond, father of Queen Anne Boleyn.
21. Lord Wentworth.
22. Lord Chancellor Rich.
23. Lady Rich, his wife.
24. Sir Thomas Wyatt, the poet.

25. George Brook, Lord Cobham.
26. Edward VI. when a child, very like Henry VIII.
27. Jane Seymour.
28. John Russell, first Earl of Bedford.
29. Anne Savage, Lady Berkeley; she held up the train of Anne Boleyn, at her coronation.—*Vide Stow's Chron.*, p. 543. (This is really Elizabeth Dancy, More's second daughter.)
30. Sir W. Sherrington, Master of the Mint, whence he furnished Admiral Seymour with money.
31. Sir John Gage.
32. Sir Richard Southwell, one of the accusers of the Earl of Surrey.
33. Queen Mary, when princess.
34. Thomas Duke of Norfolk, beheaded in the reign of Elizabeth; young.

CATALOGUE.*

PORTRAITS BY HOLBEIN IN HIS MAJESTY'S COLLECTION.

TOM. I.

Lords and Ladies of the Court of Henry VIII.

1. HARRY GULDEFORD KNIGHT—a finished head nearly life-size; in a light cap, and with a short stubble beard: a three-quarter face turned to his left. On unprimed paper; slightly stained: 15 in. *h.* by 11 in. *w.*

   Sir Henry Guildford, of whom the Queen has the fine half-length picture, for which this drawing is a study, was made Comptroller of the Household in 1523: he died in 1532 aged about fifty-four.

2. WARHAMUS ARCH Bᴾ CANT:—bust, nearly full face, looking to his right; in doctor's cap, and with a sable collar to his coat. On unprimed paper, somewhat rubbed and damaged: about 17 in. *h.* by 12 in. *w.*

   Thomas Warham, Archbishop of Canterbury, who died also in 1532. Of this grand drawing there are several pictures, two of which, one at Lambeth, and another in the Louvre, are excellent; but the Lambeth picture is much more like the drawing than that in the Louvre.

3. THO: MOOR Lᴰ CHANCELOUR—head life-size, three-quarter face looking to the left: sable collar. On unprimed paper, rubbed and stained; it has been pricked for tracing: about 16 in. *h.* by 12 in. *w.* Most of the More family are sketched on a larger scale than common, and all on plain white paper.

   In this drawing Sir Thomas has a small moustache, which is not decidedly shown in the painted portraits, except in that at East Hendred, and in the Thorndon "Family picture." Beheaded in 1535, eight years after the date of the drawing.

* The names and the numerical order of this catalogue are taken from an old list in the Royal Library at Windsor. I have elsewhere called this list the original catalogue, but it appears to be nothing more than a list of names taken from the drawings, when they were removed from their frames, and arranged in two volumes for George III. The descriptions of the drawings and remarks on their state are added by me.

Lords and Ladies of the Court of Henry VIII.

4. Sier Thomas Mooer—the well-known head, nearly life-size, of the painted portraits, nearly identical with No. 3; the face is modelled in red chalk, the cap tinted, the fur collar of the gown only outlined. On unprimed paper; somewhat rubbed.

5. Fitz Williams Earl of Southampton—a fine head, in cap, three-quarter face looking to his left, a knightly collar on his shoulders. The face in fine condition, the rest in outline.

Sir William Fitzwilliam, created Earl of Southampton in 1538, died at Newcastle in 1543. He was the Earl Southampton concerned in the Anne of Cleves catastrophe.

6. Judge Moore, S[R] Tho. More's Father—an excellent drawing of a head, nearly full face, with black cap and yellow sable collar: the study for the portrait in the "Family picture." On unprimed paper; stained.

Sir John More was created Judge of the King's Bench in 1518, and died in 1530.

7. J. Russell L[D] Privy Seale (with one eye)—an old bearded head in a black skull-cap, showing a little more than the profile, turned to his right. About 14 in. *h.* by 11 in. *w.*; rubbed.

He was the first Earl of Bedford, and died in 1555.

8. Rich L[D] Chancelor—head, in cap, three-quarter face, turned to his left, completely shaven. Much rubbed and damaged, little more than the outline remaining.

Sir Richard Rich became Lord Chancellor in 1547, and died in 1566.

9. John Poines—nearly three-quarter face, looking up, showing the right side, in a kind of black skull-cap: face completely shaven. Dark-lined with the brush; in fair condition, and a fine drawing, notwithstanding the hard lines objected to.

John Pointz of North Wokendon, in Essex, was in the King's Household, and died in 1558.

10. L[D] Wentworth—head, in cap and feather, with entire beard; three-quarter face turned to his right: small life-size. Unfinished, rubbed.

He died in 1551.

11. S. G. Carow Knight—a dark round-bearded head, full face, small life-size, with brimmed cap inclining on the left: salmon-coloured priming; rubbed.

Sir George Carew commanded the "Mary Rose," and went down with that ship, when it was sunk in an engagement with the French, in 1545.

Lords and Ladies of the Court of Henry VIII.

12. A Gentleman — named by some, Charles Brandon Duke of Suffolk. Conjectured also to represent Edward Stafford Duke of Buckingham. A good drawing full of black lines, of a middle-aged man with a dark beard and black hair, and a round Scotch bonnet on his head; nearly full face, with a somewhat flattened nose.

Some colours are written in, with the same brush that has made the black lines in this drawing.

13. Cha. Winhfield Knight — a bare head with receding forehead, bearded; a little more than the profile turned to his left: hair on his chest, and a medal suspended by a cord round his neck. Brush lines in the beard: rubbed.

Supposed to have been a son of Sir Richard Wingfield.

14. Phil. Melanchton — nearly three-quarter face turned to his right, shaven; with a small cap on his head. Much rubbed.

This drawing must be misnamed, as Melancthon was never in England. What opportunity Holbein may have had of drawing him, abroad, is not known.

15. S. George of Cornwall—a profile showing the left side; a fine but stern face, with a moustache, a short beard, and very short hair; his black cap with a white feather in it, inclined on the right side of the head: body indicated only. Strongly black-lined.

Simon George of Quocoute.

16. Edward Stanley Earle of Darbey—nearly full face, in cap and beard; body indicated only. Black-lined and stained.

The third Earl of Derby, who died in 1574.

17. Reskemeer a Cornish Gent.—bust, in profile, with cap and a long pointed yellow beard, showing the left shoulder. Damaged from having been laid down on an old bordered mount of smaller size than the drawing, the old border lines still showing through the paper, though remounted on clean white board; otherwise in fair condition. A picture from this drawing is in the Hampton Court collection.

John Reskimer, of Murthyr, Cornwall.

18. Tho: Wiatt Knight—head in cap, nearly full face, small life-size, with a long beard: a fine head, the hair and beard modelled with the brush. Rubbed and stained.

Lords and Ladies of the Court of Henry VIII.

Sir Thomas Wyatt was born in 1503, and died in 1541. A profile picture of him is in the possession of Lord Romney.

19. N. Poines Knight—bust, small head in profile, showing left side, with short youthful beard and moustache; in round cap with white feather; a gold chain on his shoulders. Finely lined, in fair condition. Mr. Holford, of Dorchester House, has a miniature on vellum, corresponding with this drawing; with a plain blue back-ground.

Sir Nicholas Pointz of Iron Acton, in Gloucestershire: he died in 1557.

20. Rich. Southwell Knight—inscribed anno ettatis suæ 33. Head and shoulders, three-quarter face turned to his left, close shaven; he wears a black cap with a medallion in it: head in fine conditon, body in outline. Nearly 16 in. *h.* by 11 in. *w.* The original drawing of the portrait in the Uffizj Gallery at Florence.

Sir Richard Southwell died old, Master of Ordnance to Queen Elizabeth.

21. Ormond—half-length, with a fine bearded head, in a red cap, and black slashed doublet; the body done in outline with the brush. Nearly a full-face, turned slightly to his left, and showing the right hand. About 15 in. *h.* by 11 in. *w.*

Supposed to be Thomas Boleyn, father of Queen Anne Boleyn, and Earl of Wiltshire and Ormond; he died in 1538.

22. Gage—a bearded head in a slouching brimmed cap, covering the forehead; three-quarter face looking to his left. Salmon-coloured priming.

Sir John Gage was Constable of the Tower to Henry VIII.; he died in 1557.

23. William Sharinton—red-bearded head, in brimmed cap, nearly full face. Rubbed.

Sir William Sherrington of Norfolk.

24. Fisher B^p of Rochester—inscribed *Il Epyscopo de resester fo taiglato il Capo l' an°* 1535—The Bishop of Rochester beheaded in 1535—which inscription (quite unintelligible in Chamberlaine's Work) would imply that the drawing was once in the possession of an Italian.

A fine head in doctor's cap, nearly full face, turned to the right; very thin; body in mere outline. The hard lines spoken of in this case are very serviceable, giving great force of nature at a little distance. There is a finished drawing of the sketch in the British Museum, bequeathed to it by the Rev. C. M. Cracherode; it was once Richardson's.

Lords and Ladies of the Court of Henry VIII.

25. A GENTLEMAN—in cap and feather, and with a fur collar to his coat, a three-quarter face looking to his left; body indicated only. Finely lined with the hair-pencil; in good condition.

26. THE LORD VAUX—a small bearded head, three-quarter face, turned to his left, with a round black cap on the right side of the head: the proper colours, and other observations written in with a pen or brush. A superb drawing, and full of the hard lines referred to; the beard seems entirely executed with the hair-pencil or brush: it is on three separate pieces of paper: in good condition. (Photographed for this volume.)

Thomas second Lord Vaux of Harwedon. He was born in 1510, made a Knight of the Bath at the coronation of Anne Boleyn, and died in Queen Mary's reign.

27. THOMAS PARRIE—a fat shaven face, with hat and feather, turned slightly to his right: face highly finished. Rubbed.

Sir Thomas Parry was a short time Comptroller of the Household to Queen Elizabeth: he died in 1559.

28. GAWIN CAROW KNIGHT—head, three-quarter face, with a long pointed beard, and a broad-brimmed hat; he is looking up to his right. Much rubbed.

Sir Gavin Carew made his escape from Exeter Gaol in 1553. There is a picture corresponding with this drawing at King' Weston near Bristol.

29. A GENTLEMAN—head of a young man, three-quarter face, looking to his left, with a black bonnet or cap on the right side of his head· fur on his shoulders. Finished with the hair-pencil; the body very slightly sketched: on salmon-coloured priming.

30. NICHOLAS BORBONIUS (POETA)—profile in cap, half-length, with a pen in his hand; body slightly sketched: a beautiful drawing. Black-lined, and in fine condition.

This name is doubtful. N. Bourbon, noticed in the text, was still living in 1530.

31. SIR JOHN GODSALVE—finished half-length, with a letter in his hands, bright blue back-ground; three-quarter face turned to his left, but looking at the spectator; he is dressed in a purple coat, and black overcoat edged with yellow sable: the hair and eyebrows are finished with the hair-pencil: about 15 in. *h.* by 11 in. *w.* Somewhat rubbed. The black outlines noticed lose all their prominence in this finished drawing.

Lords and Ladies of the Court of Henry VIII.

Sir John is represented in a picture at Dresden, painted in 1528 (see text, under date), but younger than in this drawing. He died in 1557.

32. Tho. Strange Knight—small bearded head, in a black cap, a little more than the profile, turned to his right. Very finely modelled, almost exclusively with black chalk: in fair condition.

He died in 1545.

33. A Gentleman—bust portrait in black, a young man with a yellow beard, and a small round cap on his head; full face. This is something like the portrait of Lord Cobham. In fair çondition.

34. Th. Eliott Knight—bust, a fine drawing, with three-quarter face looking to his right; black cap, hair long at the sides of the head, with stubble beard; fur at the neck. In fair condition.

Sir Thomas Elliot was a man of letters; he died in 1546. The head somewhat resembles that of Sir John Godsalve.

35. Tho. Earle of Surry—the same as No. 6, Tom. II., but somewhat older. Hair unfinished; cap and body indicated in outline only. Rubbed.

36. N. Poines Knight—nearly full face, with beard, and bare head: a free drawing, without the black lines; rather rubbed. Does not seem to be the same head as No. 19, but there appears little or no difference in the ages of the two. I imagine some confusion in the naming.

37. John Colet, Dean of St. Paul's—a very fine small head with a shaven face; in cap and cape, a little more than the profile, turned to his right. Remarkable for its delicate line-modelling with the brush.

This drawing can scarcely be correctly named, as the dean died in 1519, some seven years before Holbein came to England.

38. Clinton—a fine small head, with a black cap on one side, and a slight beard; little more than a profile, turned to the left. Face in fair condition.

Edward Lord Clinton was born in 1512, and died Earl of Lincoln, in 1584.

39. A Gentleman—a yellow-bearded man with a small slouching cap, nearly full face, and looking hard to his left: body in outline. Rubbed.

Lords and Ladies of the Court of Henry VIII.

40. S^{r} THO. WIAT K^{T} —unfinished; a much rubbed copy of No. 18.

41. THE LORD VAUX—nearly full face, with cap and feather; body indicated only. Much rubbed.

42. JOHN MORE, S^{R} THOMAS MORE'S SON—in cap, half-length, looking down, reading, and showing the right hand holding a book. A coarse chalk sketch, on unprimed paper: face injured.

43. A COPY.*

44. BROOKE L^{D} COBHAM—a fine drawing, a full face, with a beard but with very little hair; a flat-brimmed cap is lying just upon the top of his head; his chest is naked. About 11 in. *h.* by 7½ in. *w.*

There is a picture of George Brooke Lord Cobham, at Littlecote, Hungerford, Wilts, belonging to F. L. Popham, Esq.; it was exhibited at the British Institution in 1846.

TOM. II.

1. EDWARD PRINCE—full face, as a young child, with a close skull-cap, and a common cap with feather, above it; a single frill round his neck: very much rubbed.

This agrees with the Duke of Northumberland's portrait, and much with Lord Yarborough's likewise.

2. EDWARD PRINCE OF WALES—full face in cap and feather; not an effective drawing; the often-noticed hard lines are here less skilfully put in than in other instances: much rubbed.

This drawing, of a child somewhat older than in No. 1, is like the miniature of one of the Dukes of Suffolk, Henry, who was born in 1535: the proportions of the face do not quite agree with that of the infant prince.

3. EDWARD VI.—a head in profile with hat and feather, and almost yellow hair: slight, but tolerably well preserved. It may represent a boy about six years of age.

4. FRANCIS RUSSELL EARL OF BEDFORD (some time after)—full face with a broad slouching cap on the back of his head, inclining to the right. Once a fine drawing, now nearly defaced.

A boy, he was born in 1528, and died in 1585.

---

* What this copy may have been cannot be ascertained; but of late years two drawings of the old series have been eliminated as works of Jacob Binck.

Lords and Ladies of the Court of Henry VIII.

5. William Par Marquis of Northampton—small half-length, showing part of the right hand; a three-quarter face turned to his right: a cap with a feather, stuck on the right side of his head. A medallion is hanging to his neck, and he has a sable collar to his coat. Details of the ornaments to be introduced, are drawn on the back-ground with a brush.

He died in 1571.

6. Thomas Earl of Surry—full face in cap and feather, the body outlined with the brush; small: highly finished, but rubbed.

A boy, the eldest son of Henry Earl of Surrey, beheaded in 1547; he became fourth Duke of Norfolk, and met his father's fate in 1572.

7. Philip Hobbie Knight—a head in a soft brimmed cap, three-quarter face, with a very scant beard, looking to his left; small life-size; body merely indicated.

Sir Philip Hoby was resident ambassador at the court of Charles V.; he died in 1558.

8. Tho. Howard E. of Surrey—small drawing of a head with a slouching brimmed cap, a three-quarter face turned to the left, but with the eyes looking out of the picture at the spectator. The beard is put in with a hair-pencil. Rubbed.

This drawing is supposed to represent Henry Howard, who was beheaded; it is something like the portrait of the earl, once at Arundel, and which is represented in the picture of Fruytiers. It is a very unpleasant face.

9. A Lady—called by some, Queen Catherine Howard—bust, three-quarter face looking to her left, in a small round bonnet, and fall or veil, hanging behind; with a cameo on her bosom, attached to a small chain only partly seen. Face tolerably perfect, body in mere outlines with the brush.

10. The Lady Hobbei—bust, a three-quarter face turned to her right, in a black bonnet, tied under the chin. Hard-lined and rubbed.

She was the wife of Sir Thomas Hoby, who died in Paris in 1566.

11. A Lady—a young lady in a short spencer, and in a white cap, with a kerchief tied round her head, and a man's black cap over all: three-quarter face looking to her left. Somewhat rubbed.

Lords and Ladies of the Court of Henry VIII.

12. DITTO—Cicely Heron, Sir Thomas More's youngest daughter; a bust to the waist, three-quarter face looking to her left, wearing a white veil as a bonnet; on her neck a small cameo showing a female head in profile; yellow petticoat body. On unprimed paper, somewhat rubbed.

 A study for the "Family picture."

13. DITTO—an effective drawing of a middle-aged woman, in a large white hood and fall, and a light dress, edged with velvet? A three-quarter face turned to the right, with the eyes looking at the spectator. On unprimed paper; somewhat rubbed. About 17 in. *h.* by 11 in. *w.* It seems to have been executed about the same time as the drawings of the members of the More family.

14. A LADY—a woman with a white kerchief on her head, covering her ears, and a large round cap such as men wear, over it; three-quarter face turned to her right. On unprimed paper; slightly rubbed.

 Is this possibly "Mother Jack," or perhaps some German woman?

15. THE LADY RATCLIF—bust, full-face; in a diamond-shaped hood, with a large black fall, partly turned over the hood. By the side are slight sketches of ornament for the details of the dress, done with a pen or the hair-pencil. Strengthened with lines about the face. Rubbed.

16. THE LADY MARCHIONESS OF DORSET—bust, three-quarter face looking to her left; in a diamond-shaped hood with a large back to it. She shows part of her right hand, holding some flowers and a stick. Lined over, and rubbed.

 Lady Dorset, afterwards Duchess of Suffolk, was the daughter of Charles Brandon, and Mary Queen Dowager of France, the sister of Henry VIII. She was the mother of Lady Jane Grey, and died in 1559.

17. THE LADY OF RICHMOND—full face in black cap and feather, looking down; the cap and feather put in with a brush: face much rubbed.

 Mary only daughter of the third Duke of Norfolk, and sister to Henry Earl of Surrey, who was beheaded in 1547. She married the natural son of Henry VIII., the Duke of Richmond, who died, still a youth, in 1536.

Lords and Ladies of the Court of Henry VIII.

18. Anna Bollein Queen—a profile looking down, dressed in a gown with a fur collar, and a cap with a kerchief twisted round her head. She is neither pretty nor queenly, but the mouth is certainly sensual. This name is questionable.

19. The Lady Eliot—a small head a little more than in profile in a yellow diamond-shaped hood, with a large black fall, and an embroidered partlet collar: the body slightly sketched: rubbed. It constitutes a companion drawing to that of her husband, Sir Thomas Elliot. She died in 1569 as Lady Dyer.

20. The Lady Meutas—bust, full face, straining her eyes to her right. In diamond-shaped hood, with the black fall folded over it. Rubbed.

Wife of Sir Peter Meutas.

21. The Dutchess of Suffolk—bust, three-quarter face turned to her right, brown eyes (very rarely seen in these drawings). In diamond-shaped hood, and with an embroidered collar round her neck. Something like the pictures commonly called Jane Seymour. Lined and somewhat rubbed.

Catherine Willoughby, fourth wife of the duke, and mother of the two boys, of whom the Queen possesses miniatures by Holbein, and who both died of the sweating sickness, on the same day at Bugden, July 14, 1551. The duchess died in 1580.

22. Jane Seymour Queen—half length, with the hands clasped, in diamond-shaped hood, 20½ in. *h.* by 11 in. *w.* Hard-lined and in fair condition.

This is a straight-nosed blue-eyed woman, not like the Queen in Van Leemput's picture. This designation, if incorrect, should throw a doubt on the story that the names were given to the drawings by Sir John Cheke, while they were in the possession of Edward VI. About such a personage as Jane Seymour there could be no mistake under the circumstances supposed.

23. The Lady Borow—head, three-quarter face turned to her right; hood outlined only; no body; rubbed.

Wife of William Lord Borough.

24. The Lady Surry—bust, full face; this drawing is very similar to that of Lady Ratclif, both in pose and costume, and the faces are not very different. Lady Surrey has on a pearl necklace, with a locket pendant: the hoods and falls are very similar, and both have a pearl enrichment or knotted stuff in imitation

of pearls, round the front edge of the hood. The countenances differ in expression; Lady Ratclif has an arch character, Lady Surrey's is much softer. The latter is something like the portraits of Anne of Cleves.

Lords and Ladies of the Court of Henry VIII.

25. THE LADY HENEGHAM—bust, profile showing the right side; she wears the diamond-shaped hood with the large black fall. Strengthened with lines, and rubbed.

Supposed to represent the wife of Sir Anthony Henningham, but the drawing has a remarkable resemblance to the portrait of Margaret Roper.

26. THE LADY LISTER—bust, three-quarter face, in diamond-shaped hood, with the black fall turned over the head: strengthened with fine lines.

Wife of Sir Richard Lister afterwards Lord Chief Justice, who died in 1552.

27. M. SOUCH—bust, full face, yellow hair, with a small round jewelled bonnet, or veil, giving the effect of a coronet; on her bosom a large cameo showing a seated woman.

Probably the wife of Richard Zouch son of Lord Zouch of Haringworth.

28. THE LADY PARKER—bust, full face, also with a coronet-looking bonnet on her head: eyes far apart. Much rubbed.

Sir Drue Drury, the keeper of Mary Queen of Scots, was her third husband.

29. A LADY—bust, three-quarter face turned to her right, representing a very handsome girl. She has on a close white cap, and a man's cap with a gold medal or jewel, put on over it; black embroidery on the collar. The lines on this face are certainly by Holbein: the body is rubbed. Can this be the drawing of Anne Boleyn? In the vestibule of Windsor Castle there is a picture somewhat resembling it.

30. THE LADY VAUX—small bust, nearly full face, with diamond-shaped hood, and a large fall behind. Lined; in fair condition. There is a faded picture of this fine drawing at Hampton Court, but apparently repainted, or a copy from some other.

Wife of Thomas second Lord Vaux.

31. THE LADY AUDLEY—bust, three-quarter face turned to her left, with a large veil tied over her head, and jewels on her neck and bosom, indicated in outline. Rubbed.

Lords and Ladies of the Court of Henry VIII.

Elizabeth daughter of Sir Brian Tuke, and wife of George Touchet Lord Audley, who died in 1559. There is a good miniature of this lady, similar to the drawing, in her Majesty's collection at Windsor.

32. The Lady Montegle—bust, nearly full face, looking to her left; in a bonnet having the effect of a veiled coronet: she has jewels on her neck and a medallion on her bosom. On salmon-coloured priming, slight, and rubbed. It has some hard brush lines, with writing.
Wife of Thomas Stanley second Lord Monteagle.

33. A Lady—a little more than the profile, looking to the right, with diamond-shaped hood, and black fall turned up. A fine drawing delicately lined, in fair condition.

34. The Lady Barkley—bust, profile showing the right shoulder, with the diamond-shaped hood, and black fall folded over the hood. On unprimed paper, rubbed, but in fair condition.
This drawing is wrongly named; it represents Sir Thomas More's second daughter Elizabeth Dancy; her portrait is in the "Family picture," in which she is putting on her gloves.

35. A Lady—bust, showing the right side, a three-quarter face looking out of the picture, with the diamond-shaped hood with yellow edges, and the black fall hanging down behind. On unprimed paper, 15 in. *h.* by 10 in. *w.* In fair condition.
This is the portrait of Anne Cresacre, John More's wife; as seen in the "Family picture."

36. The Lady Butts—bust, nearly full face turned to her right, with diamond-shaped hood and black fall, and a sable collar to her cloak. About 15 in. *h.* by 11 in. *w.* Outlined heavily.
Wife of Sir William Butts, physician to Henry VIII. An excellent portrait of her by Holbein, similar to this drawing, is in the possession of Mr. W. H. Pole Carew.

37. The Lady Rich—bust, three-quarter face turned to the right, in diamond-shaped hood; companion drawing to her husband's. A very expressive head, lined, but not very prominently: the painter has introduced some hair on a wart, on the right side of her chin. The body is only outlined. Mr. Walter Moseley of Buildwas Park, has an oil picture from this drawing.
Lady Rich was daughter of William Jenkes, a grocer of London, and wife of Lord Chancellor Rich.

38. A Lady—full face, diamond-shaped hood, and black fall partly over the hood. A handsome face: on salmon-coloured priming; much rubbed. *Lords and Ladies of the Court of Henry VIII.*

39. Lady Mary, after Queen—bust, three-quarter face turned to her right, in diamond-shaped hood with a large fall turned over her head. On her neck a pearl necklace, with a very large pearl pendant. Hard lines conspicuous in this drawing: on salmon-coloured priming; rubbed.

It does not much resemble the ordinary portraits of Queen Mary.

40. Mother Jak—a fine bust in profile, with a fur cap on her head, and showing the right shoulder. About 15 in. *h.* by 10 in. *w.* On unprimed paper, in fair condition.

This is the portrait of Margaret Gigs afterwards Clement, related to Sir Thomas More's family, and she is in the "Family picture." If Mother Jack or Jackson be in the set, there are two other drawings which look much more likely than this lady—No. 18, 'Anna Bollein Queen,' and No. 14, the anonymous portrait of a woman in a very homely dress.

41. A Lady—bust, three-quarter face turned to her left, with round bonnet and fall, jewelled; the jewels indicated in parts only with the black brush-lines. Round her neck a pearl necklace. Body sketched in with the brush.

42. A Copy.*

A portrait of a lady, described as Anne of Cleves, formerly in Dr. Mead's collection, was added to these Windsor Drawings by Benjamin Way, Esq. It represents a full face in a close white cap, over which is placed a round projecting black cap, after the fashion of the other sex. It is a small drawing 9½ in. *h.* by 6½ in. *w.* and has been cut round the edges of the figure. The face is spare rather than fat, but has something of the character of the Louvre portrait of this princess. Can it be the missing drawing of the Lady Amelia, Anne's sister?

In Chamberlaine's published work from these portraits, several of the sketches are omitted, but two plates from water-colour drawings of a man and a woman, now at Windsor, called Holbein and his wife, are added: one forming a frontispiece to each volume. I feel satisfied that they do not represent Holbein and his Basel wife, and am also disposed equally to reject them as drawings by Holbein. They were presented to Queen Caroline by Sir Robert Walpole.

The End of the Appendix.

* See note to No. 43 of the first series.

INDEX

TO THE

LIFE AND WORKS OF HOLBEIN.

A.

B.

C.

D.

I.

J.

K.

L.

M.

N.

O.

P.

Q.

R.

S.

T.

U.

V.

W.

Y.

Z.

www.ingramcontent.com/pod-product-compliance
Lightning Source LLC
Chambersburg PA
CBHW030945110726
47900CB00004B/1134

* 9 7 8 3 3 3 7 3 9 4 1 1 0 *